EVA IBBOTSON

The Dragonfly Pool

MACMILLAN CHILDREN'S BOOKS

First published 2008 by Macmillan Children's Books

This edition published 2013 by Macmillan Children's Books
a division of Macmillan Publishers Limited
20 New Wharf Road, London N1 9RR
Basingstoke and Oxford
Associated companies throughout the world
www.panmacmillan.com

ISBN 978-1-447-24631-2

1 3 5 7 9 8 6 4 2

A CIP catalogue record for this book is available from
the British Library.

Typeset by Intype Libra Limited
Printed and bound by CPI Group (UK) Ltd, Croydon, CR0 4YY

I would like to thank my son
Toby Ibbotson for the help he gave me
in the writing of this book

A NOTE FROM THE AUTHOR

The story of *The Dragonfly Pool* is an imaginary adventure. But Delderton Hall is based on a school which I went to many years ago, and which surprised me when I first arrived there as much as it surprised Tally.

I came there as a rather shy and well-behaved little girl from a convent in Vienna, where I was born. The first thing I did was to curtsy to the headmaster when he greeted me in the school courtyard, which made the children watching laugh so much that one of them fell out of a tree.

But I soon realized that this was a school like no other. Amazing biology classes which sometimes began at four in the morning, a school cook who had been an artists' model, the pet hut with its collection of weird animals – these were all part of my school life. Like Tally I found it difficult to be 'free' and 'progressive' – yet soon I thought of this strange place as fondly as the home I had lost when I fled Vienna – which did not mean we were untouched by the war. From the flat roof of the school gym, my friends and I watched as Plymouth, thirty miles distant, went up in flames.

PART ONE

CHAPTER ONE

BALLOONS OVER LONDON

'I don't think you ought to be crying at your age. People of fifty-two don't cry,' said Aunt Hester sternly.

'I'm not crying,' said her sister May. 'Not really. And anyway, I heard you blowing your nose three times last night when you went to the bathroom.'

'Anyone can blow their nose,' said Hester.

'Not three times. And you're older than me.'

But then they stopped arguing and clung to each other because the news their brother had given them the night before was so awful that they could only bear it if they were standing side by side.

'The house is going to be like a tomb without her,' said May. 'She's far too young to go away.'

'Of course we knew she'd go away to get married,' said Hester.

'But people don't marry when they're eleven years old.'

'Except in the olden days, perhaps. And in very hot countries.'

But England was not a hot country. Now, on a fine spring day in 1939, it was only pleasantly warm. The men digging trenches in the little park opposite had not removed their shirts, and a fresh breeze stirred the silver barrage balloons that floated over the houses. The government was trying them out to protect the people of London against enemy aircraft if the war, which everyone was expecting, really came.

Tally loved the barrage balloons.

'They're like really kind great-uncles,' she said, 'only a nicer colour.'

All the children of Stanford Street walked home with their heads turned to the sky when the balloons went up.

The war against Hitler seemed likely to come; no one really thought now it could be prevented – the poor man could be heard raving on the wireless, his mad eyes and loathsome moustache appeared each day in the newspapers on Mr Pepper's paper stall. But it was not the thought of the war that was upsetting May and Hester now. They had been quite excited when they were issued with a stirrup pump to put out the flames from incendiary bombs – and the air-raid shelters delivered in sections to the houses in the street were a great comfort, though nobody could quite work out how to put them up. Hitler was nasty; if there had to be a war, they would put up with it. But this was different . . .

'Help me to make her see what a chance this is for her,' their brother James had begged them. 'Help me to keep her cheerful.'

The aunts had kept house for their younger brother since his wife had died, leaving him with a baby less than a week old. For nearly twelve years now that baby had been the centre of their world.

'We'd better do something about our faces,' said Hester, looking in the mirror. 'She mustn't see we're upset. She'll be home from school soon and James wants to tell her himself.'

But the only powder they could find was some talc that May used on her feet in hot weather, and once they had covered their faces with it they returned to the bathroom to wash it off. It would not help Tally to stand up under the blow that awaited her to be greeted by two white-faced clowns.

It was a friendly, bustling little street, shabby but cheerful. The houses sloped a little downhill in the direction of London's river and the dome of St Paul's Cathedral, which you could see from the attic window on a clear day. There was a row of shops – a greengrocer, a butcher, a cobbler and a baker – and at the end of the street a small park with a slightly muddy pond and ducks. On the other side of the road from the little shops was a row of terraced houses. The end one of these –14 Stanford Street – was the one everybody knew. It was a tall house with a wrought-iron balcony and built on to it on the ground floor was a red-brick surgery, where the patients waited. For number 14 was the Doctor's House; it belonged to Dr James

Hamilton, and to see him, rather than other, more fashionable doctors, the people of East Stanford would have walked miles. But the people were poor and Dr Hamilton charged them only what they could afford. So in the Doctor's House the rugs were threadbare, the fires were lit as late in the day as possible, there was only a cook general to serve the house, instead of the maid and cook and handyman that other houses in the terrace kept. None of which mattered to the people who came there because, lighting up the house with her warmth and her energy and her laughter, was the doctor's daughter.

There was unrest among the patients waiting in the afternoon surgery. The plain little room was packed because Dr Hamilton was the doctor on duty and not his partner, but there were mutterings and murmurings of discontent.

No one knew if it was true for certain, but if it was, it was bad news indeed.

Joe Smithson sat with his sore leg stuck out in front of him, thinking about his wife. Mrs Smithson was an invalid; she seldom left her room and Tally came to read to her – actually more to read *with* her. They were in the middle of *The Prisoner of Zenda* – both of them liked sword fights and plenty of swashbuckling and people leaping off parapets. On the afternoons that Tally came after school his wife was always cheerful. Should he ask the doctor if the rumours were true? Well, they'd know soon enough – nothing stayed secret in the street for long.

Old Mrs Dawson, whose chest was bad again, stared at the notices pinned to the wall and thought about her dog. Tally took the dog out for her and said she didn't want to be paid, because she liked dogs. She even liked Horace, who was a dachshund and that was not a popular breed just now. Tally had punched a boy who'd sneered at him for being a German sausage dog. There wasn't anyone else who'd take him out for free, and Mrs Dawson's budget was tight. Surely the rumours couldn't be true? Everyone knew that the doctor thought the world of his daughter. Why, it would break his heart to part with her.

'Next patient, please,' said the receptionist, Miss Hoy, and Mrs Dawson made her way into the doctor's room. She'd ask him whether it was true – after all, she had a right to know.

'Have you heard?' said Mr Cooper as his son Kenny came in from the park. Kenny was the same age as Tally; they'd played together all their lives.

'Yes,' said Kenny and went past the cabbages and the sacks of Brussels sprouts and out of the back of the green-grocer's shop into the mews. He'd be going to the stables, thought his father. When things were rough with him, Kenny often went to talk to Primrose. She was only an old Welsh cob who pulled the vegetable cart, but she was one of those horses that understood things.

Tally's friend, Maybelle, at the corner shop, was angry when she heard the news. She became angry easily, and now she picked up the trowel with which she'd been spooning lentils from a sack and threw it across the room. Tally wouldn't fight, Maybelle knew that. She wouldn't bite and kick and lie down on the floor till she got her own way. Not where her father was concerned. It was going to be a nuisance, doing without her friend. And she'd miss

Maybelle's debut as a powder puff in the Summer Show at the Hippodrome.

'Come on, girl,' said her grandmother. 'We've got all those bags to tie up before tomorrow.'

'Shan't,' said Maybelle, and she marched out of the shop and past the butcher's and the cobbler's till she came to the greengrocer's. She'd see if Kenny knew.

Why can't children be left alone? thought Maybelle angrily.

The nuns were used to children being taken away.

'But I shall be sorry to lose her,' said the Mother Superior.

Sister Felicia, who produced the end-of-term plays in the convent, was feeling guilty. I should have let her be the Virgin Mary, she thought. She was always a sheep or a cow coming to the manger. I know how much she wanted the star part but she was so good at controlling the little ones.

Tally, coming down the hill like a lamb to the slaughter, was the last person to know. She was carrying a rolled-up sheet of paper with on one side a painting of St Sebastian stuck with arrows, and on the other a diagram of the life cycle of the liver fluke. The nuns were poor, and one sheet of paper had to go a long way.

Dr Hamilton came in from the surgery and made his way into the house. A thin, dark-haired man with a high forehead and concerned brown eyes, he was looking very tired. Friday was always a long day: the surgery stayed open till eight o'clock so that patients who came from the factories and the dockyards could come without missing work.

He was a man who told his patients exactly what to do – to eat regularly, take exercise, get plenty of fresh air and go to bed early – and he himself did none of those things. He snatched meals between the surgery and his sessions at the hospital where he went two days a week, he went out on night calls that often turned out to be unnecessary and stayed up till the small hours catching up with the new medical research.

The hallway was dark – his sisters, so much older than him, were good about saving electricity. Supper would be left for him in the dining room, but he wasn't hungry. He'd come in late like this so often, looking forward to an hour with his daughter before she went to bed. He could hear her upstairs, talking to the aunts. Well, he'd better get it over.

'Ask Tally to come and see me in my study,' he said to the cook general.

Five minutes later the door opened and his daughter came in.

Oh Lord, I can't do it, thought Dr Hamilton. What will there be left when she is gone?

Already as she stood there in the lamplight he was memorizing her face. The pointed chin, the straight fawn hair lapping her ears, the enquiring hazel eyes. Her fringe had a nibbled look – Aunt Hester insisted on cutting it herself.

When his wife had died of puerperal fever a week after their daughter's birth, Dr Hamilton had been completely overwhelmed by guilt and grief. How could it be that he, a doctor, could not save the woman that he loved so much? For several weeks he scarcely noticed the baby, fussed over by his sisters and a nurse. Then one day, coming in late, he passed the nursery and heard a sound coming from his daughter's room. It was not a cry, nor was it a whimper. It was the sound of . . . conversation. His five-week-old daughter was talking to the world.

He walked over to the cot. The baby's eyes, properly focused now, were wide open. She did not smile at him; she *looked*.

What an idiot I've been, he thought. This is a *person*.

Things had happened to this person in the weeks he had ignored her that he might not have permitted if he'd been aware of what was going on. For example, her name . . . His sisters had had the child christened Talitha, after their grandmother.

'She was a saint,' they reminded their brother. 'She used to wash the socks of the tramps she met on the London Underground. Wash them and dry them and give them back.'

Dr Hamilton would have preferred to call his daughter something simpler: Ann, perhaps, or Jane. Yet as she grew, her name seemed entirely suitable, for in order to wash the socks of tramps you have to get them to take their socks *off*, and it was the kind of determination this would need that Tally showed from a very early age.

Tally meanwhile had crossed the room and come over to his chair to give him a hug. She could see that he'd had a bad day – he looked like that when a patient at the hospital died who should have lived, or when the pile of bills on his desk became unmanageable, or, lately, when he had been listening to Hitler raving on the wireless, and she was already thinking of ways to cheer him up. Sometimes they played chess, and sometimes she told him about something funny that had happened at school, but today she had a feeling that neither of these things would work.

'I've got something to tell you, Tally,' he said, putting his arm round her shoulder.

'Is it important?' she said apprehensively. She had learned early in life that important things were usually not nearly as nice as unimportant ones.

'Yes . . . I suppose it is. At any rate, it's good news,' said the doctor resolutely.

Tally looked at him suspiciously. She knew his face better than she knew her own, and the lines round his mouth and the furrows on his forehead did not seem to indicate good news.

'Perhaps I'd better explain. I have a patient at the hospital – I won't tell you his name but he is someone important in education – a professor and a very nice man. He thinks I saved his life, which is rubbish, but it's true we were able to help him. Afterwards, while he was waiting to be discharged, we talked about you, and . . .' Dr Hamilton paused, looking at the window, which was just a square of darkness now, 'he told me about a school he knows – he's on the governing board and he thinks very highly of the staff and the ideals of the school. It's in the country, in south Devon, not far from the sea.'

Tally waited. Her heart was beating fast; but surely it was all right? A school in south Devon must be a boarding school, and one of the advantages of being poor was

11

that she could never be sent away to those places that cost the earth.

'Apparently they give scholarships from time to time. Not for schoolwork but to children who they think might benefit from being there. Complete scholarships, where everything is taken care of. He says he thinks he could get you a place there.'

'I don't want to go away.' She tried to speak in a sensible, grown-up way, but already her voice was letting her down. 'I'm all right here. I'm fine.'

Her father was silent, jabbing his pencil on to his blotter. The blotter was a present from one of his patients: four sheets of pink paper pasted on to a piece of lumpy leather. His study was full of presents his patients had made for him: knitted sausages to keep out draughts, lopsided letter racks . . . Among all the strange objects was a plaster head of Hippocrates, the patron saint of medicine, who, two thousand years ago, had laid down the rules for treating patients with dignity and respect.

'I don't want you to go away, Tally, believe me . . . We will all miss you very, very much.'

'Well then, why do I have to go? Why? Why?'

'The nuns are very kind but I want you to have a broader education. Science, modern languages . . .'

'But I'm learning French. And you could teach me science. You've always said, as soon as one can read one can teach oneself anything. Please, oh please, don't make me go away.' She looked at him. Then: 'It isn't about the teaching, is it? It's because there's going to be a war.'

There was a long pause. Her father reached out for comforting words, but he had never lied to his daughter.

12

'Yes,' he said heavily. 'I think there's going to be a war. There may not be but . . .'

But if there was, everybody expected that London, like all big towns, would be heavily bombarded. A man who did not protect his daughter from that horror must be the greatest criminal on earth. This chance to send her to safety in one of England's loveliest counties had been a godsend.

But Tally was angry.

'Well, what if there is going to be a war? Why can't I share in it?' Kenny's father says we're all getting gas masks and they're digging a big shelter in the park and Aunt May has got lots of khaki wool to knit balaclavas for the troops, and anyway we've got the balloons to protect us. Why should I miss everything just because I'm a child? And why should I be buried in the country and you be in danger? Everybody talks about sharing – you and the aunts and the nuns. Well, why can't I share the war?'

Dr Hamilton leaned back in his chair and closed his eyes for a moment. 'Most of the children will be sent away. The government's made all the plans for evacuation. You don't want to go to strangers with a label round your neck.'

'No, I don't. And I wouldn't go. They tried to make Maybelle go to a rehearsal for evacuation at her school and she just screamed and kicked and bit and now they've said that she can stay.'

But even as she spoke Tally knew that she wouldn't scream and kick and bite. Not about something that concerned her father whom she loved so much.

'I think sending children away like parcels is wicked

13

and wrong,' she said. 'I could take messages and look out for nuns coming from the sky. At school they say Nazi spies are going to come down on parachutes disguised as nuns. Well, I know nuns; I wouldn't be fooled – you can tell by their shoes. And anyway, there may not be a war in the end. You always say the German people are good, it's only the Nazis who are wicked, so maybe they'll rise up and overthrow Hitler and everything will be all right.'

But her father was near the end of his tether.

'Delderton is a first-class school,' he said, making a final effort. 'Children come there from all over the world – and with the kind of scholarship they give, you can do all the extras: music and horse riding . . .'

'I don't want to ride a horse, I've got Primrose. I want to stay here and be part of things and help. And anyway, who's going to look after you?'

But she had lost, and she knew it.

CHAPTER TWO

RICH COUSINS

For two nights Tally cried herself to sleep. Then she pulled herself together. What was done was done and she would have to make the best of it.

It was her father who had taught her that knowledge is power – that if one could find out about something one is afraid of, it made the fear less. So now, when she wanted to know what to expect when she went away to boarding school, she decided to consult her cousin Margaret.

James Hamilton had a brother called Thomas, who was also a doctor but a very different kind of doctor. He saw only special patients in his elegant rooms in Harley Street and he charged them about ten times as much as James charged his patients, so that his family was as rich as his brother's family was poor.

The house he lived in was in one of the smartest streets in the West End, with a gleaming brass plate on the door giving a list of all his degrees and qualifications – and his two children, Margaret and Roderick, went to the most expensive boarding schools in the country.

Margaret and Roderick were obedient, tidy children. Their manners were good but inside they were chilly creatures, thinking of themselves the whole time – and they looked down on Tally, who lived in a shabby street and wore old clothes and played with the children of greengrocers and butchers.

But when they heard that Tally was going to go to boarding school and wanted some advice they were ready to be helpful, and their mother, Aunt Virginia, asked Tally to tea.

So now Tally rang the bell and followed a maid in uniform up the thickly carpeted stairs to Margaret's room, which looked like a room in a furniture catalogue, with looped curtains and a kidney-shaped dressing table and fluffy white rugs.

'I was wondering about – oh, you know . . . well, everything really . . .' said Tally. 'I mean, is it true you have prefects and feasts in the dorm and pashes on the head girl and all that? And . . . do you like being away? asked Tally, longing to be reassured. 'Do you like your school?'

'Oh yes,' said Margaret, 'I like it very much. I couldn't bear to stay at home' – and Tally sighed, thinking how very much she could have borne just that. 'It's strict of course, but all boarding schools are strict, and St Barbara's has everything. We have four titled girls there and a millionaire's daughter and the head girl is related to one of the queen's ladies-in-waiting. She's absolutely super; we all want to do things for her. And we have such fun. Last term we had a midnight feast in the dorm and one of the girls stepped on a tin of sardines, and she shrieked like mad – the tin was open – and that brought Matron rushing in. Only they couldn't do much to us because the girl who was the ringleader had a terribly rich father who'd just given the school a new sports hall. And we're always making apple-pie beds for people we don't like and putting spiders in Matron's slippers.'

'Yes, I see.' Tally was trying not to think of the poor spiders, squashed to death by unexpected feet. But Margaret was in full cry now, explaining the rules.

'You have to curtsy when you meet the headmistress and call her Ma'am and always walk on the left side of the corridor, but you soon get the hang of it. And of course you have to have exactly the right clothes. We've just finished buying my uniform for next term and you wouldn't believe how expensive it was. Mummy nearly died when she got the bill from Harrods!'

She went to her wardrobe and took out, one by one, the clothes she would need for St Barbara's and laid them on her bed. There were two bottle-green gymslips with pleated skirts and a matching sash to tie round the waist. There were four pale blue flannel blouses, a tie, a pudding-shaped velour hat with a hat ribbon, a straw hat for later in the term and a blazer edged in braid. The blazer, like the tie and the hat ribbon, was striped in the St Barbara's colours of bottle green and blue, and the motto on the pocket said: 'BE THE BEST'.

'The best at what?' asked Tally.

'Oh, everything,' said Margaret airily. She picked up one of the gymslips and held it in front of her. 'There's always a big fuss about the length of the skirt. Matron makes us kneel down and if the hem is more than four inches off the ground we get detention.'

Tally tried not to panic. The whole bed was covered in clothes; there was a smell of starch and newness.

But Margaret had not finished. She went back to the wardrobe and brought out a big carrier bag full of brand-new shoes.

'The lace-ups are for out of doors, and indoors we have strap shoes and on Sundays we wear these pumps. Then there are plimsolls and dancing shoes . . . and I have skating boots . . .'

After the shoes came Margaret's underclothes: woollen socks and garters and a liberty bodice that buttoned into Margaret's bottle-green knickers. The knickers had pockets and elastic round the knees.

'Mummy thought I could wear the same knickers as I had last term, but I told her I couldn't. They have to be new because people can see you take your handkerchief out of your knicker-pocket. And here are the things we have for games . . .'

From another cupboard Margaret produced a pair of nailed hockey boots, a brand-new hockey stick, a woollen bathing costume with the St Barbara's crest on the chest and the school scarf. Like the blazer and the tie, the scarf was striped in the school colours of bottle green and blue. It was not a joyful colour scheme.

Like a bruise, thought Tally, but a very expensive one.

'And we have to have regulation nightclothes too: some

18

schools are sloppy – they let you wear what you like at night – but not St Barbara's. Even the slippers are regulation – and on Sundays we wear special dresses: green velvet with lace collars; I can't show you everything because the maid is still sewing on name tapes. But here's my satchel – we have to have proper leather ones with our names stamped on, and hymn books, of course, and a tuck box.'

But even Margaret, who seldom noticed other people, saw that Tally was beginning to look worried and now she said, 'The school will send you a list of the things you need and your aunts will help you buy them. Only you must have absolutely the *right* things – a girl came last term without her Sunday shoes and she got into awful trouble. Being different is the thing you mustn't do.'

At this point Roderick came into the room. He was nearly two years older than Margaret – a fair, good-looking boy who seldom spoke to girls if he could help it. Roderick's school was so famous and so grand that he didn't really need to show off about it, but since Tally wasn't usually easy to impress he mentioned that the Prince of Transjordania was in the class above him and that this term they were expecting a boy who was related to the family of the ex-Emperor of Prussia.

'But we don't treat them any differently from the other boys at Foxingham,' he said carelessly.

The rules at Foxingham were of course even stricter than those at St Barbara's – there was fagging and caning – and it was a famous rugby school, which had beaten Eton at the game.

'Have you bought your uniform too?' asked Tally.

'Of course,' said Roderick.

For a moment he hesitated. Then he went to his room and came back with his brand-new blazer, his tie and his cap.

All of these were striped fiercely in red and yellow. Walking out together the boys, thought Tally, must have looked like a swarm of angry wasps or ferocious postmen. The motto on Roderick's blazer was: 'OUT OF MY WAY'.

'I'll lend you some books if you like,' said Margaret. 'School stories. I want them back of course, but I've read them millions of times. They'll give you an idea of what to expect.'

She went to her bookcase and took out *Angela of the Upper Fourth* and *The Madcap of the Remove* and gave them to Tally, who thanked her warmly.

Aunt Virginia came in then and told them to come down to the dining room because tea was ready.

'You needn't bother to do that,' said Margaret as Tally began to gather up the clothes on the bed. 'The maid will do it.'

But after tea, just as Tally was getting ready to go home and was alone with her cousins, Margaret said: 'By the way, what's the name of your school? The one you're going to.'

'It's called Delderton.'

Margaret and Roderick looked at each other. 'Delderton? Are you sure?'

'Yes. Why?'

There was pause.

Then: 'Oh, nothing,' said Roderick, shrugging his shoulders. 'Nothing at all.'

But as the maid opened the front door to let her out, Tally heard them titter. The titter turned into full-scale laughter – but the door was shutting, and Tally was out in the street.

CHAPTER THREE

THE TRAIN

Aunt Hester and Aunt May had always done their best to share in Tally's life. When Tally was six years old and had been cast as a sheep in the nativity play they had read books about agriculture and sheep farming and taken Tally to the zoo to watch the way the cloven-footed mammals moved their feet – and Tally's performance on the day had been very much admired.

So now they tackled *Angela of the Upper Fourth* and *The Madcap of the Remove* and enjoyed them very much, though they were a little worried about how Tally would get on, having to say 'spiffing' and 'ripping' all the time, and shouting, 'Well played, girls!' on the hockey field.

What they couldn't do however was get Tally's school uniform together, because no list came from Delderton.

'You mustn't worry, dear,' said Aunt May. 'The school will let us know in good time and then we'll go and fit you up. They'll pay – it's a full scholarship.'

'Yes . . . but there are so *many* things . . . Eight pairs of shoes; I'll get muddled. And a liberty bodice . . . I don't really know what that is,' said Tally.

She was worried too about the rules: the curtsy to the headmistress and remembering to call her Ma'am. And if the rules were going to be difficult, breaking them in the right way was going to be difficult too. The midnight feasts in the dorm, for example . . . What if *she* stepped on an open tin of sardines and brought Matron running?

Because Aunt May's letters in violet ink were apt to be rather emotional and Aunt Hester's in green ink were almost impossible to read, Dr Hamilton asked his receptionist, Miss Hoy, to write to the school asking for a list of the things Tally would need.

But before they got a reply Hitler invaded Czechoslovakia, and after that no one had time to worry about braided blazers and green knickers with pockets in them, let alone about feasts in the dorm.

The milkman's son got his call-up papers for the army and Dr Hamilton spent more and more time at the hospital, where they were arranging for the evacuation of patients to the country; posters appeared telling people to grow vegetables and 'Dig for Victory', and Aunt Hester said she wanted to go and entertain the troops.

'I know I'm not young,' she said, 'but my voice is still good.'

Then, just a week before the beginning of term, a letter came from the school secretary at Delderton announcing the departure of the school train from Paddington Station at ten o'clock on 13 April. There was still nothing about the school uniform or the rules and regulations.

'They'll probably fit you out when you get there, like in the army,' said the aunts consolingly.

And Tally tried not to panic because she was going to an unknown place without any of the right things and without at all knowing how to behave. After all, men were joining the army or going to fight in aeroplanes or drown in ships, and here she was fussing about liberty bodices and stepping on sardines.

Two days later there was a phone call from Aunt Virginia. Margaret was not starting school till the day after Tally, but Roderick's school, Foxingham, which was also in the West Country, started the same day and his train left Paddington at almost the same time.

'So we could take Tally to the station,' she said. 'There's plenty of room in the Rolls.' To her husband she had said, 'It would be nice for the girl to arrive in a decent car instead of that old crock her father drives. First impressions are so important.'

Tally looked in anguish at her father. 'Oh please, I want you to take me.'

'Don't be foolish,' said Dr Hamilton. 'You don't suppose we'd let anyone else see you off?'

Because of course May and Hester were coming too. Actually, rather a lot of people had wanted to come and see Tally off: Kenny and Maybelle; the receptionist, Miss Hoy; Sister Felicia from the convent . . . but Dr Hamilton had persuaded them that Tally would do best with only her immediate family to say goodbye.

*

24

Paddington Station on the morning of 13 April was in a state of bustle and confusion. Parents towed their children to what they hoped was the right barrier; loudspeakers crackled, announcing changes of platform; porters with their trolleys tried to avoid the passengers who asked them things they didn't know. From time to time a waiting train would hiss fiercely and a group of agitated mothers or worried children would vanish in a cloud of steam.

Tally stood with her father and the aunts beside the bookstall. Her stomach had dropped down into some place deep inside her and didn't seem likely to rise up again for a very long time . . .

Into this confusion there marched the boys of Foxingham, in their red and yellow uniforms, looking like a line of soldiers or regimented bees. There was a teacher at the head of the line and another at the tail. The boys had said goodbye to their parents at the barrier – the school did not permit parents to come on to the platform – and of course no one showed signs of emotion or looked as though they might cry. Homesickness was not in the Foxingham tradition. Tally had tried to say goodbye to Roderick earlier, but he had been far too lordly to speak to her, and now she did not dare to wave. At the end of the line was a very dark, serious-looking boy and she wondered if he might be the Prince of Transjordania and, if so, how he felt, so far from home.

The Foxingham school train left from Platform 2. It looked as though it might be late leaving, but the well-drilled boys stood beside their carriages waiting for the sign that they could board the train.

'It must be Platform 1 that you're going from,' said

Aunt May, looking at the departure board. She had been awake most of the night, but she was determined to be cheerful and brave. 'Look, what a nice lot of girls!'

Platform 1 had no barrier; it was the end one, by the ticket office and the refreshment room, and the girls who were gathered together there did indeed look very nice. They were all identically dressed in smart navy-blue blazers and straw hats with navy ribbons, and their white knee socks gleamed with cleanliness. Beside them stood calm and elegant parents tweaking at their daughters' clothes. Two teachers in grey coats and skirts with whistles round their necks moved among the girls. Cries of 'Had a good hol, Daphne?' or 'Wait till you hear what I did, Cynthia!' filled the air. They were exactly like the heroines in the books that Tally had been reading.

Tally bit her lip. How was she to join those beautifully turned-out girls, dressed as she was in her shabby tweed coat?

But at that moment the loudspeaker crackled into life.

'This is a platform change. The school train for St Fenella's Academy will now depart from Platform 6.'

And in an instant the beautifully turned-out girls and their parents hurried away.

'Oh dear,' said Aunt Hester, who had been much taken by the well-behaved children in their straw boaters. 'I did hope they were bound for Delderton. They seemed so suitable.'

For a while Platform 1 was empty.

At least it was empty of anyone who might have been going away to school. There was a girl doing a handstand by the ticket office: her skirt swirled round her head; her knickers were white and pocket-less. A boy with wild dark hair appeared, carrying a glass tank containing something bald and white. His shoelaces were undone; water from the tank slopped on to his unravelling jersey. Another boy, wearing a boiler suit, was holding a banner that read: 'Down with Tyrants!' Behind him came a very pretty girl with bare feet.

'Are they from a circus,' wondered Aunt Hester aloud, 'or can't they afford shoes? Her poor feet . . .'

More children arrived. Here and there were grown-ups: a woman dressed like an Aztec peasant with a blanket round her shoulders . . . a man in corduroys with huge patches on the sleeves and a rent in his trousers . . . a small fat man with an enormous beard . . .

The train steamed in.

'Excuse me . . .' Dr Hamilton had waylaid a porter. 'Is this the train for St Agnes? The Delderton train?'

'Aye,' said the porter. 'Better keep out of the way, sir — they're savages, this lot,' and he hurried off down the platform.

But now a woman in a loose cloak, with long, red-gold hair tumbling down her back, came hurrying down the platform. She carried a clipboard, and when she came up to a child she spoke to it and ticked off its name and the child wandered off to the train and got into one of the carriages and opened the window and went on shouting to its parents.

Now she came up to Tally and said, 'Are you by any chance Augusta Carrington?'

'No, I'm afraid I'm not.'

'Oh dear. This list . . . I don't know why they bother

with lists, they never seem to be right. In that case who would you be?' She peered in a worried way at her clipboard.

'She's Talitha Hamilton,' said Dr Hamilton, frowning.

'Ah yes, that's all right, I've got you down. You can go to the train – sit anywhere you like. And if you do see Augusta Carrington send her to me,' and she moved away towards a boy with a birdcage who had just come out of the refreshment room.

'Well, at least it doesn't seem to matter too much what you wear, dear,' said Aunt Hester, looking very pale.

Tally said nothing and her father put his arm round her shoulder. He was remembering some of the things that Professor Mayfield had said when he told him that he thought he could get Tally a scholarship to Delderton.

It's an unusual school and very highly regarded. All sorts of eminent people send their children there. The school believes in freedom and self-development, and not forcing the children.

Perhaps he should have found out more before he'd agreed to send Tally – but the part he had taken notice of was the description of the beautiful Devon countryside, the healthy food . . . the safety it would provide in times of war. And of course he himself believed in freedom and self-development – who didn't?

Now quickly he tried to explain to his stricken daughter that Delderton was what was known as a progressive school.

But Tally was beyond help. She would rather have gone into a lion's den than into one of those compartments.

'I don't know how to be progressive,' she said in a small

voice. 'I don't know how one does it.' Tears sprang to her eyes. 'And I don't know about self-development. I don't know about any of these things.'

But it was too late. As for Augusta Carrington, it was quite obvious to Tally what had happened to her. She had stayed at home with her head under her pillow and refused to leave the house.

'We'll write to you every day,' promised Aunt May – and Dr Hamilton, blaming himself utterly, took his daughter's hand and led her to the train.

People don't die from getting into school trains and Tally, as she leaned out of the window to wave, stayed incurably alive, but as she saw her father and the aunts standing very upright on the platform she felt a sense of desolation such as she had never known.

Doors slammed; the guard waved his flag and put his whistle to his lips and the train began to move. Her father lifted his arm for the last time and turned to lead his sisters to the exit, and Tally, following him with her eyes, saw some of the other parents hurrying away blindly, as if these odd people too might be sorry to see their extraordinary children go. For a short time the Foxingham train ran beside hers, and she could see the fierce-striped boys in a blur of red and yellow. Then their train accelerated and they were gone.

She took a deep breath and opened the door to a compartment.

There were three people inside. A thin girl with two long sandy plaits sat in one corner, turning the pages of a film magazine. She had grey eyes and a narrow face covered in freckles. People with freckles usually look cheerful, but this girl seemed listless and rather sad, hunched in her seat. Yet the smile she gave Tally was welcoming and friendly.

'You'd better sit over here,' she said. 'Not under the salamander. He slops.'

'He doesn't,' said the wild-haired boy crossly, looking up at the luggage rack. His legs were stretched out so as to leave little room, but he moved them for Tally to get past. 'I got him a new tank.'

Tally peered up at the strange pale creature, like an overgrown newt, lurking in the waterweeds.

'Is it an axolotl?' she asked, remembering her father's zoology books.

The boy nodded. 'I got him for my birthday.'

'Are we allowed to keep animals then?' asked Tally.

'Not cats or dogs, but small ones that can stay in cages,' said the girl, putting down her magazine. 'There's a pet hut where they live.' And then: 'My name's Julia.' She pointed to the boy with the axolotl. 'He's Barney. And that's Tod.'

Tod was the boy who had carried the 'Down with Tyrants!' banner, but the banner was now rolled up and he was reading the *Dandy*.

'You'd better come and sit next to me,' Julia went on. 'There's a little fat boy who was sitting where you are. He's called Kit and he's new like you. He's in the lavatory. They sent him in a shirt and tie and he's very upset. I think he's trying to flush his tie down the loo.'

'But it won't go down, surely?' Tally was instantly concerned. 'He'll block everything.'

Julia shrugged, but Tally was not good at leaving well alone. 'I'll go and see,' she said.

She made her way along the corridor. The girl with bare feet was hanging on to the window bars. She wore a green shirt with a rip in it and a gathered skirt with an uneven hem and looked very confident. Obviously the rip was in exactly the right place, and the hem needed to be uneven.

The lavatory door was locked, but after she had banged several times it opened and a woebegone face appeared round it. In one plump hand the little boy held a bedraggled tie.

'It's no good – I looked but the hole's too small. No one's wearing a tie. *No one*. And there's a girl without any shoes and I want to go to a proper school where they have prefects and play cricket,' he wailed, and a tear fell from his large blue eye.

'We could throw your tie out of the window,' suggested Tally. 'That would be simpler. Or I'll keep it for you till you go home.'

The idea that he might one day go home again cheered Kit up enough to stop him crying and he followed her out into the corridor.

'Wait a minute,' said Tally. 'Just let your shirt hang out over your shorts. And take off your socks. I'm going to take mine off too; they're a bit clean and white.'

Back in the compartment they found the teacher with the clipboard. She seemed to have forgotten about Augusta Carrington and looked relaxed and cheerful. Her amazing russet hair tumbled down her back and her amber eyes were flecked with gold.

'Oh, there you are. Good.' she said, smiling at Tally and Kit. 'Is everything all right?'

Tally nodded, and Kit, who had been about to repeat that he wanted to go to a proper school where they played cricket, decided not to.

'Well, if you want anything I'm in the next carriage,' she said. 'I'd better go and see how the other new people are getting on.'

'It's not fair to make Clemmy take the school train,' said Barney when she had gone. 'She hates all those lists and things, and somebody always does get lost. They could get someone boring and bossy like Prosser.'

'Who is she?' asked Tally.

'She's called Clemency Short. She teaches art and she helps out in the kitchens. She's a marvellous cook.'

'I thought I'd seen her before, but I can't have done.'

'Actually you can,' said Barney. 'She's in the London Gallery as the Goddess of the Foam coming out of some waves, and on a plinth outside the post office in Frith Street standing on one toe – only that's a sculpture.'

'And on the wall of the Regent Theatre as a dancing muse,' said Julia. 'She looks a bit cross there because the man who painted the mural was a brute and made the girls stand about in the freezing cold dressed in bits of muslin and Clemmy got bronchitis. That's what made her decide to stop being an artist's model and become a teacher.'

It was a long journey. The children brought out their sandwiches; they grew drowsy. Julia had stopped turning the pages of her magazine. Tally thought she might be asleep, but when she glanced at her she saw that she was looking intently at one particular picture: a photograph of a woman with carefully arranged curls drooping on to her forehead, a long neck and slightly parted lips. The caption said: 'Gloria Grantley: one of the loveliest stars to grace the firmament of film'.

'Isn't she beautiful?' said Julia, and Tally agreed that she was, though she didn't really care for her. Gloria looked hungry, as though she needed to eat an admiring gentleman each day for breakfast.

The train stopped briefly at Exeter and Clemmy came past again, checking that everybody was all right.

'By the way, you're in Magda's house,' she told Tally. 'And Kit too. Julia will show you; she's with Magda as well.'

'Oh dear, that's bad news,' said Julia when Clemency had gone.

'Isn't she nice? Magda, I mean.'

'Yes, she's nice enough. Kind and all that. But she feels bad about things, and her cocoa is absolutely diabolical.'

'Cocoa can be difficult,' said Tally. 'The skin . . . but why does she feel bad?'

'She teaches German and she used to spend a lot of time in Germany, and every time Hitler does something awful she feels she's to blame. She's really a philosophy student – she's writing a book about someone called Schopenhauer – and her room gets all cluttered up with paper and she can't sew or sort clothes or anything like that.'

'Perhaps we could help her to make proper cocoa,' said Tally. 'She probably needs a whisk.'

But Kit had gone under again.

'I don't like cocoa with skin on it,' he began. 'I want to go to a proper school where they –'

But just then the train gave an unexpected jolt and a shower of water from Barney's axolotl descended on his head.

When they had been travelling for more than three hours Tally looked out, and there was the sea. She had not expected it; the sun, the blue water, the wheeling birds were like getting a sudden present.

They went through a sandstone tunnel, and another one . . . and presently the train turned inland again. Now they were in a lush green valley with clumps of ancient trees. The air that came in through the open window was soft and gentle; a river sparkled beside the line.

The train slowed down.

'We're here,' said Barney.

'Really?' said Tally. 'This is Delderton?'

Her father had spoken of the peaceful Devon countryside, but she had not expected anything like this.

'My goodness,' she said wonderingly. 'It's *very* beautiful!'

CHAPTER FOUR

DELDERTON

Tally was right. There was no lovelier place in England: a West Country valley with a wide river flowing between rounded hills towards the sea. Sheltered from the north winds, everything grew at Delderton: primroses and violets in the meadows; campions and bluebells in the woods and, later in the year, foxgloves and willowherb. A pair of otters lived in the river, kingfishers skimmed the water and russet Devon cows, the same colour as the soil, grazed the fields and wandered like cows in Paradise.

But it was children, not cows or kingfishers, that Delderton mainly grew.

Twenty years earlier a very rich couple from America came and built a school on the ruins of Delderton Hall, with its jousting ground and ancient yews, and they spared no expense, for they believed that only the best was good enough for children and they were as idealistic as they were wealthy.

The new Delderton was built round a central courtyard; the walls were lined with cream stucco, the windows had green shutters, the archway that led into the building was crowned by a tower with a blue clock adorned by gold numbers and a brilliantly painted weathervane in the shape of a cockerel.

And the ancient cedar that had sheltered the lawns of the old hall was saved and grew in the centre of the courtyard.

Inside the building too the American founders spared no expense. Each child had its own room: only a small one, but private. The common rooms had well-sprung sofas, the pianos in the music rooms were Steinways and the library housed over ten thousand books.

But what was important to the founders was not the building; it was what the school would mean to the children who came to it. For Delderton was to be a progressive school – a school where the children would be free to follow their instincts and develop in a natural way. There would be no bullyings or beatings, no competitive sports where one person was ranked above another, no exams – just harmony and self-development in the glorious Devon countryside. A school where the teachers would be chosen for their loving kindness and not their degrees.

And this was exactly what had happened. But now, twenty years later, the building looked . . . tired. The cream walls were streaked with damp from the soft West Country rain; the paint on the shutters was flaking – and the beautiful cedar in the courtyard was supported by wooden props.

And the nice American founders were tired too. In the autumn of 1930 they sold the school to a board of trustees who appointed a new headmaster. His name was Ben Daley: a small, portly man with a bald head and a nice smile, who now, at the beginning of the summer term, was looking out of his study window at the pupils coming in through the archway from the station bus.

And at one pupil in particular – a new girl with straight fawn hair who had stopped and laid her hand on the trunk of the cedar as though she was greeting a friend.

'It's three hundred years old,' said Julia, looking up at the tree. 'The headmaster's mad about it – if anyone climbs it or throws stuff into the branches he comes rushing out of his room. No one ever gets expelled here, but if they did it would be because of the tree. That top branch broke off because a horrible boy called Ronald Peabody climbed it though it was already weak. He fell and broke his arm, but nobody cared.'

'I wouldn't have cared either,' said Tally.

The rooms where the children slept were on corridors on either side of the courtyard. Inside, the building was divided into four houses separated by a double door. Each house had a room for the housemother, a common room and a pantry. Tally was in the Blue House; her room overlooked the courtyard and the tree.

'You mean we each have our own room?'

Julia nodded. 'I don't know for how much longer; I think the money's running out a bit, but for now.'

Tally's room was very small, but it had everything you could want: a divan bed, a washbasin, a bookcase and a built-in wardrobe. The door of the wardrobe was somewhat battered and one desk leg was propped up on a wedge, but Tally was delighted. And it solved at once the problem of the feasts in the dorm. No one could have a feast in a dorm which was not there.

Julia was in the room next to hers; then came Barney, then two children she had not met yet. Kit was at the far end of the corridor.

As she was putting her things away there was a knock on the door.

'Do you need any help with unpacking? I'm Magda – your housemother.'

Magda was thin and very dark with large black eyes and wispy hair.

Tally shook her head. 'No, I'm all right, thanks.'

'Good. Well, high tea's in half an hour. You'll hear the gong. And after that you're to go along to the headmaster's room.'

Tally looked stricken. She had not quite shaken off the memory of the books she had read before she came. 'I can't have done anything yet – I've only just got here.'

Magda smiled. 'No, no. Daley likes to welcome new children individually. Julia will show you where to go.'

The headmaster's study was large and light. One window looked out over the courtyard; another faced the terraced garden leading to the playing field and, beyond it, the rolling hills. Now, hearing a quiet knock at the door,

Daley said, 'Come in,' and a girl with a nibbled fringe and interested eyes came into the room.

'Ah, Talitha Hamilton, is that right? And they call you Tally.'

'Yes.'

Clearly this wasn't a curtsying situation, though the headmaster sat behind an impressive desk, so Tally smiled instead and put out her hand.

The headmaster had a headache. He always had a headache for the first three days of term, but for a moment the throbbing grew less. For this child was actually on the list, she was expected, she looked intelligent – and she had taken notice of the cedar tree. And this was important because she was on a scholarship and he couldn't console himself with thinking that she brought much-needed money with her. One child, however awful, provided the salary for a teacher for a term, or a year's worth of books. He shouldn't of course have given any more scholarships, but his friend Professor Mayfield had spoken so enthusiastically of the selfless work done by Tally's father that he had agreed.

'Now,' he said, when he had welcomed her to Delderton, 'have you any questions you wanted to ask me?'

'Well, I do have. I mean, I thought I was coming to an ordinary school where girls lived in dorms and shouted, "Well played, Daphne!" – and all that . . . but this isn't like that, is it?'

'No.'

'I'm not reproaching anybody, but what is it exactly? People say it's a progressive school and I know what progressive means – at least I think I do. It means going from somewhere to somewhere else. But where to?'

'Ah yes.' The headmaster for a moment looked sad. 'That is a good question. I suppose we want children to take responsibility for their own lives. To choose what is right rather than to have it forced on them.'

'Yes, I see. Of course, one would have to know what is right.'

'Don't you think one does know?'

'I suppose so. Usually. But oughtn't . . . the *whole school* to be going from somewhere to somewhere else? To somewhere better . . . if it's being progressive? I mean, the world isn't very good, is it, with this war coming and everything?'

Daley was silent. The child was certainly right about the state of the world. For a moment he saw what she saw: a whole school marching like an avenging army on the side of The Good.

'We do what we can to help: we take a lot of children from abroad. Staff too, and many of the people who help with domestic work come from oppressed countries. And there's a council meeting every other Monday: if you have any ideas you could put them forward then.'

Tally nodded, screwing up her face. 'I expect it's more difficult than I realize.' And then: 'Is it true we don't have to go to lessons?'

'You don't have to, but I hope you will. We have some excellent teachers.'

'So it's all right to go to lessons? We don't *have* to be free if we don't want to?'

The headmaster smiled. 'No, Tally, you don't have to be free.'

But Tally had another question. 'I was wondering about Augusta Carrington. Did anyone find her?'

'Yes, they did,' said the headmaster, looking pleased. 'She's turned up at a school in Wales. She got on the wrong train at Paddington – it happens from time to time.'

He looked down at the note he had made on his writing pad. All the children had a tutor chosen from among the staff, whom they saw once a week and to whom they could take special problems. Against Tally's name he had written: 'David Prosser'. There was nothing wrong with the chemistry teacher; he was a perfectly sensible and responsible man. But now he crossed it out and wrote a different name.

'Your tutor will be Matteo von Tarlenheim. He takes biology . . . and other things.'

Now why did I do that? he wondered when Tally had gone. He usually kept Matteo for difficult boys or for children like Julia Mecklebury who had a special problem – and Tally was in neither of these groups.

But he did not change his mind.

When she got back to her corridor Tally found that Julia had finished unpacking and arranging her room. She had tacked up two posters of landscapes – an autumn wood and a rocky beach – and plumped up an embroidered cushion on the bed. Everything looked cheerful and nice, except for the photo of Gloria Grantley, the film star with sausage curls and pouting lips, which was in a silver frame by Julia's bed.

'Is she a friend of the family?' asked Tally, but Julia just shook her head, and Barney came in then to say he was going to settle the axolotl in his proper tank in the pet hut and, if they came with him, Tally could see where everything was.

The pet hut was behind the gym, which was a separate building set in trees. On the wooden steps leading up to it sat a small, very pretty girl talking in French to an enormous white rabbit that drooped down on either side of her slender knees.

Inside, the hut was full of cages from which came the squeals and snuffles of various rabbits and mice and guinea pigs. In one corner, however, there was an unexpected pet: a large striped snake, which opened one gummy eye as it felt the vibration made by their footsteps. It looked unhealthy and dry.

'That's Verity's,' said Julia. 'She's an awful show-off. You wouldn't catch Verity with anything as ordinary as a guinea pig.'

Verity, it turned out, was the girl who had been barefoot on Paddington Station.

They decanted the axolotl into a bigger tank and gave him some bloodworm pellets and he settled down at once and began to eat – but Barney was still worried because he hadn't got a name for him.

'It's so rude having pets that aren't called anything,' he said.

But it was difficult. The axolotl's head, with its piercing black eyes and feathery gills, could have been called something Mexican and royal-sounding, like Protaxeles, but his legs were not royal at all. They were short and

42

bandy – and if you had been naming his legs he would have been called Cyril or Alf.

'It'll come to you suddenly,' said Tally. 'Probably in the middle of the night.'

After that they took Tally on a tour of the school buildings. As the school had grown, classrooms and workshops and studios had sprung up outside the courtyard in places that had been part of the gardens of the old hall. There were only a few gardeners and groundsmen left now, so that creepers grew up the side of the gym and there were patches of moss and wild flowers between the paving stones. In the early-evening light everything looked dreamy, like an illustration in a book of watercolours.

They went down a sloping field to look at the school farm: a huddle of sheds with three goats, a cow, a handful of sheep and some chickens which an African boy called Borro was shutting up for the night. As they made their way back they passed the open door of the art room and saw Clemmy bent over some dishes, mixing powder paints. She looked serene and happy – and Tally saw what Barney meant when he said that she should not be in charge of trains. Last term's paintings were still on the wall: monkeys swung through jungles, underwater creatures wreathed and coiled . . . and in one corner was a blood-red painting of excited workers carrying sickles and hammers towards a palace gate.

'That's Tod's picture,' said Julia. 'He's sure the revolution will come soon, and that will be the end of tyrants and kings.'

*

Julia had not been exaggerating when she said that Magda was not good at making cocoa. When they had washed and put on their pyjamas, all the children in the Blue House met for cocoa and biscuits in Magda's room. Magda had a little kitchenette adjoining her room and she disappeared into it, emerging with a huge jug and a tray of cups.

The cocoa she poured out was quite extraordinary – blackish and grainy with a thick layer of skin – but she seemed so relieved when she had made it and poured it into the cups that even the rowdiest children said nothing. Then she played a Mozart sonata on her gramophone and everybody went to bed.

'You see what I mean about the cocoa,' said Julia.

'Yes, I do. Perhaps something could be done,' said Tally.

Julia looked surprised. 'How could it? She always makes it like that.'

'Maybe we could make it?' suggested Tally.

But now, as the lights went out, the homesickness that had been lying in wait for Tally gathered itself together and pounced.

She thought of the aunts, waiting for her as she came home from school, eager for every detail of her day. She thought of her friends in the street – Maybelle and Kenny, and Primrose in her stable.

But above all she thought of her father. Coming in from the surgery asking, 'Where's Tally?' as soon as he entered the house . . . teasing her about something foolish she had said . . . walking with her along the river on a Sunday, while they talked about anything and everything on earth.

It would be months before she saw him again and they had scarcely been separated for a day.

The lump in her throat was growing bigger. She groped for a handkerchief.

And then she heard the sound of sobbing. The sobbing grew louder, was muffled, then grew louder again.

Tally had expected tears from Kit but he had gone to sleep at once, his thumb in his mouth, and anyway his room was at the other end of the corridor. She waited, but the crying went on. It was none of her business, really – but she had not been brought up to ignore distress. She got out of bed, opened her door and listened.

The sobbing came from a door opposite. She knocked very quietly, then pushed it open.

She was in the housemother's room. Magda was sitting at her table, which was piled high with manuscript paper. Clearly she had intended to work on her book about the philosopher with the diffficult name, but she wasn't. Her head had fallen forward and she was crying bitterly; strands of hair lay on the paper and there was ink on her face.

When she saw Tally she sat up suddenly and blew her nose. 'Is anything the matter?' she asked. 'Are you homesick?'

'No . . . well, not really. But are you all right?'

Tally's enquiring face, tilted in concern, brought on another attack of weeping.

'Yes . . . yes. Of course. I'm not starving or being shot at so of course I'm all right.' Magda sniffed and dabbed at her eyes. 'You must go back to bed – you'll be so tired in the morning.'

But Tally knew what one had to do when people were in trouble; her father had told her often enough. One sat quietly beside them and waited. And indeed, almost at once, Magda began to speak.

'It's just . . . when everything's quiet, one can't help remembering. You see, I studied in Germany, in Weimar. It's such a beautiful city, the old squares, the gardens . . . so peaceful, so full of interesting people and everyone so well-behaved. Scholars, professors . . . the lectures were remarkable. There was a young professor there . . . Heribert. I was going to go back to Germany to live when I had finished my book, and I thought that we might get married. But not now. Not with the Nazis marching about in jackboots spoiling everything – and anyway, I have a Jewish grandmother. But for me,' said Magda, and her eyes filled with tears again, 'Weimar will always be home.'

'Yes, I see.' Tally put out a hand and laid it on Magda's arm. 'I'm so sorry.'

She stayed for a while, and before she left Magda's sobs had died down. She even offered to make Tally another cup of cocoa.

Back in her bed, Tally found she was too tired to go on with her own longings. She had expected anything except to go to a school where it was the *teachers* who were homesick – and almost at once she fell asleep.

CHAPTER FIVE

BECOMING A FORK

Perhaps it was a pity that the first lesson on the timetable the next morning was drama. Tally had thought that drama was about doing plays and had been looking forward to it, but it wasn't. It was taught by a woman with grey hair called Armelle, wearing a leotard, and took place in the hall.

'Now I want you to spread yourself out on the floor,' she said. 'Give yourself plenty of space because we're going to do an improvisation that covers the whole of our lives. We're going to start by giving birth to ourselves. We're going to imagine that we're an embryo waiting to be born. Waiting . . . waiting . . . Don't hurry it . . . that's right . . . Then we're going to learn to walk . . . slowly . . .

very slowly . . . crawl first . . . then upright. Good . . . good . . .'

Tally was between Julia and Kit. She had hoped that Kit would decide to be born near some boys on the other side of the room, but he settled himself down as close to her as he could and now she heard his anguished whisper.

'I don't want to give birth to myself, Tally. I don't want to. I want to go to a proper school, where they have prefects and play cricket.'

When they had finished giving birth to themselves they had to stand up and become rigid and pronged like a fork, and then curved and bountiful like a teapot, and then soft and yielding like a pillow.

'If we don't have to go to classes, why does everyone come to drama?' asked Tally when they were out in the courtyard again.

'It's because Armelle's son was killed in Spain, fighting for the Republicans,' explained Julia. 'She used to be quite fat and bossy, and now she's all skin and bones.'

After drama came 'handicrafts'. This was taught by a cheerful plump woman called Josie, who took them out into the fields behind the school to look for sheep's wool.

'When we've got a sackful we're going to wash it and card it and dye it – using natural dyes, of course. Lichen and moss and alder bark . . . It'll keep us busy most of the term,' she said cheerfully.

Tally thought that this was likely: the fields round Delderton seemed to be inhabited by cows rather than sheep and wisps of discarded wool were scarce, but as they searched the hedgerows Josie pointed out all sorts of interesting plants which they would pick later and grind up and boil in vats.

'I've been experimenting with woad,' she said, and rolled up her sleeves to show them her forearms, which were mottled with blue, 'but I haven't got it quite right yet. It makes you realize how clever the ancient Britons were.'

After break they had a double period of English; it was taken by a quietly spoken man in spectacles called O'Hanrahan. They were studying Greek myths and he told them the story of Persephone, who was carried away by the King of the Underworld and kept prisoner there, guarded by a dreadful three-headed dog, while her sorrowing mother, the goddess Demeter, searched and lamented, and the trees and flowers withered and died. He didn't read the story, he told it, and the class listened to him in total silence.

'It would make a good play,' said a boy with ginger hair.

'Perhaps next term,' said O'Hanrahan. He turned to Tally. 'What do you think?'

Tally nodded. 'Yes, it would. The spirits trapped in the Underworld would be interesting to do. Writhing and shrieking and begging to be let out.'

'Oh, not a play,' said Julia nervously. 'Not proper acting.'

O'Hanrahan looked at her quietly for a moment before he said, 'No one has to act if they don't want to, Julia. You know that.'

When they were back in Julia's room getting ready for lunch Tally asked, 'Don't you like acting?'

'No. I mean, I don't do it. Not ever.'

She had on her worried look and Tally did not ask any more. She knew already that she and Julia would be friends, but there was something puzzling about her. It was as though she would do anything not to be noticed, as though she needed to be younger and less important than she was.

Later, as Tally walked over to the dining room with Barney, he said, 'She's silly. Julia, I mean. O'Hanrahan got her to do a bit in *Much Ado About Nothing*. It was just in the classroom, but Julia was amazing. Only when we told her how good she was, she clammed up completely and went off in a state and she's never done anything since. Whereas Verity always wants to be the star. You'll see – if we do *Persephone*, she'll try to be the heroine.'

'I was wondering about her feet. Verity's, I mean. I can see it's fine to go barefoot in the grass, but in Paddington Station . . . Doesn't she get splinters?'

Barney shrugged. 'Someone told her she had beautiful feet and that was that. She's the vainest person I know – she'll spend an hour tearing her skirt in exactly the right place or un-tidying her hair.'

In the afternoon they had games and Kit's hopes of playing cricket were finally dashed. The only team game they played at Delderton was rounders, and people who didn't want to play that went for cross-country runs, used the apparatus in the gym, or worked on the school farm.

Tally went down to help Borro clean out the goats. Borro's father had been a chieftain in Bechuanaland before he was deposed by a rival and now had a job lecturing in the University of London, but Borro was determined to go back to Africa and reclaim his father's land and farm it. The walls of his room were covered in pictures of cattle: Friesians and Aberdeen Angus and

Longhorns, whose mild eyes gazed down at him as he slept. Not only that, but he was going to breed a new kind of cow, which would grow fat even on the parched soil of his native land.

Meanwhile, since cattle breeding was not really practical at school, he and Tod had decided to breed edible snails and sell them to restaurants. Tod wanted the money for the revolution and Borro wanted it for his fare back to Africa. Unfortunately the few snails they had managed to collect so far did not seem to be remotely interested in mating.

Tally's friends discussed this, sitting on the steps of the pet hut after tea, watching the snails crawl over each other in a bored sort of way.

'I suppose it's because each snail is both a male and a female,' said Tally, 'so they get muddled.'

'Matteo would know what to do,' said Barney.

But Matteo was not yet back at school, and his first biology lesson had been postponed.

It was surprising how quickly one could get used to a completely new life. Some of the lessons were quite ordinary: Chemistry, say, when a man called David Prosser did the experiments for them on a bench and then told them what to write up, but mostly going into a classroom was an adventure that might turn out in any sort of way.

Art, for example . . . Clemmy took a double period of art on Tally's second day at school except that she didn't 'take' it – she just seemed to wander round the art room, which looked out over fields and the distant trees that lined the river. Paper and paints were laid out and Clemmy murmured something.

'Most people don't believe in guardian angels, but what exactly is a guardian angel?' she said. 'Could it be something quite different to what people think . . .?' And almost at once everyone had started working, completely absorbed. Tally found that she was painting her street: the rows of houses, her father's surgery and above them, flying over the roofs, London's own guardian angels, the barrage balloons – and it felt as though she was joining her life in London with her new life at Delderton.

But the lessons everyone spoke about were Matteo's biology classes. 'They're special,' they said, and when Tally asked in what way, they said it was no use explaining; she'd see.

Making friends was the most important thing, but what Tally loved was the way Delderton grew out of the countryside. Going over to the gym she would meet a red squirrel or pass a great bank of primroses as scented and rich as if they had been planted there. And each morning, as she woke, she heard a thrush singing in the cedar tree.

Kit, though, had still not settled in and followed Tally about lamenting from morning till night. Kit did not want to be a fork or pick worts to dye his sheep's wool – and he did not want to go 'ping' on the triangle when they played the Toy Symphony in music lessons.

Music was taught by an elderly professor of harmony who had hoped for a quiet life by returning to teach in the country. New children were usually persuaded to learn whatever instrument was needed for the orchestra, but when he met Kit the professor knew he was beaten.

'Oh Kit, surely you can just go "ping",' said Tally wearily. 'It doesn't take a minute.'

But she was really very sorry for the little boy, who had just started at a small prep school down the road from his house and made friends with a boy called Horlicks Major and been picked for the cricket team, when a rich friend of his mother's had come to stay with the family and said that Kit was repressed and should be sent to Delderton, and had offered to pay the fees.

'But I don't mind being repressed,' Kit had told his new friends. 'I don't like it when people tell me I can do what I like. I want them to tell me what to *do*.'

Magda had stopped crying after lights out and did her best to be a good housemother. Nothing could be done about her cocoa, and she got very confused about checking the laundry – it was a question of luck whose clean washing landed on one's bed – but her German lessons were good, and she was particularly kind to Julia on the morning when the first letters came.

The post at Delderton came just after breakfast, so that there was time before lessons began for the children to go to the pigeonholes outside the school office to see if there was any mail.

The aunts had kept their promise. There were three letters in Tally's pigeonhole: one in green ink from Aunt Hester, one in violet ink from Aunt May and one in ordinary ink from her father, which she pounced on and read first.

There was a letter for Barney and one for Tod and for Borro and for Kit.

Only Julia had no mail.

*

On Tally's third day at Delderton the headmaster gathered the school together in the hall. He said that it was easy to forget, in the peace of the countryside, that Britain and France and so many of the free people of the world were in danger. Here in Devon we were unlikely to be bombed, he said, but we must be ready to do everything to help the war effort if the worst happened.

At this point the older children looked at each other hopefully, ready to man a nest of machine guns if one was set up in the courtyard, but what the headmaster said was different.

'Already two of the domestic staff have had their call-up papers. So I think it would be fair if every child did half an hour of housework before the start of lessons.'

Everyone agreed with this – except Verity, who said that she didn't think her parents had sent her to school to scrub floors – but of course it was a disappointment. When one has hoped to man the barricades, it is difficult to get excited about doing the dusting or polishing the furniture.

Actually, it was not easy to forget that there might be a war, even at Delderton. Most of the staff had their own wirelesses and at six o'clock the children would make their way to the housemothers' rooms and listen to the news.

Not only was Hitler braying and strutting and threatening, growing madder and wilder in his demands by the day, but Mussolini, the Italian dictator who copied him in everything he did, had invaded Albania, a defenceless country which had done him no harm whatsoever, and the Albanian ruler, King Zog, had fled his country and gone into exile.

*

On the following day as Tally was walking across the courtyard she saw a girl standing alone by the archway with a suitcase and a violin case beside her. She was tall and thin with frizzy black hair, and for some reason Tally knew at once who she was. She had the look of someone who had come far, like a camel across the desert.

'You're Augusta Carrington,' she said.

Augusta nodded and said, 'Yeth, I am.'

She had a ferocious metallic brace on her teeth, which made her lisp.

Clemmy now came out of the school office, holding a list and looking shaken.

'Are you sure, Augusta?' she asked. 'It says here that you can't eat cheese or strawberries or wheat or eggs or nuts or rhubarb. You're allergic to all of those.'

Augusta nodded.

'And fur and feathers,' she said, spitting a little through her brace.

Although Tally and her friends all took to Augusta, the allergy to fur and feathers made it difficult when they brought her to the pet hut, where they had their meetings. If she sat on the top step she sneezed all the time, and on the second step she sneezed often, but on the bottom step she was all right, and able to be sympathetic about their problems.

'You could call the axolotl Zog,' she suggested.

Actually she said 'Thog' because of her brace, but they understood her.

'You shouldn't call anything after a king,' said Tod. 'Kings are evil.'

But Barney said it wasn't Zog's fault he had been born

a king, and when they had looked carefully at the creature's bandy legs and round black eyes he really did look quite like a Zog.

So that was one problem solved. The snails on the other hand were still lying about on other snails as though they were old sofas.

'I wish Matteo would come back,' said Borro restlessly.

But Matteo was still away, and biology had been postponed again.

Tally had heard a lot about Matteo as a biologist – but it was what he was like as a tutor that she wanted to know.

'He's your tutor too, isn't he?' she asked Julia as they were getting ready for bed. 'What's he like?'

Julia had been re-plaiting her hair. She put down her hairbrush and didn't answer straight away.

'He's not like anybody else,' she said.

'But do you like him?'

'Yes, I like him very much, but that isn't what it's about. You'll see . . .'

CHAPTER SIX

LONDON INTERLUDE

After they watched the Delderton train steam out of Paddington Station, the aunts felt completely wretched, and Tally's father vowed that he would take her away at the end of the first term.

Then came Tally's letters and everything changed.

'This is a very interesting school,' she wrote on her second day. 'The first night I thought I would be homesick, but it was my housemother who was homesick . . . Being a fork is a bit odd but it can be quite peaceful because you can think your own thoughts . . .' and she described the cedar tree the headmaster loved so much, and the art classes and Clemmy. By the time her second letter came it was clear that Tally was enjoying herself – and as it was a sunny morning the aunts, who always took such an interest in Tally's life, set off for the Thameside Municipal Baths.

They were not going swimming. It was a long time since they had cared to plunge into chlorinated water in their bathing costumes, which no longer looked quite right. They were going to look at Tally's art teacher.

'She's in a mural in the Thameside Baths,' Tally had written. 'Barney says it's easy to see her there because you can get quite close. She's coming out of the water holding up a garland of seashells.'

So now the aunts paid their admission fee for 'Freestyle Swimming' and took their rolled-up towels (which had no costumes inside them) into the entrance hall and there, sure enough, was a large mural of some girls coming out of a very blue pool surrounded by flowers.

'That's her,' said Aunt Hester straight away. 'I remember her hair.'

Now that she wasn't looking for Augusta Carrington, the woman who had been in charge of the school train was smiling very happily as she held up her necklace of shells. After that the aunts went on a proper Clemmy trail, searching her out in the London Gallery and the Battersea Arts Museum as instructed by their niece, but not tracking her down as she stood on one toe outside the post office in Frith Street where, as Tally had explained, she was cast in concrete and couldn't really be seen.

In her second letter Tally also mentioned the problem of Gloria Grantley, with whom her friend Julia was so besotted.

'Could you ask Maybelle if she knows anything about her?'

So the aunts went to the corner shop, where Maybelle was weighing caster sugar into blue bags, and she was very helpful and came round after the shop closed with a pile of film magazines in which she had marked a great many photographs of Gloria Grantley.

'She's a big star all right,' said Maybelle. 'She usually plays in those gloomy films where she's on trial for murder or her lover tries to kill her and all that kind of thing. You know, melodrama.'

Maybelle herself preferred musicals – she was taking tap and stage-dancing classes and definitely intended to break into films. 'She must earn millions,' said Maybelle. 'And she's beautiful all right, but . . .' She shrugged.

The aunts dutifully studied all the copies of *The Picturegoer* Maybelle had left.

There were photos of Gloria on a tiger-skin rug and in a hammock and coming down a flight of stairs.

'I think her throat is a little . . . excessive, don't you? I mean . . . almost too swan-like?' said May.

Hester agreed: 'But it says here that she's only twenty-five years old, so maybe she'll settle down. People of twenty-five don't always know how to behave sensibly.'

As Tally's letters continued to come, the aunts became more and more involved with her life and that of her friends. They searched the ironmongers for a whisk that could be used to froth up Magda's cocoa, and they went to the library to look up the philosophy of Schopenhauer and agreed that someone who was doing research on him could not be expected also to be good at housework. And when Tally added an excited postscript to her fourth letter to say that Augusta Carrington had turned up, they shared the relief of the staff, even though poor Augusta had serious problems.

'She's allergic to absolutely everything,' wrote Tally. 'Magda says she is used to allergies because Heribert, the professor she loved in Germany, was allergic to cheese and strawberries – they brought him out in lumps – but Augusta mostly lives on rice and bananas, though she can eat weird things like tripe and dark chocolates with gooey centres. It's no wonder she got on the wrong train.'

And the aunts in their turn wrote almost daily to Tally to tell her what had happened in the street: about the new air-raid shelter at number 4, in which the dog across the road had had her puppies, and about old Mrs Henderson, who had attacked the gardener in the park with his own shovel for digging up the wallflowers and planting cabbages, which would help us to win the war if it came, but did not smell nice.

When Tally had been at Delderton for a week, Dr Hamilton's brother, Thomas, came to see him to consult him about a patient. Thomas was the richer and more fashionable doctor, but James had a special instinct for what was wrong with people. And with Thomas came his wife, Tally's Aunt Virginia, the mother of Roderick and Margaret. She said she had come to sympathize with Tally's family, but actually she came to gloat.

'My dear, we were so horrified by what we saw at the station. Those dreadful children and everything so out of control and no uniforms! I suppose you're going to take her away?'

Tally's father looked at her. 'I don't think so, Virginia.

Not yet, at all events. We have had some very interesting letters from Tally.'

'Letters! But she hasn't been away for a week. At Foxingham they're not allowed to write at all the first week while they settle back into school.'

'Well, at Delderton they write when they like and Tally has been very good. Her letters amuse us very much.'

Actually, thought Dr Hamilton, Tally's letters had done more than amuse him. They had interested him and consoled him and touched on some things that he cared about deeply.

'Really?' This was not at all what Aunt Virginia wanted to hear. 'Margaret never has time for more than a few lines.'

'Of course, the letters at Foxingham are censored by the teachers,' said her husband. 'Just as well, really. One doesn't want to get oneself upset by any nonsense the boys can come up with.'

'We saw something about Foxingham in the newspaper, didn't we, May?' said Hester. 'A boy who tried to run away because he was afraid of being punished.'

'Well, that's the kind of nonsense I mean,' said Thomas. 'There have to be punishments – they have pupils there from the royal houses of Europe, so the strictest discipline must be maintained. The Archduke of Hohenlohe has just sent his nephew there, and of course the Prince of Transjordania has been there for over a year. The boy who ran away was obviously a coward. He was supposed to go to the Head for a caning and he just bolted like a scared rabbit. They found him the next day hiding in some wood about a hundred miles away. If Roderick did that I'd be ashamed, and I certainly wouldn't want to hear about it in a letter.'

'Roderick would never get into that kind of trouble, dear,' said Aunt Virginia. She turned to her brother-in-law. 'Well, I suppose you know what you're doing, James, but I'd take Tally away at once if I were you.' She lowered her voice. 'Mrs Trent-Watson, who was at the train seeing Bernard off, says she's seen that woman who was in charge of the children before. She says she's an artists' model – and you know what that might mean. Life classes and all sorts of dreadful things! Of course it may not be true . . .'

Hester and May smiled. 'Ah, but it is true, Virginia. We've seen her on the walls of the swimming bath. Such a lovely girl. And Tally says she's a wonderful cook!'

Aunt Virginia sniffed. 'Well, all I can say is I wouldn't let Margaret associate with anyone like that, not in a million years.'

After they had left and Dr Hamilton was alone in his study, he took out his daughter's last letter again. Tally had described a strange, slightly mad but very beautiful world, a world in which the trees and the river and the hills at Delderton seemed to be as much a part of her life as the teachers and her friends.

And she wrote that she was waiting for her first biology lesson.

'The man who takes it is my tutor and he's supposed to be terribly good. He's been all over the world and done some important scientific work. I'm really looking forward to it.'

Dr Hamilton missed his daughter more than he would ever admit, but he was very pleased about that last sentence. Biology, the science of life, how it had begun and where it was going . . . this was what had started him off on his studies as a doctor.

That his daughter should take the same journey made him very happy.

CHAPTER SEVEN

MATTEO'S MOAN

As it happened, Tally was late for the first biology class. She had cut her knee, tripping on a paving stone, and gone back for some sticking plaster, and everyone was already settled when she slipped into a desk near the back.

The man standing at the blackboard wore a grey flannel suit. He had sparse ginger hair and a pointed ginger beard and he wore rimless spectacles.

'Today we are going to study the life cycle of the liver fluke,' he said in a high, slightly squeaky voice. 'Look at page seventy-six of your textbook and keep it open.'

Tally fought down a wave of disappointment. The life cycle of the liver fluke might be necessary. It might be important. But it does not make the heart beat faster. The nuns had taught it also.

'The history of this organism begins in vegetation in slow-moving streams, where it exists in the form of slime-encrusted eggs. You can see a picture of these in your textbook, labelled diagram A. Please copy it carefully into a blank page of your exercise books.'

He waited, the chalk in his hand, till everyone had finished.

'The eggs are then eaten by a sheep and make their way through the animal's bile duct into the liver, where they become adult flukes.'

He drew a liver (but not a sheep) and put in the adult flukes, explaining their effect on the animal, which was bad. 'I will allow five minutes for you to copy from the blackboard,' he said.

Tally, filling her liver with the flattened parasites, felt increasingly miserable, and angry too. Why did everyone tell her how wonderful biology was? The nuns had taught it better.

'There now follows hermaphrodite fertilization, and the resulting eggs pass out through the alimentary canal and on to the grass, where they turn into conical organisms which are known as miracidia,' he droned. 'You will find these on the next page, page seventy-seven . . .'

When the lesson was over Tally hurried out past Julia and her friends. She wanted to be on her own, for it seemed clear that they had been playing a joke on her, pretending that the biology teacher was special. She didn't mind being teased usually, but she had written to her father about him because she knew how much he wanted her to enjoy science.

But they caught her up.

'I'm sorry – that was a shame,' said Julia. 'We should have warned you – but everyone was sure that Matteo would be back today.'

'What do you mean? Wasn't that Matteo?'

Julia stopped dead and glared at her friend. 'Well, really, Tally! I may not be a genius, but I would hardly tell you that Smithy gives brilliant biology lessons.'

'I don't understand.'

'Smithy stands in when teachers are ill or away. He lives in the village; he used to teach at the High School in St Agnes, but he had to retire early. He's the most boring teacher in the world, but Daley keeps him on because he's good at getting people through external exams when we have to take them.'

But two nights later, as Tally drifted into sleep, Julia knocked at her door.

'Wake up! Open your window and listen.'

The courtyard was deserted; the cedar tree stood silvered in the moonlight. And floating towards them, very faintly, came the sound of a long-drawn-out and very melancholy noise.

'What is it?' asked Tally.

'It's Matteo's Moan,' said Julia. 'He likes to play it on the sackbut last thing at night. He says it's a folk song from the mountains – but we think he's made it up, it's so weird.'

The headmaster, sitting in his study, was frowning over documents and decisions. The founders of Delderton, who were still very much concerned with the school, had written from New York suggesting that if war came, Daley should evacuate the school to America. They offered the use of a large farmhouse in Maine, which could be the basis of a school while the war lasted.

Daley had read this letter a dozen times and pondered it, but he didn't know what to do. He didn't want to leave Delderton and he knew that many children – especially those on scholarships – would not be able to go; the fare to the States would be far too expensive. But did he have the right to turn down such an offer?

This was a big issue, but there were other annoyances. The parents of Philip Anderson wanted him to learn the accordion so that he could mix with the Common People. And the Ministry of Culture had written asking Daley to send a folk-dance group to a festival in an obscure country in central Europe.

This last letter annoyed him particularly. Delderton did not go in for folk dancing – the mere mention of Morris dancers with bells and funny hats would have the children up in arms, and it was not exactly a time when schools wanted to send their pupils gallivanting all over Europe. The man from the ministry had written very earnestly: there was nothing, he said, so likely to increase goodwill among nations as an exchange of cultural activity, especially if it involved children or young people – but the whole idea was ridiculous. All the same, Daley would bring it up at the council meeting at the end of the month – it would take everybody's minds off the Free Period the children had decided they needed on Wednesday afternoons, not to mention the matter of the dustbins which came up at every meeting.

And at least Matteo was back.

It was through the founders – Mr and Mrs Ford-Ellington – that Matteo had come to Delderton, arriving two years earlier with nothing but a leather holdall and his sackbut in a battered case.

No one knew much about his early life. He was a European who spoke five languages and had a Nansen Passport – the document given to those who no longer have a country of their own – but he had spent most of his adult life travelling and working in the wild places of the world: the Galapagos islands, the Mato Grosso, the high peaks of the Andes.

The founders had come across him on the Amazon, where he was doing research on the harpy eagle. They were with a party of tourists in the charge of a tour guide who turned out to be incompetent and lazy, and when they met Matteo they left the party and persuaded him to take them into the jungle for a week.

It was a week that they never forgot. Matteo took them through a maze of secret rivers to a valley where the morpho butterflies, in a shimmer of ultramarine and turquoise, came down to the water's edge to drink, and the trees were brilliant with hummingbirds and parakeets. He told them nothing about himself, but one night as they lay sleepless under their mosquito nets, watching the stars moving like fireflies between the waving branches, he admitted that his mind was once again turning to Europe. He foresaw great trouble over there, but at a time when so many people were planning to flee from the dangers they foresaw, Matteo wanted to return.

The founders offered him the cottage they had kept in Delderton village when they sold the school, and he had accepted. He had meant to stay for a few months at the most but now, nearly two years later, he was still in Devon and living in a room in the school. Yet Daley, as he greeted him and ordered coffee for them both, knew that at any moment he might move on. Like so many people during this uncertain time, Matteo was waiting.

'I've given you another girl to tutor,' Daley said when they had talked for a while. 'She's new. Her name's Tally.'

'Oh? And what particular problems does she have?' said Matteo suspiciously, for he knew that the headmaster liked to send him the most difficult and troubled children.

Daley smiled. 'It is rather you who will have the difficulties, I'm afraid. She is a girl who wants to make the world a better place.'

A few days after Matteo's return, Julia called Tally into her room and asked her if she would come to the cinema in St Agnes.

'Daley says I can go but I have to take someone with me. The buses don't fit so we have to walk, but it's only an hour and there's a matinee.'

They were sitting on Julia's bed, and from the way she spoke Tally realized that this was no ordinary visit to the cinema. She looked at the photograph on Julia's bedside table and her heart sank.

'Is it a film with Gloria Grantley in it?' she asked.

'Yes, it is. It's called *I'll Always Be Yours*. It's got an "A" certificate but one of the maids will go with us and then go and sit with her boyfriend.' As Tally hesitated Julia went on, 'Please, I'd rather it was you. The others tease me.'

'Yes, of course I'll come. Is she a good actress? I mean, I can see she's beautiful, but can she act?'

Julia flushed. 'She's an absolutely marvellous actress.'

Later Tally thought how different her life would have been if she had refused to accompany her friend – so much happened as a result of that visit to the cinema. But she did not go back on her word, and the following Saturday they set off to walk to St Agnes. The cinema was in the market square and already there was a queue of people waiting for the doors to open at two thirty.

'Her films are always terribly popular,' said Julia.

They decided to go for the good seats, which cost sixpence, and settled down to enjoy themselves.

The newsreel came first. The queen had launched a big aircraft carrier, releasing a champagne bottle to swing on to the hull, only it didn't smash the first time and had to be swung back again. The little princesses, Elizabeth and Margaret Rose, looked worried, but the second time the bottle smashed properly and the ship slid safely into the water.

After that came some pictures of Hitler and his followers yelling, 'Sieg Heil!' and goose-stepping in jackboots. Hitler said Germany needed more room for the German nation and he wanted Danzig, which really belonged to him and not to the Poles, and if they didn't give it to him he would take it by force. And an American had invented a new kind of bath plug.

Tally had hoped that there would be a cartoon: *The Three Little Pigs* perhaps . . . but what came next was a travelogue about a country called Bergania.

Bergania was in the news because the King of Bergania had just refused to allow Hitler's troops to march through his country if there was a war, and this was brave because it was a tiny kingdom, one of the smallest in Europe, and everybody feared the worst.

Though she was disappointed about the cartoon, Tally enjoyed the travelogue very much indeed. Bergania might be small, but it seemed to have everything one could want. A ridge of high mountains with everlasting snow, wide valleys planted with orchards and vineyards, and meadows where children herded goats like in *Heidi*. The capital of the country, which was also called Bergania, was a pretty town on the banks of a river, and overlooking it on a hill was the royal palace, guarded by soldiers in splendid uniforms.

The last part of the film showed the king on horseback at the head of a procession making its way towards the cathedral, where they were celebrating the birthday of Bergania's patron saint, a brave woman called Aurelia who had been beheaded by the Romans because she wouldn't renounce her faith.

Obviously St Aurelia was important to the Berganians. They had draped their balconies with flags and decorated the streets with flowers and the procession was very grand. Behind the king rode courtiers and soldiers in splendid uniforms – and beside him, on a spirited pony, rode the Crown prince, who was only a boy.

Tally was staring at him, wondering how it felt to be a prince so young, when the ancient projector gave a hiccup and the image on the screen stayed frozen. But though she saw the boy's arm held up to acknowledge the cheers of the crowd, she couldn't catch even a glimpse of his face. It was completely hidden by the gigantic feathery plumes on the helmet that he wore.

The film ended with a close-up of the king looking stern and resolute but rather tired, while the voice of the commentator said: 'To the brave ruler who defied Hitler's bullying, we, the people of Great Britain, send our greetings. Well done, Bergania!'

Then came the film they had come to see.

I'll Always Be Yours was not a good film. In fact, it was a perfectly awful film.

Gloria Grantley played a poor girl who went to work in a department store where she caught the eye of a handsome millionaire. She fell in love with the millionaire and he promised to marry her but it turned out he was married already, so Gloria jumped off a bridge and everyone thought she had drowned and the millionaire felt terribly guilty. But it turned out that she hadn't, and she became a nun and looked after little children in a convent and taught them to sing. It ended with her on her deathbed looking up to heaven and saying the millionaire's name (which was Lionel) in a throbbing voice before she closed her eyes for ever.

Tally was glad it was over; she couldn't wait to get into the fresh air, but although people were streaming out of the cinema, Julia hadn't moved. She was sitting with her shoulders hunched and her hands over her face.

'What is it, Julia? What's the matter? It ended all right – she's perfectly happy with God. It's what she wanted.'

Julia shook her head. She was crying – not at all in the way that Gloria Grantley had cried, with glycerine tears rolling down her perfectly made-up cheeks, but hopelessly, her face scrunched up, her shoulders heaving. She had no handkerchief and Tally hadn't got one to give her; the children in Magda's house did not come easily by handkerchiefs.

'Come on,' Tally urged her friend. 'Let's go outside.'

She took Julia's arm and led her across the square and down some stone steps to the towpath along the river. There was a bench looking over the water and they sat down on it side by side.

'If you feel like telling me what's the matter, I wouldn't tell anyone. It isn't because she didn't get Lionel, is it? It's something else.'

Julia went on sniffing and gulping. Then she lifted her head and said, 'I miss her so much!'

Tally stared at her. 'Who? Who do you miss so much?' And then: 'What is it about Gloria Grantley that you—'

'She's my mother.' Julia's voice was flat and exhausted. She sat bent up like an old woman.

'Your mother?' It seemed incredible, but now that Tally looked out for it she could see a likeness . . . something about the set of Julia's mouth and her eyes.

'No one knows except Daley and Matteo, so you mustn't tell.'

'I won't say anything. But if she's your mother . . . you

73

mean you miss her during term time? I miss my father but—'

'No. I miss her all the time; I don't see her even in the holidays. Well, hardly ever – just in secret places for a very short time. I'm too old, you see. I'm nearly thirteen, and it wouldn't do for her to have a daughter my age. She's supposed to be twenty-five so I have to be kept out of the way, but I just want to be able to be with her. I love her so much.'

Tally knew what she should have done next – sat quietly beside Julia and let her talk – but she couldn't. She got to her feet and collected the largest stones she could find and hurled them one by one into the river. Except that in her mind it wasn't stones she was throwing, it was Gloria Grantley she was sending into the swirling, icy water. Gloria with her pout and her bosom and her fluttering eyelashes, who was too busy being famous to acknowledge her daughter.

It was a while before she could come back to comfort her friend.

'I expect it's just as hard for her. She must long to be with you, but I expect it's her manager who told her she has to be careful.'

Julia looked at her with gratitude. 'Yes – he says it's only while her contract lasts. Then when she's saved lots of money she can retire and we can be together.' She looked wistfully at Tally. 'There's another performance at five o'clock. I'm going to stay for it – even if I get into trouble. Will you tell Magda?'

Tally sighed. 'I'll stay with you,' she said. 'You shouldn't go home by yourself in the dark.'

The thought of another two hours of the swan-necked Gloria was appalling. But at least she'd get another look at the brave King of Bergania, not to mention the prince-under-plumes.

CHAPTER EIGHT

BIOLOGY AT DAWN

Dr Hamilton was reading the latest letter from his daughter:

We had our first biology class with Matteo today. Only it wasn't a class really. It was a sort of walk . . . or an exploration . . . or an expedition. It was like being hunters on a trail and having your eyes sharpened with special drops so that you saw things that you didn't think you could see and yet they had been there all the time.

Matteo is tall with broad shoulders and very dark hair and eyes. He looks foreign and he is – he has a slight accent and his voice is very deep. He can look quite scary but he has a very funny laugh. I'm not describing him well because he isn't really like anybody else I've met. And the biology class wasn't like anything I'd imagined either.

For one thing it started at four o'clock in the morning. You wouldn't think a class could start then, would you, but Matteo's classes start at whatever time he thinks we will see the things he wants to show us.

So I was woken by him walking down the corridors and opening our bedroom doors and saying, 'Out' – and then we were all huddled in the courtyard, trying to wake up.

But we didn't stay huddled for long because as we followed him into the copse where the path goes down to the river we were greeted by the most incredible noise! I'd read about the dawn chorus, but I thought it was just a gentle twittering. I didn't realize that while I was asleep all the birds in England were singing their heads off.

Matteo made us stop to listen but actually he didn't have to make us – it was so beautiful we couldn't help listening. He didn't tell us the names of the birds – it was about listening not identifying. Barney told me later that there were thrushes and robins and warblers and wrens – but I heard them like instruments in an orchestra, each one distinct and separate but joining up to make a marvellous whole.

Then we went on through the wood and no one said a word. If anyone starts talking when they're out with Matteo he bites their head off.

It was getting lighter now, and when we came to a boulder lying on the side of the path, Matteo stopped and said, 'Well? What do you expect to find?'

All the others stood round and Barney said, 'Snail's eggs,' and Tod said, 'Centipedes,' and Julia said,

77

'Woodlice,' and Matteo nodded and said, 'Anything else?' and when no one said anything he said, 'What about the humidity?' and one of the other boys said, 'Violet ground beetles,' and Matteo said, 'And a sheltering toad perhaps?'

So then he turned the stone over – and all the things were there, and I know it sounds silly but he made us all so pleased – I suppose because he was so pleased himself. It was as though what was under the stone was a splendid present that God or whoever does these things had put there for us. Then he put the stone back – putting things back is the core of fieldwork, he says. And we walked on a bit further and crossed a paddock and he bent down to a tuft of rough grass by a hedge and parted it very carefully, because he said it was the sort of place where there might be a field vole's nest but there might not.

Only of course there was. Right at the base of the tussock was a round ball of chopped grass like a tennis ball and inside were three tiny squirming babies as pink and bald as sugar mice. We had to look at them very very quickly so that they wouldn't get disturbed, but I think I'll always remember them – they were so small but so alive.

The river is about twenty minutes' walk from the school, and we have to ask permission to go there without an adult because the current is quite fast in places. It's a really beautiful river, with banks full of balsam and bluebells everywhere, and there are sandy coves. We went to a place where there is an island which you can reach because a beech tree has fallen across from the bank. When we got to the island we had to lie down in the grass and be absolutely silent, and being absolutely silent didn't just mean not talking; it meant more than that.

We lay there for a while and nothing happened and then there was a silver flash and a fish jumped out of the water and made a great arc . . . and behind the fish – we could see it quite clearly now – were two otters.

I've never seen otters before. They are amazing – so swift and so . . . graceful but funny too. It was a mother and a nearly full-grown cub and they started rolling over and over in the water, trying to grab the fish, and at first they lost it and there was a lot of splashing, but then they caught it and swam with it to a big flat rock in the water and settled down to their meal.

But it was what came next that I liked so much.

When they'd finished eating the fish they swam back to the shore and started grooming themselves. They licked their fur and they polished their heads on each other and they went on rolling and polishing, till they were quite dry and fluffy, and only then did they dive back into the water and swim away.

We were there a long time because the otters were like people one was visiting and one didn't want to leave them.

There was more we saw on the way back: a woodpecker very close to, and a buzzard. It was as though Matteo knew where everything was – he would just go there and wait and there it was – and he said that we had to remember that everywhere was somebody's home and tread respectfully and reverently.

You might think it wasn't proper science, it was just a nature walk, but it wasn't like that. When we got back we wrote down the date and the temperature of the water in the river and the exact location of the field-vole nest and I don't feel that I will ever forget what I saw. Not ever.

*

When he had read Tally's letter through twice and taken it upstairs to the aunts, Dr Hamilton made his way to the surgery. He walked with a light step, ready for the question his patients always asked about his daughter.

'Tally is well,' he would tell them. 'Tally is very well indeed.'

CHAPTER NINE

DUSTBINS AND A FESTIVAL

The term, which had begun slowly, suddenly seemed to gather speed. Armelle stopped asking the children to be forks and told them to become victims of the bubonic plague. Josie sent them out to collect bunches of motherwort, which they had to boil up in a vat.

Clemmy gave an art class in which she told them about a Spanish painter called Goya, who fell ill and became deaf and rather mad and shut himself up in a gloomy house away from everybody and people thought the poor old man was finished – but afterwards they found that he had covered all the walls of his house with strange, dark pictures. Then she drew the blinds in the art room and told the children to select their paints without turning on the light, and they grumbled and fussed – and found that they had made paintings in colours they hardly knew existed. The next day she retired to the kitchen and made pancakes for the whole school.

Magda allowed Tally to froth up her cocoa with the whisk sent by the aunts, but she lost page thirty-two of her book on Schopenhauer and became troubled again. As spring turned to early summer and some of the other children began to go barefoot, Verity took to wearing shoes.

And Matteo solved the problem of Borro's snails in two minutes.

'They're the wrong kind. Edible snails are *Helix pomatia* – these are *Cepaea hortensis*.'

And he suggested that Borro should tip them out and let them go, which Borro did.

Tally's first tutorial with Matteo took place in his room, which was not in the main building but above the row of workshops behind the gym. It was reached by an outside staircase and had the look of a mountain hut: very plain, with wooden walls, a scrubbed table, a narrow bed and a case full of books in various languages. The sackbut lay on a chair; it looked like a battered trombone and far too harmless to make such a howling and melancholy sound.

'Come and sit down,' he said.

He had come straight from taking a fencing class; his foils and mask were propped up in a corner and Tally looked at them wistfully.

'Could anyone take fencing?' she asked. 'Could I?'

'Next year would be better,' said Matteo. 'You're still rather young.'

Tally nodded, accepting this. 'I really liked your

82

biology lesson. I liked it so much. I always thought science would be different – sort of cold and impersonal – but it isn't, is it? It's all part of the same thing. My father tried to make me see that, but I didn't listen properly.'

'Listening is one of the most difficult things.'

He talked to her for a while about the river and what else might be seen in it later that year. Then he said, 'But what about you personally? Your problems.' He smiled. 'Tutors are for problems, you know.'

'Yes. Well, I do have problems. There's Magda, you see. I found her crying on the first day about Germany and Heribert and I can't do anything about that, but now she's worrying again and it's about the blackout curtains and Magda can't sew. Of course, there may not be a war, but if there is we're going to need an awful lot of them. So I think we should find some way of helping her so that she can get on with her book and stop the pages flying about so much, but I haven't been here very long and I'm not sure how to do it. Could it be part of the domestic work we do before school?'

'I don't see why not. That would be a way of doing it which would not upset her, and I'm sure you could manage it.'

'And there's Kit,' Tally went on. 'Of course, he can be very annoying, but he does so very much want to play cricket. I don't know anything about it – we didn't play it at my convent – but I thought . . . there's the High School at St Agnes and they do play cricket – I asked Daisy who I do housework with, and she says they do; her brother goes there. So couldn't Kit go there one afternoon a week, maybe?'

'One could certainly ask,' said Matteo. 'It seems a perfectly sensible suggestion to me. Any other problems?'

'Well, there's Verity's snake. It looks really ill and I can't say anything because—'

Matteo's face darkened. 'You can forget the snake. It's being collected this afternoon and returned to the shop.'

'Oh, good.'

Matteo waited. 'Anything else?' he asked, for he had the feeling that Tally's biggest worry was still to come.

'Well, yes. It's about Julia. When I got on the train to come here I was so homesick you can't imagine – I just wanted to cry and cry – but Julia was so welcoming and so kind, and I like her so *much*, but I could see she was worried about something. It was as though she had a great weight on her mind, and she was so odd sometimes – Barney says she's a marvellous actress, but whenever O'Hanrahan tries to get her to do anything she just curls up . . . and no one could be kinder than him. And then last week she asked me to go to the cinema with her and it was Gloria Grantley, and Julia broke down completely and told me she was her mother. I promised not to tell the others, and of course I haven't, but really I can't bear it.'

'What is it that you can't bear?'

'That ghastly woman – how can she think it's more important to be famous and earn lots of money? Julia's so sad, having to be kept secret, and she won't do anything that makes her stand out, and she can't get ordinary letters like the rest of us – her mother just sends awful boxes of chocolate with liqueur centres that nobody can eat except Augusta Carringon – but Julia doesn't want chocolates; she wants a letter. And I think there has to be something one could do. I thought maybe I'd write to her and tell her how miserable she's making Julia. She may just be stupid and not realize.'

Matteo looked at her gravely.

'I'm afraid you'd only make trouble for Julia. I know it's hard, but sometimes there are situations where one can help only indirectly. And you do help Julia enormously just by being her friend.'

'Yes . . . but I do so hate not being able to make things better. And she's so awful – Gloria Grantley, I mean. The way she looked up to heaven and said, "Lionel!" and fluttered her eyelashes. You wouldn't believe what a bad actress she is!'

'I would actually,' said Matteo. 'I saw the film.'

Tally looked at him in amazement. 'You went to the cinema in St Agnes? To see *I'll Always Be Yours*? Did you really?'

Matteo was looking past her at the open window, and he did not speak at once.

'I had my reasons,' he said.

Tally waited, but whatever his reasons were he obviously did not want to share them.

She thought it was time to go, but as she was getting up Matteo turned to her.

'But what about you, Tally? Don't you have any problems of your own?'

Tally thought for a moment. 'No, I don't think so. I do miss my father very much, but that's not a problem, is it? It's just part of life.'

'Yes, you're right.' Matteo's face was sombre. 'Missing people is definitely part of life.'

An unusual child, he thought when she had gone. I wonder where that comes from in someone so young – that concern for other people.

But almost at once he forgot her, lost again in a vision of his own.

In O'Hanrahan's English classes the discussions about doing the legend of Persephone as a play became serious. The story seemed to have everything: all kinds of devils and demons and monsters, not to mention the three-headed dog, Cerberus, whom everybody liked; a beautiful and innocent heroine carried off by the King of Darkness and forced to live as his wife in the Underworld; a distraught mother, the goddess Demeter, who mourned her daughter so dreadfully that she could not attend to her duties and so let the corn wither and die. And it was a story about the earth being renewed in the spring, when Persephone returns from Hades, which seemed to be a good idea at a time when the world appeared to be doing anything rather than renewing itself.

In one lesson Barney, who had helped to produce the play they had done the previous year, attacked Julia directly.

'You ought to be the heroine – you'd be good. You know you would.'

But Julia only shook her head. 'I wouldn't mind being one of the heads of Cerberus if they wear masks,' she said, 'but that's all.'

When they were alone Tally tackled her friend.

'Julia, *why* won't you do any acting? Everyone says you're good, and we don't want beastly Verity being the heroine and tossing her hair about. Perhaps you've inherited your talent from your mother,' said Tally, trying to forget Gloria Grantley raising her eyes to heaven and saying, 'Lionel!'

'No, I haven't. *I haven't!*' Julia, who was usually so gentle, was getting angry. 'It's my mother who acts. If she thought I was trying to compete she'd be terribly upset. Once when I was small she was making a film in Spain and I was able to be with her and I started to make up a funny dance – well, it wasn't really funny but I thought it was – and the people who were watching laughed, and she told me not to be silly, and that I was embarrassing her. She said it would be very wrong if I thought I had any talent – I would only be miserable. She was thinking of me, she said – and she must know because it's her profession.'

'Unless she's jealous,' said Tally.

'Jealous!' Julia rounded on her. 'Jealous of a freckled beanpole like me? You must be mad!'

So that was the end of that conversation.

The school-council meeting on the following Monday took place in the hall. It was open to staff and pupils alike and Daley usually swallowed a couple of aspirins before it began because the meetings were apt to go on for a long time. The agenda lay in front of him. It read:

Vegetables
Cricket
Visit of Spanish Children
Complaint from Great Western Railway
Domestic Work Letter from Ministry of Culture.

*

Daley was declaring the meeting open when, to his surprise, the door opened and Matteo slipped into the hall. Matteo never came to meetings if he could help it, and even now he took a chair at the very back and leaned back as though he might be about to drop off to sleep.

The first item did not take long. The waste ground behind the gym had been dug up and cloches were going to be put down for vegetables. Children could submit a list to Clemmy of plants they would like to see growing, and she would discuss it with the gardeners.

'Why is that with the vegetables we will win the war?' asked the small French girl with the large white rabbit, and Daley explained that by growing vegetables instead of importing them, Great Britain would save space on ships, which could bring over ammunition and armaments instead.

Then came cricket, which Tally had put on the agenda, and now she stepped forward and launched bravely into her speech.

'I know we don't play team games at Delderton, but there are people here – well, there's Kit, and there may be others – who would like to play cricket. And I thought . . . there's the High School in St Agnes, and they do play cricket. So might Kit go there one afternoon a week, maybe? Could one ask?'

'Who would do the asking?' said Daley. The headmaster of St Agnes did not approve of Delderton.

'Well, Kit could . . .' and as the little boy squeaked agitatedly, 'and I could go with him. If you'd give me a letter?'

No one saw anything wrong with this, and the visit of the Spanish schoolchildren to give a concert came next.

Everyone wanted to hear the children sing; they had been made homeless when their country was split by civil war and they were going to spend the night camping on the playing field.

'Couldn't they stay longer?' suggested Tally 'One day isn't very long. Maybe we could have one child each in our rooms.'

Everyone agreed with this, and Daley said he would suggest it to the person who was in charge of the Spanish children, but Tally realized that she must now be quiet and not have any more ideas and she put a peppermint in her mouth, the kind with a hole in it, and put her tongue through it so as to stop herself from speaking.

Daley now read out the complaint from the manager of Great Western Railways, who said that passengers on the 11.15 from Paddington had been shocked to see Delderton pupils bathing in the river with nothing on when they went past. This happened every year, like hearing the first cuckoo in spring, and the older children sighed.

'That's just silly,' said Ronald Peabody, the boy who had broken the topmost branch of the cedar tree. 'There's nothing to be ashamed of in the human body.' And he flexed his skinny biceps as though he was a weightlifter.

'Perhaps not,' said O'Hanrahan in his quiet voice. 'But it seems a good idea to live in harmony with our neighbours.'

'Well, I think we're being bullied. It's like the dustbins,' said Ronald – and the children were off!

The bins at Delderton had large metal lids which made

excellent shields, and the kitchen staff had taken to locking them up in a compound so that the children couldn't get at them.

'Locking things up isn't in the Delderton tradition,' said a boy with large spectacles. 'We're supposed to be a free school.'

'Freedom doesn't mean causing distress and inconvenience to others,' said Magda, and told them what Schopenhauer had said about this, which was a lot.

Arguments about the dustbins took nearly a quarter of an hour and after that Verity said she had thought they were going to discuss the Free Period on Wednesday afternoons. She had tried to bring it up last time and Daley had promised to put it on the agenda, she said, and why wasn't it there? They had a free period in her cousin's school, and Wednesday was early-closing day in the village so they had a right to have one here. A proper one, not the kind you got by cutting classes.

After this came 'Domestic Work', which seemed to be getting on all right on the whole, and Daley then decided to bring the meeting to an end with something that would unite everybody because it was so obvious that it couldn't be done. He picked up the letter about the Folk Dance Festival.

'I have had a request from the Ministry of Culture. It's rather a strange request and I shall of course turn it down, but I thought you might like to know that we have been invited.'

And he read out the letter from the ministry in London, which ran as follows:

Dear Mr Daley

As your school is well known for its enterprise and initiative I am writing to ask whether you would consider sending a group of children to a Folk Dance Festival to be held in Bergania in the second week of June.

The Berganian authorities are very anxious to make stronger links with other European democracies and to foster friendship between the children of different nations as one of the most effective ways of securing world peace.

Quite a small group would suffice, and we would offer you assistance in the matters of group passports, visas and travel assistance generally.

Should you feel able to comply with this request, please get in touch with me at the ministry.

Yours sincerely,

(Sir) Alfred Hallinger

*

Daley folded up the letter and looked round at the meeting.

'It's quite an honour to be asked. As I say, I shall of course turn it down but—'

'Why?'

The clear voice carried to all parts of the hall. Julia grasped her friend's arm, trying to quieten her but without success. The peppermint disappeared down Tally's throat.

'Why?' she said again. 'Why would you refuse?'

She had forgotten that she was not going to speak again. One word had leaped out at her from the letter that Daley read.

'Bergania' – it was more than two weeks since she had seen the travelogue, yet she found she could remember the film in detail. She could see the snowy mountain range with the central jagged peak, and the fir trees running up the slope towards them. She could see the river and the spire of the church where St Aurelia was buried, and the palace. She could see the proud king on his horse and, as clearly as if she was there, the young prince in his troublesome helmet trying to blow the plumes out of his eyes.

'Why can't we send anybody?' said Tally yet again. 'The King of Bergania is very brave; he said no to Hitler.'

'Because,' said the headmaster patiently, 'we have never done folk dancing here at Delderton and it is less than a month till the festival. And there are other reasons.'

'Just because we've never done it doesn't mean we can't do it. There's probably a book about it; there's a book about everything. It must be very difficult to stand up to Hitler. It wasn't just that he said no about letting the troops go through his country, but he also won't let Hitler dig up minerals in his mountains to use for armaments. And I know people like Tod think there shouldn't *be* kings, but if there are and they're brave and resolute then surely we should show them that we're on their side.'

'I don't see how it would help the Berganians if we went and did folk dancing all over them,' said one of the senior girls, 'especially when we haven't any idea how to do it.'

'It's to do with just being there,' said Tally. 'They invited us so they must want us to come, and refusing would be a snub.'

She looked round the room for support but no one seemed ready to back her up. Even her own friends were silent.

'Folk dancing's silly,' said a boy with huge spectacles. 'People wind ribbons round a pole and get tangled up.'

'Or they wear idiotic clothes – trousers with bells on them and bobbles on their hats,' said Ronald Peabody.

'Only sissies do folk dancing,' came Verity's disdainful voice.

'Really?' The deep voice came from the back of the hall. Matteo had appeared to be asleep. 'You surprise me.' He uncoiled himself and moved forward to the centre of the room, and the children made way for him. 'You surprise me very much.'

Everybody fell silent, watching him as he turned and faced the meeting.

'You might of course call the Falanian Indians sissy. Certainly they do a folk dance before they dismember their enemies and nail them to trees. There are even bells – or rather gongs – involved, though not, if I recall, ribbons. It takes an Indian child five years to learn the steps, and they are not allowed to take part in it till they can crunch up the skull of a jaguar with their bare hands.

'And there are the leopard hunters of Nepal. They do a folk dance to prepare themselves for the chase, which includes leaping over pits of burning cinders with a fire-brand in their mouth. The steps go something like this.'

And without any warning Matteo leaped high into the air, seemed almost to hang there and came down with a blood-curdling howl almost on top of David Prosser, who stepped back with an agitated squeak.

'I could give you more examples,' said Matteo, 'but I just wanted to make the point that whatever folk dancing is, it's not sissy.'

Daley shook his head. That Tally wanted the school to march to the help of the Berganians was to be expected – but he had not thought that Matteo would stab him in the back.

'I suggest you set up a working party to see if it can be done. You have one week to prepare a suitable dance.'

Nothing would happen in so short a time; Daley was sure of that.

CHAPTER TEN

THE FLURRY DANCE

Tally was right. There was a book about folk dancing, several books in fact, but they were not very helpful.

'There's Scottish dancing and maypole dancing and morris dancing,' she said.

But Scotland was a long way from Devon and they did not feel they had a right to pretend to be Scottish, and anyway the steps were difficult.

'Maypole dancing looks nice,' said Julia. 'All those ribbons.'

But Barney said that disasters happened very easily with maypole dancing. In his village the vicar at the garden fête had been completely trussed up when one of the children had taken her ribbon in the wrong direction.

'He had to be cut out in the end,' Barney said.

So that left morris dancing, which was derived from the ancient sword dances of medieval England, only instead of swords the dancers had wooden sticks – and it was danced by men.

'Well, we can't have only boys,' said Julia. 'We'd never get enough.'

They had of course consulted Armelle, but she was so horrified at the idea of a dance that did not come spontaneously from inside the soul that she was not helpful at all.

'It says here that they hit each other with the sticks – they're called staves – at least they bang them together and they flap at each other with handkerchiefs,' said Tally, looking at the book. 'And they have bells on their ankles, rows and rows of bells, and more bells tied round their knees so that their trousers look baggy.'

'And they wear hats with flowers sewn on to them. There's one dance called the Helston Flurry Dance, which is danced in Cornwall. Flurry means flowers,' said Tod. 'It's not exactly a morris dance, but it's that kind of thing.'

He had at first wanted to have nothing to do with the trip to Bergania. The king who had said no to Hitler might be brave but he was still a king, and all kings belonged in dungeons – preferably with their heads chopped off. But when his friends all became involved he had joined in and put in some very useful work in the library.

'I don't want to flap with my handkerchief,' said Kit, looking even more woebegone than usual.

'There's one person who rides a sort of hobby horse through the dancers,' said Barney. 'The Devil, they think.

Or maybe the Fool. It's a very old dance. "Full of antiquity", it says here.'

It certainly looked old from the few pictures they could find. Not only old but exceedingly odd.

'What about the music?' asked Borro.

They went to consult the old professor who taught music and he said it would probably have been danced to pipes and tambours but perhaps a violin would do.

'Augusta's got a violin,' said Tally. 'I remember when she came.'

So they went to find Augusta, who was eating a banana and reading a detective story, and she said she *could* play the violin, but she couldn't play it well.

'I don't really like the noithe it maketh,' she said.

But she fetched it and played a slow tune full of double stops and they thought it would do if she could play it faster and maybe learn a more jigging sort of piece as well. Taking Augusta to Bergania would be complicated because of her only being able to eat so very few things.

'But if we stock up with bananas you'll be all right, won't you?' said Julia, and Augusta agreed that she probably would. She was really a very good-natured girl and they were glad she had come back from Wales.

'Of course, the other groups will probably have all sorts of instruments – an orchestra even – all those Swiss and Bavarian people in lederhosen slapping their thighs will be terribly good – but we can't compete with them. All we want is to be there,' said Tally.

'I don't,' said Kit. 'I don't want to be there.'

'We could always alter it a bit and make a Devon version,' Tally went on. '"The Delderton Flurry Dance".'

Getting a team together was the next problem. Tally's immediate friends all rallied round, and Verity after watching snootily for a while said she would come, which was a pity but they couldn't afford to be fussy. Kit of course was really too small, but they couldn't get people who were matched in size; they would just have to make do with what they had.

The next day the rehearsals began, and they did not go well.

'Form a circle,' said Barney with the book in his hand. 'Now pick up your sticks . . . Then bow to each other. Now lift the right foot . . .'

Augusta took up her violin, and the dancers lifted the staves they had begged from the gardeners, who used them for staking peas.

'Move towards the centre . . . hold the sticks up high . . . now flap your handkerchiefs. One, two, three and hop . . .'

None of the children in Magda's house had handkerchiefs; they flapped their headscarves or borrowed tea towels. Borro flapped his shirt.

'Ow!' said Borro, as Tod's stick went into his cheek.

Kit said he couldn't do it – it was too difficult. Augusta snapped a string on her violin.

'We have to be able to do it,' said Tally. 'We *have* to.'

At night the Delderton Flurry Dance ran through their dreams. They thought of it as a kind of sick animal that had to be nursed into health.

'It's like those runts you get in a litter of piglets,' said Borro. 'You know, the one that can't feed itself.'

They ran into each other's rooms at all hours, suggesting changes – making the steps simpler. Nobody now

98

would have recognized it as a known morris dance or anything else, but it didn't matter.

Gradually, very gradually, the children who had scoffed wandered away. The snooty Verity turned out to be the best at dancing, which was a pity but the kind of thing that happens in life.

Matteo came past once when they had got into a hopeless coil. He gave some orders that freed them, but if they had hoped that he would stay and help, they were disappointed.

Next came the clothes. White trousers or white skirts . . . bells . . . and flowers for their hats.

'Real ones will wither,' said Julia.

'We could buy artificial ones from Woolworth,' someone suggested. They were surprisingly expensive, but everyone gave up their pocket money.

The girls looked very weird in their hats so Clemmy suggested they make wreaths and wear the flowers in their hair, which gave Verity the chance to nab all the forget-me-nots because she said they matched her eyes.

By the end of the week they were ready to show what they had done to the headmaster.

They took him down to the playing field. Augusta struck up on her violin. Borro, who was the hobby-horse rider, galloped round the circle. The dancers began.

The Delderton Flurry Dance was bad. It was very bad indeed. But it was *there*.

'All right,' said Daley wearily. 'You'll have to work on it solidly till you leave – but, yes, you can go.'

*

It should have been a day of triumph and then suddenly everything went wrong. It was Verity of course who gave Tally the news that devastated her, but it was not really Verity's fault; Tally would have found out anyway soon enough. But now she walked blindly away from the school and down the sloping, tangly path that led towards the river and sat down with her arms round her knees, trying to fight down the misery and wretchedness that engulfed her.

She must fix her eyes on the things that were outside herself. The new beech leaves, with the sun on them . . . the bluebells shimmering like a lake through the trees . . . A thrush flew by with his beak full of twigs, and a water vole ran along the bank of the little stream.

These were the things that mattered – not her own wishes and hopes and needs.

But it didn't work. Tears welled up under her eyelids and she felt completely desolate.

From the moment she had seen those images of Bergania, she had felt as though the country somehow spoke to her. And now though her friends would go, she would stay behind.

'You realize that all the parents have to pay thirty pounds for our fares,' Verity had said. 'The school can't afford them. Daley's going to write a letter to everyone and explain.'

Verity always knew things before other people.

Thirty pounds. It was nothing to Verity's parents, with their estate in Rutland, and most of the others came from well-to-do families. But Tally would never ask her father for so much money. His patients were poor; he had both the aunts to support. He mustn't be asked in case he felt he had to make the sacrifice and, whatever Tally wanted from her father, it was not a sacrifice.

'It doesn't matter,' she told herself.

But it was no good. Perhaps it didn't matter compared to people dying in famines and earthquakes and wars, but it mattered to her.

After a while she got up and brushed the grass off her skirt and made her way back up the hill to school.

She would see if Matteo was free.

She found him in his room, looking down a microscope on the windowsill, but when he saw her tear-stained face he pulled out a chair for her at the wooden table.

'I see you have a problem,' he said. 'A proper one, for yourself.'

'Yes, I do.' She felt better now that she was taking some action. 'It's . . . I want you to tell the headmaster not to write to my father about the fare to Bergania. Verity says it's thirty pounds – that's right, isn't it?'

'It sounds about right. Why?'

'Well, I know my father can't afford it, and I don't want Daley to ask him in case he . . . I don't want him to be asked. I don't have to go. I can show one of the others how to take my place.'

'I see. But you want to go, don't you?'

Tally wiped her eyes with her sleeve. 'Yes, I do. I wanted to go from the minute I saw the travelogue about Bergania. But—'

'Why?'

Matteo had spoken sharply. Tally blinked at him. 'I don't know really. It's very beautiful . . . the mountains and the river . . . And the procession. Usually processions are boring, but the king . . .'

'Yes?' Matteo prompted her. 'What about the king?'

'He looked so strong and . . . brave – except I know you can't really look brave just for a moment in a film. Only he did. But tired too. And there was the prince . . . he was hidden by plumes . . . feathers all over his helmet. I was sorry for him.' She shook her head. 'I don't know . . . there was a big bird flying above the cathedral.'

'A black kite, probably,' said Matteo. 'They're common in that part of the world.' But he seemed to be thinking about something else. Then: 'I'll speak to the headmaster.'

'You'll tell him not to write to my father about the money?'

'Yes, I'll tell him that.'

As Matteo knocked on the door of Daley's study, four children came out – Julia and Barney and Borro and Tod.

'You've had a deputation, I see,' said Matteo. 'Not connected with the trip to Bergania?'

'Yes,' said the headmaster. 'They want the school to pay for Tally's fare to Bergania – they don't think her father could afford it. I must say that girl has made some very good friends in the short time she has been with us.'

'And will the school pay it?'

Daley looked worried. 'The trouble is if you do that kind of thing once you have to do it again, and we simply don't have funds for that.'

'So it would have to come out of the Travel Fund. The fund that exists for worthy cultural exchanges to broaden the minds of the young and all that.'

Daley looked at him blankly. 'There isn't such a fund.'

'There is now,' said Matteo. 'I shall pay in thirty pounds this afternoon.' And as the headmaster continued to stare at him he said, 'Don't worry, I have the money – after all, I got paid last month. Who are you sending with them?'

'I thought Magda should go – her German is fluent, of course, and she also speaks Italian and French. But one will need somebody who can actually cook because they'll be camping some of the time, and I can't send Clemmy – I shall need her here to look after the children left behind in Magda's house. And I'll want a man as well. O'Hanrahan is rehearsing a play for the younger ones and the professor is too old. I thought maybe David Prosser.' The headmaster sighed. 'It has to be someone who can be spared.'

Matteo nodded. Prosser could certainly be spared. He was famous for being the most boring man in the school, and for being in love with Clemency – but for not much else. There was a pause. Then: 'I can cook,' said Matteo.

'Good God!' said Daley, staring at him. 'Don't tell me you meant to go yourself all along?'

'Only if the children had been serious. Only if they really meant to work. Not just Tally, all of them.'

'And if they hadn't been?'

Matteo shrugged. 'Who knows?' he said.

PART TWO

CHAPTER ELEVEN

THE PRINCE AWAKES

It was a very large bed – a four-poster draped in the colours of Bergania – red, green and white. Green was for the fir trees that hugged Bergania's mountains, red for the glowing sunsets behind the peaks, white for the everlasting snows. On the headboard were carved a crown and the words 'The Truth Shall Set Thee Free', which was the country's motto.

The bed was too large for the boy who now woke in it – but then everything in the palace was too large for him. His bedroom could have housed a railway carriage; in his bathtub one could have washed a company of soldiers. Even his name was longer than he needed it to be: Karil Alexander Ivo Donatien, Duke of Eschacht, Margrave of Munzen, Crown Prince of Bergania.

He was twelve years old and small for his age, with brown eyes and brown hair and an expression one does not often see in the portraits of princes: the look of someone still searching for where he belongs.

Now he stretched and sat up in bed and thought about the day that faced him, which was no different from other days. Lessons in the morning, inspecting something or opening something with his father in the afternoon, then more lessons or homework . . . and always surrounded by tutors and courtiers and governesses.

For a moment he looked out at the mountains outside the windows. On one peak, the Quartz Needle, the snow never melted entirely, even now in early summer. He imagined getting up and escaping and walking alone up and up through the fir woods, across the meadows where there were marmots and eagles . . . and up, up till he reached the everlasting snow and could stand there, alone in the cold clear air.

There was a tap on the door and a footman entered with his fruit juice and two rusks on a silver tray. Not one rusk, not three, always two. After him came the major-domo with the timetable for the day, and then another servant to lay out his clothes: his jodhpurs and riding jacket, his fencing things and the uniform of the Munzen Guards which Karil particularly hated. The stand-up collar rubbed his neck, the white trousers had to be kept spotless and the plumes on the helmet got in his eyes.

And now came the woman who would scold him and hover over him and criticize him all day. Frederica, Countess of Aveling, was tall and bony and dressed entirely in black, because someone in the Royal Houses of Europe had always died. She was in fact a human being, but she might as easily have been a gargoyle that had stepped down from the roof of a dark cathedral. Her ferocious nose, her grim mouth and jagged chin looked as though they could well be carved in stone.

Officially she was the First Lady of the Household, but she was also the prince's second cousin and had come over from England after the death of the prince's mother in a riding accident when he was four years old.

Queen Alice of Bergania had been British – the daughter of the proud and snobbish Duke of Rottingdene, who lived in London, in a large grey mansion not far from Buckingham Palace. Although English was the second language of the Berganian court, the duke did not trust foreigners to supervise the education and behaviour of his grandson and had sent the fiercest of his unmarried relatives to see that the boy behaved correctly and with dignity at all times – and never forgot exactly who he was.

In the palace, and to Karil himself, she was known as the Scold, because scolding was all she seemed to do.

'Good morning, Your Highness,' she said, and curtsied. She always curtsied when she greeted him in the morning, and from the depth of her curtsy Karil could tell how badly she was going to scold him. The more displeased she was, the deeper did she sink towards the ground. This morning she practically sat down on the floor, and sure enough she began to scold him straight away.

'I really must speak to you about the way you have been waving to children when you are out driving. Of course, to extend your arm slightly and bring it back again is right and proper. It is expected. But the way you greeted those children outside their school yesterday was quite inexcusable, leaning out of the window. You cannot expect your subjects to keep their distance if you encourage them like that.' She broke off. 'Are you listening to me, Karil?'

'Yes, Cousin Frederica.'

'And when will you realize that servants are not to be addressed directly except to give orders to? I heard you yesterday asking one of the footmen about his daughter in a way that was positively chatty.'

'She was ill,' said Karil. 'I wanted to know how she was getting on.'

'You could have sent a message,' said the Scold. She moved over to the chair on which the valet had laid out the prince's uniform, picked up the helmet and peered at it suspiciously. There had been a most shocking incident once when Karil had cut the plumes off the helmet of the Berganian Rifles just before an important parade.

'I haven't done anything to it,' said Karil. 'It was only once, because I wanted to be able to see.'

'I should hope not. Cutting the ends off valuable ostrich feathers! I've never heard of anything so outrageous. However . . .' the Scold's face changed and took on a coy and simpering look, 'I have something here that will please you. A letter from your cousin Carlotta. It encloses a photograph which I will have framed so that you can have it in your room.'

She handed Karil a letter which he put down on a gilt-legged table.

'Well, aren't you going to read it?'

'Yes, I will – later. I want to go outside for a moment before breakfast.'

'I'm afraid that won't be possible.' She consulted a large watch on a chain which she wore pinned to her blouse. 'We are already four minutes late.'

Karil sighed and took out the photograph. Carlotta von Carinstein was a year younger than the prince and very pretty, with ringlets down to her shoulders. She was wearing a floating kind of dress with puffed sleeves and holding a bunch of flowers, and she was smiling. Carlotta always smiled.

He already had three of her photographs.

The countess controlled her irritation. It was obvious that Carlotta and Karil would marry in due course and it was time that the boy realized this. Carlotta lived in London with Karil's grandfather, the Duke of Rotting-dene. Of course, both the prince and Carlotta were very young but it was sensible in royal households to have these things understood from the beginning.

'Now, Karil,' she said, 'here is the programme for the day: maths and French with Herr Friedrich as usual, then history and Greek with Monsieur Dalrose. At luncheon you will sit next to the Turkish ambassador's wife – she has asked to meet you because she has a son your age, and you will talk to her in French. Your fencing lesson with Count Festing is at the usual time, but your riding lesson has been put forward to allow you to change for the inspection of the new railway station at which you will accompany your father.'

'Are we riding or driving?'

'You are driving. Your father will be in the Lagonda;

111

you go in the next car with the Baron and Baroness Gambetti.'

Karil tried to hide his disappointment. He saw his father so seldom – rarely before dinner and often not then. Days passed when he did not see him at all. Even though he was not allowed to chat in the royal car, it was good to be beside him. His father was a stern and conscientious ruler, and he seemed to care for nothing except his work. Sometimes Karil felt that his father had really turned into that bewhiskered, solemn person – King Johannes III of Bergania – whose pictures hung in the schools and public places of his country.

But the countess was still scolding. 'And I don't want to have to tell you again that your manner to Baron Gambetti is not satisfactory.'

'I don't like him.'

'Like him? *Like* him? I hope you don't imagine that princes of the blood can have likes and dislikes. You are entirely above such things.'

'He wants us to give in to the Nazis. And his wife sleeps with a picture of Hitler under her pillow.'

'I beg your pardon? I dare not wonder how you have come by that piece of tittle-tattle. Now hurry up and get dressed.'

Breakfast was taken in a room that overlooked the moat and had a view down the hill to the town and the river which wound through it. Karil had it in the company of his Cousin Frederica and three Ladies of the Bedchamber, who were also the king's aunts: plump turnip-shaped ladies with big bosoms and short legs, like roots, on which they tottered round the palace giggling and gossiping and finding fault. Karil's Uncle Fritz was also at breakfast: a vague-looking man with long silver hair and dreamy pale blue eyes. Nobody had known quite what to do with him so the king had made him Minister of Culture. It was a job he took very seriously, organizing singing competitions and literary events and folk festivals. The politicians in the cabinet laughed at him behind his back, but Karil was very fond of him.

The king never breakfasted with his family. He had a tray sent to his bedroom and started to work on state papers as soon as he woke.

Conversation at meals was supposed to be 'improving' and to show Karil what was happening in the world and today there was plenty to discuss. Hitler had again sent envoys to Bergania asking the king to allow troops to march through the country in case of war, and the king had again refused. Bergania had always been neutral, he said, and neutral it would remain.

'It was very brave to refuse a second time,' said the oldest Lady of the Bedchamber, slicing the top off her egg. 'Very brave indeed.'

'Perhaps a little foolhardy,' said the second lady. 'Hitler is not to be trifled with.'

'And look at what happened to poor Zog,' said the third.

All three ladies shook their heads, thinking of poor Zog of Albania, who had lost his throne and was now having a miserable time in a villa in Spain without proper drains.

'There were other demands,' said Uncle Fritz. 'Hitler wanted all the refugees returned – the people who had fled

Germany and come here, and that's quite out of the question. The leader of our orchestra is a German Jew and the best musician we've ever had.'

Cousin Frederica broke her roll in half with her bony fingers. 'Herr Hitler has might on his side.'

Karil looked at her across the table. 'But my father has right on his.'

It was not a big procession – opening a railway station is not as important as signing a treaty or welcoming a foreign ruler. All the same, the schoolchildren were let out of school early, people lined the streets, there were flags and bunting among the flowers in the window boxes, and at least five cars filled with various dignitaries stood ready to set off.

Karil had hoped to get a chance to talk to his father before the procession left, but the king was flanked by the Prime Minister and the mayor and escorted to his favourite car, the Lagonda, with the royal pennant fluttering on the bonnet. Following in the Rolls-Royce with Baron Gambetti, Karil tried hard to be civil. Gambetti was a thin man with a yellow skull, sneering lips and a pointed beard like a goat's stuck on the end of his chin. Everyone knew that he was trying to persuade the king to give in to Hitler and that the baroness egged him on. Trying to be polite, trying not to wave too enthusiastically to the children lining the route, kept Karil busy till they reached the station and there it all was: the red carpet, the officials with their chains of office and their medals, the band of the Berganian Rifles breaking into the national anthem . . .

A small girl in a white dress came forward to curtsy and give the king a big bouquet of lilies, and an even smaller girl was pushed forward and gave Karil a posy of sweet peas – and then the speeches began.

Karil had liked the old wooden station, with its single waiting room hung with posters of Italy and Austria and Spain, and a black iron stove. The new one was of brick, faced with yellow stucco, and had a fanciful blue roof, and the architect who had designed it was presented to the king and made a speech and so did the mayor and the Director of Railways.

Karil found it difficult to concentrate on the speeches; they always seemed to be the same, whether it was a railway station being opened or a football team being presented or a bishop being buried, but he managed to stand up very straight and not to blow the ostrich feathers out of his eyes even though a breeze had sprung up and they were tickling him badly. Then the king cut the pink ribbon stretched across the platform and declared the station open, and everyone got back in their cars for the drive home. As they made their way along the promenade beside the river Karil noticed some workmen putting up bell tents on the level ground at the edge of the park.

'What are those for?' he asked Baron Gambetti.

'Oh, some nonsense of your Uncle Fritz,' sneered the baron, who made no secret of his contempt for the Minister of Culture. 'A folk-dance festival or some such thing – children coming from all over the place.'

'I hope they will behave,' said the baroness. 'There are some from one of those free schools in England. They will carry on like savages, no doubt.'

Karil looked at the tents, imagining them full of busy children from all over the world. But it wouldn't help him. Maybe one child would be scrubbed clean and presented to him for a few minutes, but he would never know what was really going on in their lives . . . or make a friend.

When he was younger and had read fairy stories, Karil had always been angry with all those goose-girls and milk-maids who wanted to marry a prince.

'Don't do it!' he had wanted to shout at them. 'Don't go and live in a palace. You'll be bored and bullied, and everybody you meet – absolutely everybody – will be old!'

Back at the palace Karil changed out of the detested uniform, but the working day was still not over. A professor came from the College of Heraldry to give him a lecture on the different methods of saluting and showed him pictures of the exact angle of the hand in relation to the lobe of the ear. This was followed by the visit of a sculptor who wanted to measure Karil's head for a bust which the Youth Centre had ordered for their sports hall.

'Do I have to do this now? There's time for a ride before dinner,' said Karil.

'Certainly you have to do it now,' said the Scold. 'You really must stop making an unseemly fuss about this kind of thing.'

It was true that Karil hated being painted and photographed and modelled. It had begun when he was small and a photographer's flashlight had exploded in his face – but even now he was frightened by the way his father had turned into a portrait and his mother had become a marble statue in the park.

The king was not at dinner. A special meeting of his cabinet had been called to deal with Germany's new demands and it was still going on.

'Couldn't I go and say goodnight to him?' asked Karil. 'Just for a minute?' He had not spoken a single word to his father all day.

'Now, Karil,' said the Scold, 'you know you mustn't disturb him in a meeting.'

The meeting had already lasted for four hours. The king looked grey and tired. Baron Gambetti, the Foreign Minister, sat next to him, leaning forward. His goatee waggled on his chin; his yellow skull glistened with sweat as he stabbed his pencil against the paper.

'In my view it would be extremely unwise to refuse Herr Hitler his requests. He has made Germany into a great power and those who oppose him will be crushed.'

On the other side of the king, the elderly Prime Minister, Wolfgang von Arkel, shook his head. A loyal and faithful servant of the king for many years, von Arkel supported his master in his stand against the German Fuehrer.

'Giving in to bullying has never been a wise policy,' he said now, stroking his long white beard. He turned to the king. 'I have to assure Your Majesty that your people are behind you. No one wishes to see storm troopers marching through our country. As for forcing those people who have sought shelter with us back into Nazi hands, it is not to be thought of by decent men.'

Gambetti snorted. 'A sensible compromise in which we grant a few of Herr Hitler's demands in exchange for—'

'In exchange for what?' put in von Arkel. 'Empty promises and then more demands.'

The king leaned back in his chair. He agreed with his Prime Minister, a good man whom he trusted absolutely. The head of the army was behind him too. But there were others . . . He looked at his watch. There was time still to say goodnight to his son. He half rose to his feet and then sat wearily down again. He could not afford to let Gambetti bring the waverers round to his point of view.

The day ended as it had begun, only in reverse. A footman came to turn down Karil's bed, a second one brought two rusks and a glass of fruit juice on a silver tray. The uniform of the Munzen Guards was put back in the cupboard and the uniform of the Berganian Rifles was taken away to be pressed for the following day. The countess came with Carlotta's latest picture in a frame and put out the light.

Left alone, Karil got out of bed again and drew back the curtains. The mountains were dark against the sky; the rosy light of sunset was gone. He went over to the other window and looked down at the river and at the row of lamps on the promenade. He could make out the bell tents, and inside them a glimmer of moving lights as the workers finished the preparations for the Folk Dance Festival.

He turned, startled, as the door suddenly opened. Someone had come in with a firm stride and without knocking.

In a second Karil had run forward to embrace his

father. He had come to say goodnight after all, and at once the world seemed to be a different place.

The king did not ask his son whether he had had a good day. He knew full well about Karil's day; he had had so many days of his own like that when he was a boy. Days when he felt trapped and weary and wanted nothing except to escape into the hills and never return.

'When this crisis is over we'll go out together, you and I, and hide,' he said, 'and they can look for us as much as they want.'

Karil nodded. 'Can we go to the dragonfly pool?' he asked. 'It's the right time of year.'

'Yes. That's where we'll go.'

For a moment the king stood looking down at his son. The dragonfly pool belonged to his own childhood, before he was weighed down by duties. To the days when he had had a friend to share adventures with. The friend had betrayed him in the end, but the memory of those days still warmed his heart.

After the king had left, Karil stood by the window, looking down at the tents in the park below. Perhaps he would not always be cut off from real people and real life. Perhaps he would get to know the children who were coming. Those few moments with his father had given him courage and hope.

CHAPTER TWELVE

ARRIVAL IN BERGANIA

The Deldertonians came by train through one of the longest tunnels in Europe and suddenly they were in a valley that seemed to be a kind of garden because everywhere there were flowers – in the window boxes of the little houses, trailing round lamp posts, hanging down from verandas. Yet when one looked upwards, leaning out of the windows of the train, there were the mountains, cold and majestic and very, very high.

For Tally it was as though the newsreel she had seen in the cinema had burst into colour and life. She had wanted to come to Bergania because of the bravery of the king and his people, but now she was just glad to be there, in a country she had never dreamed of seeing.

'Make sure you leave nothing behind,' said Magda –

and Tally and Julia exchanged glances, for it was Magda who left things behind: her handbag when they changed trains in northern France, her scarf on the boat. As long as she had her briefcase with her notes on Schopenhauer in it, she felt herself fully dressed.

The children scrambled for their belongings. Kit had sat on a tomato sandwich and Julia dabbed at him with a paper napkin. Verity was tossing out her hair – it had to be untidy in just the right way and this took time. Matteo was out in the corridor. Whenever Tally woke in the night he had been standing there with his back to the crowded compartment, looking out at the landscape.

The children from Delderton had three compartments in the front of the train. Then came the group from Germany – well-behaved, good-looking children in dark blue shorts and spotless white shirts. In the second carriage were the Swedes and the French; then came the Italians, the Norwegians, the Spaniards . . . They had all just begun to make friends at Innsbruck, where the train had halted for a couple of hours.

The station came in sight, its pillars wreathed in roses. As the children got out they were greeted by a blast of music.

'My goodness, they've sent a band to welcome us,' said Barney.

At the end of the platform stood a distinguished-looking man with long silver hair, wearing a loden jacket, flanked by two officials with badges and golden chains.

'A reception committee,' said Borro. 'Well, well. They must think we're important.'

'We are important,' said Tally firmly. 'We're here because of good will between nations and all that.'

All along the train, children tumbled out on to the platform and re-formed in a line beside their teachers. The Delderton children, who were not used to standing in line, stayed in a huddle, blinking in the warm sunshine.

The band, which had played various national anthems, broke into 'God Save the King'. Then the distinguished gentleman with the long grey hair, flanked by the mayor and his aldermen, came down the platform, greeting each group, shaking hands. It was the Minister of Culture, Prince Karil's Uncle Fritz, who had come in person to welcome them.

When he reached the Deldertonians he spoke to them in perfect English.

'We are particularly glad to welcome you to Bergania,' he said, 'because as you may know our beloved queen came from your country. The links between Bergania and Britain have always been strong.'

Everyone looked round for Matteo, expecting him to reply, but he had vanished and Magda was silent, overcome by shyness. But the minister had seen the book under her arm and reached out for it.

'Ah, Schopenhauer,' he said. 'You are interested in his work?'

Magda blushed. 'I am writing a thesis on his stylistic influences,' she said.

'How interesting. I myself have always been fascinated by his views on Reason and the Will, but alas there is so little time to pursue such things.' He pulled himself up. 'Now here is the programme for the week,' he said, handing Magda a brochure. 'There will be two days to rest and to see our beautiful country. Then on Monday the festival will be opened officially and the dancing will begin. We have buses ready to take you to your camp, and tonight there will be dinner at the Blue Ox. Here you have a map of the city, a timetable and a list of excursions.'

It was only as they were making their way to the buses waiting in the station forecourt that Matteo came to join them.

'Where have you been?' asked Barney. 'You were supposed to greet the minister.'

Matteo gestured to a clump of aspens on the embankment.

'The perfect habitat for the poplar moth. I saw one as long as my thumb.'

The children did not ask if he had brought it back. Matteo never killed the butterflies he found . . .

The field in which the dancers' bell tents had been pitched was a pleasant place – by the side of the river and adjoining the park with its bandstand and pavilion and its pool full of carp. At the far end of the park, the ground sloped upwards towards the hill where the palace stood. Behind the palace – as everywhere in Bergania – one could see the mountain peaks.

Each group of dancers had been given two tents, and there was a flag on top of the tent poles to show which nationality they belonged to. The British were in the tents next to the bridge which crossed the river on to the promenade and into the town. Beside them were the Germans, with the other nationalities strung out along the bank.

There was a wash house and toilet block shared by all the groups. The Yugoslavs, who had arrived earlier on a bus from the south, were already busy splashing and showering and singing, while their teachers, two large and cheerful ladies, were cutting their toenails in the sinks meant for washing up.

A wooden platform had been erected close by so that the visitors could practise their dances, but the actual festival would be held in the town's main square. Fortunately Matteo had stopped chasing butterflies and looking at the view, and in a short time the sleeping bags were arranged in the two tents, with Magda and the girls in one, and Matteo and the boys, with the boxes of costumes, in the other, and it was time to cross the bridge and make their way to the Blue Ox for supper.

The Blue Ox was on the promenade: an old-fashioned hotel and inn which was the favourite gathering place for the people of the town. It had a big terrace overlooking the river, and tables with red-and-white checked table-cloths were set out under a chestnut tree. Inside, everything was very large and very solid and made of wood. The benches gleamed with polish, there were stands with salted pretzels on the tables, and the walls were covered in antlers and the stuffed heads of mountain goats.

The landlord, Herr Keller, was the kind of man one would expect an innkeeper to be: genial and burly with a big stomach and a loud laugh.

It was clear that he was a staunch royalist, because for every pair of antlers or stuffed goat, there was a portrait of the king. Johannes III was pictured with whiskers and before he had grown them. He was pictured on horseback and at the head of a procession and just standing very straight in his uniform with his decorations on his chest. There were a number of pictures too of Queen Alice but these were draped in black crepe and had been for the last eight years, since she died.

Herr Keller spoke a little English and, with Magda translating, the children were made acquainted with the history of the Royal House of Bergania.

'What about the prince?' asked Tally. 'Aren't there any pictures of him?'

Herr Keller frowned and said that His Highness hated to be photographed.

'Why?' asked Verity. 'Is there something wrong with him?'

'Certainly not,' said Herr Keller, offended. 'He is a very nice-looking boy. I can show you a picture in the smoking room.'

But the picture was of a very small boy in a sailor suit, his face hidden by an enormous sun hat.

He led them into the dining room, where the other children were already sitting.

The food was delicious and the waitresses were very helpful about bringing a plate of boiled rice for Augusta Carrington. Only the head waitress, a middle-aged woman with ginger hair and a square, plain face, behaved oddly; they caught her again and again staring at Matteo and it was not till he glared at her angrily that she stopped.

'Perhaps she just wanted you for a friend,' suggested

Tally, who was sitting next to him, but then he turned and glared at her instead. Well, he can suit himself, thought Tally as she helped herself to a gigantic pancake oozing with apricot jam.

When the Deldertonians returned to the camp, the German children were already in their tents, their belongings stacked neatly outside. From inside their tent came the sound of an old Bavarian folk song sung in perfect harmony.

'Why are they so good at everything?' said Julia irritably. 'If they weren't so nice one would be really annoyed.'

But the German children were nice: friendly and helpful and kind. They could not have been less like those Hitler Youth corps one saw on the newsreels, saluting and stamping and marching about.

'Right, it's time for bed,' said Matteo.

One by one they crawled into their sleeping bags. Magda and Matteo stayed up a while, talking very quietly, but at last all the tents were silent.

Tally fell asleep at once, but two hours later Verity turned over in her sleep and kicked her. The soles of Verity's feet were very hard from walking barefoot even in Paddington Station, and Tally was jerked into instant wakefulness. She tried to go back to sleep again but she was overtired; images from the journey kept running through her brain, and presently she gave up the attempt.

Matteo had insisted that everyone bring a torch, which they put beside their pillow. Now, as she slipped into her gym shoes and put on a jersey over her pyjamas, she reached for hers and crept out of the tent.

But when she got outside and straightened up she found there was no need for a torch, because she had come out into a world of silvery brightness: the moon was full over the mountains; the single snow-covered peak dazzlingly white; the trees in the park standing out black against the sky.

She left the tents behind and made her way towards the little pavilion, built like a Greek temple, but her eyes kept being drawn upward to the moonlit palace on its hill. Now, in the night, it looked like the impenetrable fortress it must once have been, not a place of pleasure.

The statue appeared before her suddenly as she crossed a footbridge and rounded a bend on the path. It was very white in the moonlight, and when Tally got close to it she saw that the woman was wearing a long white dress, and in her hair was a kind of tiara – or was it a crown?

Tally switched on her torch. The woman was very beautiful, though her face was sad. In her hands, which were loosely clasped, was a bunch of flowers. At first, because of the unreal white light Tally thought they were made of marble like the rest of the statue, but as she went closer she saw that the flowers were real; she could even smell, very faintly, the scent that came from them. Someone must have brought them and put them in the statue's hands.

At the base of the statue was a plaque. Like all the notices in Bergania it was in three languages – Berganian, English and Italian.

ALICE, QUEEN OF BERGANIA, BORN 10 APRIL 1900, DIED 15 JUNE 1931. DAUGHTER OF THE DUKE AND DUCHESS

of Rottingdene, wife of His
Majesty King Johannes III and
mother of the Crown Prince Karil.
She served her people well.

Tally switched off her torch. The marble face looked down at her, thoughtful and sad. The prince had been four when his mother died, so he would remember her, thought Tally, but only just. She herself had no memories of her mother, but one could manage without a mother if one had a good father, and both she and the prince had that. The prince would be all right.

She was turning away when she heard footsteps and saw, coming over the little bridge, a man in dark clothes. He was walking very fast, almost running, and from his hurrying figure there came a sense of menace. He looked dangerous and angry.

Tally braced herself. She was quite alone. There was nothing to do except wait and hope he would go past.

But he did not go past.

'What the devil are you doing out here alone?' came Matteo's furious voice. 'You must be out of your mind. Surely it's obvious that you should stay in the camp?' He shone his torch, infinitely stronger than her own, and transfixed her in a beam of light. 'You're in a strange country – anything could happen to you.'

But Tally stood her ground. 'I don't feel as though I'm in a strange country,' she said. 'I feel as though I'm in a place where nothing bad could happen.'

But Matteo was not appeased.

'There is no place where nothing bad could happen,' he said. 'Not in the world we live in now.'

CHAPTER THIRTEEN

THE PRINCE WATCHES

Karil had removed the latest photograph of Carlotta from the table by the window so that he could rest the arm with which he was steadying the big telescope he had borrowed from the library. Usually when he looked down at the town he used the binoculars his father had given him for his birthday, but to make out actual people he needed a stronger magnification.

But even with the telescope he saw the children only as scurrying ants, not as individuals. The British tents were the closest, next to the bridge; the other tents were partly screened by the trees that grew along the river, but he could see the wooden platform which had been put up so that the dancers could practise.

There was a group there rehearsing now, stamping and

swirling. They were brightly dressed in red and yellow – Spanish perhaps, or Portuguese? He could hear very faintly the sound of guitars and tambourines.

He directed the telescope back to the British tents. The children there seemed to be doing chores: shaking out sleeping bags and fixing a clothes line. Two boys were banging wooden sticks together – one girl, small as a grasshopper, was taking a little boy through the steps of a dance. Karil tried to follow her with the telescope, but she was like quicksilver and he kept losing her.

An angry voice behind him made him turn round.

'May I ask you what you are doing, Karil, staring out of the window when Monsieur Dalrose is waiting to give you your history lesson?' said Countess Frederica. She walked over to the window. 'And where is the photograph of Carlotta? What have you done with it?'

'It's on the chest of drawers.' Karil sighed and put down the telescope. Actually it seemed to him that the whole room was full of pictures of Carlotta. She was like those earthworms that one cut in half and each half grew again. 'I only wanted to see what the folk dancers are doing. Especially the British ones.'

'The less said about the British team the better,' said Countess Frederica. 'I saw the Baroness Gambetti this morning and she told me that their behaviour is shocking.'

Karil turned away from the window. 'How? How is it shocking?'

The countess drew her ferocious brows together. 'I'm afraid I can't tell you that. But I can only say that you can stop showing an interest in what appear to be ruffians with no discipline and no manners.'

The Scold did not normally spend time with the Baroness Gambetti. Whether the wife of the Foreign Minister did or did not sleep with a picture of Hitler under her pillow, she was certainly a woman who disagreed with the king, and whatever the countess's faults she was utterly loyal to Johannes. But they had met in the salon of the dressmaker who made clothes for the court, and the baroness had been full of gossip and indignation.

'The British rabble have no uniform – they came with a ragbag of clothes and not one of them can curtsy. And they call their teachers by their Christian names. But that's not all – they wear nothing in the shower rooms.' She lowered her voice. 'Nothing at all.'

Countess Frederica had tried to be fair. 'Of course, it would not be sensible to shower in one's clothes,' she pointed out.

'No, of course not,' snapped the baroness. 'But it is customary to slip off one's bathrobe at the very last second, whereas these children just wander about in the washroom till it is their turn. They have no modesty and no shame. And the man who is in charge of them looks like a bandit. My husband says his face is familiar – he's probably wanted by the police.'

There had been no time to hear more about the British children but the countess had learned enough.

'Put the telescope away, and put Carlotta back in her rightful place, please.'

But at lunchtime Uncle Fritz seemed to be very pleased with the way things were going down in the park.

'Everyone has settled in very well,' he said. 'It's so good to have young people' he sighed. 'They're going to have a tour of the town today,' he went on. 'They'll come to the palace – only the staterooms, of course, and the ramparts – but if you look out of the window you'll be able to see them. Fortunately they seem to be getting on very well, the different teams. That's because it's not a competition, just people coming together to make music and dance,' said Uncle Fritz happily.

But the best news was still to come. After the meal was over, an equerry sent for Uncle Fritz and asked him to come to the council chamber because His Majesty wanted to speak to him. When he came back he was beaming.

'Your father will come himself to the opening ceremony,' he told Karil. 'It is quite unexpected – no one thought the king would have time to open what is after all only a children's festival. You will accompany your father, of course. The master of ceremonies is arranging the details now.'

But if Uncle Fritz was delighted and the prince, too, the chief of police and the head of the army were appalled.

'It's madness – trying to arrange proper security at such short notice. Two days! My reservists will be away at camp,' said Colonel Metz.

'We'll have to use the trainees,' said the chief of police. 'And he's going on horseback – both he and the prince will ride. He thinks the children will prefer it. What's got into the king – and just now when everything is so tense?'

The king himself could not have told them what had got into him. He only knew that after yet another week of endless meetings, threatening telegrams from the German

132

chancellor, heckling and nagging from Gambetti and his followers, he was reaching the end of his tether. He had forgotten what it was like to be a human being, to have a son whom he loved, to live in a world where children came together to make music and to dance.

That night he left a meeting of his defence committee early and made his way to Karil's room.

'Is it true?' was the first thing his son said. 'We're going to open the Folk Dance Festival together?'

'Yes, Karil. We'll give them something to remember! I'm calling out the Mounted Guard. And I shall see that the children are presented to you.'

The prince was silent for a moment. Then: 'Couldn't I actually meet them? Not just have them presented – meet them properly?'

It was the king now who was silent. 'Karil, it never works, trying to make friends with people from outside our world. Believe me – I know what I'm talking about.' His face was sombre as he looked out at the mountains. 'You will only get hurt.' He put his hand on his son's shoulder. 'Perhaps we shouldn't put it off any longer, going to the dragonfly pool. I can't promise, but there are no meetings tomorrow. I'll see what I can do.'

Chapter Fourteen

Sightseeing

The Berganians had done their best to make the camp-site comfortable for the visiting teams, but camping is camping – there is nothing to be done about that.

Kit found a toad on the slatted floor of the shower and came back to tell Tally that he did not like it. He did not like it at all. Then there was breakfast. Matteo had gone off early, no one knew where, and Julia and Tally tried to light the Primus while Magda was still in the shower, but it was an ancient, temperamental contraption with a will of its own and, however much they pumped, it wouldn't get going.

'I can perhaps help?' said a boy from the German tent. He had a mass of brown curls and a friendly smile, and with him came his sister, whose hair was even curlier and whose smile was as broad.

And he did help, without any fuss, so that in a few minutes the stove was roaring like a furnace.

At this point Magda appeared and decided that she would make the porridge, and she began well, stirring the pot with a big ladle – only then she had an important thought about Schopenhauer – you could tell when this happened because her eyes glazed over – and the ladle moved more and more slowly, and though Barney rushed to take it from her, it was too late.

'It's funny – you can eat burnt toast and it isn't too bad at all,' said Borro, 'but burnt porridge!'

After breakfast they started on their chores. Augusta Carrington must have swallowed something which disagreed with her – perhaps a piece of meat that had got stuck to her plate of rice – and had come out in lumps on her back, and Verity needless to say did nothing to help but wandered past the tents of the other children, showing them how beautiful she was, but the rest of them worked with a will.

The Deldertonians were in their ordinary clothes, but most of the children wore their national costumes and the campsite was a blaze of colour – the orange and yellow of the Spaniards and the Italians, the cool blue and white of the Scandinavians . . . the fierce black-and-red embroidered shirts of the Hungarians . . .

The buses that were to take them on a tour of the town were not due till eleven, and while they waited some of the teams took it in turns to rehearse on the wooden platform. The Germans had gone through their dance early. It was beautiful and didn't involve anybody hitting themselves on their own behinds, though there was a certain amount of yodelling.

'But yodelling is a good thing really because it's how people call each other in the mountains,' said Barney.

After the Germans came the Yugoslavs, whose dance was very ferocious with a lot of stamping, and music from a very strange instrument which was covered in fur and had a horn sticking out of each end.

'Do you think we should be stamping more?' asked Julia anxiously but Tally said no, she didn't think the British did much in the way of stamping.

'It's no good worrying about the poor Flurry Dance – it may be odd but it got us here,' said Tally. 'And the people are pleased to see us; they really are.'

This was true. The assistants in the shops, the waiters in the Blue Ox, mothers strolling through the park pushing prams – all greeted them and said how good it was to see children from other countries.

'You really like it here, don't you?' said Borro. 'I mean, *really*.'

'Yes,' said Tally, 'I really do.'

The Swedes were on the platform, their blue skirts swirling gracefully as they waltzed, when the two buses drew up on the other side of the bridge.

They drove to the cathedral first. Tally and Julia remembered it from the newsreel – a solemn gothic building with a tall spire. Inside, among the dark paintings of crucifixions, was a portrait of St Aurelia, the saint whose birthday the Berganians had been celebrating in the film.

'She was so young when she died,' said Anneliese, the curly-haired German girl whose brother had helped them to light the Primus. 'Only thirteen. I would not wish to die so young.'

After the cathedral they drove to the covered market, where they seemed to be selling everything in the world. There were cake stalls piled high with gingerbread hearts, and meat stalls where enormous pink sausages swayed like Zeppelins, and fruit such as the children from the Northern countries had never seen properly ripened: peaches and apricots, nectarines and great succulent bunches of purple grapes.

Then back into the buses for a drive to the town's main square, the Johannes Platz, named for the king.

It was very large and covered in cobbles. On the north side was the Palace of Justice, on the west side the town hall, with a famous clock tower from which carved figures of the Twelve Apostles came out one by one as the hours struck, and on the south the Blue Ox, with its beer garden and terrace.

But what the children from Delderton were staring at with dismay was the wooden platform in the centre of the square which had been put up specially for the festival.

It looked as though the whole town meant to come and see them dance.

They had lunch in a cafe in a side road and then everybody got into the buses again for a tour of the royal palace. By now the children had all mixed. Borro was talking to a pretty French girl with long blonde hair. They sat with their heads close together, discussing milk yields and grazing acreages, because her parents kept a herd of Charolais cows on their farm in Burgundy. At the back of the bus the Danish girls were cutting up bunches of grapes with their nail scissors and handing them round. Verity was flirting with an Italian boy, who listened to her politely but seemed more interested in the mountains they could see out of the window.

Matteo was not on the bus. He had counted everybody in, exchanged a few words with Magda and walked away.

'He's getting really good at not being there,' said Tally.

They drove through a sun-drenched valley covered in vineyards and orchards, and past little wooden houses with flower-filled balconies, and the people they passed all waved. It seemed to her that she had never been in a happier place.

The palace appeared and disappeared as the road snaked round the side of the hill. It was not a big palace, just as Bergania was not a big kingdom, but everything was there: turrets and towers, a moat, and a flagpole with the royal standard raised to show that the king was in residence. There were two sentry boxes, striped red, green and white in the Bergania colours, and a soldier stood guard on either side of the tall, gold-spiked gate.

As they drove into the forecourt an eagle soared up over the battlements and Tally, her head tilted to follow its flight, gave a sudden intake of breath.

'What is it? What's the matter?' said Julia.

Tally could not answer. What she had seen had both frightened and shocked her.

A figure dressed in black was pulling someone roughly away from a high barred window. She could not make out the person who was being dragged away; it was someone small, a child probably – and already out of sight – but the black-clad figure stood for a moment looking out through the bars. It was a woman – but a woman out of some cruel and ancient story: a witch, a jailer. Even so far away, one could see the anger that possessed her.

Tally was right about the anger. Inside the tower room, the Countess Frederica had lost her temper and lost it badly.

'What is the matter with you, Karil?' she shouted. 'Why do you do this – stand and look out like an orphan waiting to be adopted instead of a prince of the blood? Have you no *pride*?'

It's insufferable, she thought. She knew the boy to be physically brave: he rode fearlessly in spite of his mother's accident; he was a skilled rock climber and a talented fencer . . . but this ridiculous need to belong to children who should be proud to black his boots was not to be endured.

Carlotta would not behave like this. Carlotta knew her worth.

She lingered for a moment, watching the children spill out of the buses and make their way towards the gates. Then she turned to speak to the prince again, but he had gone.

Tally's mood had changed. It was such a strange image – the black-clad woman pulling someone away from a window as though looking out was a crime. Were there things she did not understand about Bergania? It had seemed to be a sort of paradise, but perhaps she was wrong. She remembered Matteo's words in the park, his grimness.

They were led through the palace by a guide who spoke in three languages, and those children who understood English or German or French translated for the others. The staterooms were very grand, but the truth is that one ballroom is much like another, with mirrors on the walls, a dais for the musicians and crystal chandeliers. The state dining room had what all state dining rooms have – a massive polished table, set with exotic place mats and gold-edged plates – and the library, like most royal libraries, was lined with bookcases that kept the leather-bound books firmly hidden behind a trellis of steel.

'They have put the books in prison,' said a little Finnish boy, and his friends nodded and translated what he had said.

'It's absolutely ridiculous,' said Tod, 'one family living in all this space. It ought to be given to the workers of the country.'

But Tally, thinking of the trim pretty houses they had passed in the town, wasn't so sure that the workers would want to live in the palace. As they walked from one grand impersonal room to another, passing dark paintings of Berganian knights in armour and courtiers in ruffles, she found it difficult to keep her attention on the guide's patter. What would be interesting would be to make one's way down one of the corridors that was barred to visitors by a red satin rope and a notice saying: '*No admittance past this point.*' Tally longed to lift up the rope and slip under it and see where real people lived –

where the king slept, where the prince did his lessons and ate his breakfast and the servants cooked their meals. Once she even went across to one of the ropes and lifted it but immediately a guard came and spoke to her sharply and she put it down.

As they trooped out again Barney called to her. 'Look,' he said. 'This is the best bit.'

Tally came to join him. Barney was standing by a large window at the end of a corridor, and as Tally came to join him she saw what he meant.

The window faced the town below, and one could make out everything. The river with its sheltering lime trees and the people taking the air; the spires of the cathedral and the clock tower and – amazingly clear – the field with their tents and the practice dance floor . . . even the marble statue of the queen.

'If I lived here I'd spend most of the time looking out of the window,' he said.

Tally gave a little shudder.

'What's the matter?'

Tally didn't answer. She had remembered the woman in black and her gaunt arm as she pulled away someone who was probably doing just what she was doing – looking out.

He climbed steadily; there was no need to seek the way. The fifteen years he had spent away from his country had not blotted out any memories.

The sights were familiar: the way the clouds were massed above the high peaks, the exact shade of azure of the sky, the shape of the clump of pines that edged the meadow he was crossing. The flowers were the same: the vetches in their tangle of blue and yellow, the delicate harebells growing out of sparse pockets of earth between the rocks, and now, as he gained height, the edelweiss, which no one was supposed to pick then, as now, because it was so rare.

There had been a burrow by the side of the path made by a family of marmots – and the burrow was still there. A kestrel circled, lost height to show its chestnut plumage and rose again. As a boy he had watched such birds a hundred times.

The sounds were the same too: the soughing of the wind in the pines, the droning of the bees clustering in the clover. And the scents too were utterly familiar: pine needles warmed by the sun, the tang of resin . . .

His feet made their own way, recognizing now the roughness of stone, now the softness of the earth as he walked through a patch of woodland. His time in the Amazon, in the Mato Grosso, might never have been.

Now he could see the hut; not the kind of place a woman of such great age should be living all the year round – isolated, exposed to the weather, often snowed up in the winter – but no one had been able to persuade the king's old nurse to come down off the mountain and settle in the town.

He left the path and followed the track to the hut. For a moment he was afraid. She had been old when he left Bergania – anything could have happened.

Then the door opened and she came out carrying a basket of washing. She had not seen him yet, and he watched as she began to hang up her aprons – checked aprons in red and white, hemmed with a row of cross stitch. She had always worn them to work and suddenly he remembered the comfort of their clean and starchy smell.

But now he moved out of the shadow of the tree and she saw him. Would she remember, after so long?

She remembered. She looked at him in silence – she did not shout or exclaim or drop the pillowcase she was putting on the line. She just looked. Then as he came up to her, she opened her arms and called him by his name.

CHAPTER FIFTEEN

TREACHERY

The man who sat in the best bedroom of the Blue Ox could not be mistaken for anyone but a very high-ranking army officer – and a Nazi officer at that. Though he was still eating breakfast, Reichsgruppen Fuehrer Anton Stiefelbreich was fully dressed in a khaki jacket so covered in medals that they dazzled and caught the eye, and afterwards people who met him never quite remembered his face. His cap lay ready beside him, adorned with the swastika of the party he now served, and he wore jackboots even while buttering his roll.

As much as Karil detested his uniforms, with their scratchy collars and showy buttons and infuriating plumes, so did Colonel Stiefelbreich love his. Back in Berlin, where he now worked at the headquarters of the

Gestapo, he had a whole cupboard of uniforms. That was one of the many things he valued in his new job – the job of stirring up trouble in those countries that did not understand how important it was to cooperate fully with Herr Hitler's dreams for a united Europe. United, of course, under the German flag.

And to impress foreigners one had to be properly dressed. The colonel was waiting for Gambetti, the Berganian Foreign Minister, who was coming to see him on a private visit here in his room. Meanwhile, to make certain that his bodyguards were in place, he walked silently to the door and opened it.

The two men who had been sitting in chairs in the corridor got to their feet.

'Got any jobs for us to do, Colonel?'

'Not at the moment. But stay in position – I'm expecting the Foreign Minister. Make sure no one follows him upstairs.'

The two men Colonel Stiefelbreich had recruited as his bodyguards could not have been more different, nor were they simply bodyguards. They were more by way of being spies and sleuths and he used them for all the work that he wanted to be kept secret.

One of them was good at his job simply because of his enormous size and strength. He was one of those people who seemed to be made of something inorganic like iron or stone – in fact his huge, stupid face might well have been carved from granite, except that granite, when it catches the light, sometimes sparkles, and the thug's face had never sparkled in its life. He was known as Earless, because he had lost his left ear in a fight. He had lost a lot of other things too – the tip of one finger, part of a nostril and more teeth than he could count – but it was his ear he worried about because his wife, Belinda, had been fond of it. She was a tiny blonde woman and Earless, who would throttle someone with his bare hands without thinking twice about it, was completely soppy about Belinda.

The other man was called Theophilus Fallaise and he had been brought up in a library where his father was Keeper of the Books. One can read about all sorts of wonderful things in a library but the things that the young Theophilus had chosen to read about were not wonderful. He read about the tortures they had used in the olden days: the rack and the iron maiden and thumb screws – and about the punishments they had used in foreign countries like China, where people were driven mad by having water dripped on to their skull.

The library was in a castle belonging to an eccentric nobleman in a country about which Theophilus never spoke, and because the boy had hardly ever gone outdoors, but only deeper and deeper into the basements in search of more and more horrible books about inflicting pain, he had grown up very unhealthy. His skin was pale and clammy, he blinked in the light and his upper lip was lifted by a wrinkled scar that parted to show a filed gold tooth.

But as a sleuth and a spy he was second to none. He could see in the dark, because of the years he had spent underground, and wriggle through the narrowest spaces – and there was nothing he didn't know about the more silent and sinister ways of getting rid of someone.

The two bodyguards did not like each other. Theophilus thought that Earless was a stupid thug – which he was – and Earless thought that Theophilus was a slimy creep – which was true also – but the two men made a good pair. One had brains and the other had brawn – and Stiefelbreich had taken a lot of trouble to get hold of them for his latest assignment in Bergania.

Baron Gambetti arrived in Stiefelbreich's room through the back entrance of the Blue Ox. He was extremely nervous; his goatee beard trembled slightly and he was sweating, but when he entered the room and saw the colonel he took heart. The bodyguards at the door, the glittering medals, the man's air of importance were reassuring. In encouraging the Gestapo to come to the aid of Bergania he was doing the right thing, Gambetti told himself. He was saving his country from the king's foolish obstinacy. The future lay with the people that Stiefelbreich represented.

'Heil, Hitler!' said the colonel, and Gambetti cleared his throat and said, 'Heil, Hitler,' in a slightly squeaky voice.

'I have messages for you from our headquarters. The chief of the Gestapo is appreciative of the information you have sent to us. I take it there has been no change?'

'Not as far as I know, Colonel,' said Gambetti.

'Good. Good. In that case I think it is time for us to act for the good of your beautiful country. We have great affection for Bergania – I used to come skiing here with my family when the children were small. It will be a pleasure for us to rescue the country from the king's obstinacy and folly.'

Baron Gambetti nodded. 'It seems impossible to make him see that there is no future for countries that oppose the might and strength of Germany. We must join the great German Reich or be trampled underfoot. But the king is obstinate – his Prime Minister too, old von Arkel. As a Berganian patriot I feel it is my duty to help you,' he said.

'Quite so,' said Stiefelbreich. 'In that case we had better get down to details.'

An hour later Gambetti let himself into his villa behind the botanical gardens and found his wife in her dressing room.

'I hope you didn't weaken, Philippe,' she said. 'If we dither now, we are lost.'

'No, I didn't weaken. But I hope he means what he says. That everything will be . . . civilized . . . an orderly takeover without any bloodshed or violence.'

'Of course he means it,' said his wife, taking the curlers out of her dyed blonde hair. 'It will be perfectly simple. And you will at last have the honour and glory you deserve. I'm sure he promised you your reward.'

'Yes, he did. Only . . .'

'Only what? For heaven's sake – why can't you be a man?'

'I am being a man,' said Gambetti plaintively. 'But it isn't easy to do this – the king has been good to me.'

'Bah! Milksop,' said the baroness. 'Thank goodness you are married to somebody who isn't afraid of a bit of adventure. Now pass me my hairbrush, please.'

*

Back in the Blue Ox, Stiefelbreich was questioning his bodyguards.

'Find out if Stilton has arrived – he should be here by now.'

'He has, sir,' said Theophilus. 'Checked in to room 23, on the third floor. Next to the attic . . .'

Stilton, like Earless, was an Englishman. He had led a perfectly normal life for many years, working as a sanitary engineer who specialized in bathroom fittings, so that he earned good money, but after a while he decided it was his duty to travel round the simple peasant houses of Europe and persuade their owners to get rid of their old-fashioned outdoor toilets – just a hole in a wooden bench – and order a proper, indoor, flush sanitation system.

But that wasn't all he did. Stilton had a hobby – more of a *skill*, really – and it was because of this that Stiefelbreich had tracked him down. Now, hearing that Stilton had arrived safely, the Nazi smiled and rubbed his hands, knowing that everything would go exactly as planned.

There was only one more thing for Stiefelbreich to do. He picked up the phone and put a call through to the German consulate.

'I take it you have my instructions about the German children on the campsite? I have made enquiries and they are quite unsuitable. Children like that should never have been sent to represent our glorious country and the new order that Herr Hitler has established.'

He listened, frowning, to the voice on the other end. The man seemed to be arguing, almost pleading.

'I'm afraid that has nothing to do with it,' Stiefelbreich

barked. 'Please see that my orders are carried out without delay.'

Satisfied that the matter was settled, he ordered a large beer. The middle-aged waitress with ginger hair who brought it to him was unfriendly – but it didn't matter. This infuriating country was about to get a lesson it would not forget.

CHAPTER SIXTEEN

THE DRAGONFLY POOL

They had worked all morning but now, the last day before the festival began, everyone was relaxing. Tally and Julia had finished disentangling the wreaths and straightening the flowers for their costumes and were playing cards on the grass with Anneliese, the curly-haired German girl who had befriended them. Borro was demonstrating slingshots to his French friend, whirling his scarf round his head and sending missiles unerringly into the river. Kit and two Dutch boys were trying to catch a carp, lying on their stomachs by the pool and using willpower to make the fish come to the surface.

Matteo was organizing a game of football on a patch of level ground further along the bank, and Magda was playing chess with the teacher in charge of the German

151

group. He was a serious young man with horn-rimmed spectacles and reminded her of Heribert, the professor she had hoped to marry.

It was a glorious day, sunny and still.

A woman carrying a posy of sweet peas came out of the Blue Ox, crossed the river and made her way towards the marble statue of the queen. She removed the withered flowers and put the fresh ones in her hand. As she came back she smiled at the children. It was the middle-aged waitress who had stared at Matteo.

From the Spanish tent came the sound of a guitar, and the dancers in their bright red skirts and yellow boleros made their way to the wooden platform for a last rehearsal. Their music drew a few of the other children to the platform. Those who had been dozing lifted their heads.

'We did it,' said Tally happily. 'It worked – here we all are from everywhere.'

And their new friend nodded and taught them a German word: *Bruderschaft*. 'It means a band of brothers – and sisters too,' she said.

It was at that moment that they looked up and saw three men in uniform come across the bridge – and with them was the Minister of Culture. His silver hair was dishevelled and his face pale. Two of the men were in the light blue uniform of the Berganian Police and one – who walked in front with a swagger – wore khaki with a swastika on the sleeve. It was this man who marched up to Magda and the teacher with whom she was playing chess and said sharply, 'Where are the German children? Which tent?'

The teacher stood up and looked about him. 'They are everywhere,' he said, startled by the sudden command.

And indeed they were. Some were playing football with Matteo. A little girl with a crown of flaxen pigtails, her arm round her new friend from Portugal, was sitting on the steps of the platform listening to the music.

'Call them at once,' barked the Nazi officer. 'Get them together. Why are they not in an orderly group?'

The teacher looked bewildered. 'They have made friends,' he said. 'It is—'

'Round them up,' repeated the officer. 'They have one hour to get ready. A bus will take them to the station.'

'But—'

'They are leaving. The King of Bergania has again insulted the people of Germany and no child of the Fatherland will remain in this country. Hurry!'

The Minister of Culture had taken Magda aside.

'A directive has come from the Gestapo in Berlin,' he said hurriedly. 'I've tried to make them listen but it's impossible.'

On the platform the music ceased; the dancers came to rest. The sudden silence was ominous. The two policemen stood by, looking embarrassed. Gradually, as they understood what was happening, the German children, one by one, came towards their tent. At the same time the other children, in every language, expressed their indignation.

'We want them to stay.'

'They're our friends.'

'They haven't done anything.'

And repeated again and again: 'It isn't *fair*!'

Only the German children were silent. They had lived

153

for too long in an oppressed country. They knew there was no hope. The small girl with flaxen pigtails was crying. Her friend from Portugal tried to comfort her and was turned away by one of the policemen.

Then Tally saw red. She ran up to the Nazi officer and began to pummel him with her fists. 'You can't do this,' she yelled. 'You can't, you can't!'

Strong arms pulled her back. 'Stop it, Tally,' said Matteo. 'Stop it at once.'

Within an hour the tents had been stripped and the German children herded away.

Karil woke in high spirits. For once it was going to work; he was going to have a whole day alone with his father in their favourite place. The Scold had gone to visit a friend – there was nothing in the way. The king, when he came to fetch him, looked more relaxed than he had done for a long time. He carried his hunting bag filled with their picnic, and his collapsible fishing rod.

They made their way out of the palace by the secret door the guards had opened for them and set off along the turf path that led up towards the mountain.

'Look, a lammergeier,' said the king.

Karil, following his pointing arm, saw a tiny speck in the sky.

'How can you tell, so far away?'

'It's the flight pattern and . . .' He shrugged. 'I had a friend once who could identify birds that I could hardly see with the naked eye. He was uncanny – he could lead you up to a stone in a place he'd never been before and tell you what was underneath it. Almost exactly. It was as though he'd placed the creatures there himself.'

'Like giving you a present,' said Karil.

The king looked at him, startled. 'Yes, exactly like that.'

'What happened to him?'

The king shrugged. 'He went away, just when I needed him most. People do that with us.'

They walked for a while in silence. Then Karil said, 'We're sort of freaks, aren't we? I mean because we're . . . royal or whatever. It's not real, being a king or a prince.'

The king turned to him. 'Good heavens, Karil! Is that how you feel?'

Karil nodded. 'When I wake up in the morning I think, why me? Why did it happened to me, being kept apart? Why didn't I just get born as an ordinary person? Well, I am ordinary, but nobody realizes that. Why can't I be like anyone else and belong?'

'There are good things too,' said his father. 'Sometimes we can help. Not often, but when we can . . .'

They came to a division of the path. The main track led up to the high meadows, to old Maria's hut and the peaks. The smaller one veered off to the left, towards the hunting ground. This was a green and shady place of great trees and running water, of moss and unexpected pools. Nowadays it was more of a nature reserve. The king had little time for hunting; the dappled deer roamed without fear, and the hares when disturbed sat up and gazed at the intruders before lolloping away.

They passed a wooden lodge, now boarded up, and plunged into the cool greenery of the forest. There was a place here to which the king had come as a boy, a hidden pool known only to the foresters and groundsmen who worked there. He had taken his queen there when she came from England; Karil had taken his first steps on its mossy banks and caught his first trout in its waters. The dragonfly pool was outside time: safe, beautiful and private.

They had not walked more than a few hundred metres into the forest when they heard the sound of hoof beats. Turning, they saw a palace messenger riding a black mare and leading a second horse.

The messenger slid to the ground and bowed to the king.

'Your Majesty, there has been a crisis. The Prime Minister requests your presence most urgently.'

The king frowned. 'Not today, Rudi. I'm going into the woods with my son.' And again, firmly, 'Not today. Tell von Arkel I'll deal with the matter tonight.'

The messenger leaned forward and whispered in the king's ear. Karil caught a few words. 'Troops mustering . . . urgent telegram from the border station . . .'

The king's face changed. All the weariness and strain of the last weeks returned.

'This is serious, Karil. You will understand; I have no choice.' He laid a hand on the boy's shoulder. 'Next Sunday, by God's grace – next Sunday we will go.'

But the boy pulled away and would not look at him.

'Please, Karil,' said the king. 'Please try to understand.'

'All I understand is that you don't care about me,' muttered Karil. 'You care about everybody in the world except me. A few hours can't matter; there's always a crisis. Always.'

156

The king's voice was suddenly the voice of an old man.

'A few hours can topple a kingdom, Karil.'

'Then let it,' said the boy furiously and began to walk off between the trees.

The king stood for a moment, looking after him. The weight on his chest was almost more than he could bear.

'You must come back and fetch him, Rudi,' he said to the messenger. 'He shouldn't be out alone.'

And he took the second pair of reins and mounted, and they rode away.

Left alone, Karil walked without any sense of direction. His anger was like cold steel going through his body. He hated his father. All his life the king had put anything and everything before his son. The thought of this day had meant so much to Karil – they had begun really to talk – and then it was over before it began.

'But I don't care,' he said aloud. 'I'm not going to try any more. I'm going to learn to be completely on my own. People you love just die or ignore you.'

He had cut a switch from a hazel branch and slashed at the undergrowth in a relentless and sullen rage. He wouldn't make his way to the pool – what was the point? But he would not return home either. Not yet. They could worry about him if they wanted to – but they wouldn't. What would his father care, busy in useless meetings and conferences that led nowhere?

Without thinking, he had turned away from the forest and come out on the meadows. The sun was very hot, but what did it matter if he got sunstroke? Who would be sorry if he died? Nobody – nobody at all.

He had not gone far when he saw, sitting by the side of the track, a small hunched figure. Coming closer, he made out a girl about his own age. She had light hair cut in a fringe and wore shorts and a blue shirt. Not a local then – probably one of the folk dancers. As he came up to her she lifted her head and he saw that she had been crying.

'Are you all right?' he asked in English.

For a moment she looked at him blankly, and he was about to try another language when she focused on him.

'No,' she said furiously. 'No, I'm not all right. How can one be when things like that go on?'

'Like what?'

'The Nazis. Hitler. I'm so *tired* of Hitler. I'm so terribly tired of him.' She began to cry again. 'We were all so happy. I thought we had done it.'

'It's when you're happy that God strikes you,' said Karil.

She shook her head angrily. 'Its nothing to do with God. It's people who spoil things.' She went to wipe her eyes on her sleeve and Karil felt in his pocket for a handkerchief, which he gave her.

'Thank you. I really like my school and I really like Magda – she's our housemother and very clever – but she can't manage handkerchiefs.'

'Keep it,' he said. 'I've got another one.'

'Two?' said Tally, momentarily diverted. 'Lucky you!'

'No,' he said vehemently. 'I'm not lucky. I'm not lucky at all.' He looked away, then turned back to Tally. 'You're from the camp, aren't you? One of the folk dancers?' He thought now that he had seen her through the telescope, helping a little boy. 'It looked so nice down there – what happened?'

'They came and marched all the German children away. They said the king had insulted Hitler again, but I don't see how you can insult Hitler enough. There was a horrible Nazi . . . There's been a crisis.'

'There's always a crisis,' said Karil bitterly.

'They were so sad to go, the German children. There was a very little one with plaits wound round her head who couldn't stop crying. I went for the Nazi, and Matteo – he's in charge of us – pulled me away and I was so angry I just ran off. There'll be a row – we're not supposed to leave the camp alone.'

'No, children are never supposed to do anything sensible alone.' He hesitated, then made up his mind. 'I'll take you to a place where no one will find you. You'd better come out of the sun. Then you can tell me . . . if you want to. But you needn't.'

She followed him willingly. He was surprised at himself: the dragonfly pool was his secret and his father's – yet he was going to show it to an unknown girl. But then, what was the point of sharing anything with his father – what did his father care?

They plunged into the cool of the forest. He led her down a mossy path, along a stream in which a heron stood on one leg, fishing. The path was dappled with pigeon feathers, and small fir cones lay on the ground; there was the faintest of breezes. The relief of the shade and moisture after the heat of the meadow was overwhelming.

Karil turned along beside a smaller stream; Tally heard the sound of rushing water and they came to a waterfall, tumbling down between rocks. Running up its side was a narrow track almost hidden by creepers and overhanging bushes. Still following the boy, she scrambled up to the top – and stood there, silent and amazed.

They had come to a pool so still and dark and deep that it hardly seemed to belong to the real world. The branches of great trees spread their arms over the surface of the water; a bright green frog plopped suddenly from a leaf into its depths. A kingfisher flew off with a flash of blue and emerald.

And over the surface of the water there danced and swooped and circled a host of dragonflies. Shafts of sunlight turned them every colour of the rainbow and in the silence she could make out, very faintly, the dry clatter of their wings.

She said nothing, just shook her head in wonder – and Karil knew that it was all right to have brought her here. He could not have borne it if she had gushed and exclaimed.

'There's a place there behind those boulders where no one can see us.'

He led her along the side of the pool and they scrambled over the flat stones into a kind of hollow soft with fallen leaves and moss.

'Are there otters?' she asked.

Karil nodded. 'You have to come at night to see them.'

'I think this must be the most beautiful place I've ever seen,' said Tally as they sat down side by side, resting their backs on the cool stone. 'But then, this is a marvellous country. I knew it would be. I wanted to come from the moment I saw it on the newsreel.'

'You're with the British team, aren't you?'

Remembering the rumours he had heard about the British 'savages' he smiled, and Tally stared at him. He looked quite different when he was no longer serious and stern.

'Yes. We're very bad – in fact we're terrible – everyone's going to laugh at us. We invented this thing called the Delderton Flurry Dance and it's really weird, but it was the only way we could get here.'

'Why did you want to come here so much?'

Tally had been watching a tiny spider crossing the stone.

'It was because of the king.'

'What king?' said Karil, startled.

'The King of Bergania, of course. I saw him on the newsreel and he looked so strong and brave – but tired too. And when they wrote and said they wanted people to come to a festival, I sort of bullied everyone into coming.'

'But what could you know about the king?'

'I knew he had stood out against Hitler . . .' She saw the spider safely into his hole and went on. 'We have a king too in England and he's really nice – absolutely decent. George VI he's called . . .'

Karil nodded. Carlotta had played with his daughters in Buckingham Palace.

'He has a stammer, and when he makes his speech on the wireless at Christmas my aunts get terribly worried in case he's going to break down and not be able to finish. They sit there clutching their sherry glasses, just willing him to go on. But he's not like the King of Bergania. He's not a ruler.'

'I can't see how you could tell what he's like just from watching a film.'

Tally shrugged. 'I don't know . . . but I felt it. I was sure. Perhaps it's because of my father. He's not a king, of course, he's a doctor, but he's like that. He knows what's right and he does it whatever it costs. I get annoyed when he's back late and I wanted to be with him, but I wouldn't want him to be someone who had nothing to do except look after me. Anyway, when I saw Bergania and the king I wanted to come here. I felt I had to. And I thought Matteo was behind me – he persuaded the others that folk dancing wasn't sissy – but he's been so odd since we came. He never seems to be there when you want him; it's as though he's hiding all the time. And just now he was furious with me for attacking the Nazi.'

'Well, of course. You could have got into serious trouble.'

'He can't want me to just let things happen without fighting.'

Karil had been pulling the seeds out of a fallen pine cone. Now he threw it into the water. 'Tell me again about the Bergania film. Tell me exactly.'

'I was with my friend Julia. She wanted me to come to the cinema and we saw an awful film – but before that there was this travelogue. And it was as though the country sort of spoke to me – it was so beautiful. It was silly, because I'd only been at school half a term and I was still settling in – progressive schools are hard work – but I knew I had to come.

'Because the country was beautiful?' he asked.

She shook her head. 'No, I've told you. It was because

162

of the king. Because he was brave and true to what he believed in and wouldn't let himself be bullied. Because he knew that if you have power you must use it well and not be afraid.'

Karil said nothing. Something inside him was changing . . . a knot was dissolving.

She turned to him. 'You live here,' she said. 'You must know. Is he like that?'

Karil took a deep breath. 'Yes,' he said joyfully. 'He is like that,' he said. 'That is exactly what he is like.'

They were silent for a while, watching the ripples made by a fish as it jumped for a fly. Then he turned to this unknown girl who had given him back his father and said, 'Thank you. Thank you very much.'

'For what?' she said, surprised.

'Oh . . . just . . . never mind.'

She had taken out the handkerchief and was flattening it on the stone. She had not guessed, yet when she saw the initials and the crown embroidered in the corner, she was not surprised.

'Of course,' she said. 'I've been an idiot. I know who you are.'

He braced himself, waiting for a fuss – she would be too respectful, or angry – or back away, make him feel 'different'.

'You're Karil,' she said – and because she had used only his name and not his rank he allowed himself a moment of hope.

'I would have liked us to be friends,' he said, looking down at the ground. 'I would really have liked that.'

'Well, of course we're going to be friends. That's obvious. It's what's going to happen.'

He shook his head. 'It won't work,' he said wearily. 'They read my letters and the doors are locked and . . . Oh, you've no idea what it's like.'

'Look, Karil, if I want to be friends with someone, nobody is going to stop me. Absolutely nobody. Perhaps I should tell you that I'm named after my great-grandmother who washed the socks of tramps in the London Underground. She came over as a young girl from America to marry my great-grandfather and she used to go up to these fierce men, some of them dead drunk, and make them take off their socks and give them to her to wash. Now that *is* difficult.' She folded up the handkerchief and put it in her pocket. 'And I think you should stop feeling sorry for yourself. It's not the end of the world, being a prince.'

In the palace the king came out of his emergency meeting with a lagging step. It seemed there was no end to the bullying his country had to endure. More than anything he wanted to see his son, but he had left Karil in a temper. Perhaps it was better to let the boy calm down in his own good time.

He had taken only a few steps down the corridor when he was almost knocked off his feet by someone who had been waiting half hidden by the velvet curtains.

'Karil! Are you all right?'

'Yes. I'm absolutely all right. And I'm sorry – I'm very, very sorry I was angry. It won't happen again. I'd like to help more . . . if you tell me . . . I'm . . .' He swallowed. 'I'm so proud of what you do.'

The king put his arm round the boy's shoulders. Just when one thought one couldn't carry on any longer something happened to make life bearable.

'And I'm proud of you, Karil. Prouder than you can imagine.'

CHAPTER SEVENTEEN

THE FESTIVAL BEGINS

The town square had been bustling with people and carts and carriers since dawn. Everybody seemed to be involved in the preparations for the folk-dancing display and for the opening ceremony that preceded it.

Workmen hammered, putting finishing touches to the platform on which the important people of the town would sit and from which the king would declare the festival open. The wooden stage for the dancers at the other end of the square was bedecked with flags and bunting; extra tubs of flowering trees had been brought in and there was hardly a windowsill or lamp post which was not festooned with greenery.

At the Blue Ox the waiters hurried from the kitchens to the restaurant and the beer garden, bringing bottles of champagne or lemonade or jugs of coffee and cream. There was a good view to be had from the windows of the inn and all available tables were taken very early in the day.

In his bedroom Colonel Stiefelbreich put the finishing touches to his uniform. He had been offered a seat on the platform and was making sure that every single medal was polished and in place. His bodyguards were going to mingle with the crowd, but Mr Stilton did not intend to leave the Blue Ox. He had spent the previous day trying to persuade some peasants to buy his indoor flush toilets, but they had behaved in a very stupid way and told him that they preferred the wooden huts they had always used. It gave them some peace from their families, they told him, to go across the fields with their newspapers. Well, if they wanted to go on living like savages, let them, thought Stilton; he had other things to do, and now he left his room and made his way up a narrow flight of stairs to an empty attic which had an uninterrupted view across the square to the town hall. He would get a much better view of the procession from here than jammed in a crowd of unwashed yokels.

Once inside, he locked the door behind him. Then he opened his case, took out a packet of sandwiches – and certain things which had absolutely nothing to do with lavatories – and settled down to wait.

Countess Frederica, who would be sitting near the front of the platform, stood before her mirror, wondering whether to add a touch of colour to her outfit. Her dress was black of course and so were her vest and her knickers, but she could perhaps add a coloured scarf. Karil seemed to set great store by this occasion – and it was quite a long time since anyone had died. But in the end she decided against it; there was no need to dress up for a lot of unruly children.

Everyone else though seemed to be in their best clothes. The Baroness Gambetti was dressed like a peacock in a gaudy blue and orange two-piece and as much jewellery as she could get round her neck. She was in excellent spirits but her husband, who was trying to eat his breakfast, looked like a ghost, only yellower.

'He promised me it will all be very civilized,' he kept muttering, 'a peaceful takeover,' while his wife told him to shut up and finish his egg.

In the square, the brass-band players rubbed up their instruments, workmen sprinkled sawdust along the route of the royal procession, policeman put up ropes. Wooden benches were brought and set out for those who wanted to watch the dancing, and coloured lights were strung between the trees – for the evening would end with a great open-air party for anyone who cared to come.

The Berganians had always been good at celebrations.

Now that the festival was really upon them everyone felt better. Even if they made fools of themselves it would soon be over. Tally, helping Kit fix the bells on to his ankles, had quite forgotten her black mood of the day before, and now that they were all dressed they didn't look too bad. In fact, suddenly they looked unexpectedly nice, and this was because of Magda.

Magda had stopped having Important Thoughts about Schopenhauer long enough to notice that the girls' wreaths had not really recovered from their bashing in the luggage van of the train and had suggested they go to the market early in the morning and buy some fresh flowers to fill up the gaps.

'But have we enough money?' Julia had wanted to know.

And again Magda had surprised everyone, by groping about among her notes and card indexes and extracting her purse.

So Tally and Julia had got up very early and come back with roses and lilies of the valley and cornflowers still moist with dew and everyone had set to, healing the poor wreaths.

'What about our hats?' Kit wanted to know. 'Don't the boys get any flowers?'

So Julia pinned a hyacinth to the brim of his hat and, though it would probably fall over his nose once he began to dance, he was pleased.

'We may look a bit odd, but no one can say we're not fresh and floral,' said Tally.

And for the first time they wondered whether after all it might turn out all right, this Flurry Dance which had given them all so much trouble.

The broken staves had been mended, Augusta's bananas had been stowed in her violin case and Matteo, looking more like a bandit than ever in a black corduroy shirt and dark trousers, had assembled his sackbut, so there was hope that he would come in with his *oom-pa-pa* at important moments.

It was still difficult not to be upset by the empty German tent, but the other teams, all dressed now in their dancing clothes, looked really festive. The Italians with their sashes and bright kerchiefs, the French girls with their white headdresses . . . the Yugoslavs in goatskin jackets with feathers in their caps . . . Lots would be drawn after the ceremony to decide the order in which the teams would dance.

They made their way over the bridge, joined by crowds of people in their best clothes and children waving flags. In the square they were given their places. The Deldertonians were in the front, against the ropes that marked off the route the king would take as he rode towards the platform on which the distinguished guests would sit. The visitors would come on through the double doors of the town hall, but the king and the prince would mount by special wooden steps from the square.

The crowd was in a party mood, wanting to forget the crises and threats that beset their country.

Now the great doors opened and the mayor, in his gold chain, took his seat on the platform, followed by the Lord Chief Justice and the Prime Minister. When Gambetti appeared with his wife there was some booing in the crowd, but it was quickly hushed – today was not a day for politics.

Stiefelbreich marched on in his jackboots. For a moment his face turned towards the attic of the Blue Ox and then away again. More and more people filed on to the platform. The clock in the tower on the north side of the square struck eleven, and eleven apostles came out, marched woodenly out of their niches and went back again.

'We've got a really good view,' said Tally.

'Matteo hasn't,' Julia pointed out.

This was true. Matteo was standing behind an exceptionally tall and heavily built policeman in a brass helmet, one of a whole contingent who was lining the route.

'There's room here,' called Tally, but Matteo only raised a hand and stayed where he was.

There was the sound of rousing music, a rustle of excitement from the crowd – and the procession which had set off from the palace entered the square.

'We'll give them something to remember,' the king had told his son, so he rode the grey thoroughbred that was kept for state occasions and wore his most dazzling uniform, that of the Berganian Rifles in scarlet and white and gold. The prince, riding his favourite chestnut, was hardly less grand. Ignoring the discomfort of the scratchy braid round his throat and the ludicrously tight trousers, he had chosen the uniform of the Mountain Cuirassiers because here was something worth dressing up for: not a dead saint or a railway station but a festival made by children who had come together from everywhere – and a girl who had brought her friends to honour the king.

Behind them rode Uncle Fritz, the Minister of Culture, then came the Household Cavalry, the men-at-arms, the band of the Fusiliers . . .

There were shouts of 'Long live the King! . . . Long live Johannes!' People climbed up lamp posts to see better. There had never been such enthusiasm for this ruler, who had become a hero to his people.

The procession was drawing level with the place where the children from Delderton were standing. Everything was going as expected – the marching men, the trotting horses, the band . . .

Then the burly policeman who was standing in front of Matteo shifted to one side – and everything changed.

The king reined in his horse and came to a stop – and as the king stopped so did those who were behind him. The sound of the band spluttered and died away, and in the silence that followed, the king's words rang loud and clear.

'Seize that man!' he cried. 'Hold him! Don't let him go!'

And he pointed directly at Matteo, standing very straight among the children he had brought.

The policeman who had been standing in front of Matteo grabbed his arm, and a second officer came forward to help restrain him. Matteo did not struggle. All the time he stood erect and looked steadily at the king.

'Bring him here,' ordered the king.

While the crowd murmured and wondered and craned their necks to see the criminal, Johannes dismounted and handed the reins to his son.

Then he stepped forward and lifted the rope that separated him from the crowd and let it fall, and at the same time Matteo freed himself and moved towards the king.

There was a moment of total silence. Then the king's arms came round Matteo and the two men embraced. The throng of people might not have existed; they saw only each other.

'My God, Matteo,' said the king. 'It's been so long.'

No one could hear the words the men now spoke.

'Later,' said the king, freeing himself reluctantly. 'As soon as this is over.'

Then Matteo went back to stand beside the children and the king with his son rode to the platform and dismounted and climbed the wooden steps – and old von Arkel, the Prime Minister who had served him for many years, thought that Johannes looked as he had not looked since before his wife had died.

The ceremony began. The Lord Mayor made a speech. The Countess Frederica scowled and speculated. Who was this bandit whom the king had embraced so publicly, and how could she make Karil behave as he should when his father so forgot himself?

Then the king stood up. He had written a short speech in Berganian, saying all the proper things. Now he tore it up. He looked once across the square, and when he spoke it was in English, but there was not a person listening who failed to catch the joy behind his words.

For Johannes was giving thanks.

He said that today had been a special day for him because a friend he had loved as a boy had returned.

'And he did not come alone,' said the king. 'He came with children from all over Europe who have brought support and encouragement to our country. We are accustomed to using big words: Cooperation Between Nations, International Treaties, Political Solidarity . . . But cooperation begins with one thing: with friendship between ordinary people, with the love we bear one another – and with citizens who refuse to hate, or to judge.

'It has not been easy to stand firm in these hard times, but I am the most fortunate of men because I rule over people who understand this. Who are tolerant and forgiving and *good*.

'And because of this, we shall prevail!'

He stepped forward to the edge of the platform. 'And now let us forget wars and threats and invasions, and celebrate. I declare the Bergania Folk Dance Festival open. Let the dancing begin!'

Cheers rang out over the square, and curious faces turned to look at Matteo. The band began to play again and the king made his way to the steps.

Only the people sitting close by heard anything – a short crack, nothing more. The king paused on the top step for a moment. Then he stumbled and missed his foothold. His arms came out and slowly, very slowly, almost as though time had stopped, he began to fall.

It was so strange and unexpected that no one could take in what had happened. No one except Matteo. With a few bounding steps he reached the king almost as his crumpled body came to rest on the ground.

He loosened the glittering tunic, saw the blood seeping through the fabric – and the king tried to push his hand away.

'There is . . . nothing to be done, Matteo. It is . . . over.'

'*No!*'

But he had seen the wound now.

The king tried to speak, and Matteo put his ear to the king's mouth.

'Do you . . . remember?'

'I remember everything,' said Matteo. 'Everything.'

But there was one last desperately important thing that had to be said, and with a tremendous effort the dying man forced out the words.

'I have a son, Matteo. Will you . . .?'

His breath was failing; with his eyes he entreated his friend.

'Yes,' said Matteo. 'I will. I swear it.'

And he stayed on his knees beside the man he had loved beyond all others as a boy, while the storm broke about him and men came from everywhere and there were shouts of 'Get a doctor!' and 'Call an ambulance!'

Till a great wail of despair ran through the crowd and from a thousand mouths came the unbelieving cry: 'The king is dead.'

CHAPTER EIGHTEEN

FINDING THE PRINCE

It was Tod who couldn't stop being sick. He hung over the basin in the toilet block, retching and shaking. His room at Delderton was hung with posters of fierce revolutionaries attacking palaces, he had thirsted for the blood of kings – but now, seeing the real thing, he was helplessly ill.

Tally sat on the grass with her hands over her knees and tried to stop shivering. It wasn't cold; the sun shone as it had done every day since they had come, but she was cold through and through.

At first she hadn't taken it in . . . the tall figure of the king breaking, Matteo's incredible leap to be by his side . . . It had seemed like something out of a film.

But it had happened. It was real.

Julia crouched beside her – one of her plaits had come undone; her freckles stood out dark against the pallor of her face.

The children still wore their dancing clothes, but now, with their exhausted tear-stained faces, they looked more like sad clowns than dancers.

Two girls came over from the French tent.

'So we are not to dance at all,' said one; 'and we have worked so hard.'

Everywhere on the campsite groups of children huddled together, trying to grasp the fact that all their efforts and preparations had come to nothing. For the festival had been cancelled; there would be no dancing – and all foreigners were to leave the country on the following day.

'We should begin to pack,' said Magda.

But nobody moved. They were waiting for Matteo.

'Take them back,' he had said hurriedly to Magda. 'I'll be along as soon as I can. Keep them together whatever you do.'

After the ambulance came and the king's body was carried away, there was complete uproar in the square. People cried and screamed; some struggled to their feet. The guests on the platform pushed their way in an untidy scrum to the door.

Then the loudspeakers took over, telling everyone to leave the square and go home in an orderly manner.

'Keep calm; the situation is under control,' the voice kept repeating.

But the people of Bergania did not feel calm. They wanted to know who had done this terrible thing. Even when the procession had returned in confusion to the palace and the mounted police came to clear the square, groups of angry people re-formed on every street corner.

No one could believe it. In the Blue Ox, Herr Keller was unashamedly weeping. The waitress who had brought flowers to the statue stood with her hands over her eyes. She had been a maid in the palace when the queen was still alive.

In the middle of the uproar Mr Stilton came quietly downstairs, paid his bill, loaded his case of samples into his car – and drove away.

The fee from Stiefelbreich was in his pocket and his expression was cheerful and serene; everything had gone without a hitch. The first bullet fired from the attic window had hit its target; it was no wonder, he thought, that he was now considered to be the best assassin in the world.

On the campsite, the children waited. Augusta Carrington ate her last banana. A Norwegian girl in a blue skirt twirled alone outside her tent. She had spent hours sewing on the braid.

Then came a fanfare on the loudspeaker. There was going to be an announcement in the square. Baron Gambetti, the Foreign Minister, would address the people.

Gambetti had been in a state of terror since the assassination – all he wanted to do was to run home and hide under his bed.

'I didn't want him to be killed,' he quavered. 'Not *killed*.'

'Well, he has been, you lily-livered coward,' snapped his

178

wife. 'And you're going to be in charge; so get up there and do what Stiefelbreich tells you.'

So now Gambetti was pushed on to the platform. He was still shaking with fear, but he managed to read the speech which Stiefelbreich had prepared for him, addressing the weeping population with much emotion and stopping every so often to wipe his face with his handkerchief.

'People of Bergania,' he began, 'I come to offer you the deepest sympathy for the vile deed that has been perpetrated here today against the beloved ruler of our country. I promise you faithfully that the person who was responsible for this crime will be brought to justice and that all revolutionaries and anarchists will be hunted down without mercy. Meanwhile, the German people are prepared to offer you protection and to ensure that order will be maintained. There will be further bulletins every hour but for now please go quietly to your homes. A state of emergency has been declared.'

From the crowd came a shrill voice.

'Where is the prince? What has happened to the prince?'

Gambetti threw a frightened glance at Stiefelbreich, who whispered something in his ear.

'The prince's whereabouts are being kept secret for his own protection,' said Gambetti.

But this was a lie. The prince was nowhere to be found.

'What do you mean, he's disappeared?' said Stiefelbreich furiously.

He had moved to a room in the German embassy, which

had already filled up with SS officers and Nazis in brown shirts.

'No one knows where he is,' said Earless. 'They're running through the palace like maniacs, calling and looking.'

Theophilus sneezed and squirted something up his nose. 'The head groom says the prince stabled his horse, but the master-at-arms swears his horse came in alone. There was such uproar after the king was shot that no one knows anything for certain.'

Stiefelbreich's jaw tightened. 'He must be found at *once*,' he shouted, thumping the table. 'At once, do you hear?'

Everything had gone according to plan. Gambetti would be allowed to strut about as a figurehead until the king was buried. Then, when suspicion was lulled, he would be got rid of, the German troops already mustered on the border would march in, and the thing was done.

But the prince must on no account be allowed to go free – there could be nothing more dangerous. Berganian patriots could use him as a rallying point, or there could be an attempt, now or later, to restore the monarchy.

'Somebody has blundered and will be punished,' said Stiefelbreich. 'I made it perfectly clear that the prince was to be seized immediately after the assassination. Our plans for him have been in position from the start: he is to be taken to Colditz and kept there as a prisoner of the German Reich.'

Earless and Theophilius looked at each other. The bodyguards had heard of Colditz – everyone in their business had heard of the grim fortress in east Germany from which no one could escape. It had been a mental hospital for years; the cries of the patients incarcerated there were apparently still heard at night by superstitious peasants who lived nearby. Since the Nazis had come to power, Colditz had been used to shut up all the people who had displeased Herr Hitler: social democrats, gypsies, Jews. No place in Europe was more feared.

'The prince will be well treated,' said Stiefelbreich. 'There is a special part of the castle kept for political prisoners. Later, if he cooperates with our plans for Bergania, he may be released, but if not . . . Well, children do sometimes have to be sacrificed to a Greater Cause. But he must be found, and quickly.'

'The trouble is,' said Theophilus, 'we've only seen him from a distance, riding in the procession, and there are hardly any photographs so if he's hiding on purpose it might be tricky. He seems to be a very ordinary-looking boy – brown hair and brown eyes, they say, but that doesn't tell you much. Now, if he belonged to the Royal House of Habsburg it would be easy. The Habsburgs are so inbred that their upper lips reach right up to their nostrils – you can recognize a Habsburg anywhere, especially if you see them trying to eat. And if we were looking for a Bourbon, like in the Royal House of France, we'd be searching for someone without a chin. But as it is . . .'

'I suppose he doesn't have a birthmark?' said Earless hopefully. 'They're a big help, birthmarks are.'

But Stiefelbreich had lost patience. 'You can question the palace servants – no doubt you'll find ways of making them talk. But if the boy isn't found and brought here in the next twenty-four hours, God help you both.'

*

181

Matteo returned to the camp in the late afternoon, looking as though the devil was at his heels.

'He's vanished,' he told the children. 'There's no sign of him. If he falls into the hands of those traitors . . .' He broke off. And under his breath. 'Oh God, where *is* the boy?'

Julia brought him a piece of bread and a hunk of cheese and he took it, but it was obvious that he had no idea what he was eating.

Then Tally put a hand on his arm.

'I think I know where he might be,' she said.

Matteo went so fast, scrambling up the side of the waterfall, that Tally could hardly keep up with him.

He knew the place so well; his happiest times had been at the pool with the king. The woods surrounding it, the creatures in its depths, had helped to make him a naturalist.

They reached the top and the pool lay before them. There was nobody there. The water was as still as glass; the water lilies might have been carved in stone.

Then, behind a large boulder on the other side of the pool, something stirred.

Karil had not been crying. The boy was a long way beyond tears, in a state of shock so extreme that he could barely connect with the world, but after a moment he recognized Tally, and Matteo was glad that he had brought her in spite of his misgivings.

'We came to help,' she said, taking his hand.

Matteo waited, letting Tally talk quietly to the boy. Then came the moment when he focused on Matteo and said, 'I saw you in the square. You were my father's friend, and . . .' But he could not go on.

Matteo knelt down beside him. It was time to tell his story.

'Yes, your father was my friend, the truest friend I ever had. We shared a tutor, we rode together, we went climbing together. I looked up to him, but really we were like brothers. We used to come here and talk about all the things we were going to do. He knew he'd be king one day, and he was going to be a different kind of ruler – give his people more freedom and more say in how the country was governed. Bergania was going to be a model for the world.

'When the time came to go to university we went to Basel in Switzerland. It was a heady time for Johannes – for your father – it was like the door of a cage opening. He was so happy to be free of the bowing and scraping. We met all sorts of people – idealists and dreamers and poets who wanted to make everybody free. And Johannes was going to do that, with me to help him. I suppose most people guessed who we were – but it didn't matter; we were students first and foremost.

'And then, while we were in our last year, the old king – your grandfather – died and Johannes had to go back to Bergania to be crowned.

'From the moment the courtiers came to fetch him, calling him "Your Majesty" with every second breath, everything changed. To me it seemed that he became cut off from his people, giving in to ceremony and pomp. But I had promised to help him and I stayed.

'Then a young hothead we'd known as boys got into

trouble. He'd been giving out leaflets about the Brotherhood of Man, saying there shouldn't be kings.'

'Like Tod,' said Tally.

Matteo nodded. 'They put him in prison, and I went to see the king to ask for his release – he was only a boy – and the king refused to see me. He was in consultation with his ministers.

'You have to know what friends we were to understand what happened next. I have a temper; when I found that Johannes wouldn't see me I went home, packed a bag – and went.' He paused. 'That was fifteen years ago, but I've never been back. And then when I returned to Europe I learned what he had done, how brave he had been, standing up to Hitler, and I was ashamed of having deserted him. I realized too that he must be in danger and I longed to see him again. So I came back.'

'But too late,' said the boy.

'Yes, Karil. Too late.'

The boy could not blame him more than he blamed himself, thought Matteo. He should have made himself known to the king as soon as he arrived, but he had wanted to find out who the conspirators were and how serious the danger to Johannes. So he had hidden from those who might recognize him – the Minister of Culture, the waitress at the Blue Ox – and pursued his enquiries in secret. By the time he spoke to the king he knew where the danger lay – but not that it would come so soon.

Karil had been listening intently, but it was a tremendous effort: his eyes clung to Matteo's face almost as though he was lip-reading.

'I saw how my father held you . . . how he wanted to

be with you. I will remember.' He looked round at the trees and the pool as though wondering where he was. 'Now I must go back.'

'No!'

Matteo spoke more loudly than he meant to and Karil shrank back. 'I must,' he repeated. 'I must see my father buried.'

'No,' said Matteo again, making an effort to speak calmly. 'No, you must come away with us. You must carry on somewhere else. It is what your father would have wished.'

'I don't want to go on being a prince,' said the boy in a thread of a voice.

'You don't have to be a prince – only the person that you are and the man you will become.'

But the boy shook his head.

Matteo changed his tack. He took him by the shoulder. 'Listen, Karil, the men who killed your father are not isolated criminals. They are part of a conspiracy that will take over Bergania and perhaps the whole of Europe. Once they have you in their power they will do one of two things. They will use you. Or . . . He paused deliberately, judging how much the boy could take. 'Or they will kill you.'

There was silence after that. Tally looked aghast at Matteo, then at the boy still deep in shock. But Karil had understood.

'I have to trust you,' he said. 'I see that. But . . .' He made a hopeless gesture.

Matteo turned to Tally. 'I'll take him over the

185

mountains. You'll have to make your way back with Magda. We can stay overnight with the king's old nurse.'

But as soon as he had said it he realized it would not do. Old Maria's hut would be searched straight away by anyone looking for the boy.

'No,' said Tally, 'you'll be caught.' And then: 'There are better ways of getting Karil out of the country.'

Matteo was about to cut her short. Yet it was uncanny, the feeling she had had about Bergania from the start. Perhaps she deserved to be listened to.

'Karil said he had to trust you,' Tally went on. 'Well, you have to trust us. All of us. Barney and Julia and Borro . . . even Verity.'

Matteo waited.

'It's quite simple,' she said. 'Karil must become a Deldertonian.'

CHAPTER NINETEEN

THE LAST DANCE

As soon as she returned to the campsite Tally was surrounded.

'Where have you been?' everyone wanted to know. And then, lowering their voices: 'Did you find him?'

Tally nodded and told them what had happened.

'Matteo's with him. But we have to get him down from the hill and into our tent. And then smuggle him back to England. We're going to pretend he's one of us.'

Magda frowned. 'Does Matteo agree to this?' she asked.

'He didn't like it, but there's no other way. Matteo wanted to take him alone over the mountains but they'll already be watching the borders.'

'There have been announcements the whole time on the

loudspeakers,' said Barney. 'Everybody is to keep off the streets.'

'But do they say anything about keeping off the mountains?' asked Tally.

'How are we going to bring him down without being seen?' Julia was very worried. 'I suppose in the dark—'

'No, we're not going to wait for the dark. And we're not going to creep about or slink. I've had an idea.'

Julia sighed. 'I wish you'd stop having ideas.'

'This one is about trust. Karil said he'll trust Matteo, and I told Matteo he'll have to trust us. And we'll have to trust the other children here. We'll have to tell them what we're doing so that they can help us and know what to do.'

'And what are we going to do?' asked Borro.

'We're going to do what we came to Bergania to do. We're going to dance.'

There was a pause while the others stared at her.

'All of us,' Tally went on. 'In full costume. And we're going to sing too, and maybe recite – I don't know exactly; we may have to improvise. It'll be a sort of homage to the king, a . . . a rite for his passing. Only the point is, there'll be so many of us that no one will notice if we come down with one more person. There's a meadow by the entrance to the hunting ground that's almost flat – that will make a kind of dancing floor. We'll wear our Flurry clothes and make sure that we're closest to the entrance, and while the ceremony is going on, Karil can slip out and join us. Only we'll need some clothes for him.'

'I've got a spare shirt,' said Tod eagerly. 'And he can have my white trousers – I'll find something else.'

He was desperately keen to help the prince.

'He can have my hat,' said Kit. 'It's got the most stuff on it. It'll hide his face.'

'There'th a lot of ivy under the bridge,' said Augusta. 'We can drape our headth so that you can hardly see our faces. Ivy's uthed a lot for funeralth.'

But the most important thing was to get the other groups to join in, because Tally's plan depended on a swirling mass of people in which one extra dancer would not be noticed and it was this that everyone was worried about.

'There must be more than a hundred children here,' said Julia. 'We can't trust so many children not to give anything away.'

'Why not?' said Tally. 'Why should anyone betray the prince when they know he is in danger? Why do there have to be traitors?'

'Not traitors,' said Barney, 'but idiots who blab.'

'We have to trust them,' repeated Tally. 'We have to. If they don't know what's happening, they won't be able to cover up if anything goes wrong.'

But the others still looked doubtful.

'Do we know them well enough?' Borro wondered.

'How long does it take to know whether people are decent?' Tally demanded. 'One can make friends in a minute. Look at the little German girl with the pigtails round her head and Conchita? They only knew each other for a day and Conchita's still crying. When I was six I fell on the pavement outside my father's surgery and Kenny came past driving Primrose and stopped to pick me up – and that was that. I'd trust him with my life.' She looked round entreatingly. 'Only we haven't got much time,' she said. 'Matteo is sure it was the Gestapo who organized the shooting of the king, so the prince is in dreadful danger.'

'I could ask Lorenzo,' said Verity – and for the first time she spoke about the Italian boy she had been flirting with without her usual simper.

'I'll talk to Jacqueline,' said Borro, thinking of the French girl who had been so informative regarding the milk yield of her mother's dairy cows.

Barney said the Scandinavians would join in, he was sure. 'They're really keen on justice and things being fair.'

'The Spaniards did that lovely saraband when they were practising,' said Julia. 'That would work beautifully for a funeral dance.'

'You see, we do know them,' said Tally joyfully. 'Even after two days we know they'll help. Only we must hurry – any minute now they could be closing in on the prince.'

And they did hurry. Even Augusta who didn't speak much because of her lisp, even Kit who was so easily frightened of people, ran to the other tents. Magda watched them go, crouching on her camp stool, desperately worried. The whole plan seemed mad and dangerous to her, but the headmaster had made it clear before they left Delderton that it was Matteo who was in charge of the trip, and if Matteo knew what was going on, there was nothing she could do.

Not all the teams could come – some of them had packed up already, some had teachers who refused. But less than an hour later, a most unexpected cavalcade set off across the park and made its way up the hill.

The Deldertonians were in the lead; they had draped their hats in so much ivy that it was almost impossible to see their faces. Borro, who was the hobby-horse rider, carried a bundle shaped like the medieval bladders that jesters used to hit each other with. It contained the clothes that Karil would have to change into before he joined the dancers.

Behind them came the others. Some of the boys had found black scarves, which they had tied round their throats; some of the girls wore black ribbons round their sleeves or in their hair.

At first they walked in silence. Then from the group of children in red skirts and boleros there came a lone voice, singing a song: fado; the saddest, most heart-rending music in the world.

And with this lone song, the whole ceremony became real. The children did not forget that they were here on a quest to save the prince, but they remembered too that a just and noble king had died that day.

When the voice of the singer died away, there came a hymn from the heartlands of Sweden, sung by the children in blue and white, and after that, from the Yugoslavs, the mournful wail of the fur-covered horn, like an animal in pain.

And as they made their way up the hill, every single child in the throng knew exactly what they were doing and why they were there and was proud to be helping the boy whose father had died so cruelly before their eyes.

'Look!' said Herr Keller, standing on the terrace of the Blue Ox. 'It's the foreign children.'

'They're paying homage to the king,' said his wife, and the waitresses nodded and said, 'Yes, they are honouring the king.'

But if the decent people of Bergania understood what the procession was about, the Gambettis were horrified.

'It's an outrage – the noise, the disrespect,' said the baroness, peering out of her bedroom window. 'They must be stopped at once. Look at those British savages in the front.' She turned to her husband. 'You must do something. Call out the police.'

But Gambetti, who had been getting steadily feebler and more afraid since the king's death, said he had no instructions to call out the police. 'And Stiefelbreich's in a meeting and mustn't be disturbed.'

'Well, if you won't call out the police, I will,' said the baroness, and reached for the phone.

'Listen,' said Matteo. 'They're coming.'

Karil crouched beside him on the bare wooden floor of the boarded-up hunting lodge. Matteo had prised aside a couple of planks and they had crawled inside: it was closer to the entrance of the hunting ground than the pool. Matteo had wrapped the prince in his own jacket and was talking to him quietly, telling him stories about his father as a boy. Karil, fixing his eyes on Matteo's face, tried to listen, but he was still so deep in shock that he heard only the words, not their meaning. The uniform that Karil had worn had been tied round a stone and dropped into the water; everything was ready.

The music came closer. They could make out the sound of Augusta's violin as she played a Celtic lament.

Matteo prised open another board and now Karil could see them: a whole hillside of children coming to fetch him away. Tally was near the front; she looked very small down there.

'Are they really coming for me?'

Matteo nodded. 'You'll be safe with them. Just join in and do what they tell you, and you'll be in our tent in no time. And in the morning we'll get you away to England.'

It was what Karil had longed for as he looked down at the lighted tents from the palace – to belong to the children that lived in them. Now he wanted nothing in the world except to have his father back.

The procession had reached the meadow. Now they formed a circle with the Deldertonians closest to the gates of the hunting ground and the wooden lodge. Soon Borro would slip in with Karil's clothes and bring him.

But the farewell for the king had taken on a life of its own. Here on the dancing ground Johannes III had to be honoured and now everyone was looking to the children from Delderton, who had brought this ritual into being.

'We absolutely can't do the Flurry Dance,' whispered Tally. 'It isn't suitable at all.'

But what could they do?

'Someone ought to recite a poem,' said Barney. 'Something noble.'

And one and all they looked at Julia.

'You can do it,' said Barney.

'No!' Julia's voice was anguished. 'Not in front of all those people.'

'This isn't about you,' said Tally. 'It's for the king. Say

the piece we did in class, about the hunter coming home from the hill.'

Julia looked round the circle of children waiting in silence.

'Please,' said Tally.

Julia did not fold her hands or step forward. She only lifted her head and began to speak the words that Robert Louis Stevenson had written for a much-loved friend. The poem that began:

Under the wide and starry sky
Dig the grave and let me lie

No one needed to know English to understand what she said. Julia's voice did it all.

When she had finished there was complete silence. Then suddenly a tall boy in a tunic and leather boots began to click his fingers. A second boy joined in – and a row of boys formed, resting their arms on each other's shoulders. Music came now from an accordion and a drum, and now the girls broke ranks and twirled in and out of the men. This was not national dancing now; it was dancing that broke all the barriers. It was dancing for everybody who had ever sorrowed and lost somebody they loved.

'Now,' whispered Tally – and Borro picked up his bundle, ready to run for the gate.

And then everything changed.

They heard the roar of motocycles coming up the path behind them, and three men in police uniform dismounted. They were part of the new force recruited in readiness for the takeover.

'What's going on here then?' said the tallest. 'You're not supposed to be out.'

'There's a curfew,' said the second man. 'You're breaking the law.'

The children clustered round. In a babble of languages they explained what they were doing.

'We are honouring the king.'

'We are performing a funeral dance.'

'It is what we do in our country.'

The policemen, if they understood what was being said, took no notice.

'You must stop this nonsense now, at once, and go back to your campsite or you'll be in serious trouble.'

The tallest of the policemen lifted his truncheon. 'Let's get going,' he ordered threateningly.

There was nothing to do but obey. As slowly as they dared, the children began to walk down the hill. But the Deldertonians had not started to move yet; they lingered still near the gate but how long could they hang back? One of the policemen was making his way towards them.

And then suddenly a truly terrible scream came from the front of the procession and everybody stopped. A second scream followed, more dreadful than the first, and two little girls could be seen rolling over and over each other, pounding each other with their fists. A third joined in; they were the smallest and frailest of the dancers, wearing flounced petticoats with ribbons in their hair, but now they fought and clawed and kicked like maniacs.

The scuffle turned into a fight and spread. Two tall

youths in crimson sashes attacked each other with the flags they carried. These children, who had lived together in harmony ever since they came, were shouting appalling abuse at each other.

'You're a garlic-eating peasant!'

'Everybody knows that in your country they cook babies and turn them into soup!'

'You're nothing but a fascist beast!'

And all the time the fighting got worse – two boys were pounding each other with their fists. Another came up behind a youth and wrestled him to the ground.

'Look out, he's got a knife,' shouted a girl, her face contorted with fear.

There were cries of 'She's bleeding!' and 'Oh help, help – he's coming for me!'

The policemen abandoned the loitering Deldertonians and ran downhill towards the disturbance. It was only what they had expected – that these unruly foreigners would start attacking each other. They waded into the middle of the fight, taking the youths by the scruff of the neck, pulling the little girls apart.

Musical instruments were tossed aside, the furry horn let out a frightful cry as they stepped on it with their heavy boots. As soon as they had quietened one group of children, a scuffle broke out somewhere else.

No one took any notice of the children left on the meadow at the top. No one saw a boy run into the forest with a bundle of clothes under his arm, or another boy come out and join the dancers.

It took a long time to control the fighting. Dusk had set in by the time everything was quiet.

'If there's any more fuss you'll be locked up,' threatened the policemen.

The children obeyed. They knew that their diversion had worked, that Karil had had time to join the Deldertonians, and they marched proudly down the hill and into their tents.

And Karil, on the day his father died, somehow managed to march with them.

Matteo watched till they had gone. Then he slipped through the trees and made his way towards the back entrance of the palace. There were things he wanted to know before he left Bergania on the following day.

It was after midnight when he returned. Karil was lying in a sleeping bag in the boys' tent. Tod lay beside him wrapped in an old blanket; he had insisted on giving his sleeping bag to the prince.

Karil was sobbing, trying to stifle the sound he made, and Matteo was relieved. The boy's silent grief had been dangerous. He slipped off his shoes and lay down across the entrance to the tent, but he made no attempt to comfort him. A whole ocean of tears would not be enough to wash away what the boy had endured that day.

CHAPTER TWENTY

GOODBYE, BERGANIA

They packed up before daybreak.

The children dressed in silence – they had decided the night before that they would travel in their dancing clothes; the hats festooned with ivy gave some measure of disguise. If they looked mad and dishevelled, all the better. They already had a reputation for being the sort of people it was best to keep away from, and they meant to keep it like that.

There was time only for Tally to whisper her thanks to the little girls who had started the fight on the hillside and saved the prince. They looked smaller than ever, like sleepy butterflies in their flounced dresses, and it was hard to believe that they could have screamed so loudly.

Then the buses came, and the children piled inside.

They had been afraid of what would happen at the station – there had been no time to buy a ticket for Karil – but the sudden evacuation had put everything in a state of muddle and confusion. The station master didn't take tickets or examine passports – his instructions were to get rid of the foreigners as quickly as possible and, along with their friends from the other groups, the Deldertonians were pushed on to the train. Safe in their compartment, they clustered together in as small a space as possible, pushing Karil in between Barney and Tally and making as much mess as they could, spreading out comics, putting their feet on the seats, living up to their reputation as hooligans.

More and more children climbed on to the train, and adults too – people who were no longer desired by the new order in Bergania. There was an atmosphere of tension and bustle. The contrast with the hope and happiness that had marked their arrival four days ago was heartbreaking.

Matteo, who had been keeping watch in the corridor, let down the window.

'Listen!' he said to Magda, who stood beside him.

Carrying towards them from the mountainside was one of the most dreaded sounds in the world – that of a pack of baying bloodhounds following a scent.

The guard blew his whistle. The train began to move.

On the tower of the palace on the hill the flag was at half mast, but Karil did not turn his head. The vineyards and orchards flashed past as lovely as ever, but there were signs that Bergania was now a threatened land. They could see armoured vehicles on the road, and clumps of soldiers.

'You'll be all right now, you'll see,' said Tally, putting a hand on Karil's arm. 'In less than two hours we'll be at the border.'

But before he could answer her, the train plunged into the famously long tunnel.

The sudden darkness sent the boy's thoughts plunging down. The thunder of the carriages, the bare black wall, forced him into a world without hope. His face, reflected in the sepulchral window, was that of a stricken ghost – and still there was no glimmer of light.

Then at last it was over – but as the train emerged the door of the carriage was thrown open and everybody gasped, for it was as though the person who stood there had gathered all the darkness of the tunnel into herself. Dressed entirely in black, scowling furiously as she stared into the compartment, was the Countess Frederica.

Instantly the children sitting next to Karil drew closer, trying to shield him, but Karil made no attempt to hide behind his companions. The woman who had looked after him since he was four years old would know him instantly wherever he was and whatever clothes he wore. And of course she would give him away. She would see to it that he was stopped on the border and brought back to the palace and it would all go on again: the scolding, the etiquette . . . She would never let him go.

The Scold's black eyes were raking the compartment. Barney's shoelaces were undone, Kit's comic had fallen to the floor. Verity's bare feet rested on the seat opposite. Magda had handed out her egg sandwiches, but in the agitation of the night before she had not boiled the eggs hard enough and the children were dabbing at their clothes.

'I thought I had made it perfectly clear,' said the Scold, fixing Karil with her steely gaze, 'that sandwiches may only be eaten if a clean napkin is first spread across the knees. Both knees.' She took a large starched handkerchief out of her pocket and handed it to Karil. 'You may return this when we reach Switzerland. I shudder to think what Carlotta would say if she could see you now. And if you continue to sit hunched up in your seat you will get a crooked back. Posture is everything for those of royal blood, as I have told you many times before.'

And she slammed the door shut again and marched away down the corridor.

For a while after the countess left everyone was silent. Tally had recognized the witch-like woman she had seen at the barred window of the palace and a shiver went down her back. But what she said was, 'Who's Carlotta?'

Karil wiped the egg yolk off his trousers and said, 'She's a sort of cousin of mine. She has ringlets and wears white dresses and smiles a lot.'

'Do you like her?'

'I've never met her.'

But now, for the first time since the death of his father, he thought about where he might be going if he reached England safely, and it seemed as though it must be his grandfather's house in London.

'She lives with my grandfather.' And then wearily: 'I suppose that is where I shall have to live if I get across the border. It's full of my relations.'

'No, you don't have to,' said Tally. 'Not unless you

201

want to. You can come to Delderton with us. You'd like it.'

The others nodded.

'There's lots going on. You could have an animal to keep,' said Barney. 'I've got an axolotl.' He was about to say that the axolotl's name was Zog and then thought better of it. After all, Karil himself was now a sort of Zog.

'We're going to do a play of *Persephone* next term,' said Verity.

'Matteo gives amazing biology lessons,' said Tod.

'And there's a river with otters,' said Tally. 'It's almost as nice as your dragonfly pool. And even the awful lessons are quite funny, like when you have to be a fork or boil up motherwort.' She described the gentle countryside, the cedar tree in which a thrush sang every morning, the white-painted rooms, one for each child, which they could decorate in any way they liked. 'Of course, being free can be exhausting, but you soon get used to it.'

'I can't imagine being free,' said Karil, 'being allowed to do what you want.'

Kit however felt that something should be made clear. 'We don't play cricket. Not ever. You'd have to put up with that.'

But Karil did not mind about cricket, which was not played much in Bergania.

'Would they let me come?'

'Of course.' As far as Tally was concerned the matter was settled. 'Even if you haven't got any money, the head-master will probably give you a scholarship. I'm on a scholarship, so why not you?'

'You wait till you see Clemmy,' said Barney. 'She teaches art and she's the best cook in England.'

The train steamed on towards the border and Karil closed his eyes, dreaming of a place where one could wake each morning among friends, and choose one's day. And Matteo would be there – the man who had been his father's friend.

Tally, on the other hand, was thinking of Carlotta.

Should I smile more? she wondered. But it wouldn't really help. There was still the question of the ringlets. Aunt May had tried to curl her hair once and the results had been disastrous.

And she had never in her life worn a white dress, let alone owned one.

It had not taken long for the people in the palace to realize that the prince was not in a safe place for his own protection, but quite simply missing, and a great search had begun.

The Countess Frederica had rampaged through the rooms, lifting the lids of chests, opening cupboard doors, scouring basements and attics. The king's turnip-shaped aunts searched too, calling and imploring. So did Uncle Fritz and those of the servants who had not run away in terror after the assassination – for order and discipline were breaking down fast.

After a few hours the countess had swallowed her pride and gone to see the Baroness Gambetti.

'If you know anything about the prince, please tell me,' she begged. 'The king put him in my charge, as you know.'

But the Baroness Gambetti knew nothing. 'The

wretched boy's hiding somewhere, I suppose,' she said. 'As though there wasn't enough trouble. Poor Philippe is at the end of his tether.'

And indeed Gambetti could be heard in the bathroom, groaning and being sick.

When the countess returned to her room in the palace she found two army officers who informed her that she would be put on a train and sent back to England first thing in the morning.

'British subjects are no longer welcome in this country,' they said.

'I'm not leaving without the prince,' she had said. 'It's out of the question.'

The officers belonged to the new order: men who supported Stiefelbreich.

'You can take one suitcase,' was all they said, and left, locking her into her room.

The countess fought all the way to the station. Her shoes were as spiky as her elbows and her nose; one of the officers who manhandled her had thin legs. Now, sitting in her compartment, the countess allowed herself a sour smile as she recalled his yelps of pain.

Even on the platform she went on struggling. Then, in the crowd of children making their way to the train, she saw a boy wearing an absurd ivy-wreathed hat and surrounded by a group of hooligans who seemed familiar. And at that point she had ceased to struggle and allowed herself to be escorted to a first-class compartment at the front of the train and locked in.

'The guard will open the door when the train is under

way,' said one of the officers. 'But I warn you: if you attempt to return to Bergania it will cost you your life.'

The door slid open and, looking up, the countess saw the bandit who now had Karil in his charge.

'What happened?' Matteo wanted to know. And when she told him: 'What about the bloodhounds? Were they out for the boy?'

'Yes. There are two lackeys of Stiefelbreich's – vile-looking men who look as though they will stop at nothing. They set them off.'

'Can you describe them?'

'One is huge, with a missing ear. But the other one is worse – a slimy little worm of a man with a scar on his lip and a gold tooth.'

Matteo nodded. It was what he had expected.

'But at least they still think that Karil is somewhere close, which gives us a little time.' He turned to the countess. 'You do realize, don't you, that once they suspect that the boy is fleeing the country you will be followed. They know how close you were to the prince.'

The countess drew her fierce eyebrows together. 'Thank you, it is not necessary for you to tell me this. I am perfectly aware that it would not be wise for me to be seen with the prince when other people are nearby. But whenever it is safe for me to do so I shall appear and do my duty towards him as I have always done. Even on a short journey it is possible for a boy to get into bad habits, and this I shall prevent with all the power that I have. You may expect to see me again in Zurich.'

Left alone again, the Scold allowed herself to lean back

against the cushions. She was not a woman who gave in to her feelings, but now she closed her eyes and permitted a few tears to well up behind her lids. She wept for Bergania and the dead king, for old van Arkel, who had been taken away for questioning . . . Above all she wept for the boy who was now an orphan and eating egg sandwiches among children who walked without clothes on towards the showers.

But she did not weep for long, for it was clear that she had one overriding duty and that was to take Karil to Rottingdene House, where his grandfather would keep him safe. Things were done properly there; there was no place where rules were stricter or etiquette was enforced more strongly – and the boy would be surrounded by nobly born relations to make sure that he did not lapse. In Rottingdene House, with dear Carlotta at his side, Karil would be safe until this nonsense was over and he could return to Bergania to be crowned as the country's rightful king.

CHAPTER TWENTY-ONE

THE PURSUIT

The campsite was deserted. A coloured kerchief caught in the branches of a tree, a mouth organ forgotten in the grass, were the only signs that a few hours ago children had stayed here and been happy. Soon workmen would come and surround the site with barbed wire – the tents were going to house soldiers of the occupying army.

In the cathedral the king's body lay in state, ready for burial.

So everything was going according to plan. Yet in his room in the German consulate, Colonel Stiefelbreich paced the floor, angry and frustrated. His thoughts were on one thing and one thing only.

Where was the prince?

Every nook and cranny in the palace had been gone

over; the king's aunts – tiresome women who would have to be sent to a convent to get them out of the way – had been questioned. The mountain hut of the king's old nurse had been searched, and every stick and stone of the surrounding countryside had been scoured. On the hill, the bloodhounds had drawn a blank.

This meant trouble for Stiefelbreich. He was supposed to hand the prince over to his superiors as soon as they entered Bergania – failure to do so would have serious consequences. A radio message had just come through from the commandant at Colditz to say that everything was ready to receive the prince. A cell had been prepared for him in the High Security Block, the commandant had said. Not that it mattered whether it was a high-security block or not – the whole of Colditz was high security. No one had escaped from that doomed fortress and lived to tell the tale. Stiefelbreich picked up the telephone.

Earless and Theophilus were resting in their room after their all-night search. They were not pleased with the accommodation they had been given above the consulate garages. Theophilus was worried about the effect of the fumes from the cars on his lungs and was spraying disinfectant up his nose.

Earless was sitting on his bed, which sagged under his weight, and worrying about Belinda. There was a man who served in the corner shop at the bottom of their street at home who smiled at Belinda in a way which Earless did not like. He thought of writing to Belinda and warning her, but reading and writing were very difficult for him and as so often before he thought how different things would be if he still had his other ear. The man in the corner shop wouldn't have had a chance if Earless had both his ears.

But when they heard that Stiefelbreich wanted them, both men cheered up. There is nothing like work for taking your mind off your troubles.

'Tell me again exactly what happened with the bloodhounds,' he said when the men stood before him.

'They followed the scent easily enough into the hunting ground, up to that lodge by the gates, but then they started going all over the place, running down the hill and coming back. But that's not surprising – there was a whole stampede of kids up there last night,' said Theophilus.

'Exactly,' said Stiefelbreich, rubbing his chin. 'So I think we must face the fact that the prince may have been among them, that somehow he has sneaked out of the country with the children that left on the train this morning. He can't have gone on his own – the passes have all been watched and the roads checked. And if so it's likely that he might be trying to get to Great Britain – after all, his mother was British.

'So we'd be looking out for that man the king spoke to in the square perhaps,' said Theophilus.

Stiefelbreich nodded. 'Or that woman who looked after him. Mind you, she still thought the boy was here when we put her on the train so she didn't know anything then. But the main thing is that you must leave at once.'

'Trouble is, they've got a good start on us, on that train,' said Earless.

Stiefelbreich shook his head. 'I'll let you have one of the consulate cars – a Mercedes. The train will go slowly –

everything's disrupted; we've seen to that, and it stops altogether in Switzerland. But he mustn't get away. If he reaches the Channel and gets over to England, we've lost him. The Fuehrer doesn't want any trouble with the British government – or the Americans.'

'And if we find him—' began Theophilus.

'Not *if*,' snapped the colonel. '*When*.'

'When we find him,' said Theophilus, 'do you want him brought back here?'

Stiefelbreich shook his head. 'You'll be in radio contact with the SS patrols; they'll take him straight to Colditz. As soon as you have the prince, arrange with them to hand him over. You'll get your bonuses just the same.'

But Theophilus had one more question: 'If there's any difficulty . . . there might be a struggle perhaps . . . I take it you want the boy alive?'

'Certainly we want him alive,' snapped Stiefelbreich. 'Unless . . .' He walked over to the window and stood looking out. 'He mustn't get across the Channel,' he said. 'But yes, if possible we want him alive.'

Left alone again, Stiefelbreich sent a message to the commandant at Colditz.

'Expect prisoner hourly. Inform time of arrival,' it said, and it was signed with his code name, which was Iron Fist. It was a good name, thought Stiefelbreich; he had chosen it himself.

CHAPTER TWENTY-TWO

THE BERGANIAN MOUNTAIN CAT

The train was travelling more slowly now. The stops grew more frequent; convoys of army trucks passed on the road. The time for Bergania to be 'protected' by the brave soldiers of the German Reich was coming very close.

In their compartment the children waited anxiously. The ordeal that faced them was not far away now. At the border with Switzerland there was a checkpoint where passports and permits were examined. The Deldertonians were travelling on a group passport. It contained photographs of Matteo and Magda; the rest were mentioned only by name: four girls, four boys . . .

Only now there were four girls and five boys. Somehow

they would have to lose a boy or confuse the customs officials and persuade them that the numbers were right.

As the train reached the beginning of the Altheimer Pass, which crossed the last mountain range into Switzerland, it stopped in a final sort of way and the guard came down the corridor and said everyone was to get out. The rest of the journey was to be completed by bus.

Everyone grabbed their belongings and piled out of the train. At the other end of the platform, keeping her back to them, they saw the Countess Frederica standing with the other first-class passengers.

They waited for nearly an hour and then three buses appeared labelled 'Zurich'. The first-class passengers were led to one of them, the children scrambled into the others and they set off.

The pass was dramatically beautiful; the bus climbed and snaked and climbed again. The land below them was neutral and safe as it had been for centuries. Switzerland had kept out of the last war; it had given sanctuary to thousands of refugees in the centuries that had gone by. It wasn't just chocolate and cuckoo clocks and cheese that the Swiss were famous for, but safety and peace.

Then as they approached the top of the pass the buses drew into a lay-by and stopped. The drivers got out and stretched and lit cigarettes. They seemed to be waiting for orders.

Inside the bus, Matteo suddenly spoke. 'Out,' he said. 'All the Deldertonians out. Quick.'

The children stood up. This was how their biology lessons began – with Matteo ordering them out. Matteo strung his binoculars round his neck and said a few words to the driver, who shrugged and turned back to his colleagues. Then he turned to the children.

'We're going up the path to that rocky ledge. No one must make a sound.'

'What is it?' whispered Barney.

'Probably nothing,' said Matteo below his breath, 'but possibly – just possibly – one of the rarest mammals in Europe: the Berganian mountain cat.'

The wind at this height was piercing; the quartz in the rock sparkled; the sun beat down. Tally was completely bewildered. Was this part of the prince's escape or was it a biology lesson?

It was a biology lesson. Nobody was allowed to talk, anyone not picking up their feet was glared at, and strangely, all of them, in spite of what they had gone through, were focused on one thing and one thing only: the snow leopard of the Alps, the Berganian mountain cat. Matteo had described it. Fur pale as honey, black tufted ears like a lynx . . . a predator who could leap a hundred metres down on to its prey . . .

They climbed until the buses below them had turned into toys. Tally and Julia tried to keep Karil between them – shielding him had become a habit – but the boy moved at speed. Even in his exhausted state he knew exactly where to put his feet; the mountains were his home – and when Augusta stumbled it was he who steadied her.

They saw marmots and goats and an ibex – and found the nest of a kestrel from which the young had just flown – but they did not see a Berganian mountain cat.

They had reached the top of the pass now with a clear view of the valley they had driven through. Matteo, who

213

had been raking the mountainside with his binoculars, suddenly became very still and they all froze, trained as they had been not to interrupt his moments of concentration. But whatever Matteo had seen it was not something he meant to show them, and down below they could see the tiny figure of their driver waving his arms and heard the tooting of horns.

As they ran down the hill Karil stopped for a moment and bent down to pick up something from the path. Not a valuable stone or a rare plant . . . just an ordinary pebble of Berganian quartz.

'Is it to remind you?' asked Tally.

'I shan't need reminding,' said Karil.

It was not until they were back in the bus and had been driving for several kilometres that Barney spoke.

'How is it you never mentioned the Berganian mountain cat to us all the time we were there? Or before we went? And how come it's not mentioned anywhere in the guidebooks if it's so famous?'

Matteo did not answer. When they were safely over the border he would explain, but to confess now that the noble and rare animal had come out of his own head would be to explain why he had invented it, and he was not ready for that. He had needed a chance to reconnoitre and what he had seen through his binoculars had relieved his mind. The road behind them had been clear; there was no sign of a black Mercedes of the kind that the Germans had brought to Bergania. He would never relax his vigilance, but so far at least there was nobody on their tail.

The buses stopped at the checkpoint and everyone scrambled out. They had expected to go all the way to Zurich in the same transport but now there was a change of plan again. The buses were required by the army in Bergania so they would travel on in charabancs provided by the Swiss on the other side of the border post.

'So for goodness sake make sure you have all your belongings,' the teachers instructed their charges. 'We can't go back once we're through.'

The children grabbed their bags and books and scarves and the souvenirs they had bought in the market and made their way to the customs shed. It was a small building, not accustomed to receiving hordes of people, and the officials manning the three gates looked startled at the mass of children rushing in.

This was the last chance that all the different groups would have to say goodbye properly; after that they would be driven to different destinations: some to trains going west or north, some to bus stations for the journey south.

And it was the last chance for the children who had danced the prince down from the hill to give their help.

The first-class passengers were allowed through straight away, and Countess Frederica marched off with her ramrod back and got on to the waiting bus. Then came the folk dancers.

The Deldertonians were by Gate number 2. Magda and Matteo stood in front, the rest bunched behind them. Matteo showed his group passport. The official counted the children.

'It says here, four boys and four girls. You only have three boys,' he said in his strong Swiss German dialect.

Magda looked round. There were black rings under her eyes from thinking about Schopenhauer in the night and she blinked at the customs official like a troubled owl.

'Oh dear,' she said. 'We have lost a boy. Tally, see if you can find him.'

Tally came back with Barney and Karil.

'Here they are,' she said.

'That is two boys,' said the customs official. 'Which one is with you?'

Magda pointed to Karil. 'This one,' she said. 'Look, here is his name.' And she pointed to Tod's name on the list.

One of the Swedish boys now came running up and took Barney's arm.

'Hurry up, Lars,' he said in his own language. 'We're just about to go through.'

Barney went with him, but now there was a fuss at Gate 3, where there were too many Greeks. Two of the boys from Italy had got into the wrong queue.

The teachers were getting rattled.

'Keep still,' they shouted. 'Stand by your group.'

But the children did not stand still. Verity broke away and rushed at Lorenzo, throwing her arms round him. Two French girls came hurrying up to Tally, waving address books. A Spanish girl started to cry noisily and abandoned her group to hug a girl from Norway.

The Swedish boy who had fetched Barney away called, 'Lars! Where are you, Lars? – Come over here,' but 'Lars' was nowhere to be seen.

The Italians now had too many children whereas the Dutch had too few, and still the children swirled about and merged and parted while the harassed customs officials counted and recounted.

The Deldertonians, by Gate 2, at least had the right number – four boys, four girls.

'All right, you can go through,' said the man in charge of the gate. He lifted the barrier and they rushed out and climbed into the nearest of the waiting charabancs.

One by one the children in the other groups gathered themselves together and passed through into Switzerland.

The customs officials wiped their brows and closed the gates. It was the end of their shift and they were going for a beer.

And at that moment a boy with long hair and desperately untidy clothes came running into the shed from the Berganian side.

'Wait!' he called. 'Wait for me! Don't close the gates. I had to go back to the bus – I left my camera.'

He held out a Brownie box camera, and the customs men glared at him.

'Who do you belong to?' they asked.

Barney, dishevelled and distraught, said, 'I'm British. I come from England. Look, I belong to those people over there – they're waiting for me. Please let me through. His face puckered up; he looked as though he was going to cry.

The men muttered together. 'I counted the British,' said one.

'You can't have done.'

The men conferred. Should they call everybody back and count them again?

From the buses waiting to depart came the tooting of

a horn, and now a man leaned out of the nearest one and yelled angrily.

'What do you think you're up to, Barney?' Matteo sounded like a public schoolmaster of the sternest sort. 'Get over here at once. I told you you couldn't go back to the buses. You're holding everybody up.'

The customs men gave up. They opened the gate.

'Yes, sir. I'm coming, sir,' called Barney and scrambled on to the bus. It was the first time he had called anybody sir and he thought it sounded rather good.

'We did it,' said Tally exultantly when they had been driving for some time, and they patted Barney on the back, because it had been his idea to get left behind and confuse the guards still further.

'Everybody did it,' said Barney.

'Yes.'

Karil was silent, He had expected to feel devastated as he left his country behind, perhaps for ever, but what he felt was gratitude and wonder that all these strange children had conspired to help him.

They drove on steadily towards the clean and shining city lying beneath them in the valley. Their thoughts were with the future; no one looked back, not even Matteo, who was busy planning the next stage of their journey.

So no one noticed the black Mercedes, with smoked windows, snaking behind them down the hill.

CHAPTER TWENTY-THREE

THE CHEESE MAKERS' GUILD

'What a good job I learned about having feasts in the dorm,' said Tally, 'because this seems to be what we are having. The important thing is not to step on the sardines.'

But actually there weren't any sardines.

There were rollmops and there were slices of Gruyère cheese and there were crunchy rolls and boxes of dates and apples – all of them bought in the market which was being held in the square down below.

They had been driven straight to the Hotel Kaiserhof, where they were to spend the night. Their travel arrangements had been disrupted by their sudden departure from Bergania, and the through train which was to take them to catch the boat at Calais did not leave till the following afternoon. Matteo had been at the British embassy arranging for their tickets and visas.

Meanwhile they had been given vouchers for a large room with two rows of beds on the top floor, and a small sitting room. Looking out, they could see the beautiful city of Zurich and the Limmat river which flows through its heart.

They had wanted to go out and eat in a restaurant but money was tight – and though Matteo was reasonably certain there was no one following the prince, he wanted to keep Karil safely indoors and out of sight.

So Tally and Julia had stayed in the hotel with Karil while the others went shopping and came back with bags of delectable food.

'It's a pity it isn't midnight,' said Tally when everything was spread out, 'but you can't have everything. Let's hope Matron doesn't come in in the middle and spoil everything.'

Kit knew about feasts in the dorm too. His friend in the school where they played cricket had told him about them. 'You have pillow fights.'

'So you do.' Tally looked at Karil. 'But not when your father has just died.'

Karil had been sitting quietly on his bed. Now he lifted his head and said, 'No, that's wrong. It's when your father has died that you have pillow fights. It's when your father's died that you do everything he used to do.'

And he picked up the big, spotless pillow from the nearest bed and hurled it across the room at Borro.

There was a moment of silence. It seemed to the other children that they had witnessed someone behaving very well. Then Borro picked up his pillow and hurled it back. Soon the room was full of flying pillows and feathers. Julia managed to save the Gruyère cheese and Augusta Carrington's bananas, but the plateful of rolls tumbled to the floor.

Then the door opened and everybody stopped dead – because what Tally dreaded had come to pass. Glaring into the room, fierce and furious, was Matron. At least, she looked exactly like the pictures of Matron in the books: thin and black-haired and scowling, and she was within an inch of stepping on the rollmops.

'Karil – are you mad? Have you totally forgotten yourself?' said the Scold. 'And what is that that you are wearing?'

Karil put down his pillow. 'They're Tod's pyjamas,' he said.

The countess curled her lip.

'You cannot possibly sleep in rags like these,' she said. 'And all that food on the floor – I never thought I would live to see the day.' She raked the room with her eyes. 'Is that a *girl* I see over there?'

'Yes,' said Tally. 'It is, and it's me. And this is Julia and those are Verity and Augusta; they're girls too . . .'

'It's outrageous! Karil must have his own room. Where is the woman in charge?'

'She's with Matteo next door. They're doing the accounts,' said Barney.

But at that moment Magda came in to say it was time for everyone to wash and get into bed, and was instantly attacked.

'Ah! You there. I *demand* that the prince has his own

room. It is out of the question that he should share a bedroom with these savages.'

'I'm afraid we only have one big room for everyone. Matteo and I are sleeping on sofas next door.'

'Well then, you must erect a shelter so that the prince's bed is screened from the rest and he can sleep in privacy.'

'I don't want to sleep in privacy. I want to be with my friends,' said Karil.

The countess ignored him 'It should be perfectly possible to put up a shelter using a blanket – it can be suspended from a hook above the window.'

Magda blinked at her hopelessly. She could have climbed Mount Everest more easily than she could have erected a shelter made of a blanket suspended from a hook. 'We don't believe in segregating children,' she said.

'We are not dealing with children,' snapped the countess. 'We are dealing with the Crown Prince of Bergania. And please remember that His Highess requires exactly two centimetres of toothpaste to be spread on his brush, and he invariably has two rusks and a glass of juice at bedtime. Not one rusk. Not three rusks. Two. Moreover—'

She was interrupted by an angry voice. 'I think I have asked you already, Countess,' said Matteo, coming into the room, 'not to appear to be travelling with us. We may still be being followed, and you being the closest person to the prince would certainly be under suspicion. Once we are in Britain it will be different of course, but for now Karil must travel as one of our party and behave as our party behaves.'

'Like a savage, you mean,' barked the Scold.

But she turned and left the room, and they could hear

the lift door clashing shut as she was carried down to her apartment on the ground floor.

'I want everybody to stay here till I get back,' said Matteo the next morning, as he set off for the British embassy.

Magda had had a bad night, dreaming that she had to cover Schopenhauer with a blanket suspended from a meat hook, and had a migraine so she went back to lie down on the sofa in the sitting room.

In their dormitory the children settled down to read or play cards. It was a beautiful day; from their windows they could see white birds wheeling over the river, the green and gold domes and spires of churches and museums and a glimpse of the lake which edged the western side of the town.

Time passed very slowly. The church clocks struck the hours and still Matteo did not come.

'We're going to be cooped up in the train all night,' said Verity. 'It's ridiculous not to go out and stretch our legs. I'll bet the shops are fabulous.'

'Matteo said we were to stay,' said Borro.

'No, he didn't. He said he *wanted* us to stay,' said Tod. 'That's not the same thing.'

They waited another half-hour. A soft breeze came in through the open window. Then the chambermaid came to clean their room.

'We're in the way,' said Tally. And then: 'It's sort of our duty not to hinder people who are trying to work, don't you think? If we went out just for half an hour?'

'But let's not wake Magda,' said Julia. 'She might think

she had to forbid us and that would make her sad.' She turned to Karil. 'Unless you'd rather stay?'

But Karil was as keen as anyone to get out of the stuffy room.

They set off along the left bank of the river, across the famous Cathedral Bridge and down the wide streets that led into the commercial quarter. Beyond making sure that Karil was always flanked by at least two people, they had quite forgotten that there could be any danger.

It was a marvellously prosperous city; the shops were like museums, full of exquisite jewellery and high-precision watches and leather handbags; the pavements were wide and shaded by trees, and everything was so expensive that even Verity was not tempted to try to shop.

And keeping out of sight behind them marched the Countess Frederica.

They were walking down a particularly imposing street when Barney stopped suddenly in front of a notice set out on a wooden stand beside a big carved door.

'Swiss Guild of Cheese Makers,' it said. And underneath: 'Free cheese tasting, followed by the unveiling of the new portrait by the British painter Ferdinand Ponsonby-Smith, commissioned by the guild to mark its two hundredth anniversary.'

The notice was in German, but when Karil had translated it Barney became very excited.

'I thought I recognized the name. Don't you remember? It's the picture Clemmy posed for. They said she had to be the Spirit of Cheese, and there was a row because the artist painted her as a lot of abstract cubes and the Cheese Makers were very upset and sent it back and he had to paint it again with Clemmy looking like herself. She charged a lot of money for modelling because she had really retired.' He turned to the others. 'We *have* to see Clemmy unveiled.'

Not only Barney but all of them suddenly felt really homesick for Clemmy. She seemed to represent all that was best at Delderton: the safety, the art classes, the pancakes . . .

The unveiling was at ten o'clock, and it was half past nine. It really seemed as if it was meant that they should go.

The Swiss guilds are very important institutions. There are guilds of watchmakers and guilds of woodcarvers and guilds of yodellers – but the cheese makers' guild is perhaps the wealthiest and most important of them all. For where would the country be without its Emmental and its Appenzeller – and its world-famous Gruyère, that classic cheese which is so whole and perfect on the outside and so amazingly full of holes once it is cut.

The children followed the people going in to the building. Samples of cheese were laid out on a great number of tables in the hall. There were little red-skinned cheeses and pale cheeses wrapped in silver foil and soft cheeses rounded into pats. All the cheeses were served with small biscuits and there was a bottle of sparkling water and some glasses on each table.

The Deldertonians set to. They were very hungry. Augusta had thought that there might be one kind of cheese she could eat without coming out in lumps, but when she got closer she decided to be sensible and just looked.

The room was very crowded – no one was rude or jostled but everybody was determined to taste as much cheese as possible in the shortest amount of time.

Karil had not eaten much so far on the journey, but the little nibbles of cheese were very inviting. He was wearing Borro's blue jersey and a little colour had come into his cheeks.

The Countess Frederica had followed them into the hall but stayed near the exit, hidden by a pillar. Needless to say, she did not stoop to tasting anything: nibbles were never eaten by the upper classes.

After about half an hour a bell rang and then a very prosperous-looking man with a comfortable paunch got on to the dais and said everybody was now invited upstairs for the unveiling of the new portrait.

They followed him into a large room. The blinds were drawn and the lights shining from gilded chandeliers lit up the busts of people who had mattered in the guild. Facing the rows of chairs was a wide platform, and the wall behind the platform was hidden by a black curtain.

Everybody filed in and sat down. Barney and Kit were on either side of Karil, then came Tally and Julia. The others were in the row behind.

A number of guild members came on to the platform and everybody clapped. Then the most portly member made a speech. This was in Swiss German, which even Karil found hard to understand, but it was obviously about the importance of the occasion.

Then everybody clapped again and two men came in

from a side door. The lights went out, the curtains were drawn aside – and spotlights flashed on to the large painting which was now revealed.

And a great sigh, a kind of general 'aah' of enthusiasm, came from the audience.

Because here was the absolute essence of all that was best and most beloved in their country.

On one side of the picture stood a dairy cow, white and plump and peaceful, with a splodge of amber on her flanks. On the other side, in a meadow studded with all the loveliest flowers of the Alps – gentian and rock roses and edelweiss – grazed two eager goats. But in the centre stood a girl holding a golden globe and smiling – a great wide smile as though she was blessing everything in the world: the Swiss people, the mountains, the meadows, but most of all the Guild of Cheese Makers, who kept the citizens of their country so gloriously supplied with their favourite food.

Her amber eyes glowed with love, her russet hair tumbled down her shoulders so that its curling fronds made a frame for the globe which she was holding to her breasts.

And what was it, this perfect globe? Not a small sun, though it might well have been; not a golden ball, like the maidens of ancient Greece played with in their palaces – but a pure, round, absolutely unsullied Gruyère cheese.

The audience went mad. Anyone who thought that the Swiss were reserved and did not show their feelings had made a big mistake. They stamped their feet, they clapped, they whistled. One and all had fallen in love with Clemmy.

'You see what I mean?' said Barney, turning to Karil.

'And when you think that even now she's probably feeding my axolotl.'

'Yes, I do,' said Karil, and it seemed to him that a school where this marvellous creature could be one's housemother was a place apart.

'Gosh, I feel quite homesick, don't you?' said Julia, and Tally nodded.

But Kit did not share in the praise and pride. He had overdone the cheese tasting. His face looked green. 'I feel sick,' he said. 'I have to go to the toilet.'

Barney made room for him. 'Do you know where it is?'

'No, I don't.' Kit was feeling very sorry for himself. 'I don't know what "Gents" is in German. I'll go into the wrong one.'

'I'll come with you,' said Karil.

The two boys slipped out and made their way out of the hall across a wide landing, down two flights of stairs and into the dimly lit basement.

Kit was getting desperate, clutching his stomach.

'It's round the corner . . . Look, here we are.' Karil opened the door and Kit rushed in.

At this point a furious yell could be heard in the distance.

'Karil, what are you doing? Come back at once. You cannot go into a public toilet!'

The Scold waited, but the prince remained out of sight round the corner. Furious, she made her way back to the hall.

Karil waited for a while, then pushed open the door. Kit had finished being sick and was leaning over the washbasin, shivering. He had reached it too late and there was a considerable mess.

Karil took off Borro's blue jersey. 'Here, put this on and go back to the others. You can find the way back, can't you? I'll clear up a bit.'

'Thanks.' Kit slipped on the sweater and made his way out into the corridor.

Karil, wiping the floor with a mop he had found in a cupboard, was remembering Tally's words. 'It isn't so terrible being a prince,' she had said – and while he didn't agree with her, it was true that at this point he wouldn't have minded ringing for a valet and walking away.

He reached the hall as the speeches were coming to an end.

'Where's Kit?' he whispered.

'I don't know. Isn't he with you?' said Barney. 'Maybe he's gone out for some fresh air.'

There was a last burst of clapping and everyone filed out of the hall.

'He can't have got lost coming up the stairs,' said Tally. 'Not even Kit . . .'

But it seemed he had. He wasn't downstairs in the cheese-tasting hall or in any of the corridors or out in the street.

Frantically they searched the building again and again, they asked the attendants, they called out Kit's name . . .

But he seemed to have vanished off the face of the earth.

CHAPTER TWENTY-FOUR

A MISTAKE IS MADE

The two men had driven north out of Zurich towards a grassy hill where they expected to get a good signal for their radio and make contact with the SS patrols who were to pick up the prince and take him to Colditz.

Everything had gone well. They'd followed the children from the hotel to the Cheese Makers' Guild and bided their time till they could isolate the boy. Their chance had come at the end of the unveiling, when they saw him slip from the room and tracked him to the corridor down in the basement. He stood out clearly enough in his blue jersey, even in the gloom, and if there had been any doubts, the shrieks of the Countess Frederica when she saw him would have put them to rest. If anyone could recognize the prince even at a distance, it was that appalling woman who had looked after him since he was a baby.

Waiting till he came out and grabbing the boy in that deserted corridor had been child's play. As of an hour ago, both men were richer by a considerable sum.

Now they drove the Mercedes into a ruined shed at the bottom of the hill and Earless opened the sack which lay covered under a blanket in the back seat.

''Ere, come and look at this,' he said to Theophilus. 'Not very princely, is he?'

Theophilus came over and peered into the sack. 'No, not what you would call princely at all,' he agreed.

What they saw was a weeping, moaning blob curled up at the bottom of the sack, calling for his mother, though everyone knew that the queen had been dead for many years.

Yanking the howling boy out by his shoulders, they examined him.

It was extraordinary how far the squirming little boy was from any idea of a royal personage. Or from the two faded photos of the prince that they had been shown.

'Now don't you get in a fuss, Your Highness,' said Earless. 'We're taking you to a place where you'll be safe and looked after properly. Colditz it's called, and only important people go there. Very safe, Colditz is.'

'I'm not a highness,' wailed the terrified boy. 'I'm Christopher Hargreaves and my father is Patrick Hargreaves and my mother is Amelia Hargreaves and I live in Dene House in West Witherington.'

Theophilus leaned over him. 'It would be best not to waste our time.' He shook his sleeve and took out a thin-bladed knife with a mother-of-pearl handle. 'We've got work to do.'

'I'm not at all like the prince. He's much —' He broke off, trying for a moment to be brave and protect Karil, but the knife was moving ever closer to his throat.

Earless turned to Theophilus. 'He's fatter than I remember.'

'Yes, I am,' gulped Kit. 'I'm very fat. Princes are never as fat as me.'

'Let's get him out into the light.'

They lifted him out and dumped him on the grass. Doubts were beginning to creep in.

'Speak to him in German,' suggested Earless. 'Tell him you'll set him free if he promises to serve Herr Hitler, and see what he says.'

Theophilus spoke a few words in German, but this only brought on another storm of weeping.

'I don't speak anything except English. I'm not clever . . . I'm not clever at all.'

His terrified eyes were fixed on the two men. Tear-washed and swollen as they were, their colour, now that they could be seen in the stronger light, was an unmistakeable and vivid blue. The prince could have dyed his hair blond, but he could hardly have dyed his eyes.

'You said you're not at all like the prince,' said Theophilus. 'So you know what the prince is like?'

'Yes, I do.' Kit's moment of heroism had definitely passed. 'He's very nice. He took me to the toilet and lent me his jersey.'

The two men looked at each other. It was clear now what had happened.

And it was clear too that this moaning lump had to be disposed of, and quickly, so as to give them a chance to get back and snatch the real prince before he got on the train.

If this boy was allowed to live he could give a description of them to the police.

'Why don't we just stick a knife in him?' said Earless. 'We can dump him here.'

But Theophilus did not care for this. 'Messy,' he said. 'All that blood, and it just takes one stray dog to set off the alarm.'

But the word 'dog' had reminded him of something. For a moment he stared into space. Then his evil face became softer, and his scarred lip curled into a smile. He had remembered some of the happiest hours of his childhood, when he had come out of the library for playtime and helped with the drowning of unwanted dogs.

'Big ones, some of them,' he told Earless. 'St Bernards or Great Danes or wolfhounds. We'd muzzle them first and tie them in a sack and throw them in the river. It was so funny seeing them struggling, and the sack heaving and bobbing in the water – and then a gurgle or two and down they went.' He shook his head at the fond memories. 'Those were good times,' he said wistfully.

'Well, the river's close by,' said Earless, 'and we've just passed a bridge. So what are we waiting for?'

CHAPTER TWENTY-FIVE

A HERO IS BORN

The children sat huddled together in the dormitory at the hotel. It had not been necessary for Matteo to show his fury – they already felt as guilty and wretched as they could be for having disobeyed him and gone out by themselves.

Now they waited for news of Kit – no one could do anything; they scarcely had the energy to talk among themselves. It was incredible how much they missed the infuriating little boy and how much they feared for him.

Matteo had shut them into their room and gone to the police station. He had been there twice already and the officer in charge had promised to let him know if there was any news, but he found it impossible to keep away.

There were less than four hours to go before the night train to Calais was due to leave from the Central Station.

'I wasn't nice to him,' said Tally. 'I got so impatient.' And the others told her not to be silly.

'He used to follow you round like a half-hatched duckling,' said Julia. 'He wouldn't have done that if you hadn't been nice.'

But then they realized they were talking of Kit as though he was already dead, and they fell silent once again.

Karil sat apart from the others, on his bed. He did not doubt for a second that he was responsible for what had happened to Kit, that whatever fate had befallen Kit had been meant for him.

At the police station, the clerks sat behind their desks scratching with their pens; clocks ticked.

The phone rang and then rang again, and there was no news. The third time, the chief constable came out of his office and came over to put a hand on Matteo's shoulder.

'We've found him,' he said.

Matteo took a deep breath. 'Dead or alive?' he managed to say.

'Alive. They're bringing him in now. A fisherman found him in the river, tied in a sack. The sack got caught on a shallow bank of gravel. He can't have been in the water more than a few minutes.'

And to Matteo, the police station, with its slow clerks and the ticking clock, looked suddenly like a room in Paradise.

Kit was carried in wrapped in a red blanket; his soaked clothes had been taken away to be dried. When he saw

Matteo he stretched out his arms to him, and as Matteo took him, he began at once to pour out his adventures. Surprisingly this boy who was afraid of almost everything did not seem to be in a state of shock. It was as though he realized that he had become a person of immense importance, and sitting in the constable's office, with an interpreter taking down his words, Kit told his story clearly and well. What he described most chillingly were the two men who had kidnapped him.

'One had pale eyes and a scar on his lip and you could see his gold tooth glinting. And the other one was huge and he had only one ear. When he bent over you, you could just see a horrible hole.'

'You can take him back now,' said the constable when Kit had finished. 'We've got a good account of the men; they won't get away from us. Only there's one thing I don't understand: why did they kidnap the boy in the first place? Will you ask him if he has any idea?'

Matteo put the question to Kit – with a warning eyebrow raised – and Kit understood and said, 'I think they thought I was somebody else. Someone with rich parents who would pay a ransom, and when they found I wasn't they decided they had to get rid of me.'

Back in the hotel Kit was surrounded and hugged and praised, all of which he thought was only right and proper.

'I was a bit heroic, I suppose,' he said carelessly – and was put right by Tally.

'Not a *bit* heroic,' she said, 'absolutely heroic. Like someone in a Greek myth.'

Magda, who was always so good when things had been

sad and difficult, rubbed Kit's wrists and ankles and borrowed a hot-water bottle for him from the hotel, and it
was agreed that no one would ever be cross with him
again. But when Karil said, 'It was me they were after,
wasn't it?' Kit, after a glance at Matteo, told the truth.

'They kept calling me Your Highness . . . and they said
I would be all right with them because they were going to
take me somewhere coldish. Or something like that.'

'Colditz,' said Karil under his breath. He knew about
Colditz only too well.

So Matteo had been right about what he had said at the
dragonfly pool. The men who had assassinated his father
would stop at nothing till he too was in their possession.

'I'm sorry,' Karil said to Kit. 'I'm really sorry. I wish I
could make it up to you.'

In the old days it would have been easy: his father
would have conferred some kind of honour on Kit or his
family – a medal, a financial reward. All Karil had to offer
the little boy now was concern and friendship, but perhaps
it was enough.

The Central Station in the late afternoon was exceptionally busy. News of the takeover in Bergania was splashed
over all the newspapers, and many people, thinking that
war was very close now, wanted to be home.

The Swiss police might have been slow at first, but
when they realized the seriousness of what had happened
they could not have been more efficient. The children
arrived in two police vans and were escorted to two locked
compartments, while the superintendent and a constable
kept watch with Matteo on the platform.

'We've put an alert out all over the city and its surroundings. With the description the boy gave us, they won't get away,' said the superintendent.

They waited while luggage was loaded into the van and newspaper and fruit sellers walked up and down the platform.

Then, when the engine was beginning to let off steam and there was only ten minutes to go before departure, a police sergeant came running up to the superintendent.

'We've got them, sir,' he said, saluting hurriedly. 'Two men exactly like the boy described. They were sighted in a beer cellar. One hung up his hat – and there it was – or rather it wasn't – his ear, I mean. We've sent for reinforcements to pick them up when they come out. They haven't a chance.'

The superintendent's face lit up. 'Good. Good man.' He turned to Matteo: 'Your lot will be safe now. I'll let you know what happens, of course.'

He shook hands and hurried away, wanting to be in at the kill – and Matteo made his way to the compartment and the anxious children who awaited him.

'It's all right,' he said. 'They've found them.'

He looked at Kit, who was leaning peacefully against Magda, eating a piece of Swiss chocolate.

The boy was safe. The danger was over.

Matteo closed his eyes.

CHAPTER TWENTY-SIX

NIGHT TRAIN TO CALAIS

The Countess Frederica was travelling first class. She even had a sleeper – but she was not asleep.

Now that the danger to the prince was over she could think about the future – and the future meant Rottingdene House and that sweet child who always took such care to be pretty, and to please. Once Karil was married to Carlotta, her own work would be done and she could rest.

The children from Delderton were not travelling first class, nor did they have sleepers. They were curled up uncomfortably on the seats, dozing as best they could. Karil, sandwiched between Tod and Tally, was glad of the stuffy compartment, the huddle of people. He felt as though he never wanted to be alone again.

After a while he disentangled himself and made his way

out into the corridor. He had expected it to be empty, but Matteo was standing there, his back to the compartment full of sleeping children, keeping watch.

'Can't you sleep?' he asked, and Karil shook his head.

'Well, it's not surprising,' he said, letting his arm rest on the boy's shoulder. 'Your father could never sleep on trains either. In fact, he was a lousy sleeper altogether. We used to creep out of the palace at night sometimes – he had the key to the secret door at the back.'

'How did you get to know him?'

In the darkness, Matteo smiled.

'It was at Johannes's seventh birthday party. They'd asked a whole lot of suitable children, all scrubbed up and wearing their most uncomfortable clothes. Chosen to be the right kind of friends for him, you know. They made me come – my parents had an estate on the other side of the mountain and I lived a very rough life, more like a peasant boy. I didn't want to come and I threw a tantrum when they made me dress up in a tight collar. And your father was in a bad temper too. They tried to organize us into playing party games, but by then we'd caught each other's eye and – well, we just knew we were going to be friends. And we crept out and found a chicken in the kitchen quarters and climbed on to the roof and made it flutter down the chimney. There wasn't a fire, of course, and it was a good strong hen and it landed all right, though I wouldn't do that now. The ladies of the bed-chamber, those aunts of yours, were all in their sitting room doing their embroidery, and there was this soot-black squawking chicken rushing round the room! Meanwhile the people who were organizing the party were frantic, looking for Johannes. After that they said I wasn't a suitable friend for their future king, but Johannes dug his heels in. It ended with us sharing a tutor and more or less being brought up together.'

'Did you do other things like that . . . like the chicken?'

'Oh yes, plenty. We smuggled a piglet into a council meeting once, and there were all the usual things that children do – toads in the beds, and booby traps, and pretending to be vampires at night. But mostly we just escaped whenever we could. Your father was absolutely fearless – once we climbed to the top of the gabled roof on the palace and Johannes said we wouldn't come down unless they stopped asking him to eat semolina for ever and ever.'

'I think it must have worked,' said Karil, 'because I never got semolina to eat, not once.'

He looked gratefully up at Matteo. Hearing about his father as a boy was the best comfort he could imagine. And as if Matteo could read his thoughts, he said, 'He really enjoyed life, your father. That was why I was so angry when he became imprisoned in all that kingship. But I was wrong to be angry – he grew up to be a brave and honourable man.'

But after Karil had gone back to the compartment Matteo stood silent and perturbed outside. He had promised his friend to look after Karil and he would do so while there was breath in his body – but this war which was growing ever closer would impose duties on every able-bodied man.

'But somehow I will do it,' he vowed. 'Whatever it costs.'

When Karil slipped back into his seat he saw that Tally was awake.

'I was thinking about the play we're going to do next term,' she whispered. '*Persephone*. I sort of feel I know quite a lot about the Underworld now and the sort of people who go to Hades. Like Gambetti – he belongs there all right. We could make it really good with the right kind of music. You absolutely have to help us do it.'

'I've never done anything like that.'

'You don't know what you can do yet; you've never had a chance with all those processions and people bowing and scraping. We're going to try to persuade Julia to act in it. There's so much we're going to do at Delderton and you need to be there.'

Karil was silent. There was nothing he wanted more than to join his friends in this strange school of theirs. Because they *were* his friends. A few days ago they had been specks seen through a telescope and now they mattered more than anyone. But would he be allowed to go? His future was a blank, he had no right to make plans. And yet . . . Julia had told him about Tally's determination to come to Bergania.

'She just bullied us all,' Julia had said, 'making us invent the Flurry Dance – she seemed to know we had to come.'

So now, when Tally told him that he had to be with them at Delderton, Karil began to wonder if she might be right, and he felt hope begin to stir in him.

'I was so angry with my father when he told me I had to go away to school,' Tally went on. 'I really loved being at home, with my aunts and my friends. And London. We had a silver barrage balloon up over our house; it was like having a giant sausage to look after us.'

For a moment both children were silent, thinking about this war which everyone expected and which they had forgotten in the excitement of escaping from Bergania.

'I tried to fight him,' Tally went on, 'but he won and I'm glad he did, though I miss him horribly. You'd really like him, Karil. He's the best doctor for miles; everyone wants to come to him, and of course he doesn't charge his patients nearly enough so we've always been poor but it doesn't matter. You can't imagine how proud I am of him.'

'I'm not surprised. Being a doctor must be wonderful.'

'Yes.' She turned to him. 'You could be a doctor if you wanted to.'

'I suppose I could.' And then: 'Yes, I could. I could be anything.'

'You could be a great scientist.'

'Or an artist.'

'Or an engineer. You could learn anything at Delderton and get ready. I can't describe it, Karil, but it's such an *interesting* place – you have to come.'

As the train ran on through the night Karil's dreams, above the sorrow of his father's death, took flight. He could be a great explorer, discovering the source of an African river; he could invent a cure for cancer, or write a monumental symphony. He could own a rare and exotic animal – an aardvark or a cassowary.

Afterwards, looking back on his escape, he thought that this hour in the train, when everything was possible, was the one he would most like to have again.

*

The luggage van of the train carried the usual consignment of suitcases, trunks, wooden boxes and other things too bulky to go into the compartments. There was also a crate with a goat in it. The animal's yellow eyes peered through the bars and occasionally it let off a desperate bleat.

The two ladies who had smuggled themselves into the van were very strangely dressed. One was a woman of most unusual size, wearing a knitted bonnet pulled over her face, and a spotted pinafore. She had taken off her shoes and was rubbing her bruised and hairy toes.

'I'm not spending the night in here,' she said in a surprisingly deep voice. 'That animal gives me the creeps.'

'I could pick the lock,' said her companion, who had a feather boa thrown over her shoulder and wore a straw hat trimmed with cherries, 'but we'd only run into that blasted bandit standing guard in the corridor. He never lets those kids out of his sight.' She looked up at the ventilation grating. 'When we're over the border into France, we'll get a radio signal and alert the Gestapo. There'll be a crowd of people making for the boat and we'll be able to grab the prince. It'll be our last chance – once he's aboard we have to let him go.'

'He won't get aboard,' said the outsize lady, with a snarl.

The woman with the feather boa groped in her handbag and took out a syringe with which she squirted disinfectant on to her tonsils. 'They must be crazy, thinking we'd be trapped in a beer cellar,' she said. 'As though we'd drink anywhere with only one exit. Still, that's the police for you.'

All the same, it had been a rush: driving through the town, finding a second-hand clothes shop, kitting themselves out and dumping the car.

'I'm hungry,' said the giant in the woollen bonnet.

'Try milking the goat,' said her companion.

And the train thundered on through the night.

CHAPTER TWENTY-SEVEN

REACHING THE BOAT

It was extraordinary, stumbling out of the stuffy carriage, feeling the wind suddenly on their faces and seeing, in front of them, the harbour and the clean white world of the boats and the seagulls and the lighthouse.

The train had come to rest on the sidings beside the boat they were to catch to England. They only had to cross the tracks and make their way towards the gangway and in two hours they would be home in Britain, and safe. On the way out they had taken it for granted, travelling in a British boat, knowing they were protected, but now the ferry with her brightly painted funnels and cheerful flag seemed to be a vessel that had sailed in from Camelot to carry them over the sea.

The harbour was full of bustle and noise. Fishing boats

chugged in and out between the ferries, crates of fish and lobsters were piled up on the quayside waiting for transportation, there were coils of rope and barrels of tar and nets – and everywhere, wheeling and shrieking and diving, the fearless, hungry gulls.

The children shivered in the sudden wind and turned their faces towards the SS *Dunedin*. They were among the last to leave the train. The first-class passengers had already embarked, with the Countess Frederica in the lead, shouting instructions to her porter as she strode up the gangway.

The other passengers followed, the throng gradually thinning; then came the Deldertonians in Magda's charge.

'Go straight to the boat,' Matteo had ordered. 'No dawdling. I'll catch you up.'

They did not exactly dawdle, but Borro and Barney needed to examine the recently caught fish; Verity wanted to try out her French on a good-looking fisherman, and Tally was telling Karil about the white cliffs of Dover.

'They're not really as white as all that, but all the same when you see them you get a lump in your throat.'

Matteo watched them go and paced the train once more. Satisfied that the coast was clear, he picked up his bundle and jumped down on to the platform. He could see the children ahead of him. They had reached the boat at last.

He was just crossing the track when he heard the sound of pounding footsteps and turned to see two extraordinary-looking people running towards him. One was huge and massively built, and the remains of a spotted apron clung to his baggy trousers. The other was smaller, wearing the remnants of a feather boa, and there was a scar on his upper lip.

They were almost level with him, running hell for leather for the boat in a last effort to snatch the prince.

Matteo kicked aside a fire bucket, threw down his pack . . . and charged.

The children, with Magda, had begun to make their way up the gangway. Standing near the top was the first mate in a smart blue uniform with brass buttons and a peaked cap. And on either side of him were two men in black leather coats and jackboots. Their hats were pulled down low, and what could be seen of their faces made the blood run cold.

'Stop!' said one of them, speaking in a strong German accent. 'This is the group I have told you about. There is an extra child here – you will see. There is permission only for four boys – and if you count you will see there are five. And one of them – this one –' he pointed directly at Karil – 'is the boy we are seeking. He is a runaway – a petty criminal – and he must come with us.'

The children felt as though they were turned to stone. All the colour had drained from Karil's face. He had seen enough in the last weeks to know that the men were from the Gestapo.

'It isn't true,' said Magda, putting her arm round Karil. 'All these children are travelling with me – they're from Delderton School in Devon. We've been on a folk dance festival and we're trying to get home.'

'Can I see your passports?' said the first mate.

'They're with the gentleman who is in charge of –'

Magda turned round to look for Matteo, but he had disappeared.

'You see, it is a lie. This boy is a dangerous trouble-maker – we have a car here ready to take him back to his home. He has run away and must be returned. I have a permit from the German police. Here it is.'

The first mate examined it and handed it back.

'He is rather young to be a criminal,' he said, looking at Karil's white face, his stricken eyes.

'He must not travel,' said the other man in jackboots. 'You must hand him over now. At once.'

The first mate had been travelling the route between Britain and France for the past three years and there were things that increasingly upset him. He had seen refugees staggering on to the boat in tears – Jewish children, people with pathetic bundles from the countries Hitler had over-run – and he was getting angry. On the crossing before this one, an old man had sat in silence on the deck, tears running down his face.

'I was growing apricots,' he had said. 'Such apricots. If you could have seen my garden! And then they came and said I had to leave, I was a dirty old Jew.'

'I've no time for this now,' he said to the jackbooted men. 'If the boy's papers aren't in order it can be sorted out at the other end.' And to Karil: 'Get on board, boy!'

Tally began to breathe again. Barney took hold of Karil's hand. 'Come on,' he said.

It was all right. They were safe. The leather-clad men were scowling, one tried to grab Karil's arm – and the first mate pointed at the upper deck, where a couple of sailors were sluicing the timbers. The sailors too had seen things they did not care for on their recent trips and now they put down their buckets and came forward to the railings.

The men from the Gestapo shrugged. They had been told to avoid trouble with the British navy and now they made their way back to their car, parked on the quay.

The children were almost on board. The first mate stood aside. And then an extraordinary thing happened. Karil let go of Barney's hand, turned – and ran back down the gangway, on to the docks.

Back into certain danger . . .

'Come back, Karil!' yelled Tod.

But Karil ran on. And then they saw why. On the quayside, close to the edge of the water, Matteo was caught up in a horribly unequal fight. He was grappling with one man, trying to stop him from pulling out a knife, while a second man, a giant dressed like a pantomime dame, circled round the struggling pair, landing indiscriminate blows.

And Karil, seeing this, had shaken off the fear and exhaustion of the last days and was running like the wind to help his father's friend.

For Earless, turning his head at Tod's shout, the sight of the prince running towards him was a miracle. He abandoned Matteo and took a step towards the boy. His big, stupid face was lit up with triumph. He had only to carry the boy to the car where the Gestapo men still waited and the thing was done.

'Come on then, Your Highness,' he jeered. 'Let's be having you!'

Karil, blind with rage, threw himself at the huge man's chest. He might as well have thrown himself at an oak tree. Kicking, struggling, punching, he found himself picked up, thrown over the giant's shoulder and held there in a grip of steel.

Still grinning crazily, Earless skirted the edge of the quayside and set off towards the car.

But the other children had understood what was happening. They rushed down the gangway and, as heedless as Karil, began to attack the giant. It was ludicrous, pitting their strength against him, but there were a lot of children and there was only one of him. From carrying a single struggling boy to the waiting car, Earless found himself hung with children like a Christmas tree.

Barney was clutching one leg and Tod the other, and though he kicked them away they came back. Julia and Tally were behind him, dangerously close to the water's edge, tugging at his arms.

They were nothing – puny little flies – but Earless had to shift the weight of the boy on his shoulders. Doggedly the giant waded forward, shaking off children as he walked. Augusta had found a bucket, which she hurled at his ankles. He kicked it away, but the ground was slimy with fish scales and seaweed and for a moment he stumbled, only to right himself again.

Kit had joined in the fray even though he had recognized the men at once as his kidnappers. Now he too came at Earless, and he and Verity took hold of Karil's legs and tried to pull him free so that Earless had to adjust his grip again, bringing Karil up against the side of his face.

And at this point Karil threw off the last shreds of his upbringing. He swivelled round and in a single ferocious act he sank his teeth deep into the big man's ear.

The effect was instantaneous.

'Not my other ear! No, no . . . not my other ear!' Earless roared, and brought one hand up to his bloodied lobe, while Belinda's tearful, disappointed face swam before him.

He was still holding on to Karil with his other arm – but there was one Deldertonian who had not joined in the fight. Borro had been sorting quietly through the freshly caught seafood waiting in the crates. When he had found what he wanted, he unwound the muffler from his throat and inserted a large and exceedingly spiky crab into its folds. Then he swung the muffler once, twice, three times above his head – and let fly.

His aim was true. The crab landed full in Earless's face. The sharp edge of the shell temporarily blinded him, gouging his eye; the salty liquid and smelly gunge inside the creature ran down his face.

And this was too much. Earless brought up his other arm to clear the debris from his eyes; the children pulled Karil's legs and he tumbled to the ground.

'He's free!' shouted Tally. 'Come on – all together.'

One and all they ran forward and pushed. Even so they would not have succeeded, but as Earless stepped backwards he slipped on a patch of regurgitated fish left by the gulls. And with a monumental splash, he was gone!

As they looked into the water, Matteo came up behind them. There was blood on his arm, which he had bound up with a handkerchief, but he seem very pleased with himself.

'What happened to the other one?' asked Augusta. 'Did you kill him?'

'I don't think so,' said Matteo, 'but one can never be certain.'

In the water they saw a second head and caught a momentary glint of gold before it disappeared again under the waves.

Just then they heard the screech of tyres as the black Mercedes driven by the Gestapo's men did a U-turn and disappeared.

As they made their way back up the gangway and on to the boat, they found the Countess Frederica blocking their path.

'This way, Karil,' she said. 'I have secured seats for us in the first-class lounge.'

The others waited.

'I'll stay with my friends,' Karil said and, ignoring the scowls of the Scold, he made his way to the pile of luggage on the deck which the Deldertonians had made their headquarters.

The crossing was calm and uneventful. Magda bandaged Matteo's arm and he stood alone by the rails, looking at the water. It was time to relax now; the hunt for the prince had come to an end and he was so tired he could hardly keep on his feet.

Squashed between the canvas bags that held the dancing clothes, Tally and Karil were making plans.

'There's only another five weeks of term but you could stay with us in the holidays; there's lots of room in our house.'

'I'd like that,' said Karil. 'If I don't bring trouble.'

'You won't. You can be ordinary now. We're *very*

ordinary. Barney's family has a big house too, and his parents sound nice, if you didn't want to be with us all the time – though Matteo will probably want to see you too.'

'Thank you. I'd like to stay with you very much.'

They were three-quarters of the way across when they saw the chalk cliffs above the harbour at Dover – and though it was true they were not exactly white, more a sort of pale and slightly dusty grey, all the children, even those who had been dozing, came to the rails to look.

The boat docked smoothly, but they waited for a while in the harbour before the passengers were allowed to disembark. Then, as they crossed over to the customs shed, Karil stopped dead.

Waiting on the other side of the road was a large black Daimler with an elaborate painted crest on the doors: the coat of arms of the Duke of Rottingdene picked out in gold. And leaning out of the window was a stunningly pretty girl with fair ringlets, wearing a blue velvet beret and waving.

'This way,' she called. 'This way, Karil!'

The boy stared at her. Behind him stood the Countess Frederica and two men in the duke's livery. She had sent a cable from the boat.

'Say goodbye to your friends, Karil,' she said. 'You won't be seeing them again.'

Karil said nothing. For a moment he wondered whether to make a run for it, but what would be the use? The Duke of Rottingdene was his grandfather, not a thug or an assassin.

Tally stared at the ground, unable to bear the sight of

her friend driven off into captivity. Surely there was something he could do. Run, fight . . . he had been so brave on the quayside. But after all, he was going to his grandfather's house. He had a family. She had been stupid not to remember that.

Matteo certainly had remembered it. He made no attempt to hold Karil back but came and hugged him – and then the children shook hands one by one and said goodbye.

'This way, Your Highness,' said one of the footmen and Karil got into the car and was driven away.

The last thing Tally saw was the smug-looking girl with ringlets putting her arm round his shoulders.

PART THREE

CHAPTER TWENTY-EIGHT

SEPTEMBER THE THIRD

Nobody ever forgot where they were on the day that war was declared.

Tally was in the kitchen helping Aunt May to prepare the vegetables for Sunday lunch when the music on the wireless stopped and the announcer said that the Prime Minister would address the nation at eleven o'clock. Everyone had been expecting it; Hitler had invaded Poland two days before and the democratic countries had had enough. Aunt Hester came hurrying in from the garden and Tally's father from his study.

The Prime Minister was old and tired; he had tried to keep the peace and now he told the people of Great Britain that he had failed. An ultimatum had been sent to

Hitler demanding that he withdraw his troops from Poland.

'I have to tell you that no such undertaking has been received and that consequently this country is at war with Germany.'

No one ever forgot what happened next either. Almost straight away the air-raid sirens sounded – that hideous wailing that they had only just learned to recognize.

'Quick, into the shelter,' said Dr Hamilton, pushing his daughter towards the door.

'Oh dear, my roast will be spoiled – couldn't you go ahead, and let me—' began Aunt May, and saw her brother's face.

The shelter was at the bottom of the street. It was not really finished yet and a puddle of water had collected in the bottom. The lady from number 4 said she wasn't going down into that wetness, she'd rather be bombed than die of pneumonia. She was a very large person and the people behind her got nasty because she was blocking the door.

They had just climbed down when the all-clear went. It had been a false alarm.

'Were you frightened?' Kenny asked, when he and Tally met that afternoon in Primrose's stable.

'Yes, I was – it was the noise as much as anything – that awful wailing. But I'm glad I've got it over – the first time, I mean.'

The date was 3 September 1939. The Delderton term began in just over a week.

'Thank God you'll be out of London,' said Dr Hamilton.

That evening the king spoke to his people. The aunts

as usual were more anxious about the king's stammer than about what he said, but he got through it very well, speaking slowly and pausing when things might have got out of hand.

As she listened, Tally was back at the dragonfly pool, telling Karil about the British king. That he was a kind man and that his people loved him, but that he was not like Karil's father.

Well, now Johannes lay under a stone slab in Bergania's cathedral – and Karil too might be dead for all Tally knew of him.

There had been five weeks of term left when they returned from Bergania, and every day Tally had waited for a letter. Karil knew her address at school and at home; all the children had exchanged addresses, for while they had hoped that Karil would be able to come straight to Delderton, they knew that there might be delays.

But there had been nothing. Tally knew now how Julia felt as she waited for a letter from her mother. None of the others had heard anything either; nor had Matteo. At first Tally had written almost every day, then three times a week, then twice . . . Pride didn't come into friendship, she told herself, and she knew it might take him a while to settle down, but still there was only silence.

Now, as the king said, 'With the help of God we shall prevail,' and the national anthem was played, Tally was remembering Karil's words as they sat by the dragonfly pool.

'I would have liked us to be friends.'

She had believed him. She had believed everything he

said about wanting to be free, about being weary of being a prince.

But she had been wrong. Surely there was no one who could not write a letter and put it in a letter box.

And it hurt. For the rest of the term she had waited and hoped, and here in London too when she came home for the summer holidays, but still there was nothing. Well, she wasn't going to turn into one of those people who sighed and hovered round postmen. There were plenty of other things to do.

And indeed, during those first few days when the long-awaited war became a fact, there was hardly a spare moment.

Aunt May went off to the town hall hoping to become an air-raid warden but was directed to the wrong room and found herself lying on a stretcher, covered in bandages and labelled 'Serious Burns' in a first-aid practice. Aunt Hester and Tally filled sandbags in the park and tried to shoo off the little children who wanted the sand to make castles.

New gas masks were issued, but Mrs Dawson, whose dachshund Tally took for walks, refused to be fitted for hers unless there was a gas mask also for the dog. The blackout began and Dr Hamilton's surgery was filled with patients who had fallen downstairs in the dark or walked into lamp posts. No one knew whether laying in stocks of food was sensible or unpatriotic. Aunt Hester thought it would be hoarding and therefore bad, but Aunt May thought it must be good to save space on ships which had to bring food from overseas, and bought a large sack of pepper which she put under her bed.

'They say pepper is going to be very hard to get,' she said.

Statues were boarded up and the aunts found a paragraph in the newspaper that excited them very much. Among the paintings which were being crated up and sent for safety into a disused mine in Wales were the pictures in the Battersea Arts Museum, which included *The Angel of Mercy* for which Clemency had posed.

'So she'll spend the war underground,' they told Tally. 'She'll be as safe as can be.'

Evacuation of schoolchildren to the country began, but without Maybelle and Kenny.

'They didn't even try to make me go,' said Maybelle. 'I drew blood last time.'

Two days after the outbreak of war, Tally's Aunt Virginia telephoned to say that she was taking Roderick and Margaret down to safety in the West Country till it was time for term to begin. Fortunately she had been able to buy their new uniforms before there was talk of shortages or even rationing.

'Roderick has had such a good term,' she told them. 'He has made friends with the Prince of Transjordania – such a nice boy – and Foxingham has won their cricket match against Eton. It really is a splendid school.'

She kindly offered to take Tally away with them, but Tally told her father she would rather be hanged, drawn and quartered than go with her cousins to Torquay – and Dr Hamilton, endlessly busy at the hospital with the evacuation of patients, did not argue.

On the last night before she was due to go back to Delderton, Tally and her father climbed up the hill past the convent and looked out over London. Their own barrage balloon had been joined by dozens of others, silvered in the moonlight. They did not look like kindly uncles now, nor like benevolent sausages – but like serious sentinels protecting the much-loved city.

'We shall come through,' said Dr Hamilton, and took his daughter's hand. 'You'll see, in the end we shall come through.'

The next morning, just as the taxi arrived to take them to Paddington Station, the postman came – and there was a letter for Tally in an unfamiliar hand. In an instant she was filled with certainty and happiness. Karil had written at last – he must have been ill, she had been completely wrong to doubt him. She tore the letter open.

It was not from Karil. It was from Anneliese, the German girl who had befriended them in Bergania and who had said she did not want to die young like St Aurelia. She had managed to write before mail between her country and Great Britain ceased; she hoped that when the war was over they would still be friends and she sent 'so much, much love indeed' to Tally and her friends.

She could write from an alien country declaring her friendship, but not Karil.

At Paddington there were throngs of men in uniform and evacuees with labels round their necks saying goodbye to their tearful mothers. Among the bustle and confusion the boys of Foxingham marched, as they had done before, towards their platform, their brand-new striped red-and-yellow uniforms standing out in the gloom of the station, but Roderick was not among them. He was going straight to Foxingham from Torquay. Tally thought she could make out the serious dark-haired boy who might or might not be the Prince of Transjordania – but she turned away. She had had her fill of princes.

Then she saw David Prosser, peering at a clipboard. Even he, efficient though he was, looked as though he had mislaid a child. Not Augusta Carrington – Tally could make her out at the end of the platform. And then she saw her other friends – Julia and Barney and Borro – and ran eagerly towards them.

It was time to forget Karil and move on.

Chapter Twenty-nine

Rottingdene House

Karil stood looking out of his bedroom window at the grey London street. He had pushed aside the heavy damask curtains, and the dusty net curtains, and the blackout curtains which had just been put up, but the view of tired-looking people going about their business did little to lift his spirits.

Rottingdene House was packed from the roof to the basement with his relations, yet he had never felt so alone.

His grandfather's home was not far from Buckingham Palace where the king lived with his two small daughters, and in many ways it resembled it. Rottingdene too was surrounded by spiky railings and boasted a sentry box in the courtyard and a flagpole on the roof with a flag to raise and lower to show whether the owners were at home.

It was not till one got up close to the building that one noticed that though the house was so imposing, it was actually somewhat shabby; that the woodwork needed painting and the stonework was crumbling and that altogether Rottingdene was rather a run-down place. But if the building was run down, the people who lived in it were very grand indeed.

They never went out of doors without a footman or a maid; the carriage or motor that took them through the streets of London had the Rottingdene arms emblazoned on the side, and the soldier who guarded the door had to present arms whenever anybody entered or left.

Which was only right and proper, because the house had as many blue-blooded and royal personages living in it as there are woodlice under a stone.

The Duke and Duchess of Rottingdene had had four daughters and all of them had made brilliant marriages.

The eldest daughter, Diana, had married a Russian prince; the second one, Phyllis, had married a European archduke; the third daughter, Millicent, had captured the heart of a South American ruler who governed a country the size of France.

And the youngest daughter, Alice, had married a proper king – Johannes of Bergania.

But the map of the world had changed cruelly, and one by one the proud Rottingdene daughters came home as their husbands were deposed or hounded out of their country or fell victim to sinister plots.

In Russia, Prince Dmitri, who had married Diana, had

to flee his country after being attacked by peasants with pitchforks when the tsar was overthrown.

In central Europe, Archduke Franz Heinrich, who had married Phyllis, had to leave his land and his castles when his country became a republic. And in South America, Millicent and her husband only just escaped being slaughtered in one of the bloodiest uprisings the country had known.

Only Alice did not return home but lay in the soil of Bergania beside her husband.

The daughters who came home did not come alone. They brought their husbands – proud men with moustaches or monocles, who were used to drinking the best champagne and smoking the rarest cigars and clicking their fingers at their valets when they wanted anything. Some came with ancient relatives, who had never in their lives put on their own stockings and would have starved to death if they had had to boil an egg. Some brought nurses or governesses, who had to be crammed into distant attics and boot cupboards where they coughed and quarrelled and cried.

Prince Dmitri's mother, the old Princess Natalia, brought a small, low-slung dog with a topknot and an ancient pedigree. Pom-Pom was descended from a long line of Outer Mongolian pedestal (or snuggle) dogs, who had been bred to warm the feet of the Great Khans in their draughty palaces and now wheezed through the corridors of Rottingdene House, seeking the dark, familiar world of legs and shoes and toes.

Don Alfonso, the South American ruler, brought a monkey which shivered and gibbered from morning to night – and Franz Heinrich brought that treasured jewel, a pearl beyond price, his daughter Carlotta.

And spying on everybody, controlling everything, was the ancient, bullying, terrifying Duke of Rottingdene. The duke's teeth rode up and down when he chewed, his hearing aid fell regularly into the soup and one of his legs was largely made of metal, but he missed nothing that was going on.

It was to this house, full to the brim with discontented rulers, underpaid servants and disturbed animals, that Karil was brought after his flight.

There was a knock at Karil's door and a footman in the Rottingdene livery of purple and gold stood in the doorway.

'Your Highness is requested in the Red Salon immediately.'

'Thank you.'

Karil knew why . . . the Prime Minister was going to make a speech – and there was little doubt about what he was going to tell the nation.

The Red Salon was packed with his relations. Uncle Dmitri sat on one enormous sofa with Aunt Diana and his aged mother, the Princess Natalia, who clutched Pom-Pom on her knee. On another sofa sat Uncle Franz-Heinrich and Aunt Phyllis, and on two satinwood chairs sat Uncle Alfonso, Aunt Millicent and the monkey, looking as always as though it was about to die of misery and cold. The duke sat in an imposing carved chair, closest to the wireless, and scowled. Lesser relatives were dotted about the room.

'Here, Karil,' came Carlotta's voice, 'sit next to me.'

Carlotta looked flushed and excited, and had dressed for the expected announcement of war in a white dress with a big lace collar. The man who came to take the photographs that were sent to Karil in Bergania had told her that she resembled an angel when wearing white, and on important days like this she took care to be angelic.

Karil took the place she offered. At the beginning he had tried to keep his distance from his cousin, but he was getting very tired, and his future here in this place was so bleak that Carlotta could hardly make things worse.

The Prime Minister came on the air. It was, as everyone had known it would be, an announcement of war. When it was over, the royal uncles got to their feet and saluted the wireless set, and Karil followed suit. In his high-backed chair the ancient duke harrumphed and shook his head, and Pom-Pom coughed.

So that was that, thought Karil. Bergania, occupied as it was by Hitler, was now as far away as the moon; there would be no letters and no contact with his native land.

He was still thinking about this when the air-raid alarm sounded – and at once the seemingly moribund relatives jerked into activity.

'Down into the basement,' shouted the duke, 'but in an orderly manner.'

Prince Dmitri seized his wife and his mother and made for the door, reaching it at the same time as Archduke Franz Heinrich and Phyllis. Don Alfonso and Aunt Millicent only paused to catch the monkey before they caught up with them. Carlotta had run on ahead, looking pale and giving little cries of terror.

'Come along, Karil,' said Countess Frederica.

Although Karil was in a house full of relations, she still saw him as her responsibility.

He was about to follow her when Pom-Pom freed himself from the arms of the old Princess Natalia and dived under the piano. The old lady tried to catch him, stumbled, fell under the piano on top of him and found she could not get up again.

'Go on! I'll be all right here,' she cried.

But the people nearest the door turned back. No one minded about the old princess – she had had her life – but Pom-Pom was different. He was waiting to be united with the only other Outer Mongolian pedestal dog still in existence, a bitch now living in Brazil. When this happened, and puppies were born, they would be worth a fortune, and no one wanted him to be hit by a bomb before this happy event could come to pass.

But after a moment fear won over greed and they hurried down to the basement, where another problem awaited them. The servants who were assembled there had to be removed, since it was out of the question that they be allowed to shelter in the same place as their masters. By the time this had been done the all-clear sounded and everybody trooped back upstairs, where they found the old Princess Natalia still lying under the piano with her dog.

Karil's arrival at Rottingdene House had caused some serious problems for the duke and his household. It hadn't taken long to move out the two governesses who occupied a bedroom on the top floor and give it to Karil, and the boy did not look as though he would be expensive to feed.

No, the problem was that of precedence. Nobody had

been absolutely certain whether the son of a king, even a king who was dead, should be served first at table, or go ahead of the others into the dining room. Was he more important than Prince Dmitri, who had a crest with sixteen quarterings, or Archduke Franz Heinrich, whose family had ruled over Lower Carinstein since 1304, or Don Alfonso, who was descended from a long line of Spanish conquerers?

While the matter was being looked into, the uncles and Karil took it in turn to go ahead of the others into the dining room.

The first supper after the declaration of war was much like the other meals Karil had endured at Rottingdene House. The duke sat at the head of the table in an ancient dinner jacket which smelled of mothballs, and slurped his soup. Don Alfonso appeared in one of the twenty or so military uniforms he had brought from South America and fed titbits to the monkey, and Carlotta, who had changed her dress for the third time that day, simpered and smiled.

On the whole the uncles were pleased about the war, because they thought that once it was over they would become rulers once again. Uncle Dmitri would return to his estate in Russia with ten thousand peasants doing his bidding; Uncle Franz Heinrich would be back in his turreted castle in Lower Carinstein, and Don Alfonso would once more have charge of his vast lands on the Pacific coast. Of course it was a pity that so many people might be killed first, but if it ended with them restored to power it was all worthwhile.

They were kind too to Karil, assuring him that once

Hitler was defeated, the people of Bergania would clamour to have him back as king.

'It will all be over soon, my boy,' they said, 'and then you will be back on the throne where you belong.'

And Karil, who had begun by trying to tell them that he did not want to become king, had long since given up trying to explain.

After dinner everybody retired to the Red Salon to take coffee – and then came the ritual that took place every night, and for which Karil, when he first came, had waited with such eagerness.

A footman entered with a silver salver which he placed on a gilt-legged table – and on it were the letters that had come by the afternoon post.

When he first came, Karil had always jumped up and looked at the tray, sure that there would be a letter from Tally and his other friends. He had never doubted that they would write straight away and tell him what was happening at Delderton. When nothing had come, either by the morning or the afternoon post, he had told himself that they must be busy returning to school and catching up with their work, but as day followed day and the salver disgorged letters for everyone but him, his hopes had faded and died.

He himself had written straight away, long letters that he had been careful to seal tightly before he laid them in the brass bowl in the hall where all letters were put for the footman to stamp and carry to the letter box. It was a relief to know that Rottingdene House had a system for posting letters, because he had no money and even buying stamps would have been difficult. He had told Tally about Pom-Pom, who had to be accompanied by two footmen, one at each end, when he went out, in case he was kidnapped by anarchists and eaten. He had told her about the monkey, who looked sweet but bit as soon as one came too close, and about the duke's hearing aid, which had fallen into the soup but not actually been swallowed. Gradually he found it harder to think of light-hearted things to write – he had begun to plead a little for an answer to his letters, and then to tear them up and try again because he did not want to seem to be making a fuss or admitting his unhappiness.

But as the weeks passed and there was only silence, Karil realized he had been wrong to trust his friends so utterly – and he remembered his father's words when he asked if he could meet the children who had come to his country.

It never works trying to make friends with people outside our world, he had said. *You'll only get hurt.*

The king had been right. Karil had got hurt and it served him right for being such a fool. Yet tonight, because the outbreak of war was after all not an ordinary day, he got up and walked over as he had done at the beginning, to look at the envelopes laid out on the salver.

But there was nothing. Nothing from Tally – nothing from Barney or Julia or Tod. Nothing from Matteo, who had been his father's friend.

It was a long time before he slept, that first night of the war, and when he did he found himself floating through a dark sky trying to chase a giant tray – a silver salver from which torn pieces of paper fell and whirled downwards. When he managed to catch one it melted like a snowflake and he was left with nothing except a sense of misery and dread.

Chapter Thirty

New Term

Daley sat in his big room overlooking the courtyard and watched the children arrive. The headache he always had at the beginning of term was magnified tenfold – he had already swallowed four aspirins, but the throbbing in his temples was no better and even looking at the cedar tree gave him no comfort.

On his desk were the Blackout Regulations for Schools and Institutions and the First Aid Instructions in the Event of Casualties.

There was also an urgent letter from the founders, once again inviting Daley to evacuate the school to America. It was a generous offer, and the pictures of the bombing of Warsaw should have made the decision easy – but it was not easy. Outside, the peaceful Devon countryside slumbered in the sunshine; the idea that aeroplanes would come and drop bombs over Delderton was hard to believe – indeed Delderton village was full of evacuee children from London who had been sent here just because it was safe. But if Hitler invaded Britain, that might be a different matter.

Half an hour later, Tally knocked on the door of his room. Daley had sent for her because he had been worried about her at the end of the summer term. The adventure in Bergania and the rescue of the prince had been kept from the newspapers, and the children seemed to have settled down well – but he had an idea that Tally was still troubled about something.

'Well, how has it been? Is your father well?'

'Yes, he is. Terribly busy with evacuating the hospital and everything, but he is well.'

'And have you had any news from the prince? From Karil?'

'No, nothing. The others haven't heard anything either. We've all written and written.'

'And you think he has forgotten you, and is ungrateful?'

'What else can we think?'

'There are other things that occur to one,' said the headmaster.

But he left it at that.

'I'm going to put him out of my mind,' said Tally – and while it was a lie, it was a brave one. She changed the subject. 'Is Matteo still my tutor?'

'Yes, for now.' Everything was so unsettled and uncertain in this first fortnight of the war.

All the same, it was good not being new, thought Tally,

knowing one's way about. Magda was still Tally's house-mother and she was still worrying about Schopenhauer. She had got to the part in Schopenhauer's life where he was supposed to have thrown a washerwoman down the stairs because she was talking on the landing and dis-turbing him – and she didn't know whether to leave it in or not.

'It seems so unlike him to do that,' she told the chil-dren.

She also had a new anxiety – Heribert would almost certainly be called up to fight in the German army and she was very much afraid for him.

'I don't think he will make a good soldier; he was very absent-minded,' she said.

In the village, groups of children evacuated from London wandered about looking for fish and chips and cinemas and crying for their mothers. A fire-watching rota was pinned up – members of staff would take it in turn to watch for incendiary bombs from the flat roof of the gym.

To everyone's amazement, David Prosser volunteered for the army. No one especially liked him, but that didn't mean they wanted him to be killed. Before he went he asked Clemmy to marry him and she refused him, but so nicely that he was hardly hurt at all. The man who replaced him was as old as the hills, but he knew his sub-ject.

The children who had shared the Berganian adventure still met on the steps of the pet hut to talk about their lives. When they first came back, expecting Karil to join them, they had been full of plans. Barney had bought a tree frog in a pet shop in St Agnes as a present for the prince; it was an attractive animal with its shining pop eyes and glossy skin, but they did not try to name it – Karil would want to do that himself, they thought, but as the weeks passed the frog remained nameless.

'Amphibians don't really need to be called anything,' Borro had said. 'They're all right as they are, so there's no hurry.'

But as they met for the new term they stopped trying to make plans for Karil.

The axolotl was in good health, and Tally now had charge of the white rabbit that had belonged to the little French girl who had not returned to school. Her parents didn't want to risk sending her across the Channel and being attacked by the U-boats that now patrolled the waters. She had written to say that Tally could have her rabbit, but though Tally cleaned it out and fed it and took it on her knee, she found it difficult to love it.

'Rabbits are not really very interesting,' she complained – but Julia said that rabbits weren't meant to be interesting; they were meant to be nice, and this one was.

Barney was very indignant about what had happened in the London Zoo. On the very day that war was declared all the black widow spiders and poisonous snakes had been killed in case their cages were bombed and they escaped and bit people.

'And the boa constrictors too,' he said angrily. 'Just killed outright, which is ridiculous – people would have seen them coming. Or they could have sent them to Whipsnade like the elephants. But cold-blooded murder like that!'

It was really strange, realizing the difference these last

weeks had made to their friends overseas. Borro could write to the French girl whose mother bred Charolais cows, because France and Britain were allies, on the same side in the war, but the German and Italian children had become 'the enemy' and were as unreachable as the moon.

'It seems so silly,' said Tally. 'Only a month ago we were just people.'

As for Karil, it seemed clear now that they were not going to hear from him.

'He's obviously decided to be a prince after all,' Barney said. 'I mean, he was brought up to all that since he was a baby, and now he doesn't want to have anything to do with us. It's quite natural really.'

Only Augusta, sitting on the bottom step so that the animal fur would not set off her allergy, said:

'All the same, I think it's funny that you can save some one's life and they just forget all about you.'

Her brace had been removed in the holidays and her words were very clear.

Hearing their own thoughts spoken aloud upset the others badly – and from then on they did not speak of the prince again.

It was a beautiful autumn, that first autumn of the war, and Clemmy was busy pitting herself against the coming shortages – food rationing was expected the following month and she was determined to garner every berry, every rose hip, every mushroom before the coming frosts.

So every minute that the children were not in class she herded them through the lanes, armed with jam jars and saucepans and pots. The blackberries were more succulent

279

that year than ever, the rose hips hung like crimson jewels from the briars, and on the moors the blueberries clustered between tufts of heather. There were sloes, so dark that their blueness was almost black, and chanterelles growing between the roots of trees. Clemmy was in her element as she led her troop of helpers, her hair streaming in the late sunshine, her cloak blowing in the wind. It is very different picking berries because you feel like a mouthful of something juicy and picking them because you are helping your country and can lay by stores against hardship. Even the detestable Ronald Peabody, who had broken the topmost branch of the cedar tree, picked with the best of them.

In her art classes Clemmy had let the children paint what they wanted, thinking that they might need to depict what they were going through in the changing world. When they came back after the journey to Bergania they had painted the mountains and the palace and the folk dancers, but that was before the outbreak of war. Now they painted orange and scarlet explosions and tanks and toppling houses as they saw them on the newsreels of the invasion of Poland.

But not Tally. Tally, as the term progressed, painted the things she saw on her walks with Clemmy: rowan berries on laden boughs; late foxgloves; fallen leaves, veined and crimson on the grass – and Clemmy realized that Tally was seeking comfort in nature as people have always done when their lives have run into difficulties.

'Nothing matters really when the world is so beautiful,' said Tally – and Julia, who did not agree, who knew that for someone like Tally it is people that matter, just nodded and smiled.

All the time they were in Bergania Julia had not mentioned her mother, and Tally hoped that she was no longer so unhappy about her. But when they had been back at school for nearly three weeks she called Tally into her room and held out a copy of *The Picturegoer*.

'Look!' she said.

On the centre page was a picture of Gloria Grantley in her most pouting pose. The caption read: 'Is Glorious Gloria running out of steam?'

The blurb underneath said that the plans for her new film, *The Devil in Velvet*, had been shelved. The studio refused to comment on the reasons for this decision, and her agent was not available.

'What do you think it means?' said Julia.

'Haven't you heard anything from Mr Harvenberg?' asked Tally, who knew that Gloria's agent was a very important figure in her life.

Julia shook her head. 'Not since the holidays. My grandmother wrote when war was declared because she wanted me to go out to America and spend the war there – well, I told you – but my mother didn't want me to come. She said it was too dangerous travelling by sea because of the U-boats, but of course I knew it was because . . . she didn't want me. But do you think she's in trouble?'

'No, of course not.' Tally was very firm. 'This kind of thing happens all the time in the film business, you know it does. I expect her agent wanted more money and the studio is being difficult. You'll see, it will all resolve itself.'

'It will be awful if it doesn't. She absolutely lives for her work.'

Tally looked at the picture again. Ridiculous Gloria was lying on her stomach on some sort of animal skin with one foot in very high heels cocked up behind her. Yet it was only because she had gone to see Gloria at the cinema in St Agnes that they had seen the newsreel which had set the whole Bergania adventure off. But for this horrible woman who treated her daughter so abominably, Karil would now be in the clutches of the Nazis.

That evening Tally wrote one last letter to the prince, calling up everything she could think of to amuse and interest him: Matteo's last biology lesson, when they had camped for a night on the moor and watched the stags preparing for their annual rut . . . the visit of the Spanish children, who had given a marvellous moonlit concert in the courtyard . . . and that the cow Borro was looking after was expecting a calf.

But once again, there was no reply.

CHAPTER THIRTY-ONE

KARIL AND CARLOTTA

When you are unhappy, time goes very slowly. Karil had been at Rottingdene House for only a few weeks, but he felt as though he had been buried at the bottom of a well for years.

When he woke in the morning, he thought for a moment that he was still at home, because the first thing he saw was a tray with two rusks on it and a glass of fruit juice. But it was not an equerry who brought them; the duke's servants were so hard-pressed, looking after a household packed with people who could do nothing for themselves, that they could take on nothing extra and it was the Countess Frederica who handed him the tray. The countess had seen to it ever since they had arrived in London that Karil's life went on exactly as before, and

now she told him his lessons for the day and his engage-
ments for the afternoon.

Karil never thought he would be homesick for Monsieur Dalrose's history lessons – nor that he would miss
riding in a procession to open a railway station or welcome a foreign deputation, but it was so. For his lessons
now were given by his uncles and they taught him the very
few things that they knew. Uncle Dmitri showed him how
to design crests and mottos, Uncle Franz Heinrich taught
him how to write national anthems and music for royal
occasions, and Uncle Alfonso was a specialist in the design
of state uniforms.

No one taught him anything he might have wanted to
know, or needed, and there had been no talk of sending
him to school. For while no one spoke of money, it was
clear to Karl that however grand and pompous the duke
was, and however formal the household, there was not
much spare cash. Even Carlotta, who could usually get
blood out of a stone, found it hard to wheedle money out
of her grandfather, and when his relatives needed anything they had to scrabble about among the few jewels
that still remained to them and take something to be
pawned or sold.

While he was dressing he heard a familiar thud, but as
no cries or screams followed, Karil did not come out of
his room to see who it was that had fallen over Pom-Pom.
The little dog was black and tubular and almost impossible to see in the dimly lit corridors of Rottingdene House
as he padded about looking for feet that were worthy of
his care.

The duke himself did not come down to breakfast, but

the three uncles and their wives were there. In front of Uncle Dmitri was a marmalade jar labelled with the crest of the Drimadoffs. In front of Uncle Franz Heinrich was a toast rack decorated with a silver griffon, which was the emblem of the House of Carinstein, and Uncle Alfonso was feeding a piece of bread to his shivering monkey, who wore a jacket modelled on that of the household cavalry that had guarded Alfonso when he still ruled his lands.

When Karil entered, the three uncles very slightly raised their buttocks from their chairs, because a search through the *Almanach de Gotha* had shown that the son of a reigning king, even a dead one, did definitely take precedence over another prince or an archduke or a don, and this was the nearest they would get to bowing to their nephew.

The dining room at Rottingdene House was so dark that the light had to be put on even at breakfast, and the food was quietly nasty. The bread was never fresh, the butter slightly rancid and the bacon undercooked. The truth was that the servants were so ill paid and badly treated that they had long ago given up any attempt to do their job well.

The last to appear as usual was Carlotta, who came into the room in a freshly ironed blouse and a pleated kilt with a tartan ribbon in her shining curls.

'Here comes my little sunbeam,' said her mother, and Carlotta smiled, because in truth she knew herself to be a ray of light and cheerfulness illuminating the dark house.

Being a sunbeam is hard work, but Carlotta did not shirk her duty. She saw to it that the maids crimped and curled her hair several times a day, and that her dresses were laundered and ironed before anybody else's. She

'borrowed' any trinkets she needed from her relatives –
her dimpled wrists usually glittered with bracelets – and
she never passed a mirror without checking that everything was as it should be.

Carlotta knew that cheering up her Cousin Karil was
her job, and she rose to the task. Whenever he came into
a room she patted the chair next to her and told him about
the interesting things they were going to do that day, and
she was always thinking of ideas for refurbishing the
palace when they returned together to Bergania.

Countess Frederica had taken Carlotta into her confi-
dence when they first arrived.

'I'm afraid Karil had a really dreadful time on his journey.'

But the dreadful time, when told to Carlotta, did not
mean being chased by ruffians and nearly captured, it
meant travelling in the company of the most appalling,
unruly and impertinent children.

'I can't tell you, Carlotta, what the poor boy had to
endure. Bad language, sharing a room with utterly low-
born people, being called by his Christian name. There
was a girl there who, from the way she spoke to him,
seemed to think he was simply an ordinary person. And
I'm very much afraid that Karil was taken in by them. He
called them his friends.'

'Oh, he couldn't have done!' Carlotta was really
shocked. 'What was this girl like?'

'Rude. Abominably dressed. The children all came
from some impossible school in Devon where everybody
does as they like – and you can believe it or not, they
wanted Karil to go there with them.'

'They didn't! But surely they knew that he was a prince – and would be a king one day.'

'They knew, but they took absolutely no notice. It was the most shocking thing I've ever seen. I don't think there is any danger that they will try to get in touch with him, but you know how good-natured Karil is – he might find it difficult to snub them.'

'My goodness, yes.' And then: 'What was the name of this girl?'

'Something ridiculous. They called her Tally. I have never met anyone so lacking in respect.'

The countess said no more. Carlotta was a highly intelligent girl; no usurper would get past her. Altogether Countess Frederica was very pleased with the way things had turned out; Carlotta spent most of her free time with Karil and the countess was sure that her amusing prattle must cheer him up.

After breakfast the duke sent for Karil. He lived in a dark, fusty set of rooms on the first floor, which smelled of mothballs, tobacco and an unappetizing ointment that he rubbed into his joints to ease his rheumatism. The duchess had died three years earlier, but no one had noticed this very much. She had been a browbeaten, skeletally thin woman, usually dressed in a mountain of grey cardigans, who had followed her husband about bleating, 'Yes, Mortimer,' and agreeing with everything he said.

'Ah, there you are,' he said, glaring down at his grandson. 'I have to tell you that I'm not at all pleased with you! I'm hearing bad things – very bad things – and I won't stand for them!'

Karil waited, trying to think what he had done, but nothing occurred to him.

'You have been hobnobbing with the servants. Being familiar. Talking to the footmen, gossiping with the maids – and it must stop at once!'

And as Karil remained silent . . .

'Do you hear me, boy? I'm talking to you and I expect to be answered.'

'I don't think I was gossiping exactly. One of the maids had sprained her ankle.'

'Are you contradicting me?' asked the duke, turning crimson.

'No, sir.'

'I hope not. I really hope not. Remember you are here for one reason only, to fulfil your father's wishes. You may have a few years to wait, but you'll go back to Bergania as rightful king, no doubt about it, so I don't want to hear any more about you letting people take liberties. Never forget who you are.'

But Karil was beginning to forget just that: who he was, and where he was going.

'You should take a leaf out of Carlotta's book. She never forgets who she is. You'll be fortunate to have her to help you when you go back. And of course she has the blood. She's got the Rottingdene blood from my side, and her father is descended from Attila the Hun. You'll do very well with Carlotta when the time comes; she'll see that you behave yourself.'

Karil's lesson that morning was with Prince Dmitri, who was designing a new coat of arms to be embroidered on the sofa cushions in his room. He was a stupid man, but when he began to talk about fesses and bends sinister and gules he became quite excited.

'I've never been happy with just the lion couchant. Now what do you think about a salamander? Rampant, of course.'

After that came Uncle Franz Heinrich, who played him his latest version of a celebration march that would be performed in the great hall of Carinstein Castle when he was restored to his lands.

Uncle Alfonso cancelled his lesson because the monkey had eaten something that disagreed with him.

After lunch came the worst part of the day, because Karil had to spend the afternoon with Carlotta. He had asked if he could go out alone; St James's Park was only five minutes' walk away, but the idea had been greeted with horror.

'People like us must never go out alone. It is unheard of – and no footman can be spared,' he was told.

So he had a drive in the Daimler past the shops with Cousin Frederica and Carlotta, followed by tea with the aged Baroness Roditzky in her stifling apartment – and then back to what Karil was beginning to think of as his prison.

After dinner the silver salver was brought in again, but Karil scarcely glanced at it. He had written a last letter a week ago, trying desperately not to sound sorry for himself, and again there had been no reply. Now he had really given up; he was not going to grovel and beg for friendship.

As he was undressing he felt the quartz pebble in his trouser pocket, and for a moment he was back in

Bergania, on the mountain, with Tally saying, 'Is it to remind you?'

What were they doing now, those people who had helped him and made him feel that life could be a splendid thing?

Well, he would never know.

Karil turned out the light and pulled aside the curtains. Could it be that the duke was right, and his uncles also? His father's memory was all he had left now, alone as he was, and he began to wonder whether in his own longing to live a life without power or pomp he was betraying him. Did he really have a duty to try to follow in his father's footsteps? Were the plans he had made on the journey just a selfish dream?

Soldiers did their duty. Was he perhaps just shirking his?

There was a short cry from the homesick monkey, an oath as someone stumbled over Pom-Pom, and then silence.

'Oh, why did you have to die?' asked Karil of his father.

CHAPTER THIRTY-TWO

MATTEO'S VISIT

Everyone did their best to carry on as usual that first term of the war. O'Hanrahan, who was very short-sighted and did not expect to be called up, said that in his view the most useful thing to be done about the threat from Hitler was for the children to immerse themselves in the treasures of English literature. The class had decided definitely to turn the story of Persephone into a play. They would work on the script this term, but the actual performance would be the following term, at Easter, which was suitable because it was after all a story about rebirth and regeneration. The children found it soothing that O'Hanrahan was sure that there really would be an Easter term and that the world would not have gone up in smoke before then. At the same time they were already getting angry with Julia, who said again that she absolutely would not play the leading part.

'Does someone have to die before you stop skulking in corners?' said Tally furiously. 'There were a hundred people up on the hill when you recited that poem and you didn't seem to mind that.'

'That was different,' said Julia. 'This would be in a theatre.'

'No, it wouldn't,' said Barney angrily. 'It would be in a school hall with a stage – if it gets that far.'

Needless to say, Verity did not try to persuade Julia. She was already planning what to wear while being carried off into the Underworld kicking and screaming.

Julia's mother had sent the usual box of chocolates, and the usual note, put in by the shop, sending lots and lots of love, but there was no news about her new film.

'I'm really worried about her,' Julia said – and Tally did her best not to snarl.

Magda had lost the whisk that the aunts had sent to froth up her cocoa, and she was being persecuted by the Delderton Air Raid Warden, who kept the pub in the village and came up each night to check the blackout at the school.

'I can see chinks!' he would shout at Magda. 'There are chinks of light coming from your windows.'

'What chinks?' Magda would cry, running distractedly up and down the corridor. 'Where are the chinks?'

And the children would leave their homework and go chink-hunting in the twenty rooms of Blue House.

Clemmy, usually so serene and good-tempered, was having a hard time with the new gardener who had replaced the trusty man she had worked with up to now and who had volunteered for the air force.

'What are you doing?' she shouted at the young lad, who was pouring poison on a spinach bed to kill the snails, and she dragged him indoors to look at the beautiful striations on a snail shell under a magnifying glass before ordering him to pick off the offending animals one by one and transport them to a patch of woodland nearby.

And all the time Daley brooded over the latest letter from the founders in America, trying to make the final decision about whether to evacuate the school. With one stroke of the pen he could secure the safety of all those in his care. The Americans were famously hospitable and friendly, and the founders were ready to do everything to smooth his path.

Yet did he really want to forsake his country now? Was that what he wanted for the children? He imagined the buildings empty, the grass in the courtyard growing between the stones, the cedar tree untrimmed. Or the army would move in – they would be glad of the building.

'I *must* decide,' he said wearily and reached for the aspirin bottle yet again.

Tally, meanwhile, threw herself into all the activities that were going on. She helped Clemmy resettle the mice that were caught in the kitchen. She dealt with Kit when he said he didn't want to be an erupting seed pod in Armelle's drama class, and she stirred Josie's cauldron of whatever wort they were using till her arms ached.

But sometimes she went off on her own into the woods and made things she had not made since she was six years old: little houses of sticks and interlacing leaves which a

worm might come and live in if he felt so inclined, or a
necklace of scarlet berries which she did not put on but
left lying in the grass. Or she would wander over to the
library after supper and Julia would find her bent over a
book of those phrases that are supposed to help people
with their lives. Sayings like: '*You cannot stop the birds of
sorrow from flying over your head, but you can stop them
nesting in your hair.*'

'Well, how goes it?' asked Matteo as Tally came to his
room for her tutorial. 'Any problems?'

'No, not really. I'm all right.'

Matteo looked at her. He knew that she was not all
right and he knew why. The other members of staff,
though they watched over Tally with concern, were sure
she would soon get over her disappointment.

It was a mistake which he did not make. He and
Johannes had met when they were seven years old
and they had known in an instant that they were going to
be friends. Till Matteo was in his twenties his life had
been bound up with that of the king – his best ideas and
most selfless visions of the future had come from this rela-
tionship – and when he cut himself off and stormed away
from Bergania some part of him had died.

His friendship with Johannes had lasted for fifteen
years. Tally and Karil had known each other only for a few
days, but that made no difference. Sometimes you meet
someone – and it can be at any age or time – with whom
you should go forward into the future. All the children had
warmed to Karil, but for Tally the friendship had been
special. She had believed totally in Karil and his wish to

294

live a life that was honourable and free – and she believed that in this life she had a part to play. Now the ground had gone from under her feet. She was not the sort of child to pine, but Karil's silence had hurt her very deeply.

Matteo glanced at the sackbut propped up in a corner of the room. He had not played it since he came back from Bergania.

Then he said, 'Karil is safe, I can tell you that. Nothing bad has happened to him. He is with his family.'

Would this make it better for her? In one way yes, but in another way no. She must surely think that an able-bodied boy could write a letter and put it in a box.

There were other things he kept to himself: his visit to a lawyer who told him that there was nothing legal he could do to take Karil away from his grandfather; and the message he had sent to old von Arkel, who was supposed to have fled Bergania and be on his way to England.

Two days later a letter arrived from the War Office addressed to Matteo and he took it to Daley to ask for leave to go to London.

Even though the letter had been seen only by Matteo and the Head, its contents mysteriously went round the school and everybody knew that Matteo had been summoned.

'They'll want him to do something very important and secret,' said Tod. 'Maybe they'll recruit him to be a spy – he speaks enough languages.'

'Or they'll drop him behind enemy lines by parachute,' suggested Borro.

Barney thought they might want him to be a code

breaker. 'That wouldn't be much fun: you just sit in a sealed house somewhere and decipher things, but it's terribly important.'

Matteo, needless to say, showed no inclination to discuss his coming visit, and at the end of the week he took the train to Paddington.

The children had said goodbye to him with a mixture of pride at the thought of having a teacher who might be facing a heroic fate and sadness at the thought of losing him. But when he returned it was in such a vile temper that the idea of doing without him seemed excellent.

He came back in the afternoon, in time to give his biology class, and when they came out of it the children were stunned. Matteo had stamped up and down the classroom reciting facts about an animal called amphioxus in a manner which would not have disgraced Smith, the teacher Tally had first mistaken for him. He told them to copy things out of a book, he gave them a test on the lesson he had just given and, unbelievably, for homework set them an essay that had to be at least three pages long.

'What's the matter with him?' asked Barney, utterly bewildered. 'He never sets tests except if we have to sit a state exam.'

'And he thinks amphioxus is a waste of time,' said Borro. 'I've heard him say so. It's an animal that examiners mind about but nobody else.'

This was true. Matteo had classified a group of what he called formaldehyde animals: creatures that lived in pickle for the benefit of lazy teachers and no one else.

'Something must really be troubling him,' said Tally. 'Perhaps the War Office is sending him to certain death and he's so upset he can't remember how to teach properly.'

She was right, up to a point. Something was troubling Matteo, but it was not his interview with the War Office, which had been courteous and brief. They were recruiting a body of men who spoke several European languages for a mission behind enemy lines, the details of which were still being worked out. This first interview was simply to discover whether Matteo would be willing to risk his life in such an enterprise, and when he had said that he would the conversation had turned to the position in Bergania and ended with an excellent dinner in the Travellers Club.

If Matteo had then returned to Delderton, the children in his class would not have been writing an essay on amphioxus or avoiding him when they met him in the courtyard, but he had not. After a night with a friend he had made his way to Rottingdene House, given his name to the sentry in the box guarding the front door and rung the bell.

While he waited he looked up at the gloomy grey building with its shrouded windows where Karil now lived. The flag with the duke's crest hung limply from the top of the flagpole, so the owner was at home.

The door was opened by a footman in an ornate but shabby livery of purple and tarnished gold.

Matteo presented his card. 'I would like to see Prince Karil, please.'

The footman's eyes flickered. 'The prince is not at home,' he said.

'Very well. Then I would like to see the Duke of Rottingdene.'

'The duke never sees anyone without an appointment.'

Matteo took a step forward. He did not raise his arm, he scarcely moved a muscle, but the footman retreated.

'I will go and see.'

He returned and said, 'His Grace will see you for five minutes only. He has an engagement.'

Matteo followed the footman up a broad staircase with a carpet patterned in fleurs de lis. Everything was both shabby and oppressive, and there was a smell of some ointment that Matteo, who did not suffer from rheumatism, could not identify.

The duke's study was even darker and gloomier than the rest of the house. All the wall space that was not taken up by antlers was covered in bad paintings of horses: pedigree hunters with flaring nostrils and rolling eyes. The duke had bred these on his estate in Northumberland in his younger days. Under the painting of a particularly fearsome hunter he read the name 'Orion'. It was this horse which the duke had had shipped out to Bergania to his daughter Alice as a birthday present. The horse had kicked his stable to pieces and thrown his groom, but Alice had been too afraid of her father not to ride it. If it wasn't for Orion, Karil's mother would still be alive.

The duke, sitting behind a claw-footed desk, did not trouble to rise or offer his hand.

'Since you insist on seeing me, I want to make one thing clear. You may have brought Karil to England but this does not give you any right now to interfere in his life.

Karil will live here under my roof until he is ready to return to Bergania as the country's rightful king.'

Matteo tried to steady himself.

'I am perfectly aware that as his grandfather you have the right to determine Karil's upbringing. The law is on your side, I don't dispute that. But his father's dying words to me were about Karil. He asked me to look after him. If I can't do that, I would at least like to show the boy that I am still here as his friend.'

The duke tried to rise from his chair, collapsed and tried again. His gnarled red hands grasped the sides of the desk.

'His friend!' he spat. 'Do you seriously imagine that I would allow my grandson to be friends with an outlaw, a vagabond, a man who travels with a group of mad children without discipline or restraint? You think I know nothing about your journey here but the Countess Frederica has given me details of behaviour that makes the blood run cold.'

'Did she perhaps also tell you that we were escaping from men who would have killed your grandson without compunction?'

'I do not deny all that – it is because of this that I admitted you to my house instead of having you thrown out. But you will not come here again. Not ever. An Englishman's home is his castle, as you are aware, and if I see you here again I will have you evicted and call the police. Moreover, I know something about your past. You were responsible for the king's early escapades, a bad influence from the start. It was because of you that Johannes wanted to be one of those namby-pamby rulers who pretend that a king can consult his people. A king is a king, an absolute ruler, and one of my tasks before I die is to see that Karil does not forget this.'

For a moment Matteo saw red. He was within an ace of springing forward and fastening his hands around the raddled throat of the old bully. But he managed to get control of himself. There was one thing he had still to do, and it meant being polite when he wanted to kill.

'I shall abide by your decision,' he said, 'but I would like to see Karil once to say goodbye. I'm going off to war soon and I may not return.'

'Karil is not at home,' lied the duke.

'I am not in a hurry. I will wait till he returns.'

'No, you won't,' screeched the duke. He was suddenly crimson, a pulse going in his throat. 'You will leave my house this instant.' He pressed a bell on his desk and the footman who had admitted Matteo appeared. 'Get Henry and show this man out. Make sure the door is bolted behind him. Hurry.'

During that moment while Matteo waited for the second footman, he felt that anything would be worthwhile – prison, a hangman's noose – if he could kill the panting, slobbering tyrant glaring at him from behind his desk. He had to call up the image of Karil exposed to scandal and horror to prevent himself from leaping on his enemy.

The footmen came just in time – feeble lackeys daunted by their instructions. Matteo knocked away the arm of the first one, pushed the second one hard against the wall – and left the building.

The hour Matteo spent in the station hotel waiting for

the train back to Delderton was one of the darkest of his life. He saw Johannes's face turned to his, begging him to look after his son. Well, this was how he had looked after Karil. Left him with a power-mad imbecile who would train him to be the kind of tyrant Europe would disgorge in an instant after the war. Karil abandoned in that wretched dark house – and Matteo was powerless. He had betrayed Johannes by leaving Bergania. Now he had betrayed his son.

His rage against himself and the duke only grew on the journey back to school. He gave his lesson on the life history of amphioxus in a black cloud of fury that embraced everything and everyone on earth – and afterwards could not recall what he had said.

It was two days before any of the children dared to approach him. Then suddenly he was himself again – and at dawn on the third day he got everybody out of bed to go and look at a badger sett by the river where three cubs were hunting for wasps' nests.

Chapter Thirty-three

The Duke Is Enraged

By the beginning of November shortages and restrictions caused by the war were beginning to bite, and among the things that were in short supply was petrol for private motoring.

The duke needed the Daimler to drive to the Whitehall Bank, of which he was a director, so that the afternoon outings Karil took with Carlotta and the Scold became even shorter and less interesting. As often as not now they spent the time taking tea with whatever family lived close by and was considered worthy of knowing the Duke of Rottingdene and his dependants.

Sometimes they even went on foot, with one of the servants walking behind them, to whatever entertainment was suitable, and free.

And one of these places was the National Portrait Gallery. The sides of the building were sandbagged and only three of the galleries were open, but it was a perfectly respectable place, with no danger of seeing pictures of people with nothing on, and would provide, the Scold thought, suitable history lessons for Karil and Carlotta since the paintings were mainly of people who were both important and dead.

For Karil the hour they spent there was interesting. He had expected to see mostly kings and statesmen and governors of the far-flung empire, but he found faces that intrigued him. There were scientists and explorers and other people who had done real things: Florence Nightingale, who had nursed the dying soldiers in the Crimean War, and David Livingstone, who had beaten his way through the African jungle looking for the source of the Nile, and Shelley, who had written great poems about freedom before meeting his death at sea.

Karil had thought that Carlotta would be bored, but she came out with a rapt expression and at first she did not answer when they spoke to her, for the truth was that she had had an inspiration.

They had passed a number of paintings of little girls – the daughters of noblemen and wealthy citizens from all over the land. The girls in the pictures wore sumptuous clothes and sat on throne-like chairs – and their portraits were set in heavy golden frames – yet none of them was more important or had a brighter future than she had herself.

To Carlotta, as she came down the steps of the gallery, it was absolutely clear. She too had to have her portrait painted, and soon. It would be a surprise for Karil – a Christmas present perhaps – and when she returned with Karil to Bergania the picture would hang in the palace.

First though she had to persuade her parents.

'I'm afraid that would cost too much, my little kitten,' said her father as she sat on his knee and played with his moustache.

'Oh please, Papa,' she wheedled. 'It would be such a nice present for Karil. Think how pleased he would be.'

'I know, my angel, but really it isn't necessary, since Karil is here now and can look at you every day.'

'But I want it to happen. I *want* it. Royal people always have their portraits painted.'

'You've no idea how much a good painter would charge, and a bad one wouldn't do justice to my sweetheart,' said the archduke, tweaking her ringlets.

But Carlotta didn't want to have her ringlets tweaked, she wanted to have them painted.

'I'm being very unselfish,' she pointed out, 'because you have to sit very still to be painted, and you can get quite uncomfortable; and if I can promise to sit still, then at least you and Mama should find the money. Or Aunt Millicent – she's got a diamond-studded garter left. I know because her maid told me so.'

Her father stood firm for several days, and then Carlotta began to refuse her food. She did not refuse it completely but often she had only one bun for tea, or a single helping of custard with her pudding, sighing ostentatiously and saying she did not feel well.

'Why can't we sell Pom-Pom if he's got such an important pedigree?' she said. 'He'll never get to Brazil now that there's a war, and anyway he's far too old to be a father.'

The old princess began to lift Pom-Pom out of Carlotta's way when she came near him, and the other relatives hid the few valuables they still had as best they could. But when Carlotta had three biscuits instead of four for her mid-morning snack her mother became alarmed. She shut herself up into her bedroom and turned out her drawers and her underclothes and her make-up boxes. There was hardly any jewellery left, but she did find one shoe buckle studded with sapphires. She had been saving it for emergencies, but Carlotta going off her food was a kind of emergency. There was no need to sell it yet – the portrait might not turn out satisfactory or the artist might be persuaded that painting Carlotta von Carinstein was enough of an honour to undertake the work without payment, but at least they could get the portrait under way.

As soon as she had what she wanted, Carlotta got down to the problem of what to wear. Since the picture was to be a surprise for Karil she could not consult him, but she appeared every few hours in a different dress: pink with a broderie-anglaise collar, yellow with appliquéd buttercups, green with a row of velvet bows – and pirouetted in front of mirrors or asked advice from her relatives, which she instantly ignored. Sometimes she thought she would look best holding something – a kitten perhaps, or a bunch of flowers, but there were no flowers to be had in that dark house, and the kitten she brought up from the servants' quarters scratched and refused to sit still, so she prowled through the rooms of the aunts and the governesses, seeing what she could beg or borrow or simply steal. Bracelets tinkled on her wrists, glittering headbands appeared on her hair, necklaces circled her plump neck – only to be rejected as not good enough.

'I think it would be best if I sat in that big chair in the Red Salon,' she said. 'If it was draped in brocade it would look almost like a throne.'

The next thing was to choose a painter and Uncle Alfonso, who was artistic because of designing all his uniforms, went to his club and asked around, and came back with the name of an artist who was highly thought of and not too expensive.

The painter was approached and said he would do it – and Carlotta, for a few days, was thoroughly happy and as nearly good as she was able.

Karil, on the other hand, was in disgrace. The misery of being shut indoors all day was more than he could bear and one morning, when the servants were busy, he had slipped out of the back door and into the street.

The next two hours were spent blissfully alone in the city that was now his home and that so far he had hardly seen.

He wandered through St James's Park, enjoying the sight of the waterfowl and watching men digging trenches. There had been a group of people filling sandbags and Karil had stayed to help them for a while; they had been friendly and cheerful. He passed Buckingham Palace, but the sight of the enormous building in which he knew the two little princesses were incarcerated lowered his spirits, and he had made his way up Whitehall and stood in Piccadilly, with its shrouded fountain, and drank in the bustle, the traffic, the advertisements . . . At last for a while he was free and part of the real world.

He would have slipped back again unnoticed – the servants would not have betrayed him – but Carlotta had been looking for him, and when he returned she was there with her shocked accusations.

'You know that people like us aren't supposed to go out alone,' she said. 'I'm afraid Grandfather is very angry.'

And Grandfather was.

'You don't seem to understand, Karil, that you are not like other people. You are a future king and—'

'No.' The cry came from Karil without him being aware of it. 'I'm not . . . I'm just a person. No one knows what will happen in Bergania – even if Hitler is defeated the people might not want a king again and anyway it could be years. I've got to have some air . . . I've got to learn something. I can't live like this.'

'Can't!' roared the duke, and a shower of spittle came from his mouth. 'How dare you defy me? While you are under my roof you will do exactly as I order.' His great hands gripped Karil's shoulders like a vice. 'From now on I shall see to it that you are watched at all times. What's more, you will be locked into your bedroom at night.'

'No! Please. I've never been locked in. My father never punished me like that.'

'It would have been better if he had,' said the duke – and he sent for the servants straight away and gave his instructions.

Under this regime, Karil became more and more desperate. He even wondered if he was beginning to lose his reason – for he had been sure that he had seen Matteo, a few days earlier, walking across the courtyard away from the house. He had been standing at an upstairs window, and by the time he'd managed to pull back the curtains and struggled with the heavy sash cords, the man had gone.

'Was Matteo here?' he had asked his grandfather – and the duke had scowled and told him not to be stupid.

'The sooner you realize that those vagabonds you came over with have forgotten you, the better,' he said.

Karil did realize it. He was too proud to show his grief, but his body began to let him down. He developed a cough that did not go away, he lost weight and found it difficult to sleep.

At night, the sound of the key turning in the lock seemed to set the seal on a life to be lived without love, or endeavour, or hope.

CHAPTER THIRTY-FOUR

THE PAINTING

It was not only David Prosser who was in love with Clemmy. The children at Delderton were used to seeing young men standing outside the school with their motorbikes, hoping she would go out with them. But Clemmy had a boyfriend to whom she was absolutely faithful. She had known him since she started work as a model and she loved not only him but his work. Francis Lakeland was a landscape painter who did quiet and very beautiful paintings of the countryside. People liked these and they were shown in exhibitions, but no one bought them very much because they were too peaceful and didn't have anybody being set on fire or dismembered or sitting with their mouth open, screaming.

So, to make some money, Francis Lakeland took on

commissions to paint portraits of society people who wanted their wives and daughters to look beautiful.

A week after half-term, Clemmy had a letter from Francis in which he asked her to come up to London for a weekend because he expected to be called up for the army.

'It won't be straight away,' he wrote, 'but I want to see you badly and I need to talk to you about a piece of work I've been asked to do.'

The idea of Francis in the army made Clemmy's stomach crunch up in a most alarming way. He was a gentle, scholarly man, serious about his work but funny about everything else. It wasn't easy to think of him as a soldier.

All housemothers had a free weekend each month, and a week after she got his letter Clemmy arrived in London. She and Francis wandered hand in hand through the city and it was when they were sitting in one of their favourite places, a bench in St James's churchyard in Piccadilly, that Francis told her about his commission to paint Carlotta von Carinstein, the daughter of an exiled archduke.

'Oh Francis, do you have to?' asked Clemmy, for she knew how much he disliked the fawning and flattery that went with painting the children of rich and snobbish people.

'I don't have to – but the money would be useful. Only I have to go tomorrow and set it up and I wondered if you could possibly come along and pretend to be my assistant. She's supposed to be an absolute horror and you know how good you are with children.'

'Yes, of course I'll come. Where does she live?'

'It's a place called Rottingdene House – a great gloomy

mansion. Her grandfather's the Duke of Rottingdene –
why, what's the matter?'

Clemmy had frowned. She knew the name of Rottingdene House only too well. The children had spoken of it
when they came back from Bergania – and she could see
the name now on the envelopes that Tally left for the postman.

And she didn't want to go there. She understood how
easy it must have been for Karil to get drawn back into his
former life, but he had hurt his friends.

'What is it?' asked Francis.

'Nothing. It's all right. Of course I'll come.'

It would be as well to keep an eye on Francis, she
thought. He had a temper and had walked out of more
than one sitting when his subjects had thrown their weight
about.

And after all, they were most unlikely to meet the
prince: painters in those sorts of places were not usually
admitted by the front door.

So the following day, carrying Francis's easel and his
box of paints, they made their way down Pall Mall
towards Rottingdene House.

As Clemmy had expected, they were shown in by the
back door and told to wait in a small cold lobby. No one
offered them a cup of tea or suggested that they should sit
down, and they saw no member of the household. When
they had waited for nearly half an hour, they were shown
into a stuffy and over-furnished drawing room and into
the presence of Carlotta's mother, the Archduchess of
Carinstein.

'My daughter is preparing herself,' she announced. 'She will be with you in five minutes.'

Again they waited – not for five minutes, but for fifteen. Then Carlotta swept in, followed by one of the mournful governesses, and stretched out her hand so that Francis could bow over it. At the same time her eyes swivelled over to Clemmy, waiting for her curtsy.

She waited in vain. The painter said, 'Good morning'; his assistant smiled – and that was all. It was an outrage, and for a moment Carlotta thought of sweeping out again. But the vision of her picture framed in gold on the wall of the Berganian palace stopped her, and she walked over to a large carved chair, draped in a piece of brocade.

'This is where I'm going to sit,' she informed them.

She had decided in the end to be angelic, and wore a white lace dress and a white ribbon in her hair.

'I'm afraid there won't be enough light with the chair at that angle,' said Francis. 'It will have to be moved closer to the window.'

Carlotta scowled, but she allowed him to adjust the chair. Then she got into it, clutched the chair arms on either side and stared at Francis.

'It doesn't matter what you wear today, Carlotta,' said the painter, 'because I'm only doing the preliminary sketches, but next time I don't want you to wear a white dress. I'd like you to wear blue . . . or yellow.'

'I always wear white dresses,' said Carlotta, 'when I'm being photographed.'

'But you're not being photographed. You're being painted,' said Francis.

Carlotta's mouth shut in a tight line. 'I don't see why you should tell me what to wear.'

Clemmy now moved towards Carlotta. 'You see, Mr Lakeland has noticed how beautifully a blue dress would take up the colour of your eyes. Your eyes are a most unusual blue – it's more of an azure or ultramarine. On the other hand, yellow would blend with your hair. Your hair is such a rich blonde – not boringly flaxen. Of course you can wear white – only it is . . . well . . . a bit ordinary.'

'All right,' said Carlotta. She waved her hand at the governess. 'Go and fetch the yellow organdie,' she ordered, 'and the blue velvet. The one with the embroidered collar.'

The governess hurried away and came back with the two dresses on her arm.

'There's no need to change this time,' said Francis. 'Just tell me which one you'd prefer to wear and then I can block out the colour tones before I go.'

'I'll wear the blue.'

She sat back in the chair and Francis began to sketch the outlines of her face and arms.

'That drape is much too fussy,' he said to Clemmy. 'I'll have the chair as it is.'

'I won't sit on a bare chair,' said Carlotta.

'But surely you don't want people to look at the drapes rather than at your face?' said Clemmy, deftly removing the brocade. She was getting a little bit worried about Francis.

'Could you perhaps turn your head a little,' he said, taking up his sketchbook. 'Just find a position that's natural and comfortable.'

'I don't want to be natural,' said Carlotta. 'People like

313

me aren't meant to look natural; they're meant to look important.'

But she allowed Francis to turn her head aside, and for a short time she sat still. Then she began to wriggle and kick the legs of the chair and say she was tired.

'You've done very well,' said Clemmy. 'Have a good stretch and then you can come back for a bit longer.'

But when she sat down again Carlotta said that her foot had gone to sleep and she didn't want to sit with her head tilted, because people wouldn't see all of her face.

'You see, Carlotta,' said Clemmy soothingly, 'this painting will be shown for hundreds and hundreds of years. People will look at it and say how lucky the prince of Bergania is to have such a beautiful friend. You will be remembered long after you're dead and—'

'I don't care,' said Carlotta. 'My shoulder's stiff and I'm bored.'

'Shall I tell you a story?'

'What sort of a story? Will it be about me?'

Clemmy sighed and racked her brains. The kind of story that ordinary little girls might like, about going to live in a castle with a regiment of soldiers to salute her, would hardly satisfy Carlotta, who probably thought that all this was going to befall her in any case. So perhaps a film-star story . . . a story about being discovered and taken to Hollywood like Shirley Temple, who was driven everywhere in a white Rolls-Royce and was a millionairess at the age of seven. It was Clemmy's least-favourite topic but Francis, who had reached for his paints, shot her a look of gratitude, and she cleared her throat and began.

'Once upon a time . . .'

*

While Clemmy was telling her story, adding more and more preposterous details, Karil was walking though St James's Park supporting the old Princess Natalia, who was pulling Pom-Pom along on his lead. On the other side of the princess was the Scold, and ten paces behind came the smallest and most useless of the duke's footmen, the knock-kneed George. Because he did not trust George to restrain Karil, the duke had given the Scold a whistle to blow in case the boy showed signs of running off.

It was almost funny, thought Karil, how awful it was, this slow procession through the dank and chilly park. The old princess had arthritis and winced when she put her right foot on the ground, Pom-Pom had a cold, which made it even more difficult than usual for him to breathe through his squashed-up nose, and George had been turned down by one of the housemaids and stared ahead of him, seeing nothing but his sorrow.

The Scold had planned the afternoon carefully. They must stay out till four o'clock at least, so that Carlotta's surprise was not spoilt. The dear girl was keen that Karil should suspect nothing and be overjoyed when he received her portrait at Christmas, and this meant prolonging the walk for as long as the old princess could stay on her feet – and after that finding somewhere where they could shelter.

They had not walked far when the princess collapsed on to a damp bench.

'You had better take Pom-Pom, Karil,' she said. 'I must rest. My heart is not good.' She sighed deeply. 'Oh, when will the messenger come?'

'He will come soon, I'm sure,' said Karil.

Almost every day he had to listen to the old lady as she told him about Pom-Pom's betrothed, the only other Outer Mongolian pedestal dog in the world, who had been taken to Brazil by a Russian count now working as a stevedore on the docks in Rio de Janeiro. A messenger would come to fetch Pom-Pom, Princess Natalia had told him; puppies would be born – and the ancient line of dogs bred by the Great Khans would be continued.

'And then I can die!' was how the story always ended.

Karil would have liked to let Pom-Pom off the lead – it seemed to him all wrong that a dog bred by the Great Khans of the Mongolian steppes should be pulled along like a prisoner. Such dogs had been prized beyond rubies; they were offered as living hot-water bottles to honoured palace visitors whose feet were cold; they travelled in the Khans' own saddlebags when the rulers rode to war – lifted in and out by their topknot. And now the last survivor of this honourable race had to pad through the muddy paths of a London park and lift his leg against soiled lamp posts.

After a while the princess struggled to her feet and they set off for another laborious walk of a hundred yards or so.

'I have heard that old Simonova Ravinsky has died,' said the old lady presently. 'Ridiculous! She was only eighty-three.'

The Scold agreed that it was indeed ridiculous and they managed to cross a small bridge across a ditch. The park, on this wretched day, was almost empty – even the water-birds were silent. Only Pom-Pom's wheezing could be heard above the gathering wind.

'And they say that Count Suratov is turning an unpleasant colour,' Princess Natalia went on.

'What sort of a colour?' enquired the Scold.

'Purple,' pronounced the old lady.

'That is a bad sign, certainly,' said the Countess Frederica. 'Turning purple is definitely a bad sign.'

After three-quarters of an hour they reached a small pavilion. It was open to the weather, but at least there was a roof to shut out the rain that was beginning to fall. The Scold looked at her watch. Another hour at least before they could return.

They sat on damp, gilt-legged chairs and watched the rain fall in grey strings into the lake.

The footman shivered and took up his position at a suitable distance. It was going to be a long afternoon.

But now suddenly there was a diversion.

Two rough-looking men in shabby raincoats made their way up the steps. One had a heavy dark beard and wore a battered hat pulled down low. The other was younger, with a chin full of stubble and burning black eyes.

They lurched into the pavilion, hiccupped a few times and stopped to stare. Then they bent down to pat Pom-Pom.

'Nice little doggy,' said the bearded man. 'Come along then. Come to Jack.'

Pom-Pom rolled his bloodshot eyes and rumbled in his throat.

'Now then,' said the man, 'I'm not going to hurt you . . .'

He squatted down on his haunches and tried to pull the dog towards him.

'Careful,' said his companion. 'He might bite you.'

'No, he wouldn't. Dogs don't hurt me, not ever.'

He belched loudly and tugged at Pom-Pom's topknot.

The next moment there was a piercing scream as the old princess rose from her chair. 'Anarchists!' she screeched. 'Anarchists. They will cut him up and eat him!'

'No, no,' said the Scold. 'I'm sure they're just tramps.' And to the two men: 'Be off with you. Go away. Shoo!'

But the men, who were too drunk to understand, showed no sign of moving. They continued to sway slightly and tell Pom-Pom that he was a nice little doggy.

'I know anarchists,' shrieked Princess Natalia. 'In Russia they were everywhere! They will eat my Pom-Pom and he will never become a father in Brazil! Quick, quick, we must take him home.'

'I'll take him,' said Karil.

'No, no!' cried the Scold. 'You can't go back now; you'll spoil Carlotta's surprise.'

But Karil was getting bored with the fuss about Carlotta's surprise. 'I know all about the portrait,' he said. 'I've known about it for ages, but I'll be careful to make sure she doesn't see me.'

'We must get the police . . . the police!' shrieked the old lady, She took a step backwards, sending her chair crashing against the metal table, and the tramps, disgusted by the commotion, shuffled out into the rain.

'Silly old geezer,' one of them muttered.

But the Princess Natalia was now in the grip of fully fledged hysterics. 'They have gone to fetch bombs,' she cried. 'They will explode him and when the messenger comes he will be dead! He must go home!'

'George,' called the Countess Frederica, and the footman who had been huddled into his overcoat moved reluctantly towards her, 'pick up the dog and hurry back to the house with him.'

'He'll bite me,' said the footman, 'He doesn't like me and he's all upset now. He'll bite, as sure as eggs is eggs.'

And certainly Pom-Pom did not look friendly. He had not enjoyed having his topknot pulled by unkempt strangers. The hair on his back was standing up and his growls came thick and fast.

'Don't be such a coward,' snapped the countess, and George reluctantly bent down and then straightened himself with a cry, nursing his hand.

'I told you, the rotten little cur,' he muttered.

But Karil had had enough.

'Come on, Pom-Pom,' he said. He coiled up the lead, scooped up the little dog, and ran towards the gates of the park.

'Stop, Karil. Stop!' called the countess. She fumbled for her whistle but it had got caught under her collar.

And Karil, running like the wind, had vanished behind a clump of trees.

While Clemmy went on with her story, adding an audience of screaming fans and a bed draped in ostrich feathers, Carlotta was reasonably quiet, but as soon as it was finished she leaped up and said she'd changed her mind.

'I don't want to wear the blue dress. I want to wear the yellow one.'

Francis, who had started blocking in the colour tones, tore a leaf out of his sketchbook and let it drop.

'Very well. But there must be no more changes after this. I have to get to a particular point today or I can't promise to get your painting done in time.'

For a few moments Carlotta was quiet – then she began to fidget again. 'I'm bored,' she said, 'and I don't want to sit with my head turned like this because people won't see my ringlets. I'm going to sit the way I was before, looking straight ahead.'

Francis put down his palette. 'I think you'd better make up your mind, Carlotta,' he said quietly. 'Do you want me to paint your picture or not? Because if you do, you'd better make some effort to cooperate.'

At the other end of the room the archduchess and the mournful governess exchanged anxious looks, but it was too late. Carlotta was heading for one of her famous tantrums.

'How dare you talk to me like that?' she shouted. 'I won't be told what to do by common people.'

Blind with ill temper she leaped to her feet, knocking over Francis's easel, and rushed from the room, followed by her mother and the governess, both uttering bleating cries.

Francis put down his palette.

'I'm going to find the duke – I'm not going on with this,' he said.

Clemmy did not try to stop him. Alone in the room, she knelt down and began to clear up the mess, which was considerable. The easel had dislodged the box of paints and tubes of colour had spilled on to the floor; there was a splash of crimson on the carpet.

She had been working for a few minutes when a quiet voice said, 'Can I help?' – and she looked up to see a boy of about twelve standing in the doorway.

Karil, having shut Pom-Pom into the old princess's room, had heard the familiar sound of Carlotta drumming her heels on the floor and made his way to a quieter part of the house.

Now he moved forward to see if he could be of use, and as he did so the kneeling woman got to her feet. Her marvellous russet hair was loose, and as she shook it back from her face it was as though the dark room had acquired its own sun.

But it wasn't her beauty that held him spellbound – it was that she was familiar. He had seen her before.

'Oh, but I know who you are. You're Clemmy – you have to be! I saw you in Zurich at the cheese tasting. It was such a lovely picture.'

And suddenly he was back there among his friends in a world that had held danger, but also friendship and loyalty and hope. And surprising himself as much as her, he burst into tears.

'What is it? What's the matter? You're Karil, of course,' she said, stretching out her arms to him, and she knew in that instant that he had not betrayed his friends, that he was wretchedly unhappy and that the truth lay elsewhere.

'I can't understand why they didn't write,' Karil sobbed. 'I wrote and wrote and there wasn't a single word back. They seemed to be my friends and then they just dropped me – even Tally. And Matteo too. They might as well have let me go to Colditz. I really believed in them.'

Clemmy pushed his hair back from his forehead and waited while he found his handkerchief.

'Oh Karil, you're such an idiot! How could you think that? You *knew* them. I think Tally must have written you a hundred letters. Magda found her again and again after lights out, scribbling and scribbling. The others too, but when they didn't hear anything they thought you'd become too grand for them.'

'They couldn't have thought that! They should have trusted me.'

'Yes. And you should have trusted them.' But Clemmy was aware that his hurt, here in this wretched place, must have been even greater than Tally's. 'Matteo even came here to try to see you,' she went on. 'Did they tell you?'

He shook his head. 'I thought I saw him, but when I asked my grandfather he said it wasn't him.' He wiped his eyes and put his handkerchief away. 'When I didn't hear anything from Delderton I thought maybe it was a sign that I must forget about trying to lead my own life. That I have to follow in my father's footsteps and learn to be a king . . . that that's what he wanted . . .'

'Is that what they say? That your father would have wanted that?'

'All the time.'

Clemmy looked down into his face. 'Karil, your father was a good man, I'm sure of that. Matteo has talked to me about him a lot since he came back from Bergania. I saw a picture of him once in a gallery; I've never forgotten his face. That was a man who wanted one thing and one thing only for his son – and I'll swear to that with my last breath.'

Karil's eyes held hers.

'What? What would he have wanted for his son?'

'That he should be happy. That he should follow his star.'

CHAPTER THIRTY-FIVE

KARIL SEES HIS WAY

'Are you feeling all right, Karil?' asked the Countess Frederica nervously.

Karil looked up from his plate of lumpy breakfast porridge.

'Yes, thank you. I'm absolutely all right. I'm fine.'

The Scold frowned. That was what was worrying her. Karil looked different; he had not smiled like that since before his father's death. She was pleased of course, but it was . . . strange.

'Your cough seems better,' said Aunt Millicent, the kindest of the aunts.

Karil nodded and agreed that his cough was better, and the two women exchanged puzzled glances.

For really it was extraordinary that a bad cough should

324

almost disappear in twenty-four hours, and it wasn't just unlikely but impossible that Karil, in that short time, could have got fatter – yet the boy's face had completely lost its pinched and undernourished look.

Yet nothing, surely, had changed. Karil had not been there the day before when Carlotta had stamped out of the room and thrown over the easel of the painter who had treated her so rudely. By the time the Scold returned from the park Karil was in his room, and since then his routine had been as usual. Yet something was making her uneasy and she went on peering at him throughout the meal.

But nothing could touch Karil. He was in a different universe since he had talked to Clemmy. He could have leaped into the air and stayed there, or climbed the church steeple outside his window without a backward look. It seemed to him that the waterbirds in the park no longer screeched, they sang; the grass was greener and the sky a brighter blue. Because every moment there was a voice inside him saying, 'Your friends have remembered you.'

The first day and the second after Clemmy's visit, Karil was too happy to consider any plan of action, but on the third day he set his mind to finding out what had happened to the letters he had written to Delderton and those his friends had written to him.

Somebody had deliberately destroyed them – but who?

The duke himself? Would he have acted in secret? Or the Scold? No, she was strict but not deceitful like that. Surely they would just have told him that letters were forbidden? Karil was in constant trouble for talking to the servants but it was the servants who could help him – and he waited till he could get George alone as it was George who brought up the silver salver with the letters. At last he managed to speak to him as he refilled the decanters on the sideboard in the dining room.

'George, I've been wondering about the letters that come here. I've been expecting to hear from some friends.'

George was surprised. 'You've had a pile of letters, Your Highness. More than anyone. They came thick and fast at the beginning – wouldn't they be the ones you mean?'

Karil stared at him. 'They may have come to the house, but they never came to me.'

George shook his head. 'The little baroness always asked for them as soon as they came in. She said you were in a hurry and she'd take them up to you. I'm not allowed in the drawing room till the supper's been cleared, but she said you couldn't wait.'

So it was as easy as that.

'And what about the letters that go out of here? The ones we put in the hall,' asked Karil.

'They go out with one of the men at nine o'clock to the post office – punctual as anything.'

'But they're in the hall overnight?'

George nodded. 'Have been ever since I came.'

'I see. Thank you. Don't say I've been asking, will you?'

'No, Your Highness. I won't say a thing.'

For a few minutes after George left, Karil was overcome by a murderous rage. He wanted to put his hands round Carlotta's throat and squeeze till she fell to the ground. But killing Carlotta wouldn't really help in the long run. The letters were gone.

Or were they?

He was pushing open the door of her room before he was aware of what he was doing. Carlotta slept in a small room next door to her parents. It had been a dressing room and there were two huge mirrors on the wall and a third mirror on the table beside her bed, so that Karil saw her reflected threefold as she fixed a brooch on to the collar of her dress.

'Oh Karil,' she said, turning round and simpering a little, for her cousin had never before visited her in her bedroom, 'you can help me choose which—' and broke off, because Karil had grabbed hold of her, turning her away from the mirror, and was digging his fingers viciously into her shoulders.

'Where are the letters?' he demanded. 'Where are the letters from my friends that you stole?'

'You're hurting me,' she whined. 'I don't know what you mean.'

'Yes, you do. And if you don't tell me what you've done with them, I really will hurt you. I'll hurt you as you've never been hurt before.'

'Ow! Stop it. You've gone mad.'

'And I'll go madder. Where – are – the letters?' he said slowly through clenched teeth.

'I don't know . . . I've thrown them away. I did it for your sake.'

But Karil had seen her eyes swivel to the bureau beside her bed.

'Get them,' he ordered.

She crossed the room, crying noisily now, and he watched as she unlocked the bureau.

'I can't find—' she began, and whimpered as Karil

came up behind her and grabbed her arm. 'Don't! Let me go.'

She opened another drawer and brought out a thick bundle of letters addressed to him. He saw at once that they had been opened.

'You won't tell?' she said, sniffing.

Karil didn't answer. As soon as he had the letters in his hand, Carlotta had ceased to exist.

Back in his room he pulled a table across the door and began to read.

There were close on fifty letters. There were letters from Barney, telling him about the tree frog he had bought for him, and letters from Borro about the farm. Tod had written, and Julia, and even Kit, who was no letter writer, all looking forward to what they would do when Karil came. There was a letter from Matteo – brief but very heartening.

And there were letters from Tally – almost more than he could count. At first they were excited, hopeful, telling him about the play, about an otter cub which had become separated from his mother and they had to take back, and about Armelle who was trying to put them in touch with their internal organs – but always looking forward to when he came. Not 'if' he came. Only and always 'when'.

The letters went on through the summer holidays, describing the aunts and Kenny, who was trying to take over the vegetable round with Primrose because his father had become an air-raid warden – but the letters were shorter now, and he could sense her hurt as she asked why he didn't write back. Then a last letter written in the autumn term – a letter that did its best to be funny about the new gardener who seemed to be about ten years old.

And then no more letters as she gave up hope.

When he had finished, Karil went over to the window and stood looking out. All the uncertainties of the last weeks had gone; he felt very calm and very resolute. It was as though his father's strength had flowed into him – and he knew exactly what he would do.

Carlotta and the uncles were already at breakfast when Karil came into the dining room next morning. The uncles raised their behinds but only very slightly, and then – for some reason – raised them a little more because there was something different about Karil today.

But it was his cousin whom Karil addressed first. Carlotta looked pale and had been crying and she rubbed her shoulder from time to time to show that she was in pain.

'I'd like to speak to you privately,' he said to her. 'Will you come to the schoolroom when you've finished?' And to Uncle Dmitri: 'You will excuse me if I'm a little late.'

The schoolroom was at the top of the house – unheated and dismal. Karil had kept Carlotta waiting and the glance she gave him was full of fear and apprehension, but his first words caused her to break out in smiles of relief and even triumph.

'Carlotta, I've come to apologize. I treated you shamefully yesterday. Of course stealing is very wicked and very wrong – when I'm on the throne I shall make sure that theft is dealt with most severely – so it's not surprising that I lost my temper. After all, my great-great-grandfather was known as Karil the Cruel.'

'Was he? Was he really?' Carlotta was fluttering her eyelashes. 'I didn't know that. How . . . exciting. What did he do?'

'Oh, impaled the heads of his enemies on spikes outside the palace gates. That kind of thing,' said Karil, who had just invented this particular ancestor. 'I'll show you when we get back to Bergania.'

'We?' said Carlotta, licking her lips. 'Am I going back with you?' But she was a little suspicious. Karil had always refused to discuss his return and turned aside her offers of help.

But her cousin was coming to the point. 'You see, Carlotta, I was very angry when you took my letters, but now that I've read them I'm really very grateful to you because my eyes have been opened.'

'Have they?' Carlotta was breathing heavily, hanging on his every word.

'Yes, they have. I can't understand now how I allowed these people to be so familiar and take such liberties with me. Calling me by my Christian name, using all sorts of unsuitable phrases, thinking that I would like to come to their ridiculous school. Reading all the letters together like that made me realize how deluded I had been.'

'Countess Frederica did say she thought you were not yourself on the journey to England.'

'The countess was quite right. I see now that I was so shocked by my father's death that I had lost all judgement.' Karil shook his head solemnly from side to side. 'I don't mind telling you, Carlotta, that I have had a narrow escape. Of course, I blame myself – I must have allowed them to forget my position – but I assure you it won't

330

happen again. From now on I am going to prepare myself for my royal duties and let nothing stand in my way. And I rely on you, Carlotta, to help me.'

'Oh, I will, Karil. I will!' Carlotta's face was flushed with excitement. 'I have some really good ideas about how to decorate the palace when we get back – you know how artistic I am.'

'I shall be very interested to hear about them. Perhaps when we go for our walk in the park we can discuss this further. Be sure to be careful and button your coat up well – it's turning very chilly. That little muff of yours may not be warm enough.'

To the uncles Karil did not go into details about his conversion, but they could not fail to notice that Karil was now a different boy.

'I wonder if you could help me to design a better crest for the House of Bergania,' he asked his Uncle Dmitri. 'Our motto is too . . . well, it isn't strong enough. "The Truth Shall Set Thee Free" doesn't sound very royal, does it? A perfectly ordinary person could have a motto like that. Could we look through your book?'

'Yes, indeed, indeed,' said Uncle Dmitri happily. 'I will think about this – I have some very strong motifs. Mailed fists, of course, and dragons rampant.'

'And something metallic – crossed pikes perhaps. Or axes? Would that be possible?'

'Everything is possible for people like us,' said Uncle Dmitri proudly.

His other uncles too noticed with relief the change in Karil.

'I think I would like to learn a really martial piece of

music for my return to Bergania. Something that makes my subjects realize that I have come back not just as a figurehead but to take the reins of state into my hands. I don't know what key it should be in, but I feel there would be a lot of tubas and trombones. And a separate piece for Carlotta – a kind of theme tune for her when she alights from her carriage. I think she might have her own anthem.'

'Ah yes, dear Carlotta,' said her father. 'I was not sure if . . .'

'Yes, yes, I know. I'm ashamed to say that I was quite confused when I first came . . . my fathers' death . . .' he paused, and Uncle Franz Heinrich patted his shoulder.

'Of course, my boy. I quite understand; it takes time after such a blow to find one's true path again.'

Don Alfonso too was very sympathetic when Karil explained his change of heart – and produced sketches for a uniform which he thought might be suitable for Karil's household guards and one for Karil himself to wear on state occasions.

'You said you did not like plumes, I think?' he enquired, but Karil said he now realized that plumes were necessary to add to a monarch's dignity – and Alfonso went off happily with his sketch pad to see what he could do.

After a few days the Scold came to Karil and told him how pleased she was to notice the change in him.

'The way you helped Carlotta when we were getting ready to go for our walk and made sure she had her gloves . . . Sometimes I have felt that you would never come to your senses and see where your destiny lies, but now at last I feel I shall have my reward for all the work I have done.'

Gradually, as Christmas approached, Karil's position in the household changed. The uncles did not only lift their behinds when he came into the dining room, they stood up for him. The servants no longer dared to smile at him, and the governesses curtseyed as he passed. Karil had become more than dignified, he had become kingly.

But it was Pom-Pom who set the seal on Karil's new status. His ancestors had always known which of the Great Khan's companions were worthy of their attentions. There came an evening when Karil was reading aloud from the *Almanach de Gotha*, that historic volume which gives the titles and descendants of all the royal houses of Europe. The fire had gone out, the uncles and their wives sat dozing in the cold, when Pom-Pom rose from the hearthrug, stretched and looked about him. Then slowly he wheezed his way across the room, stood for a moment deep in thought – and flopped down on to the frozen feet of the Prince of Bergania.

CHAPTER THIRTY-SIX

CHRISTMAS

The staff had been worried about Tally being sad – but Tally *not* being sad was almost worse.

As soon as Clemmy returned from Rottingdene House Matteo called her into his room and told her what Clemmy had discovered there.

'So you see how far he was from forgetting you.'

Tally stared at him. Her face crumpled up and for a moment it looked as though she was going to cry. 'Really?' she said. 'You're not making it up?'

'I'm not making it up,' said Matteo, and he asked Clemmy to come and describe her visit to Rottingdene House.

'So we have to bring him here at once,' said Tally when she heard what Clemmy had to say.

This was what Matteo had been afraid of.

'Look, Tally, if you do anything rash you could get Karil into serious trouble.'

And later in the day he called in all the children who had been to Bergania and told them the same thing.

He might have spared his breath. Tally was transformed. The worms of Delderton looked in vain for new houses and the book of Important Sayings stayed closed, as she surged through the school getting ready for her friend.

Daley was sitting at his desk, sighing over the file labelled 'Evacuation'. He had got as far as writing letters to all the parents asking them whether they would send their children to America with the school. They were piled up on top of his filing cabinet, ready to go to the post.

A knock on the door made him close the file and call, 'Come in.'

Tally entered and the headmaster smiled; the change in the girl since Clemmy had returned from London was amazing.

'Can I speak to you?'

'Of course.'

Tally came up to his desk. 'It's about Karil.'

Daley, who had heard all about the prince from Matteo, said, 'What about Karil?'

'You have to give him a scholarship. Please. He has to come here. He can't stay in that awful place.'

'Perhaps you'd better sit down,' said the Head. And then: 'Scholarships don't grow on trees, you know. I would have to consult the Board.'

'You would give him a scholarship if he was a refugee from Poland or from Spain and he'd been bombed. Well, he is a refugee – just as much as them.'

The headmaster was silent, wondering just how much to tell her.

'When you first came back from Bergania,' he said presently, 'Matteo consulted me about the prince. I explained that I could give him a scholarship but only if he came here with the consent of his guardian. I could not shelter the boy as a runaway. And it seems that this consent will not be given.'

'It has to be given. It has to,' said Tally. 'It's not fair to keep him there like a prisoner. It's a dictatorship like Hitler and we're all fighting that. That's what Delderton is supposed to be about, fighting injustice.'

'Yes,' agreed Daley,' that is what the school is about, certainly – among other things.'

But he felt very tired.

'I told him what it was like here,' Tally went on. 'That it's a place where you can find out who you are. I told him about the river and about Clemmy moving the snails and Matteo finding the otter cub. And about the play – it's going to be *good* . . . and oh, everything. And it's wrong not to let him come. It's simply *wrong*.'

When she had gone Daley sat for a while, looking out at the courtyard while Tally's words went on sounding in his head.

I told him it was a place where you can find out who you are, she had said – and it was as though she had given him back the vision he had had when he first came to Delderton. He had spent ten years making a place where

336

children could be themselves. And suddenly he found that he had come to a decision, and he carried the letters to the parents over to the waste-paper basket and tipped them in.

He and his children would stay.

It was getting too cold to meet on the steps of the pet hut so the children sat inside on upturned wooden boxes while they discussed Karil's future. It made life difficult for Augusta, who had to wear a gauze face mask, but she was used to being uncomfortable.

'Someone should blow up the duke,' said Tod, who had reverted to anarchism again.

But Julia, who was sensible about everything except her mother, said that she saw what Daley meant.

'A school can't just kidnap a pupil,' she said, and Barney, who was convinced that the tree frog was very intelligent and was trying to train it to walk up and down its ladder, said he thought that Karil might have to arrange his own escape.

Tally, however, was deaf to common sense.

'People said we couldn't get to Bergania with the Flurry Dance but we did, and it looked as though we couldn't get Karil away from those thugs but we did. So we can do this if we have to. It's *meant* that Karil should be here. I knew it straight away.'

In the staffroom Magda, who had grown very fond of the prince on the journey, wondered about his Uncle Fritz, the Minister of Culture. 'Isn't an uncle an important relative too?' she asked Matteo. 'Perhaps he could do something.'

'I've been trying to get in touch with him – and von Arkel too. They got out of Bergania, but no one knows where they are now. And I don't know how long I'll be here – I've had another letter from the War Office and things are moving.'

But Tally listened to nobody who told her that Karil might not come. If she could, she would have told the badgers and the foxes that the prince was on his way. And so, with less than three weeks to go till the Christmas holidays, she concentrated on the play.

To everyone's surprise Tally did not want to act – she wanted to help with the lighting and the production, but she had no desire to take a part, which Julia thought was a bit much 'when you do nothing but nag me'.

But Tally said that was different. 'Karil may want to act though. He could be the King of the Underworld perhaps.'

'He won't want to be the king of anything, not even Hades,' said Borro. 'I'll bet my last sixpence on that.'

'And anyway, he may not be any good,' said Verity.

But the next thing was to get word to Karil – and now Tally wrote a letter to Kenny, who had taken over his father's vegetable round and was driving Primrose through the London streets.

Kenny was a good friend; he had never failed her yet.

It was a particularly cold winter, the winter of 1939. Coming back for the Christmas holidays, Tally found the aunts bundled into cardigans, looking like koala bears and huddled over the oil stove in the kitchen. In her father's surgery a single bar of the electric fire stopped the patients from turning blue before they got to the doctor. Aunt Hester had to bandage the pipes in the bathroom to stop them freezing – but Tally and Maybelle and Kenny went skating on the frozen pond.

The Russians had invaded Finland, where the temperature was minus forty degrees and the soldiers fought on skis. A German patriot had thrown a bomb at Hitler but it missed him, which was a shame. Skirmishes on the Western Front suggested that the war was beginning to gather pace.

All the same, Christmas was lovely – it always was in the doctor's house. Tally went with Kenny on his rounds with Primrose, delivering holly and mistletoe to his customers, and came back with armfuls of greenery with which to decorate the rooms. Aunt May cooked the turkey which the butcher had saved for them, though meat was getting scarce. The lady with the German sausage dog sent a Christmas tree from her brother's market garden, and Dr Hamilton's patients trooped in with strange presents they had made for him. Though the aunts had been worried that the king's stammer would trouble him, with the war on his mind, he got through his speech on Christmas Day with hardly a stutter, and in the evening they went to hear the *Messiah* at the Albert Hall.

Tally did her best not to spend time with Roderick and Margaret during the holidays, but a week before the Delderton term began again, her Aunt Virgina rang up to say how much her children were longing to see their cousin, and Tally was invited for tea.

This usually meant that Roderick and Margaret

wanted to show off something that they had bought, or brag about something they had done, and this time was no exception. Though they had been equipped with brand-new uniforms the last time Tally had seen them, a great deal of shopping had been done since then. Margaret had two new Sunday dresses and a new dressing gown with a St Barbara's crest on the pocket. What's more, the girls of St Barbara's did not carry their gas masks to school in cardboard boxes like common children, but had special cases in the school colours of blue and green.

'And I'm getting kid skating boots – they're being sent from Harrods,' said Margaret. 'It's that very soft leather and it's incredibly expensive. Some of the girls just have ordinary leather ones, but Mummy wanted me to have the best because my ankles are so sensitive.'

Roderick's bed was again piled high with clothes striped in ferocious red and yellow. It had been necessary to replace his blazer and his cap, and he had an entire new kit for rugger on which he had left the price tags so that Tally could see them.

'Pretty steep, aren't they?' he said proudly.

But what he particularly wanted to boast about was the kind of pupils that were coming to Foxingham. Not only was the Prince of Transjordania still there but his younger brother was going to join him, and so was a great-nephew of the Kaiser who was third in the line of succession to the Prussian throne should it ever be restored.

'I've made good friends with Transjordania,' said Roderick carelessly. 'He's not really stuck up at all, not when you get to know him. Of course he doesn't bother with everybody, but I know how to treat him.'

If it wasn't for the amazingly good tea which her Aunt Virginia served, Tally would have found the afternoon almost impossible to get through. Virginia was the sort of person who always seemed to be able to get hold of sugar and chocolate and all the other things that were in short supply. She had come back from Torquay when the expected bombs did not fall on London, but she had kept her flat down there so that if air raids did start she would be able to get away at once.

'It's all so terribly trying,' she said wearily. 'Now the maid wants to go and join the ATS. I don't know how I'm supposed to get through all the work myself. But there it is – servants never know when they're well off.'

'I tell you, it's no good,' said Kenny, sitting on an upturned crate in the storeroom behind his father's shop. 'It's a fortress, that place. I took the cart round like you asked me to, but they didn't want any vegetables and they just shut the door in my face. I had some mistletoe and chestnuts for roasting and all sorts of stuff, but they said no one celebrated Christmas there and I can believe it. You'll never get a message through to Karil like that. Just give it up, Tally.'

But giving up on things was not one of Tally's talents. 'Couldn't we try once more? Please. If you take me there I might get an idea. I just want to let him know that it's all right about the scholarship and he can come. There must be some way I can get a note to him.'

Kenny shrugged. 'I'll take you if you like, but not with

the cart. There's nowhere to leave Primrose – it's all posh streets with snooty people.'

So the following Saturday they took the Underground to Trafalgar Square and walked down the Mall to Rottingdene House.

The huge grey building with its spiked railings was a grim sight. They walked all round it, but there was no side door other than the one that Kenny had tried; it was the most sealed-up and unapproachable place Tally had ever seen.

But when they came round to the front of the house, they found a small group of people waiting on the pavement.

'It's about now they come out,' said a woman in a purple headscarf.

'Who?' said another bystander. 'Who is it comes out?'

The woman wasn't sure, but she thought it was royalty. 'My sister saw them last week; she said they were ever so friendly.'

Tally waited, keeping out of sight behind Kenny and stamping her feet on the pavement to try to keep the blood flowing. It seemed most unlikely that anyone would come out of those forbidding iron gates, but after half an hour the sentry in the box stood to attention, the front door with its heraldic crest was thrown open and three people emerged.

She saw Karil first; he was exactly the same in spite of the cap pulled over his ears against the cold. Behind him came the Scold, black as ever in a fur coat the colour of ink . . . and between Karil and the Scold came Carlotta.

Tally recognized her at once. She wasn't wearing a

white dress – or if she was, it was hidden under her velvet-collared coat – and she wasn't holding flowers. But her long blonde ringlets, her simpering smile, were exactly as they had been when she peered out of the window of the Daimler on the quayside at Dover.

It was Karil though who held Tally's gaze. He had put his arm round Carlotta's shoulders in a chivalrous and protective way, as though he was sheltering her not just from the cold but from anything bad that life might throw at her, and now he adjusted her scarf so that it covered her throat more securely and the Scold, looking down, nodded in a pleased way.

Then a footman came out of the back of the building and took his position behind them and they set off slowly towards the gate. The sentry saluted, the gate swung open and the bystanders stood aside to let the important people through.

'Long live Your Highness,' cried the lady in the purple headscarf, and Karil smiled and lifted his arm once, and twice, and three times, in that gracious wave that princes learn from infancy. Then he nodded to the footman, giving the signal that they were ready to set off, gave his arm to Carlotta, and they moved away.

Karil had not seen her and Tally stood stock-still in the icy cold. There was no escaping what she had seen. If ever there was a boy who was doing what he was best at, leading the life he was born to, it was Karil.

'Come on,' said Kenny.

And she tore up the note she had written and followed him.

Chapter Thirty-seven

The Future King

Although Karil had long ago given up expecting anything good to happen in his grandfather's house, even
he was surprised by the sheer awfulness of the Rottingdene Christmas. There was no tree, no candlelight, no
exchange of gifts, no music. The duke took morning
prayers, the cook sent up two underdone chickens – and
that was that.

Still, it meant that he was not expected to find a gift for
Carlotta. Karil was used to hard work, but being nice to
Carlotta was one of the most gruelling tasks he had ever
undertaken. Her treachery, her vanity, her lies seemed to
grow rather than lessen with each day that passed, and yet
somehow he managed to act the part of a devoted cousin
and a prince who wished her to share his life.

And still he did not know yet whether his plan was going to work. His uncles now treated him with respect, the servants scuttled past him and the governesses curtsied when he came into the room.

But it was the duke that mattered, and two days after what passed for Christmas his grandfather sent for him.

'I have to tell you, my boy,' he said, 'that I have been most pleasantly surprised by your behaviour in the last few weeks. I understand from Carlotta that you have seen the error of your ways.'

'Oh, I have, sir, I have,' said Karil fervently. 'I can't believe now how foolish I have been. And how ungrateful, when you have given me a home and a chance to fulfil my destiny. From now on I shall devote all my waking hours to preparing for kingship. I want to learn to be a proper ruler, not one of those weak kings who can't make up his mind and has to keep consulting his ministers. A king should be an absolute ruler and his subjects should obey him without a moment's hesitation.'

'Quite so. Quite right. I must say, I thought you would never see where your duty lay. What brought you to your senses?'

Karil was ready for this.

'I had a dream, sir. A dream of my future in the palace at Bergania. I was being crowned in ermine and at my side was . . . Carlotta.' Here Karil nearly forgot his script, because even mentioning Carlotta's name made his gorge rise. But he gathered himself together. 'It made me realize how fortunate I am to be here – and how lucky I am to have someone who, in good time, will share my life.'

The duke nodded, thinking of the double line of

Rottingdene blood that would flow into the restored kingdom of Bergania.

'Yes, indeed. She will make an excellent queen. There
are people who think that twelve is too young to decide
about one's future bride, but that's just poppycock. Where
duty is concerned, one can never begin too young.'

'Indeed, sir, indeed,' said Karil, and stood waiting with
his head humbly bowed. Was it going to work or had this
whole charade been in vain?

The duke cleared his throat. He harrumphed and considered. Then he said, 'Well, well, we all make mistakes. I
think it's time I called off the watchdogs. I'll get the whistles back and tell the servants you no longer need to be
followed.'

'And my room at night, sir? The locked door? Of
course I know I deserved it, but it is a little humiliating.'

The duke hesitated, and Karil felt his heart hammering
in his chest. Everything depended on this one thing.

Then: 'Very well,' said the duke. 'I'll tell the servants
it's no longer necessary.'

Left alone, Karil flopped down on his bed and punched
the pillows in triumph. Stage one was completed! Once he
was no longer watched and could get out of his room at
night he could plan the next part of his escape. For from
the moment he had read the letters Carlotta had stolen,
he had had only one idea – to escape from this house of
snobbery and deceit and arrogance and join his friends.

His troubles were far from over, but he would let nothing dismay him. Among the many unreadable books in the
duke's library were some that were not unreadable at all:

the stories of Oliver Twist and David Copperfield and Nicholas Nickleby by Charles Dickens. All these boys had run away from cruel employers with almost nothing in their pockets, and all of them had reached safety. One of the obstacles was simply getting out of the house. The back door was bolted and barred at night and the keys kept by whichever footman was on duty. To ask a servant to help him would be to risk getting him into trouble, but luck was on Karil's side. The housemaid George loved so hopelessly left to work in a munitions factory, and soon afterwards George announced that he too was leaving, going to join the Ambulance Corps.

If he was going anyway, thought Karil, perhaps he could be persuaded to leave the back door unlocked the night before he left.

Everything Karil did now had only one aim: to help him get away. He had taught himself the route to Delderton; it was nearly three hundred miles, but anything was possible when one was desperate. It was no good arriving when the school was empty, but as soon as the Christmas holidays were over he would make a break for it, and he began to assemble things he would need to disguise himself. He found some of the Princess Natalia's hair dye in a bathroom, and a pair of wire spectacles that could be made to stay on his nose – and when the Countess Frederica came with his fruit juice and rusks he thanked her nicely but he did not eat the rusks; he hid them in a shoebox in his cupboard. They had infuriated him ever since he stopped teething but now they had their uses. Rusks do not go mouldy and he could chew them on the journey.

This was the stage he had reached in his preparations when the duke sent for him again.

If he expected that his grandfather had seen through his deception, Karil's fears were laid to rest as soon as he entered the room. The old tyrant looked as affable as he was able, and sitting near him were the three uncles. They too looked friendly and relaxed, and even before the duke began to speak Karil was ready to receive good news.

And it was good news! It was incredible, wonderful and amazing news!

'I have to say, Karil, that up till now I have been utterly opposed to the idea of sending you away to be educated,' the duke began. 'Your behaviour was such that I didn't think you could be allowed to leave this house. But in the last weeks you have changed so completely that I think you may be trusted to conduct yourself properly even when you are not under my roof, so I have decided to send you to boarding school.'

He stopped to clear his throat and the uncles nodded and beamed. If Karil went away they would no longer have to give him lessons, or lift their behinds from their chairs when he came into the dining room. Only the monkey, who did not know what was going on, continued to look sad.

'As you know,' the duke went on, 'many of the world's rulers were educated at one or other of Britain's famous schools – but one of the obstacles has been money. These schools are exceedingly expensive and the cost of supporting all the people in my household is crippling. Not to mention the burden of income tax. The amount of tax

I am forced to pay by those scoundrels in Whitehall is outrageous.' The duke's face became crimson as it always did when he spoke about income tax, but he pulled himself together. 'However, Karil,' he went on, 'I have just received the most gratifying news. One of the best schools in the country has offered you a scholarship. The headmaster has just written to me.'

Karil stood stock-still. He had heard the word 'headmaster' and the word 'scholarship' and immediately he remembered Tally's words on the train.

I've got a scholarship, she had said, *so why not you?*

After that the duke's words surged over his head unheeded. Delderton had offered him a scholarship, and the duke had agreed to let him go! He'd been wrong to think nobody understood him or cared about him; underneath all his bad temper the old man wanted to do his best, and Karil felt ashamed for having misjudged him.

The duke was still talking about the school.

'Of course, I'm not surprised that they want you – to have a member of a ruling house on their books can bring them nothing but glory. But you may be sure that they understand how to deal with royalty; the place has been a cradle for princes for generations. You will be treated with all the respect due to your rank but with the iron discipline that will help you fulfil your purpose in life. Countess Frederica will take you tomorrow to be fitted for your uniform. Harrods sets aside a special changing room for pupils like you.'

Only now did Karil come down to earth.

'Uniform? But they don't have uniform. They wear what they like.'

The duke stared at him, frowning. 'Don't be foolish, boy. Of course they have uniform. Have you ever heard of a school which doesn't?'

Karil took a deep breath, steeling himself. Then he said, 'What is the name of the school, Grandfather? The one I'm going to.'

The duke told him.

Chapter Thirty-eight

The Stripy Boys

It was Magda who was in charge of the school train so the children were being very careful, making sure she had all their names ticked off and that there wasn't too much swirling about. They knew that she had been having real difficulties in the holidays with Schopenhauer and the washerwoman whom he had (or had not) thrown down the stairs, and they would not have stooped to play the kind of tricks they might have played on David Prosser.

So far she had not lost a single child – and the children in her own house were settled in their carriage even though there was another ten minutes before the train was due to go. Paddington Station was in its usual bustle: soldiers coming home on leave crossing with soldiers off to their new postings; evacuees who should have been in the country returning home – and parties of schoolchildren in charge of their teachers marching towards their trains.

And now, in spite of all their care, Magda was in trouble.

'There's one missing,' she said, poking her head round the door and looking anguished. 'A new boy called . . .' she peered anxiously at her list, 'called Stephen Bellingham. If you see him, let me know.'

They promised, and went on talking of their plans for the term. Tally was in the far corner by the window talking to Julia, who had not troubled to buy *The Picturegoer* because her mother never appeared now in film magazines. Kit, to everyone's surprise, was not crying and saying he wanted to go home.

More children got on to the train. Doors slammed. Verity took her place by the window bar in the corridor so that she could be seen in her new, suitably tattered skirt.

Seven minutes until the train was due to go . . .

'Here, you have the window seat,' said the boy who had accompanied Karil into the carriage. 'My name's Hamilton. Roderick Hamilton. If I can do anything to help you, I'll be very pleased.'

He looked at Karil with eager admiration mixed with curiosity. The same look was on the faces of the other boys in the compartment, and Karil realized that once again he was back to being a freak, a person set aside by his birth, to be fawned on to his face and sneered at behind his back. One boy handed him a bag of crisps, another offered to put his bag up in the luggage rack. All stared at him as though he was somebody out of a zoo.

'There's someone you'll like,' the boy called Hamilton went on. 'The Prince of Transjordania. He's in the next carriage – I can fetch him for you; I'm good friends with him.'

'No, it's all right, thank you. Don't bother him,' said Karil, who needed the Prince of Transjordania like he needed a hole in the head.

'Oh, it wouldn't be a bother – not for you.'

Karil was silent. It was as bad as he had feared – or worse. These boys had been brought up to be snobbish and servile and nothing he could do would break through the barrier.

How was it going to end? How would he ever get away? Escaping from Foxingham would be harder even than getting away from his grandfather's house. Already, as the boys were marched on to the platform by their teachers, he saw that it was a place where ruthless discipline prevailed. And the ridiculous uniform with its ferocious red-and-yellow stripes would make him a sitting target for his pursuers.

He turned his head to look out of the window – and found himself gazing straight into Tally's eyes.

'What is it?' asked Julia. 'What's the matter?'

Tally had given a little gasp and was staring transfixed at the railway carriage beside their own.

'It's Karil,' she said.

Julia followed her gaze and, as they looked, Karil's arm went up in greeting. It was the same gesture he had made when he was with Carlotta at Rottingdene House, or driving through the streets at home. The only greeting that he knew. A royal wave.

Tally turned her head away. 'That does it,' she said. 'He's going to Foxingham to be a prince.'

It wasn't till she finally gave up hope that Tally realized how much she minded. Fortunately Julia had a handkerchief – and the others hadn't seen. When she looked up again, Karil had gone.

'The train opposite,' said Karil, completely bewildered. 'Where does it go?'

'Oh, that's another school train,' said Roderick. 'It goes to a really weird place called Delderton. We could pull down the blind if you like, so that they can't see us.'

Karil shook his head. 'It's all right, thank you.'

'Would you like to borrow my comic?' said another boy. 'I'd be very pleased.'

Karil stared at him blankly. Then he clutched his stomach.

'Excuse me . . .' he said. 'I have to go.'

The others made way for him. 'It's at the end of the corridor,' they said, realizing that a prince would not be able to utter the word toilet – and opened the door for Karil.

As soon as he was out of their sight Karil began to run. Then he jumped down on to the platform, and as he did so he tore off his blazer and his cap and threw them on the ground. The train was wreathed in clouds of steam – no one seemed to have noticed him. He ran for dear life, ran and ran – and now he unwound his scarf and pulled his jersey over his head, and still he ran. He had reached the barrier, which was unmanned now that the train was ready to leave, and cut across to Platform 1 where the Delderton train still waited. Not once did he look behind him; he could not afford to lose a second – but he managed to pass his hand through his hair so that it looked dishevelled and unkempt. Anyone seeing him run now would see a boy in dark trousers and a white shirt who could belong anywhere.

He was on the right platform now, and the Delderton train still stood there, though the doors were being slammed and the guard had his flag at the ready. He was raising his whistle to his lips just as Karil managed to wrench a door open and leap on to the train – and the guard cursed him. Those unruly Delderton savages were always late.

The train began to move as Karil made his way along the corridor, looking for the right compartment. Then he found it – and banged on the window, and as Barney pulled back the door he almost fell into the carriage.

No one spoke at first. Then Kit said, 'You've still got your tie. It won't go down the hole – I tried flushing mine. You'd better give it to Tally; she kept mine for me.'

As Karil took off his tie and handed it to her, the door slid open again and Magda stood there with her clipboard and her list.

She peered short-sightedly at the children.

'Oh, good, you've found the new boy,' she said. 'I'm pleased to see you, Stephen. I'll just tick off your name.'

But on the way out she turned her head and winked.

Chapter Thirty-nine

Arcadia

Even before he opened his eyes Karil knew that he was happy. He had never before trusted the day, but now he sat up and stretched and looked at his little room with its small desk and the single chair and the view out on to the courtyard and the cedar tree, and though he never forgot the death of his father he knew that he was in the one place he wanted to be, and with exactly the people that he cared for.

The door opened a crack and Tally put her head round it.

'Hurry up – we're going over to breakfast. I'm just going to wake Barney.'

Karil had been fortunate. Stephen Bellingham had not ended up in Wales like Augusta, but he had chickenpox and would be late coming to school, so Karil had been given his room, two doors down from Tally and Julia.

Everything was right for Karil. Armelle was at her most extraordinary this term, asking the children to be bursting seeds about to germinate or the gaping mouths of roots as they thirsted for water, but Karil went along with her cheerfully. He would have been the gaping mouth of a cheese grater if she had asked him to, surrounded as he was by his friends.

He thought dipping sheep's wool into vats of strangely smelling dyes was splendid, and helping in the kitchen, especially when Clemmy was in charge, was the greatest fun – the warmth, the interesting smells and friendly clatter were delightful. Karil had been lonely all his life, but he was never lonely now.

Whatever lessons they did fired his imagination: in chemistry classes he wanted to be an inventor, in art he thought it would be wonderful to be a painter. When the professor asked him what instrument he would like to learn Karil wanted to say, 'All of them. The oboe and the clarinet and the fiddle and the double bass – every instrument there ever was.'

In the pet hut he was among old friends: the axolotl, the outsize rabbit . . . and the present that Barney had bought for him and that he had expected never to see.

'We didn't give him a name – we thought you should do it,' Barney said.

Karil did not have to look long at the strange creature, with its blown-out cheeks and moist pop eyes.

'Mortimer,' he said. 'No doubt about it – he's a Mortimer. That's my grandfather's name – he has those bulging eyes. But it's odd that something as nice as a tree frog can look like somebody as nasty as my grandfather.'

As soon as he found out how Karil had come to Delderton, Daley had asked Matteo to come and see him.

'I'll have to send the boy back,' he had said. 'I can't possibly be part of a deception like that. The duke must be informed and so must the headmaster of Foxingham.'

Matteo did not answer at once. He stood gazing out of the window with his back to his old friend. When he turned he looked as though the last minutes had aged him, and he spoke with more feeling in his voice than Daley could ever remember hearing before.

'I understand your position,' he said. 'No one could fail to do so. But I would ask you to wait. To do nothing for a short time. I would ask this as a last favour.'

Matteo was due to leave at the end of the month. His mission would be dangerous, Daley knew this.

'I have a plan,' Matteo went on. 'It may come to nothing, but if it worked it would clear you completely of responsibility. Give me three weeks – I won't ask for more than that. I have seen Karil happy for the first time, and I know that the king . . .' Matteo's voice broke, and Daley, knowing the guilt Matteo felt about Karil's father, did not interrupt. 'Probably it's no good,' he went on, 'and the duke will trace him very soon, but I won't be able to forgive myself if I haven't done my best. It's hard to explain the horror of the set-up at Rottingdene House.' His expression changed and he came to stand beside Daley. 'I'm bigger than you,' he told the headmaster. 'I can tell them that I threatened to knock you down or blackmail you if you didn't do as I asked!'

Daley smiled. 'Very well. You're in the wrong, as you know, and you're exposing me and the school to all sorts of risks. But . . . it isn't often you see a child so much in his element as that boy. I'll wait.'

Meanwhile *Persephone* had reached the stage of casting and rehearsals.

Kit, as they waited in the classroom for O'Hanrahan, was ready to be helpful.

'She's not called Percy Phone,' he explained to Karil. 'It's pronounced Per-Seff-On-Ee.'

Karil thanked him. No one snubbed Kit since the adventure in Zurich, but he knew the story well. He had read it with his professor of Greek in the ancient version handed down from Homer's time, and he especially liked the part where Zeus, the King of the Gods, took pity on the goddess Demeter's sorrow and sent a messenger to Hades to bring Persephone back.

But there was not an entirely happy ending. Like all the best stories, it had a twist at the end; for before she left the Underworld, Persephone's husband had forced her to eat five pomegranate seeds – and for each seed she had to return every year and spend a month back in Hades. And during these five months winter fell again on the land, until Persephone was reunited with her mother and spring and summer blessed the earth.

'It breaks down really well into scenes,' said Tally. 'There are all those maidens and things dancing with Persephone – Greek girls always have maidens – and then there's thunder and lightning and the rocks split asunder and out comes the King of the Underworld and carries her away.'

'Then there's Hades,' said Barney. 'There are lots of stories about what went on there: Sisyphus pushing a rock up a slope for ever and ever and it falling down just when he gets to the top, and Tantalus trying to get a drink of water from a spring that dries up just when he opens his mouth.'

Karil nodded. 'And everything very cold and grey and icy.'

But at this stage the most important thing was the casting of the parts.

'We thought you might like to be the King of the Underworld,' said Borro, looking at Karil out of the corner of his eye – and grinning when Karil exploded in just the way they had expected.

'Anyway, I'm not going to act. I might not be here by the time you do the play; they're going to catch up with me sooner or later. But anybody can come roaring out of rocks and carry people off. It's who will play the heroine that's important.'

There was silence while everyone looked at Julia; everyone except Verity, who looked at the floor.

'She can really act. I mean *really*,' said Barney.

'Yes, I know,' said Karil.

'How?' said Tally. 'How do you know?'

'When you were up on the hill fetching me and I was hiding with Matteo . . . I looked out . . . I couldn't hear what anyone was saying, but I saw Julia. She was standing there reciting and everyone was absolutely silent, looking at her. Even people who can't have understood a word . . . Because of the way she *was*.'

'It's called stage presence,' said O'Hanrahan, who had come in to join them.

Julia was bent over her desk, trying not to be there.

'I'm sorry . . . I can't,' she muttered.

No one tried to persuade her. They had been through this so often. And then, to his own surprise, Karil began to speak.

'At home, in Bergania, I heard a lot about duty. The Countess Frederica kept nagging me about it; it was my duty to salute properly and smile at little girls who curtsied to me and make small talk to the wives of ambassadors. Maybe it *was* my duty – I don't know; I thought it was pretty silly. But that doesn't mean that duty doesn't exist. My father knew about it. He knew about forcing himself on when he was tired and bored, or sitting on his horse in uncomfortable clothes, or listening to his ministers in meetings that went on and on. Giving everything he had to his people. Duty exists and it's real. It means sharing any gift or talent that you have with people who need it. It means not being afraid or selfish or tight – but open. And in my view,' said Karil, 'it's Julia's *duty* to be the heroine of this play.'

Then he fell back in his chair, aghast at what he had done. He had not been at Delderton for a week and here he was, lecturing and pontificating.

But now Julia had lifted her head and her voice carried very clearly, because that was one of the things she knew – how to make herself heard if she wanted to.

'All right,' said Julia. 'I'll do it.'

361

Everybody stopped dead and stared at her.

'You'll do it?' repeated Tally. 'Really? You'll be the heroine? You'll be Persephone?'

'I'll be the heroine,' said Julia, 'but I won't be Persephone. Persephone's not the heroine; she's just a pretty girl who gets carried off. Anyone can be her . . . Verity can.'

In the classroom one could have heard a pin drop.

'The heroine,' said Julia, 'the person who matters, is her mother. It's Demeter, who roams the earth looking for her daughter and never gives up. Not ever. Because loving her daughter, and finding her, matters more than anything in the world.'

Tally, who alone knew Julia's story, looked at her friend.

'And you'll be her?' she asked quietly.

Julia nodded. 'Yes, I'll be her.'

After that everything fell into place, and a few days later casting was complete and they moved into the hall to begin rehearsals. Ronald Peabody was to be the King of the Underworld.

'He's nasty enough,' Borro had agreed, but he also acted well.

And Verity got her wish and played Persephone. She took the part seriously, working out how to scream and struggle and wondering what to wear while doing it, and if her lines got fewer and fewer as Tally and Karil adjusted the script, she did not seem to notice it. Persephone was described in the old myth as having 'delicate ankles', and that was enough for Verity. And she could dance.

The rest of the casting went without a hitch. Borro was Hermes, the messenger chosen to bring Persephone back, and a tall senior whose voice had broken reliably played Zeus, King of the Gods.

And the scenes in Hades were easy. Being horrible or tortured or weird is always popular. Tod was Sisyphus, endlessly pushing his rock up a hill, Barney made an excellent Tantalus, never quite allowed to sip the water that reached to his mouth – and no one felt like refusing Kit when he asked if he could be the man whose liver was pecked out by an eagle, even though he belonged to a different myth.

As for Cerberus, the three-headed dog who guarded the gates of Hades, there was a stampede of juniors all wanting to be one of his heads. Since the heads did not speak and would be covered in masks it was difficult to choose, so they drew lots – but the good thing about Hades is that it is always full, and those children who were not picked to be a head could still gibber and wail and wobble across the stage.

Karil and Tally were joint stage managers and were incessantly busy. 'Bossy' was the word Verity used, and she had a point, but there was so much to remember.

O'Hanrahan directed, never raising his voice but holding the play completely under his hand. At the beginning Tally had been put in charge of the script; she was to gather up ideas and make notes, ready for the actual writing. So she had gone to the library, found a book called *Greek Myths for Schools* – and gone back, puzzled, to O'Hanrahan.

'It's not like you told it to us,' she said. 'It's sort of flat.

You must have made an awful lot up. All that about Persephone's delicate ankles, and Demeter tearing off her headband in grief . . .'

O'Hanrahan shook his head. 'No, I didn't make it up. The words are all there in the original Greek, just as they were nearly three thousand years ago.'

And he went to his bookcase and began to read. The musical words, serious but beautiful, went straight into Tally's soul. Understanding no word of the ancient language, she yet sensed the story's depth and resonance.

The next day she took *Greek Myths for Schools* back to the library – and they began to write their play.

Now, as rehearsals began, she was eagle-eyed, watching for missed lines – a fierce prompter protecting every syllable of the script.

As for Karil, he was everywhere, attending to the lighting, assembling props, checking the thunder sheets, experimenting with the sound of rain. To serve the play after years of being served, to be part of something and yet not singled out, was his greatest joy. He knew he was on borrowed time – any day now the duke would find out where he was, but meanwhile there was the present, there was this day – and Karil set himself to live in it.

Like all plays that take off, *Persephone* reached out into every activity in the school.

Clemmy knew all about the Greeks; she had posed for a dozen painters who had tried to show the beauty of the ancient world.

'You've got to realize that the Greeks really adored their flowers and their trees and their countryside. They absolutely worshipped them.'

She found pictures of the flowers that Persephone had been picking when she was carried away, precise botanical drawings full of detail and loving care, and she stood over the scene painters.

'Remember this was Arcadia, it was Paradise. Everything was flooded with light – that blue is far too muddy.'

Josie and the housekeeper, with a team of helpers, ran up the costumes, and the old professor left his ancient manuscripts long enough to be really helpful about the music.

'We want dreamy music for the beginning and scary music of course for Hades and a lament for when Demeter is roaming the earth, but at the end there has to be something glorious – a proper hymn praising the gods,' said Tally.

'Full of triumph,' said Karil.

'Oh, there does, does there?' growled the old man.

'Couldn't you compose one?' they asked him.

'No, I could not. If I could compose triumphant and glorious music, I wouldn't be here teaching a lot of hooligans.'

But he found a chorus from a Handel opera which made the hair stand up on the nape of one's neck – and he bullied the school choir into learning it.

As the weeks passed, O'Hanrahan began to look tired.

'You're working too hard,' Clemmy told him.

But she knew what was happening. It was possible that what they had here was not just a school play – it was a *play*. A number of things were coming together. The children acting in it had had a real experience: a king had died; a war was beginning.

And there was Julia. But about Julia's performance, nobody would speak.

Matteo had reported to the War Office and received his instructions. Now he walked down Piccadilly, turned into Old Bond Street and made his way towards Grosvenor Square. He passed Polish cavalry officers in their glamorous uniforms, come to join the Allies, sailors on leave from a British submarine, high-ranking American servicemen from the embassy nearby.

But he saw none of them. What he saw in his mind was a huddle of children, some tear-stained, who had got up at dawn to say goodbye.

Barney, whom he had turned into a biologist . . . Tally, whose problems seemed always to be about other people . . . Julia, whose mother he had mentally throttled many a time . . .

And Karil, Johannes's son . . .

If his plan misfired . . . if the people he was now seeking out refused to help him, or had not yet arrived, then Karil's future was bleak indeed.

In front of a tall narrow house, he stopped and rang the bell. The house, though in the fashionable area inhabited by embassies and diplomats, was shabby, and the servant who opened the door wore no uniform, only a leather apron. He had grey hair and a weather-beaten face and looked like a man who had spent his life out of doors.

Matteo spoke a few words and the man's face lit up.

'Yes,' he said, answering in the same language, 'they are here. Please come upstairs, Your Excellency.' And then: 'I remember your father.'

Matteo followed him up the uncarpeted stairs and into a room with a scrubbed wooden table and a few upright chairs. As he entered, the two men standing by the window turned. A man with long silver hair and light blue eyes; and an old man with a wise face and a full white beard, who came forward with both his hands stretched out.

'Welcome, Matteo, welcome!' he said in Berganian. 'As you see, we have reached safety.'

It was von Arkel, the faithful Prime Minister who had served the king for so many years, and with him was the king's Uncle Fritz, the Minister of Culture. The chief of the army was about to join them, they told Matteo, and together they meant to form a government-in-exile.

'We shall have to see what we can do,' said von Arkel. And then: 'You have news of the boy?'

CHAPTER FORTY

DRY ICE

The headmaster of Foxingham School put down the cane with which he had been beating a boy called Widdrington and went over to his desk.

Widdrington was a dreary little runt of a boy who seemed to have been made for punishment. Even before he came into the room he began to snivel and whimper, and already with the first whack on his bare bottom he was screaming the place down. It was quite difficult to stop after the regulation twelve thwacks – the temptation was to go on and draw blood, and there wouldn't have been any trouble if he had. Widdrington's parents were too grateful to the headmaster for accepting the boy at Foxingham. They were thoroughly vulgar, self-made people and desperately anxious to have their sons educated with the upper classes.

He should have been beating young Hohenlottern next, thought the Head. The boy had skived off the early-morning run, pretending to have a cold – but he was third in line of succession to the kingdom of Prussia if it was ever restored, and the headmaster preferred to deal with boys like that in other ways. Fortunately young Transjordania never gave any trouble. With his father ruling over one of the wealthiest countries in the Middle East, too much physical punishment might have been awkward.

Thinking about these two boys made the Head turn his thoughts to the Prince of Bergania. He had been happy to give the boy a scholarship; if the war went the right way young Karil would become king, there was no doubt about that, and Foxingham's reputation as a cradle for princes would be enhanced.

But how long was he going to wait for the duke to send his grandson? Karil had had an attack of homesickness and run back to his grandfather, that much seemed certain. The other boys had all described how the prince had rushed out of the train, and there was really no other explanation. Probably Karil was very attached to his grandfather, who was reported to be an upright and excellent man. So far it had seemed reasonable to say nothing to the duke and wait for the prince to come – one didn't want to expose the boy as a milksop – but the Head had his honour and dignity to consider.

He pressed the bell on his desk and his secretary, a grey-haired, sharp-nosed woman, entered the room.

'Nothing in the post from Rottingdene, is there?'

'No, sir, nothing at all. Matron was wondering how long she should keep his trunk – it's more than three weeks now. Should she send it back?'

The headmaster rose and went to the window. Outside, in the driving rain, the bottom form was doing PE. In their singlets and shorts they shivered with cold, and the headmaster was annoyed.

'Silly ass, that Johnston. He's not working them nearly hard enough. A couple of whacks on their legs and they'd soon warm up. I shall want to see him after the class.'

Then he turned his attention once more to the problem of the Prince of Bergania. The behaviour of the namby pampy PE teacher had soured his mood, and he found that his patience was exhausted.

'I'll write to the duke today. This nonsense has gone on long enough. Either he sends his grandson straight away or the scholarship is cancelled.'

The duke picked this letter off the silver salver in the dining room – and the effect was spectacular. First he turned a brilliant scarlet – his breath came in gasps, he threw the letter across the table. Then he let out a roar which sounded through the entire household. The monkey scuttled for cover; Pom-Pom hid under the sofa.

'You have had bad news?' said Aunt Diana, who was not very bright.

The duke shot her a look of contempt and loathing.

'I have been deceived. I have been made a fool of and I WILL NOT STAND FOR IT.'

His fist came down on the dining table, and a glass ashtray slipped to the floor and shattered.

'Oh poor little Pom-Pom! He will cut his feet,' cried Princess Natalia.

'Poor little Pom-Pom can go to the devil!' shouted the duke.

He had risen from his chair, and was pacing the room.

'It's an outrage and an insult and I will not forgive it. I shall sue the headmaster – the idiot, does he really think I would let my grandson skulk at home? I'm going to ruin him and ruin his school. And as for Karil . . . the boy is a deceitful monster. I suppose I should have expected it, with all that foreign blood.' He kicked a chair and swore – he had used the wrong leg, the one that wasn't made of metal. 'As soon as he's back I'm going to break his will. I'm going to beat him within an inch of his life – and that will only be the beginning. Defying me, making a fool of me.'

The uncles waited, hoping his rage would die down, but it didn't. Eventually the Archduke Franz Heinrich said, 'Where do you think the boy can be?'

The duke stopped pacing and lowered his bull-like head.

'He must have run away,' said Aunt Phyllis, 'but where to?'

The duke scowled at her. But it was true he had no idea where to search for Karil.

Then Carlotta rose from her chair. She was wearing white, which was fortunate, for she might well have been a messenger from on high as she laid her hand tenderly on her grandfather's arm.

'I think I know where he might be, Grandfather,' she said, with her most winning smile. 'I can't be sure but I think so. You see, letters used to come for him from that dreadful school . . . from the children he came to England with. I thought Karil was cured, but now I think perhaps he's run away to be with them.'

The duke shook off her arm.

'What?' he roared. 'Those disgusting delinquent brats . . . those nudist anarchists . . . those gutter rats . . . It's impossible. I won't believe it. Even Karil cannot have sunk so low.'

But the Scold now came to stand beside Carlotta. 'I'm afraid the dear child may be right. I said at the time that they had a most dangerous effect on him. I could . . .' But the Scold fell silent. She had done everything she could to keep Karil away from Tally and her friends – but though she had scolded and bullied the boy for years, she had also loved him. Suddenly she did not want him hounded any more.

The duke stopped pacing.

'I'm going to hunt the wretched boy down like the criminal he is – if it's the last thing I do!'

The day began so well.

They were rehearsing the scenes in the Underworld. They had agreed that Hades should be a place of confusion and mist, with the trapped spirits looming in and out of the vapour.

And that meant dry ice!

The blocks of frozen carbon dioxide had arrived the night before, heavily packed in straw – a special consignment as a try-out before the play at the end of term. They had to be carefully lowered into a tin bath and warm water poured over them and Karil, filling the buckets from the tap in the cloakroom, was in a state of bliss. The more water you poured, the mistier and more obscure the stage became.

The three little girls who were the heads of Cerberus were near the front of the stage; their masks had not been finished yet, but their necks swayed alarmingly. Barney was on a ladder, trying to reach his jet of water. Other spirits dashed about moaning and beseeching.

The ice was going so well that it was becoming harder and harder to make out the characters on stage.

'Isn't it amazing stuff?' whispered Tally, and Karil nodded.

More mist floated on to the stage. And more figures blundered about. One was very large and used language that was not in the script as he tripped over a rock.

'It's a policeman!' cried one of the heads of Cerberus.

'Two policemen,' called out the second head.

The men were enormous, looming in and out of the vapour with their arms stretched out in front of them.

For a moment, Karil was turned to stone. Then he threw a last bucket of water into the tub, ran out of the wings, jumped over the end of the stage and raced the length of the hall.

Straight into the arms of a third policeman, guarding the door.

It was over so quickly, all the hope and the happiness. As he was led away by two of the policemen, it was all Karil could do to walk upright and hold up his head. Knowing what awaited him, he felt a despair so deep that he did not know how he would bear it.

Behind Karil and the policemen came his friends. The officers tried to shoo them away, but they had been through too much with Karil to leave him now.

Apparently he was not to be driven straight back to the hell of Rottingdene House. The policemen were making for the headmaster's study, and Karil shivered. Had the duke come himself to clamp him in irons? Everything seemed possible.

Daley was seated behind his desk. Yet another policeman stood beside him – a swarthy man with a moustache, holding a briefcase – but this was clearly a high-ranking officer, because the men who had held Karil saluted him.

Karil's friends had followed him into the room.

'It's no good throwing us out,' said Tally, 'because we won't go.'

'Your manners are deplorable,' said Daley. 'But as a matter of fact I wasn't going to. Karil may be glad of your support.' And to Karil: 'This is Chief Inspector Ferguson from Scotland Yard.'

The inspector nodded at the policemen. 'You can let him go now,' he said. He walked over to Karil. 'You'd better sit down, Your Grace. I'm afraid I've got some very bad news for you.'

He pointed to a chair and Karil sat down, ever more confused and bewildered. Had the duke decided to send him straight to Borstal? The fact that the inspector was being so kind was surely ominous. And why was he calling him Your Grace? That was his grandfather's title.

'Perhaps a drink of water, sir?' suggested one of the

policemen, and Daley poured out a glass from the carafe on his desk.

Karil took it but could not bring himself to drink. His heart was beating so loudly that he thought it must be heard by everybody in the room.

'What is it?' he managed to ask. 'The bad news . . . ?'

The inspector laid a hand on his shoulder. 'You'd better prepare yourself, Your Grace. It's as bad as could be. Your grandfather is dead.'

Chapter Forty-one

The Play

People had been streaming into the school all day: parents and sisters and aunts. Some came by train, some by car using their saved-up petrol coupons. The hotels in the neighbourhood were fully booked, though some of the visitors were staying in the school itself or in houses in the village.

It was the end of term; the parents would see a performance of *Persephone* and take their children home the following day.

And it was spring. After days of greyness and rain, Delderton was bathed in sunshine; primroses and violets studded the hedgerows. In the pet hut the large white rabbit was moulting; Borro's cow had had her calf and Delderton was in festive mood. As well as the play, there were exhibitions of the children's paintings, and the garments made out of Josie's carded wool, and all the things that are made in school carpentry workshops the world over: bookends and small tables with wobbly legs and boxes into which things could be put (provided one didn't need to shut the lid). But the play was what everyone had come for.

Tally's aunts were among the first to arrive; her father had an urgent meeting at the hospital and was coming on a later train. They wanted to see everything that Tally had described in her letters. The cedar tree, Magda's room, Mortimer, the library, Clemmy's art room and Clemmy herself. They admired everything, knew where everything was – it was as though they had been to school there themselves.

'Oh yes, yes, of course,' they cried as Tally led them through the building. Karil they knew already; he had stayed the night with them in London after his grandfather's funeral and was coming to spend the Easter holidays. After a while they disappeared into the kitchen because it looked as though Clemmy could do with some help.

Thank God I decided to stay, thought Daley, as he watched the visitors arrive. Well-trained visitors, whose children had told them about the importance of the cedar tree and who stopped to admire it or pat its trunk. They all came: Barney's father, Borro's parents, the older sister who had brought Tod up . . .

Early in the afternoon a guest arrived in a large closed car – a man wearing a shabby dark suit, with straggles of silver hair under his hat – and was taken to Magda's room, where she was frantically sorting the children's clothes for packing.

'Oh!' she said. 'You were able to come – we hoped, but . . .'

The Minister of Culture nodded. 'There is not so very much to do at the moment – we watch and hope that things will change and that one day Bergania will be free again. But there is certainly time to visit my nephew.'

'He'll be in the hall – they're very busy with the play. We haven't said anything to him in case you were detained. It is such splendid news that you and the Prime Minister will act as Karil's guardians till he is of age.'

'Yes, we agreed as long as Matteo joined with us. Neither of us is young any more.'

But now he had seen the manuscript laid out on Magda's desk.

'Ah, Schopenhauer,' he said. 'You are nearly finished?'

'Well nearly, but not quite,' admitted Magda. 'You see, there is the question of this washerwoman. Here is a man who has devoted his life to Reason and the Will – is it likely that he would throw a washerwoman down the stairs?'

The Minister of Culture bent over the page she showed him.

'It's a problem, certainly; don't you think perhaps what really happened was that he just gave her a little push – nothing serious – and her legs were weak from standing over a washtub all day – and she fell?'

Magda looked at him gratefully. 'Yes. Yes, that seems very probable. You think I should write it like that?'

They were still discussing this urgent matter when the door opened and Karil burst into the room.

'Magda, we need –'

Then he stopped, drew in his breath – and threw himself into the old man's arms. 'Oh, Uncle Fritz – I never thought you'd be able to get away.' And then: 'Have you brought him?'

Uncle Fritz nodded. 'He's in the car.'

He led Karil to the shabby limousine and opened the door – and the last of the Outer Mongolian pedestal dogs lifted his head from the seat and wagged his tail. Committing a dreadful crime seemed to have done him good. He looked younger and fitter.

'Poor little murderer,' said Uncle Fritz, scratching his ears.

For it was Pom-Pom who had killed the Duke of Rottingdene.

Trying to get away from the duke as he stamped and raged and swore, the little dog had taken shelter on the hearthrug in front of the fireplace in the Red Salon. The room was usually quiet during the day, and Pom-Pom was fast asleep when the duke came rampaging in, looking for his hearing aid and cursing the servants who must have stolen it and sold it at a vast profit. He started to pull open drawers and throw sofa cushions on to the ground, and in his fury he knocked over a heavy brass lamp.

The lamp clattered to the floor and Pom-Pom leaped up terrified, just as the duke staggered backwards, stepped on him – and crashed with his full weight into the marble edge of the chimney piece.

There was nothing to be done. By the time the uncles came running, the duke was lying on the floor with a fractured skull – and quite definitely dead.

But that was only the beginning.

For when the lawyers and the accountants came and the duke's affairs were looked into, it was discovered not only that he had absolutely no money but that he had been cheating the bank, borrowing money and embezzling it.

And the bank did what banks do when this happens; they took over all his possessions, including his house and his furniture – indeed everything he owned.

Karil came back for the funeral but he returned straight away to Delderton. He had inherited his grandfather's title, but anyone addressing him as 'Your Grace' got thoroughly snubbed, and all he wanted was never to hear the name of Rottingdene again. Fortunately the uncles were too busy worrying about what would happen to them and their families to want to look after him.

And even if they had wanted to keep Karil they could not have done so, for by then Matteo's plan had succeeded and he had arranged for the Berganian government-in-exile to declare Karil as its ward.

But Rottingdene House now emptied as everyone left to avoid the bailiffs the bank had put in to wind up the duke's affairs. The servants were dismissed and the governesses went off to stay with relatives who were even harder up than they were themselves. And poor Princess Natalia went mad.

After she found Pom-Pom lying squashed under the duke, she scooped up the little dog (who was not dead though he ought to have been) and started rushing through the emptying rooms wailing and crying.

'Oh, when will the messenger come?' she moaned. 'When . . .when?'

She was still rampaging through the house a few days later when a tall, distinguished-looking stranger came up the steps, and with a screech that echoed to the rafters she ran towards him.

'You have come!' she cried joyfully. 'You are the messenger! You have come to take my Pom-Pom to his bride.'

And before he could protest, she had thrust the little dog into Uncle Fritz's arms.

So now Pom-Pom had become the mascot for the government-in-exile, and it was clear that Uncle Fritz was already very fond of him.

'And the uncles?' asked Karil as they scooped Pom-Pom out of the car. 'Are they all right?'

The Minister for Culture nodded.

'They've all got jobs. Uncle Dmitri is a doorman at the Ritz and Uncle Alfonso is driving taxis. And Franz Heinrich is going up to an island in the Outer Hebrides as gamekeeper to a Scottish landowner.'

'Goodness! I can't see Carlotta on a Scottish island.'

'No. Carlotta couldn't either. She threw some remarkable tantrums. But Countess Frederica has got a job as adviser to the aunt of the Prince of Transjordania, who has a house in London. She wants someone to live in and show her how things are done in British society, and the countess has accepted as long as she can bring Carlotta.'

They had reached the courtyard and a number of

children came to pat the dog, but Uncle Fritz's mind was elsewhere.

'These buildings,' he said, looking round, 'do you know what happens to them in the holidays?'

'I don't think anything does,' said Karil. And the children standing round agreed that the buildings stayed empty.

The Minister of Culture's eyes lit up. 'Good,' he said. Good. They would make an excellent centre for a festival. Not folk dancing perhaps but drama or music . . .

The hall was full, everyone was in their seats, when a large cream-coloured limousine drew up under the archway. Cars like that were seldom seen at Delderton, where the parents didn't go in for obvious luxury and were more likely to arrive on a tandem or hitchhike to their destination. Two people got out – a woman wearing a hat with a veil and a silver fox fur over her shoulder, and a small man in a raincoat.

Everyone was in the hall except for one of the maids, who had been stationed by the door to collect latecomers.

'Just take us straight in,' ordered the woman, talking with a slight American accent. 'We'd like to sit near the front.'

'I'll do my best,' said the maid, looking hard at the newcomers, 'but it's very full.'

She led them into the hall and, as luck would have it, there were two vacant seats in the third row. Followed by disapproving stares, for not only were they late, but parents at Delderton did not wrap themselves in the pelts of dead animals, the elegant woman and the small man in the raincoat slipped into their seats.

And the curtain went up.

It went up on a ravishing Greek landscape – flowers, and a view of light blue sea and streaming sunshine – and on Persephone and her maidens playing with a painted ball.

Whatever was wrong with Verity's acting, she looked lovely, with her tousled dark hair and her bare feet and the delicate ankles she set such store by, and from Verity's parents and the parents of the girls who were her companions there came a sigh of pleasure.

Musicians came in from the wings and Persephone led her girls into a dance. One of the maidens, a very small junior, stumbled and for a moment it looked as if she would fall, but Verity scooped her up and dusted her off with scarcely a break in the rhythm, and the people in the audience smiled, thinking the mishap had been meant.

The music died away. Persephone was left alone to gather flowers with which to bind her hair. She picked crocuses and lilies and asphodels – and then bent down to the narcissus with its multiple heads and roots deep in the ground: the flower that had been grown as a lure for the innocent girl.

The sky darkened. There was a rumble of thunder, faint at first, then growing stronger . . . a bolt of lightning and a grim moaning as of sufferers in the bowels of the earth . . . and with a final crash, the Lord of the Underworld burst from the rocks. This was no pantomime villain but a powerful ruler – there had been enough children at hand to coach Ronald Peabody in the true bearing of a king – and seizing the pale and trembling girl, he drew her slowly, relentlessly, down into the terrifying dark. In the moment that the light was lost to her forever, she emitted a single, piercing cry – and then all was silence.

The curtain dipped only for a moment. It rose on Demeter, the Goddess of Plenty, arriving with her entourage of nymphs and dryads.

It was necessary for Demeter to be beautiful so Julia had become beautiful. She moved across the stage, tall and bountiful, and radiant with power and grace.

But she was looking for her daughter.

'Persephone?' she called. 'Where are you? Are you hiding? Is it a game?'

The audience watched spellbound, almost unable to bear it, as Julia, still searching, became uncertain, then bewildered . . . then afraid . . . then desperate. Till she understood that the unthinkable had happened and her child was lost – and a look of such anguish spread over her face as stopped the heart.

The curtain went down to an ovation. Yet some of the parents were almost nervous that someone so young could transmit such terrible grief. The woman in the silver fox fur took out her handkerchief and sniffed.

Backstage, the scene shifters moved silently, preparing Hades.

Everybody liked Hades. The anguished figures, half obscured by mist, going about their terrible tasks; the wailing of the dead. Cerberus got a special clap, and so did Karil's dry ice. In the background Persephone languished beside her husband, toying with her pomegranate.

But the next act belonged to the sorrowing Demeter. The radiant goddess had vanished; here was a grief-stricken woman looking for her child. Julia had become old – not because of her make-up but because oldness came from inside her. It was in every movement she made, every sigh she uttered. She wore a black cloak and they could see how its folds weighed on her, how it hurt her to walk. And the world she moved in was a dead world – the crops had withered, flocks lay stricken in the fields. The grieving goddess had turned aside from her duties, and famine stalked the land.

The people she met could tell her nothing of her daughter's whereabouts.

Disguised now as an old nurse, she begged for a child to look after – and they could see how she tried to love it – tried and tried, bathing it and tending it – but failed because it was not the child she longed for; it was not her daughter.

Then came the voice of the Sun God, telling her that Persephone was lost forever, deep in the bowels of the earth – and with a cry that echoed that of her daughter as she was carried off, the broken goddess fell to the ground.

There was a short interval and the parents blinked and came down to earth. They had long since stopped watching only their own children; they were watching a play.

In the last act the gods on Olympus took pity on the goddess and the dying world and sent Hermes to the Underworld to bring Persephone back. And now the audience, watching Julia, saw a reversal. Demeter, reunited with her daughter, grew young before their eyes; she became tall and radiant and utterly beautiful.

'My God,' whispered a man in the audience. 'I swear she makes the light come out of herself.'

In the final tableau, Persephone knelt at her mother's feet, and as Demeter raised her hand the stage grew light, petals streamed down from above, and the entire cast entered, bearing fruit and flowers and garlands of leaves. The glorious hymn to Demeter was sung, the curtain fell – and the woman in the silver fox fur broke into noisy sobs.

'I'm sorry, Mother,' said Julia, 'but it's what I really want to do. Act, I mean. I know you think I can't do it but—'

'Oh no, my darling, no no. Not at all; I may have said . . .' She extracted a mauve scented handkerchief and dabbed her eyes. Daley had lent them his room, but there seemed to be nothing to drink on his desk, and she signalled to her agent, Mr Harvenberg, who slipped out for a gin and tonic. 'But I was wrong, I see that now. Only it's such a terrible profession. There is such heartbreak.' She clutched Julia, digging her long fingernails into her daughter's arm. 'I wanted to do my best for you and that meant acting younger than my age so that I could make a lot of money for us. And I have made a lot – and I shall make more when I've sued the film company. I'm going to take them to the cleaners. You've no idea how they've treated me.'

'Aren't you going back to Hollywood then?' asked Julia.

'Go back to that sewer? Never! I wouldn't go back if they asked me on their bended knees. I'm going to stay and do my bit for my country. I'm going to join the WVS.

The uniform is dreadful – that miserable bottle green – but I shan't let it put me off. You'll, see my darling; you're going to be proud of me. Now come and give me a kiss.'

Afterwards Mr Harvenberg took Julia and Tally aside.

'They sacked her. Booted her out. Said she was all washed up, too old. Don't take too much notice – she'll find someone to protect her. There's a boyfriend lined up already. Doubt if she'll last in the WVS, whatever that is. You mustn't take anything she says to heart. I'm off back to the States, but if you want anything let me know.' He extracted his card and handed it to Julia. 'It's much too early to say, but if you want to go in for the profession later, I might be able to help you. You're not a looker like your mother, but you can act and that counts for something. Not much, but something.'

Everyone had gathered together in Magda's room – the aunts, the Minister of Culture, those parents who were staying in the school . . . But Dr Hamilton had taken Karil aside and was talking to him in the courtyard.

'Matteo came to see me before he went abroad,' he said. 'He asked me if I was willing to have you to stay for the holidays. Not just these holidays, but all of them.'

Karil waited.

'I said I was more than willing. That I would be delighted, if it suited you.'

'There's nothing I'd like better,' said Karil. 'But you don't know me.'

For Tally's father had been at a conference when Karil had come to stay after the funeral.

Dr Hamilton smiled. 'Tally knows you,' he said. 'That's enough for me.'

As they made their way upstairs and into Magda's room, they heard Kit's plaintive voice.

'I don't like cocoa with skin on . . .' he began.

But there wasn't any skin on it. The aunts had made the cocoa.

And the party began.

EPILOGUE

This time they were not sleeping in tents on the edge of the park; there were no toilet blocks, no large Yugoslav ladies cutting their toenails in the sinks for washing up. They were guests of the new Berganian government, and had rooms in a wing of the palace.

Not all the children who had come to Bergania six years before were able to come. Verity was tossing her hair about in a modelling agency and Borro had returned to Africa where his father had been invited back, but the rest of them were there: Tally and Julia, Barney and Augusta and Tod and Kit.

They were hardly children now. All of them had left school at the end of the summer term. Barney had got a scholarship to Cambridge to read Natural Sciences, Julia was to start at acting school in the autumn, and Tally, to everyone's surprise, had been bitten by a thirst for the legends and teachings of the ancient world.

'There's a degree at Oxford where you can do all that,' O'Hanrahan had told her, 'but it's no use for getting well-paid jobs.'

'Would I get in?' Tally had asked. 'I'd have to get a scholarship.'

'If you work like a maniac I'll get you in,' he'd said.

And he had kept his promise.

Their rooms in the palace were crowded, for everyone wanted to come and see the ceremony in which the Berganians finally shook off the dreadful years of Hitler's occupation and took the government back into their own hands. Daley was there, and Magda, and Anneliese, the German girl with the auburn curls who had been at the festival. Even the two little girls who had started the rumpus on the hill that probably saved Karil's life had managed to make it.

VE Day, when the end of the war in Europe was celebrated, had seen the Deldertonians spilling out of school on to any train or bus or car that was available to take them to London, along with what seemed the whole population of the free world. They had climbed the railings of Rottingdene House for a view of the dancing and the revelry and the bonfires – and no one shooed them away, for the duke's old home was now a tax office, and people swore that the ghost of the old man stomped through the house at night cursing and swearing.

The city had suffered cruelly when the air raids came

at last, but already grass grew in the bomb craters and the spaces between the ruined buildings had become picnic sites.

In the following month there had been two weddings – one nice, one nasty. The nice one was between Clemmy and Francis Lakeland. It was held at Delderton on a wonderful day in June and was one of those occasions that nobody forgot, with the aunts crying in a most satisfactory way from the moment that the bride appeared.

The other wedding was ostentatious, pompous and pointlessly extravagant at a time when England was still in the grip of shortages. This was the wedding of Carlotta and the Prince of Transjordania. The nastiness was not the prince's fault, he was a modest young man, but Carlotta had to have everything – a vast guest list, costly presents, a reception in St James's Palace. Karil had been invited and asked Tally what to send her as a wedding present.

'Rat poison?' she had suggested.

In the end he did not go, and Carlotta set off with the Scold and her parents (who had had enough of their Scottish island) for a life of luxury in one of the Middle East's wealthiest states.

Before they left, Karil had a long talk with the Scold. Now that his own life was so happy he was able to value the care she had given him, and she went off contentedly, knowing she was no longer misunderstood.

The other uncles fared less well. Nobody invited them back to sit on their former thrones, so Uncle Dmitri continued to work as a doorman and Uncle Alfonso went on driving taxis.

*

The new constitution was to be celebrated in the great hall of the palace and the Deldertonians were getting ready, helping each other with pins and buckles and straps. After six years of clothes rationing they were not really ready to take part in a gala – but Bergania, like the rest of Europe, was no longer interested in show. Most of the citizens wore national dress, and whatever else was lacking, there were always the old flags and the bunting that had been kept in their attics – and above all the flowers which grew so abundantly in that lovely land.

Karil was not with his friends.

'I think we should leave him to himself,' Tally had said when they arrived. 'The whole thing's going to be an awful strain for him.'

So Karil had watched by his father's grave and then disappeared up into the mountains, getting up the strength to face the ceremony.

The waitress who had stared at them in the Blue Ox when they first came to Bergania put her head round the door to see if they needed any help. She was back in the palace now as housekeeper, and when they said they could manage, she said, 'Well, I'd better get back to him. If only he'd keep *still* – and he absolutely won't wear a sash. Just one sash across his chest to make him stand out – is that so much to ask? Really he's impossible, and I've told him so. Sometimes I wonder whether he won't turn tail and run at the last minute.'

All of them wondered this – whether they would get him on to the platform to play his part on this historic day.

The party from Delderton had seats in the front row. Uncle Fritz had retired from politics and was sitting next

392

to Magda. They had found a philosopher who was even sadder and harder to understand than Schopenhauer and were going to collaborate on a book about his life. Poor Heribert had not returned from the war, but Magda, who was helping Uncle Fritz with the Delderton Summer Festival, had quite stopped thinking about marriage.

The delegates made their way into the hall and took their seats. There were scarcely any uniforms; it was ordinary men and women now who represented their country in parliament: teachers and doctors, lawyers and farmers had been elected by the people to speak for them.

Then a man in a dark suit, with touches of grey in his black hair, came out of a side door and made his way to the place of honour: a carved chair in the centre of the semicircle.

The waitress had not persuaded him to wear a sash or anything else that would pick him out from the other people on the platform. The only decoration he wore was a medal given to him by the king for services to Great Britain in the war – the George Cross. Yet he did stand out: on account of his height, his air of authority, perhaps a certain weariness, for it had been a long war and he had suffered in it.

When they had first come to ask Matteo to be the President of the new Republic of Bergania, he had laughed in their faces.

'You are joking, of course,' he said.

He was back at Delderton, busy setting up an experiment to establish the egg-laying preferences of crested newts.

But the delegation was not joking. Bergania had

decided to become a republic, but they wanted a president. Not a figure of power, like the American president, but a figurehead who would coordinate the work of the assembly and represent the country. They pointed out that other European states had done the same thing, appointing playwrights or respected scientists to preside over the assembly, and they made it clear that as a Berganian, a friend of the former king and a war hero, he was the perfect choice.

Matteo continued to say no – but he made a mistake. He returned to Bergania to help them find another candidate, and this was his undoing. He returned to the mountains that he and Johannes had climbed as children, to the streams they had fished, to the forests in which they had roamed.

There is a saying that the landscape in which a child spends the first seven years of its life will leave a mark it cannot escape. A child brought up by the sea will always carry a longing for the ocean; a town child, reared to the sound of traffic and the warm bustle of neighbours, will never quite settle in the silence of the countryside.

So it was with Matteo. Standing on the snow-capped peaks of his homeland, breathing in the pine-scented wind, he was caught.

'I'll do it for five years,' he had said, 'and then you must find someone else.'

The hall erupted into applause. The secretary announced the historic inauguration of the new Republic of Bergania. And the president rose to make a speech.

It was the shortest speech ever made by a president, but no one forgot it.

'Today sees the start of the new Republic of Bergania. I have agreed to serve as your president, but I do so because of three things: the memory of my friend Johannes who reigned as your king and gave his utmost, the example of his son, Karil, who has had the humility to reject kingship . . .'

Here Matteo had to pause because the clapping and cheers were deafening and Karil, who was sitting with his friends, had to stand up and bow.

'And because of the people of Bergania,' he finished, 'who toiled and suffered through the years of hardship and occupation and who deserve their turn in the light.'

The party went on all night. The dancing in the square, the fireworks, all the festivities which had come to an end with the shot that killed Johannes, were unleashed. The next morning most of the visitors slept late, but two people crept out by the back door of the palace and made their way to the dragonfly pool.

It was unchanged in its stillness and its beauty.

'I suppose it all began here,' said Tally.

'Yes. When you said you would be my friend and nobody could stop you.'

'And nobody has,' said Tally. 'Nor ever will.' And then: 'Will you come back here to live do you think, ever?'

'Perhaps. I would like to work here one day. Not yet – but when I've got enough experience, try to set up clinics and hospitals. It's because you lent me your father after mine died.'

Dr Hamilton had not been able to keep Tally and Karil out of harm's way in the holidays after the bombing began. They had insisted on coming back and helping in any way they could. Digging people out of the rubble, carrying stretchers to the ambulances, Karil had seen what the arrival of a doctor could mean to the injured, and when it came to choosing his profession he found that the decision was already made. He was starting at medical school in the autumn.

'But I'd need someone to help me. Someone a bit fierce maybe. The kind of person whose great-grandmother removed the socks of tramps in the London Underground.'

Tally felt no need to answer. She had known from the start that her life and Karil's were bound up together and now she watched as he felt in his pocket for the pebble he had brought back to his homeland and dropped it into the water. Their reflections, side by side, were still there, steady and unmoving, when the surface was quiet again.

But there was one more ceremony to attend, and they had left it till the day on which they were going home. It took place out of doors, high in the mountains, at the base of the Quartz Needle, where Uncle Fritz had erected a small headstone with an inscription.

Pom-Pom had lived with the government-in-exile throughout the war, and the news that his bride had passed away in Brazil had come as a considerable relief. Uncle Fritz had intended to do what he could to save the ancient line of Outer Mongolian pedestal dogs, but the journey would have been arduous and Pom-Pom, in

396

human terms, was already over a hundred years old. When the little dog died at last (not in Uncle Fritz's arms but on his feet) it did not seem right that he should lie in a London pet cemetery surrounded by traffic and fumes, and since the mountains of Mongolia were out of reach, Uncle Fritz had brought his ashes back to the high peaks of Bergania and interred them there.

The party from Delderton had not expected a big turnout, but when it got about that the little creature who lay under their soil had freed their prince from a cruel and sadistic bully, a surprising number of people came to pay their respects – and with them came the stonemason and his family, for it had not been easy to inscribe the unusual poem in a foreign language neatly on to the gravestone and he wanted to make sure that all was well. He had been working to a deadline but now, as he removed the cloth that had been covering his handiwork, he knew that he had produced a masterpiece.

When news of Pom-Pom's death reached Delderton, O'Hanrahan had organized an epitaph competition – and now Karil stepped up to the tombstone and while everyone bowed their heads respectfully, he read out the winning entry.

The Great Khan's hunting dogs were proud
Their bite was fierce, their bark was loud
His horses always ran full throttle
But I was the Khan's hot-water bottle.

There had been some doubt about the last line, but when it was put to the vote this was the poem that was judged the best and Kit flushed a modest pink, for the winning entry had been his.

Then from higher up the mountain there came the sound of 'The Last Trump' played on Matteo's sackbut – and realizing that nobody could have had a more fitting send-off, the mourners linked hands and ran down to the buses that were waiting to take them to the station – and home.

Questions for Discussion

The following questions have been taken from the Macmillan Children's Books' reading guide prepared by children's librarian Jacob Hope, in association with Chatterbooks. To download the full guide, visit www.macmillanreadingguides.com.

1. Do you think that what we do at school and the way we are brought up are important in deciding who we are to become? Some things to think about:

- Might Tally have been different if she had attended boarding school with Margaret or Roderick rather than going to Delderton?
- Compare Tally and Karil – do they escape their upbringing or develop because of it?

2. Characters in the novel hold very strong views as to whether or not Delderton is a good school. What would you say about the school?
Some things to think about:

- The criticism its pupils attract from customers on the railway and from the Baroness Gambetti.
- Margaret and Roderick's reaction when they hear Tally is to go to Delderton.
- Professor Mayfield's comments about the school's reputation.
- Matteo and Magda's teaching methods.

3. 'It was her father who had taught her that knowledge is power – that if one could find out about something one is afraid of, it made the fear less.' (p. 15)
As the Second World War approaches, fear increases. How does this affect the characters in the novel?

Some things to think about:
- Why does Dr Hamilton send Tally away from London to boarding school?
- Tally's views that the barrage balloons are like kind great-uncles – how does this later change?
- Matteo's comments upon finding Tally out alone in Bergania.

4. Margaret warns her cousin: '*Being different is the thing you mustn't do.*' (p. 19)
Is this good advice for somebody attending Delderton school? Many of the pupils at Delderton are real individuals – what makes each of them different? Are there characteristics the pupils share?

5) Matteo tells Karil about his father: '*He really enjoyed life, your father. That was why I was so angry when he became imprisoned in all that kingship.*' (p. 241)
How might kingship be imprisoning?
Some things to think about:

- What are the reasons for Countess Frederica's behaviour on the trip to England. Is this justified or is she overprotective?
- The Duke of Rottingdene insists that Karil should not allow others to take 'liberties' with him. What might he mean by this?
- The King's warning to Karil: '*. . . it never works, trying to make friends with people from outside our world.*'
(p. 133) Why might the King have said this, and do you think kingship has imprisoned him?

Journey to the River Sea

EVA IBBOTSON

The girls in Maia's class told her what to expect when she reached the Brazilian jungle. 'There are huge mosquitos which bite you. You turn as yellow as a lemon and then you die.'

But Maia, an orphan, can't wait to start the long sea voyage. She is to begin a new life with relatives she has never met, a thousand miles up the Amazon river. Travelling with her is the mysterious Miss Minton, who has secret reasons of her own for making the journey. And Maia's classmates could never, even in their wildest dreams, imagine the adventures that await her on the shores of the river sea.

EVA IBBOTSON

Annika lives as a servant at a grand house in Vienna, a glittering city famous for its great emperor and the exquisite white horses of the Imperial Riding School. Her life there would be perfect but for the mystery of her real mother. For, as a newborn baby, Annika was found in a church, and no one knows where she came from. But every day her mind swirls with dreams of a beautiful mother arriving to finally claim her.

Then Annika is told the astonishing truth about her past and is swept on an adventure of extraordinary discovery and unexpected danger . . .

THE
BEASTS OF
CLAWSTONE
CASTLE

EVA
IBBOTSON

When Madlyn and Rollo are sent to ancient Clawstone Castle they fall in love with it – especially with the mysterious white creatures that roam the grounds. But the owners are practically penniless and the castle is crumbling away. A magnificent money-making plan is Clawstone's only hope.

Helped by a gang of hilarious ghosts – including a one-eyed skeleton and a pair of dancing feet – the children turn the castle into a genuine haunted house! Soon the money is rolling in, but just as things start looking up a terrible fate befalls the beasts. Madlyn, Rollo and their phantom friends now face some very sinister enemies . . .